The CARETAKERS

The Second Book in the Crowsbrook Chronicles

by Claire Horsnell

The Caretakers: The Second Book in the *Crowsbrook Chronicles*
© 2019 by Claire Horsnell

Cover design © 2019 by Carmen Leah at Pink Kloud

Interior design © 2019 by Jennifer Leung

Galacticor sculpted by Colin Betts. Cover photography by Janet Weldon Murray. All rights reserved.

Printed and distributed by IngramSpark.
www.ingramspark.com

Library and Archives Canada Cataloguing in Publication

978-0-9937020-2-0

Spilled Ink Books
www.spilledink.com

Copy edited by Heather Martin
www.heathermartin.com

Composition by Nelson Gonzalez

Proofread by Avivah Wargon

Printed in the United States of America.

The
CARETAKERS

The Second Book in the
Crowsbrook Chronicles

Prologue

Thirty-Five Years Ago

Hogarth Merrick was drunk and wet and cold, and the man at the crossroads was in his way.

Funny-looking bugger he was, too, long coat and flat cap—bit old-fashioned it was, like he was out of a book for kids, except it was October and pissing rain—just standing there at the crossroads in the wet and the dark, with a smile on his face like he'd just been given extra chips. Big teeth, he had; white, like on the American programs. (Not that he'd watched the American programs; Ma hadn't held with it. But you saw pictures of them in the paper.)

Ma. Hogarth just wanted to go home. To be at home.

On his way, he'd been, after he left his corner at the pub by the fireplace, few pints of Tim Taylor's in him, and would have been a few more if the dozy cow behind the bar had been doing her job instead of telling him he'd had enough, and then he'd tripped on his way out, new step it must have been, and fallen in the rain. Gotten himself up, he had—he wasn't drunk, he could take his drink—but then, turning into Green Lane, some Flash Harry shitelark had barrelled past him (no need for that kind of driving, not in Crowsbrook) and hit the pothole on the corner, not hard enough so he'd notice, but hard enough to throw a sheet of muddy water over Hogarth, drenching him from head to foot. He'd barely had time to shout three insults after the disappearing vehicle and wave a V-sign in its general direction before it turned the corner and roared out of sight. It was cold enough already, and he was soaked to the skin, and it wasn't late enough in the year to turn on the heating.

End of October, it was. Ma had never turned the heat on until halfway through November at the earliest. It just felt wrong, turning it on this early.

She'd never know, now. The thought whispered in the back of his head like the ghost of a forbidden cigarette, and he waved it away frantically and furtively.

That wasn't the point. The heating went on in the middle of November because it was the right thing to do, and putting it on earlier would be a waste. He shivered. He could put on a jumper. It was that stupid mare in the pub's fault. He belched loudly, waved another V-sign at the empty lane, and turned back toward home.

And this man was in his way. Hogarth concentrated hard and tried to step around him, but the man held up a hand to stop him.

"All right, Hogarth?" he said.

Hogarth looked carefully at him through the dark. The streetlight was yards away. The man looked vaguely familiar.

Had he been at the service yesterday? He could have been. Some distant relative come to offer condolences. Probably hoping for a pile of money or a bit of jewellery or something. Joke was on him, if he was. Ma hadn't held with jewellery. *Flashy*, she said it was. He'd never seen her wear it: no sparkly glass beads, no necklaces, bracelets, or rings and *definitely* no earrings, even the clips. No, this one wasn't getting anything. Not that there was anything to get, apart from the house, and that was Hogarth's, he knew that already. Vultures, they were, the distant relatives. Ma had always said so: vultures who gave you nothing and would have you for all they could get.

Hogarth had probably seen him at the funeral. That was it.

Or had he been in the pub? Hogarth tried to haul his brain out of its warm bath of beer. Maybe. Maybe he'd been in the pub and left just before Hogarth. Hogarth hadn't looked around much in the pub, and he hadn't gone for the company, that's for sure: parcel of pillocks laughing and joking and making stupid comments about the football and the telly. Didn't watch football, him. Didn't watch much telly either. Ma watched the nature programs and *Songs of Praise*, and he hadn't been bothered about either. He watched it a bit, sometimes, after Ma had gone to bed. Rubbish, a lot of it was. Like the pub. Bloody rubbish. But after the service and the tea yesterday (Mrs. Arbuthnot had organized the tea; she knew the secret of getting the church's leaky urn to work. Bloody thing was like an animal, it was: shooting out jets of steam to take your skin off if you tried to touch it, but Mrs. A. had the trick of it)…after the service and the tea and the morning making his own toast and going in the bathroom without having to wait, he wanted a drink, he did. And Ma didn't approve of drinking at home. Wouldn't have drink in the house, but tolerated his discreet trips to the Nag's Head, with a frosty glance the morning after, when she'd wake up half an hour earlier and clatter about more loudly than usual with the pans in the kitchen if she thought he'd stayed out too late or had one over the eight.

He'd seen this one somewhere. Maybe at the pub.

A gust of wind spat heavy rain into his face, and his mind lurched back into the moment. The funny bugger was still standing there grinning, in front of him.

"What?" Hogarth managed to ask the stranger. All dressed up

and apparently nowhere to go in the rain better than Crowsbrook. "What d'you want?"

"Quick word," said the stranger, and his eyes glittered. Hogarth squinted at him. Wasn't from Crowsbrook. Wasn't from around Crowsbrook either, talking like that. Sounded like he was from London. Not one of the posh bits. Still. Twat.

"Piss off," mumbled Hogarth, and tried to push past him. The stranger reached out and grabbed his arm, quick as a stoat. Hogarth pulled, but couldn't move. (He would wake up the next morning with a small constellation of five deep, purple bruises on his upper arm.)

"Leggo!" he shouted. He didn't struggle much.

"Just want a quick word," said the stranger, still smiling. "Need a favour." His voice was quiet and even.

"Who are you?" managed Hogarth.

"Name's Savaric," said the man.

"S'not a name. Fuck off. I'm going home." Hogarth tried to move. Savaric's grip tightened on his arm and he changed his mind.

"*Small* favour," repeated Savaric. Hogarth peered through the dark and the rain. Savaric was pale, and his hair was long and dark. His coat didn't look like it was made for the rain. But it didn't look like it was getting wet. Hogarth screwed up his eyes, and then decided it didn't matter much.

"'S raining," said Hogarth. "I wanna go home."

"Not a problem," said Savaric. "You can go in a mo." He chuckled. "That rhymes. Oh," he added, almost as an afterthought. "Just do a small thing for me when you get there, will you?"

"No," whined Hogarth. "What? K'off."

"Got a cupboard, haven't you?"

Hogarth's brain blanked.

"What?"

"Have you *got*," said Savaric, patiently, "a *cupboard*."

"What?" said Hogarth again. "Yeah. Somewhere," he added.

Savaric grinned. It was like his smile, but bigger, and seemed somehow filled with more teeth than it should have been. It made Hogarth uncomfortable.

"Great," said Savaric. "Put this in it for me, will you?" He kicked something with his foot, and Hogarth looked down to see a small hessian sack next to Savaric's foot. Hogarth thought its contents shifted. Still. Could have been the beer, could have been the kick. He stared at the bag, but it didn't move again.

"Got that?" said Savaric.

"Wait, what?" said Hogarth. "What? Why? Why should I?"

"Because I'm asking nicely," said Savaric. "And I think you'll do a good job. And it'll be worth your while."

"Good job of what?" said Hogarth. "You want me to put a bag in a cupboard?"

"I think you'll find it'll be worth your while," said Savaric, again. "Your lucky day, this is, isn't it?" His smile dropped a little. "Especially after all you've been through. My condolences, by the way."

Hogarth shrugged. He was cold, he was wet, and he was annoyed. "Full of bollocks," he said, partly to himself. "Makes no sense. Worth my bloody while? Having a laugh."

"I'm telling the truth," said Savaric. He stopped smiling, and a sudden gust of wind chilled Hogarth to the bone.

Fucking looney, he decided. He just wanted to go home.

"Whatever," he said. "Put th' bag in th' cupboard. Anything else?"

"No," said Savaric. "Only that you won't regret it." Hogarth felt a tingling in his arm. He shifted his shoulder slightly, and discovered that Savaric had let go of him.

"What is it?" Hogarth bent to open the bag, and Savaric stopped him with a hand on his chest. It felt to Hogarth like a mild electric shock.

"Ah," said Savaric. He was smiling again. "Think of it as a surprise. Don't look in the bag before you get home. You know what: don't look in it after you get home. Just—"

"Put it in the cupboard," said Hogarth. "Right."

He sighed. The man had let him go. Clearly mental, this one. Best thing to do was take the bloody thing and toss it over a hedge or something.

"Don't go tossing it over a hedge or nothing, neither," said Savaric. "I'm serious."

Hogarth looked at the bag. He shrugged and picked it up.

The rain stopped.

Wait.

The rain *hadn't* stopped.

Hogarth looked up.

The rain—

Well. It wasn't raining on *him* anymore.

He looked up. He looked down at his jacket. He looked up and then down again. It was still raining. But he wasn't getting wet.

He couldn't feel the wind either.

He looked at Savaric. Savaric smiled. It didn't make him look friendlier. His teeth were very straight and very white. And kind of *long*. He pulled a large black umbrella from the folds of his coat and put it up. It made a sound like wet crows taking off.

"Like, I said," said Savaric. "Don't chuck it over a hedge. See?"

Hogarth frowned. He was feeling warmer. He looked down at his jacket and noticed it was drying out.

"Cupboard," he said. "Right." He turned to go.

"Good man," said Savaric. "Oh," he added, "couple of things."

"What kind of things?" said Hogarth, suspicion in his voice. Too good to be true, this was. He thought about putting the bag down again, but the rain was getting worse, and he had already started to warm up a bit.

"Don't mention this to anyone," said Savaric. "And you can't let anyone else in your house."

Hogarth hated being told what to do. But he did like being dry. He held on tightly to the bag.

"House," he said. "No."

Savaric grabbed his collar and pulled him in close. Hogarth could smell his breath. It was slightly rotten. It reminded Hogarth of the single time he'd left the mince a day too long in the fridge.

Ma hadn't liked that.

"Listen, pisshead," said Savaric. His smile had completely gone now. "*Concentrate.* You take the bag. You put it in the cupboard. That's all you've got to do. You'll be looked after. But you can't let anyone in your house while h—" he hesitated for a fraction of a second "—while the bag is in the cupboard. Never. No one. *Never.* Do you understand?"

Hogarth flinched. He tried to twitch Savaric away. "Nobody," he said.

"That's right," said Savaric. *"Nobody."*

"Ever?"

"As long as the bag is in the cupboard." Savaric gently released his grip on Hogarth's shirt. "Nobody."

"Ma doesn't—didn't like company," said Hogarth. He sagged a little.

"I know," said Savaric. He pulled Hogarth in for a drunken hug. "I know. Sorry about that, mate."

Hogarth disentangled himself. He was confused, but he felt better. Almost completely dry, he was now.

"Bag," he said. "Cupboard. Nobody. Sure."

"Thanks, Hogarth," said Savaric. His voice seemed to come from a distance away, and Hogarth spun around twice before he spotted him, striding past the pub, further away than he had any right to be.

Must have made a mistake, thought Hogarth. Then something else occurred to him.

"Hey!" he roared in Savaric's direction. "How do you know my name? Who are you?"

But Savaric had gone.

● ● ●

He stayed dry all the way home. The rain got heavier.

It was impossible. Hogarth knew it was impossible. But he also knew that being cold and wet felt very different from feeling warm and dry, and he knew that putting a bag in a cupboard wasn't hard, and he knew, whether he admitted it to himself or not, that there were some people—like Ma—who, when they asked you to do a thing, *really, really, really* meant it.

Or else.

He put the bag down briefly to unlock his front door and cursed as a gust of wind lashed his face with cold rain. He picked up the bag again, stepped inside, slammed the door, and flicked on the light. The hall was clean and sparse, with a threadbare rug. Ma had always made do and mend, and that had done nicely for them, thank you very much. And it still looked fine enough. He stared at a patch that she had mended after he'd spilled hot wax from the candle on it when he was going up to bed, and the spot had had to be cut out. The hiding he'd gotten for that.

Quality work, that was, he thought, staring at the repair. All those patches, all those darns. Couldn't hardly see them, you couldn't.

He bent down to pick up the bag.

Looked better than fine, the rug did. Maybe it was—well, he couldn't put his finger on it. Maybe the light bulb was about to burn out or something. Something about the place looked different. Trick of the light, probably. Old place was looking good.

Like a home. Ma had always made a good home.

He wondered briefly if she was still around somehow, and then snorted. Going mental, he was. Like that bloke in the rain. Probably escaped from the hospital no one talked about. Him and his *bag*.

He hung up his—dry—jacket on the coat rack. He looked at the bag.

"Cupboard," he said. "Whatever."

The bag shifted. Probably the contents settling. Gravity. It was gravity.

Hogarth sighed. His brain was still soggy with beer, but it was clambering back to reality.

"All right," he said. "Cupboard."

Next to a neat line of tarnished brass coat hooks there was a door set into the wall of the entrance hall. Hogarth supposed the cupboard was for coats, if you didn't have a coat rack. He never used it. There were some bits of wood in there. He'd put them in there when he'd been tidying up a bit and had kept them in case they came in handy. They hadn't.

He opened the door to the cupboard. It smelled a bit musty, and the empty shelves were covered in a thin layer of dust. He picked the bag up, and put it on the floor. Then he looked at it, and changed his mind, and put it on the lowest shelf. He closed the door.

"Put it in a cupboard," he said. "Mental."

He turned off the hall light and went upstairs in the dark.

There was a thud as one of the planks of wood fell over in the cupboard.

• • •

He came downstairs the next morning bleary eyed and aching. His muscles all seemed to turn to cement while he slept these days. Ugh, he thought. At least it was the weekend. He didn't have to leave the house for forty-eight hours. It would be quiet and he would be alone, and that was the way he liked it now. A draft worked its way through the gaps around the front door and he shivered. First of November. Of course.

He hated November.

He shuffled into the kitchen, rubbing his forehead; he took the kettle off the hob, filled it with water, struck a match, and set the kettle on the stove to boil. As he was opening the kitchen cupboard, he cursed to himself: he had used his last teabag the previous morning, and had thrown it out, and had meant to stop by the village shop to get more on his way home.

He went to close the cupboard door when something caught his eye. He stretched up and looked more closely.

Well, wasn't *that* a turn-up for the books. Ma had clearly doubled up at the shop at some point. It wasn't the way she'd usually gone about things; they didn't have the money to go throwing around stockpiling, as if the dead were going to rise up and take over any minute (not that that would have bothered him; good riddance to the rest of the world, he thought, on the rare occasions when he'd stayed up after Ma and a late-night horror movie shuffled onto the telly and he couldn't be arsed to go to bed). But there it was: a brand new box of teabags crouching at the back of his kitchen cupboard. God knew how long it had been there, but tea was tea, and it meant he didn't have to go out.

(There didn't seem to be much dust on it, considering he had no idea when Ma had bought it—but it had been in the cupboard, after all.)

Bloody cupboards, bloody nutter at the crossroads. Bloke

was clearly a mental case. A looney asked him to put a bag in a cupboard and not throw it over a hedge. And he'd done it. Should have told him where to go instead. Could probably throw the bag out now, anyway.

He wondered what was in it. It'd be a bit before the kettle boiled. He shuffled into the hall and placed his hand on the doorknob. He hesitated for a moment, although he didn't know why.

Then he snorted and opened the door.

His jaw dropped.

It was dark in the cupboard.

Really dark. It wasn't just that there was no light bulb in the cupboard (there was, and there was a switch a few inches away from his hand, but he had momentarily forgotten about it as he stared into the blackness). It was as if light somehow *stopped* at the door frame. He couldn't see the three shelves, or the four planks.

Or the bag.

Jesus, he breathed. He closed the door. Then he opened it again. The cupboard was still dark.

He remembered the light switch and fumbled for it, staring into the cupboard the whole time. The light bulb flashed for a moment and fizzled out. The brief moment of light illuminated nothing.

Nothing. There was no back to the cupboard anymore. No walls. No floor. Just darkness. The kettle began to scream as the water boiled.

He slammed the door shut and stood there looking at it.

What the hell? The image of Sav's toothy smile floated up in his brain.

He frowned and stomped into the kitchen and grabbed the broom. Some people might say it was almost worn out, but there was still some good use in it; folk didn't have the sense they were born with, some of them. And that didn't matter, not for what he wanted it for. The kettle was still wailing on the stove. He twisted the stove knob viciously, and its screeching died away. He clenched his teeth and headed back to the cupboard, his cup of tea forgotten.

He opened the door. The inside of the cupboard was still velvet dark.

Hogarth swallowed and picked up the broom near its head. He stood back and gingerly poked the tip of the broom handle into the blackness with a short jab.

Nothing happened. He edged closer to the doorway of the cupboard. He jabbed again.

The tip of the broom handle disappeared into the darkness and then reappeared. Hogarth let out a yell of surprise and clapped his hand to his mouth. The broom clattered to the floor. He stared at it.

This is all wrong, he thought.

Breathing heavily, he picked up the broom again. He clenched his teeth and gripped the broom handle hard. In one sudden motion, he jabbed it forward. The front half of the broom handle disappeared into the darkness. He might as well have plunged it into muddy water.

It reminded him of the Foxglove Pond in the village. The water was clear at the edges—maybe a bit muddy—but somehow…there was something about the way that the light fell through the trees and dropped onto the water that made you think that you could stand on the bank and throw a pebble into the middle of the pond, and the pebble would still be falling slowly in the water, over and over, long after the ripples had reached the shore…

Spent quite a bit of time down the Foxglove Pond when he was a littl'un, he had. Ma used to sit on the seat and stare into the water while he made mud pies by the edge of the water. Didn't go there anymore. Gave him the creeps, now, it did. They said bad things had happened there a long time ago, though no one could remember quite what.

He moved the broom to the left and then to the right. There was no resistance. It felt like—well, it felt like waving a broom handle around in a cupboard. For a moment, he felt faintly silly. He pulled the broom back, and it came back easily. He examined the handle. It looked perfectly normal.

He closed the door gently. The snib clicked. He took a deep breath and let it out slowly, blowing out his cheeks.

Time for that cup of tea, he thought.

He leaned the broom against the door of the cupboard, went into the kitchen, boiled the kettle again. He poured the water and went to the fridge for milk. He hoped it wasn't too old. He opened the fridge.

"*Jesus Christ!*"

The fridge wasn't dark. It was weirder than that.

The fridge was *full*.

Hogarth's fridge, at the end of the week in which his mother died, had contained a small bottle of milk, half a brick of butter, and a small piece of cheese slowly drying out in the salad box. *This* fridge (it didn't feel like his fridge; really, it was still Ma's fridge) had two six-packs of Hogarth's favourite beer in it, an airtight box with fresh cheese in it, and a packet of ham and a whole chicken and a package of the good beef burgers and some old-fashioned sausages, linked together and wrapped in paper. There was a jar of strawberry jam in the door. That was Hogarth's favourite.

Hogarth stood there and stared at it. There was a note on top of the cheese. He reached into the fridge and picked it up. It consisted of two words, written in a very shaky script, on a plain white piece of paper.

THANK YOU, it said.

Someone had been in the house. *Someone had been in the house.* He was suddenly overcome with rage. Ma's house. *Someone had been in Ma's house.* He slammed the fridge door shut and ran to the front door. It was locked. So was the back door. He ran around the house, checked the windows. None were open. None were broken. The thin strings that Ma had tied across his windows so she could see if anyone had broken in were still intact. There was no sign that they'd been moved or broken, and neither were the plain little crosses that Ma had put on all the window-sills ("for protection," she said; he didn't know from what, but he knew better than to ask questions). He checked the hairs he'd put on the window frames himself. All still there.

It wasn't possible.

Also, it made no sense. None of his stuff was missing. Why would anyone break into his house to leave food in the fridge? Why was his cupboard full of nothing? What was going on?

He opened the fridge, took out the milk, and poured a big slug of it into his tea. He came back to the cupboard.

The broom was lying on the floor.

Hogarth spilled his tea.

Wait, he thought. *Wait. It could have fallen over.* But the kitchen was only across the hall, and he knew he would have heard it. Had he knocked it over when he was checking the house? He knew he hadn't.

None of this made sense.

He pushed the broom out of the way with his foot and opened the cupboard door. It was still the same. Same darkness. Without taking his eyes off the darkness, he bent down and picked up the broom. Slowly, he prodded it toward the back of the cupboard.

It kept going. It should have hit the back of the cupboard, but it kept going.

Hogarth whistled. Then his attention was caught by the sensation in his hand. It suddenly felt as though someone was breathing on it: hot, moist, silent breath. He jerked his hand away, and realized he had been about to plunge it into the darkness. He closed the door quietly.

He didn't exactly hear the voice. It just sort of showed up in his head, warm and moist somehow, like the darkness on his hand.

Hogarth. It wrapped itself around his consciousness like a soft blanket.

"Hello?" he said.

Hogaaaaaaaaaaaaaarth. So soft; so comforting. And he knew. He knew that the thing in the cupboard had not put the stuff in his fridge, but he knew that the stuff in the fridge was in the fridge because whatever was in the cupboard was in the cupboard.

"Hello?" he said again. "Er. Someone there? You there?"

The sound in his mind was the sound that chainsaws would make, if they could purr.

"Are you hungry?" he said. The sound changed to a kind of slobbering gurgle.

"Oh," said Hogarth. "Hold on, then."

Maybe that's why the food was in the fridge. He went back into the fridge and unwrapped the sausages. He cut one off and took it back to the cupboard. *It's a waste*, part of his mind argued feebly, *waste of a sausage*, but somehow he knew this was what he was supposed to do. He knelt down (he didn't know why) and placed the sausage carefully on the threshold, so that it was lying half in and half out of the cupboard, half hidden by darkness. He waited, still and silent. The purring in his head became deeper. Then he saw, creeping out of the darkness, the desiccated tips of what looked like a finger and a thumb. They pinched the end of the sausage and yanked it into the darkness. He felt a silent grunt of satisfaction manifest in his head.

It likes sausages, he thought. That was one thing they had in common, anyway. He unwrapped the rest of the sausages and left them at the edge of the cupboard for its new resident, because he had a suspicion that even if he gave it the good sausages in his fridge, there would be more sausages and other good things in the fridge when he went back, and when he went back to the fridge, he found he was right.

• • •

And that was how it started, the thing with Hogarth. He shared the stuff with the thing in the cupboard and talked to it, and it talked back, in its own fashion and without words. Maybe he was just talking to himself, he thought sometimes. But part of him knew that he wasn't. It was like when Ma had been around. They shared a home. The thing in the cupboard was real, and he took care of it and it took care of him.

And it was a long time before he saw Savaric again.

Chapter 1

"I have a tummy ache."

Holly tried not to grind her teeth.

"A good night's sleep'll make it better," she said. "Now settle down."

"Read me a story?"

"I just read you a story."

"A *short* one."

"It was still a story. Have you got Walter Bear?"

Jack nodded and gripped Walter Bear tightly. "I don't have Wilma Bear."

Damn it, damn it, damn it. Wilma Bear was downstairs, recovering from an earlier trip to the supermarket. Holly envied her. "Well, you can—" Even as she said it, she knew better.

"I NEED WILMA BEAR!"

I need a gin and tonic, thought Holly as she made a run down the stairs into the living room. She could hear a whole brunch-load of hypermummies twittering about her in her head as she rushed back upstairs with Wilma Bear. Her therapist said that she was too hard on herself and the tapes she had playing in her mind weren't connected to reality, that she was doing a fine job, especially under the circumstances, but then she saw the looks outside of the school gates when the toothpaste stains on Jack's jumper that had been invisible when she left the house fluoresced in the outdoor light, or his shoes were on the wrong feet (how? How? *How?*), or he reminded her that it was PE and he needed his kit, which was in the ironing pile, or a thousand other felonies that led Crowsbrook's Supreme Matriarch and Chief Prosecutor of Maternal Crimes, Allegra Valentine, to press her lips together and pull out her phone and start texting, as if Holly couldn't hear the simultaneous buzzes trilling in the designer totes of Daphne Latimer and Isabella Butterworth. Like she couldn't hear Allegra's opinions from the other side of the playground. Allegra had one of those voices that "just carried" as Holly's grandmother would have said, and she'd have been right: Allegra's voice carried right into Holly's head as she sought out Wilma Bear. *You're spoiling him, you know. He won't learn resilience. He'll treat women terribly his whole life. He'll never learn if you do everything for him. Also, you should wash Wilma Bear. He dropped it how many times? I always…*

Holly hadn't seen her therapist in a while.

Allegra and her crew had been friends since high school, where Allegra had engineered a pregnancy pact—along with a respectable timetable, taking into account higher education, sensibly long engagements, an appropriately lavish and tasteful wedding, and the time it would take to reach middle management—between the three of them. Allegra's daughter was the eldest child it had produced, but only by a month.

Eff off, the lot of you, thought Holly, and then smiled wryly to herself. Apparently she couldn't even swear in her head anymore.

"Here you go," she announced, back upstairs, in her best firm-but-fair voice (the one without the note of despair in it). "Wilma Bear."

"I need a glass of water."

"You have a glass of water."

"It's got bubbles in it."

"No, it doesn't. It's from the tap. You saw me run the tap."

"Those are *bubbles*. Look."

"I can see. That just happens. The water's fine. It's from the tap. It's time for bed, Jack."

"You're not looking."

"Yes, I am, and your water is fine. Nighty night."

"I'm hungry."

"No, you're not. You had a snack before you cleaned your teeth. It's time for lights out. Nighty night. Love you."

She kissed his forehead, turned out the lamp, switched on the mushroom-shaped night light next to Jack's bed, and got up to go. She almost made it to the door.

She heard Jack take a deep breath and a small voice came from behind her. "There's a monster in my cupboard."

Not this again. Every night for the past three weeks. She'd told him there wasn't and checked the cupboard, and checked the cupboard with him, and Googled it, and found reams of "parent-tested solutions." Some of them had been fun. They had made Anti-Monster Spray, and shouted at the monsters (quietly), and she had let Jack take his little plastic cricket bat to bed with him, knowing full well what Allegra would have to say about the dangers of permitting plastics near the bed. But after a week, she had gone up to bed herself and heard him telling Walter and Wilma why he couldn't sleep. His voice had been thin and tired. "There's a monster in the cupboard and it's *dangerous*. It wants to eat *children*."

He had told Walter and Wilma that they would be okay because they were bears.

She tried not to let her shoulders sag. *Be firm.* "No, there isn't. I checked."

"You checked *yesterday*."

"And we didn't find anything, did we? Remember? Your cupboard's all safe. There's nothing in it."

"THERE'S A MONSTER!"

Holly turned and looked at Jack. She knew that look: the fudging before bed had been a way to put off the inevitable, and all kids did it, at least all the versions of Allegra on the Internet had been clear about that. But now, he was really afraid. She'd seen him do this at the dentist. He was fighting it, and fighting it hard, but he was really scared.

He'll never learn if you always give in. She went back into the room and gave him a big hug.

"It's all safe in here," she said. "I'll leave the night light on, all right? You'll be fine, Jack. I'm not going to let anything hurt you. I love you."

"I love you," said Jack. He sounded distracted. His eyes were locked on the cupboard door.

Holly sighed. "I'll check one more time," she said.

She got up from beside the bed and crossed the room to the door of the cupboard. It was set into the wall and had slats in it. She opened it and looked inside. It was dark.

"I can't see anything," she said.

"Check all the way to the back." Jack's voice was tense.

Holly pushed Jack's clothes aside. It was really dark in the cupboard, and the nightlight didn't help much. She couldn't see much.

She reached up and pushed at the clothes; the hangers clicked as they moved, and she poked about a bit vaguely toward the back. It was too dark to see much, but she didn't want to turn the light on and get him even more unsettled. Frowning, she groped toward the back, with only the faintest sense of where it might be; she felt both relief and a childlike sense of disappointment when her fingers connected with the wall.

Something dropped onto her foot and she started, and then froze. It didn't move.

She bent down to pick it up. A rolled-up T-shirt, with Bob the Builder's face smiling up at her. She sighed and put it back on the shelf above the hangers.

It was too dark to see everything, but she'd checked and that was the point, wasn't it? She was never going to find a monster: she'd validated his feelings, and shown him that she cared and that she valued…oh, something or other. There was no bloody monster and she wanted to have a sit-down. Hopefully it was just a phase. Hopefully he'd be able to sleep. Hopefully Allegra and her phone wouldn't be judging her based on the darkening rings under Jack's eyes and his increasing inability to keep awake in assembly. Hopefully.

"Okay," she said. "There's no monster. I checked. You're all safe. Nighty night."

"Night night," said Jack unhappily. She closed his bedroom door all but a crack behind her, and took one more glance at him through the crack before she went downstairs.

His eyes were wide and remained glued to the cupboard.

• • •

Cheryl Winterfern was working behind the bar in the Nag's Head in Crowsbrook. It was Saturday night and brisk, considering it was February and raining. She looked around the bar. She could name almost everyone in the room: her boss, Ange, pulling a pint of Flowers for Gordon Chester, who was there with a couple of his mates from the sports club at the other end of the village, Jim Abbott, and Bob McEwan. There was Mary Vine, who had babysat every kid in Crowsbrook, and then babysat their kids when they had them, enjoying a quiet sherry with Florence Soames; both of them were in their eighties now, and they would still walk to Arden together a couple of times a week, and that must have been a good four miles and then back again. There were some kids she'd known in primary school, the school just opposite the rose-pink pub, which seemed tiny to Cheryl now: Stu and Emily and Kate, she'd go and have a chat and a smoke with them when she was on her break, catch up a bit—they hadn't been in for a while. And in the corner, Jake and Rose Pound, and the woman who worked for them in the shop. The woman who lived in Dot Trevelyan's old house.

The freak with one eye.

Well, now, that wasn't a nice thought, Cheryl told herself. But she couldn't help it. Sarah, that's what her name was, Sarah Trevelyan, sitting there with a pint of cider and that big patch over the side of her face, like a frizzy-haired pirate in chunky woollens. She'd been working in the shop for a couple of months now. Didn't say much. Wasn't exactly *unpleasant,* but you couldn't call her exactly *friendly* either. And she was…

Well. There were *rumours.* She was a bit… No one liked to say.

Moved into the cottage where old Miss Trevelyan had lived. Her great-aunt or something, word was. Said it all, really.

Cheryl watched the woman with one eye. She was nursing her pint and listening to one of Jake's stories, watching him like a hawk and nodding. Cheryl felt goosebumps creep over her arms, although it was warm behind the bar.

She was odd, that Sarah, that was for sure. When Shelley Boyse had gone into labour at Christmas—her Eddie was working, he worked the ambulances, made good money but had to be out at all hours, even on Christmas—Shelley had been by herself and everything was going too fast and she couldn't drive herself to the hospital in Arden, and she didn't know what to do, and this Sarah had turned up on her doorstep with her one eye and a pile of newspaper and some funny tea in jars, according to Shelley, and had put the kettle on and dealt with everything, helped her through it, even cut the cord, and everything was done and dusted by the time the ambulance got there, and they were just about to tell Sarah what a good job she'd done, and they turned round and she'd gone already. And Shelley was fine; they took her into hospital, just to make sure, and the first nurse who saw her wondered why she hadn't seen her on the ward, everything was so shipshape down there, as it were. But Sarah wouldn't go with her, not once there were other people there.

Bit funny, that was for sure. And there was the time Ethel Perkins's Alf was about to go and Ethel was exhausted from sitting up. Been a week or more, and he was still holding on. Cheryl remembered him from the pub: stubborn bugger, he always was (*no disrespect*, she thought, *people are how they are*). Sarah had turned up then as well, with bread and jam and tea and a packet of cheese sandwiches, and asked if she wanted a break, and Ethel had been so grateful, she'd had some tea and gone to sleep for a couple of hours and then woken up and was able to see Alf off quietly, she'd been with him till the end and not asleep, and Sarah had taken care of the difficult things until Ethel's daughter could get there and then disappeared when the family had arrived.

It was like she *knew*.

But then, Dot—old Miss Trevelyan—had been the same. Kept herself to herself, down in that creepy cottage, except when she was, well, *needed*. Kids had said her place was haunted for years. Cheryl remembered daring Stu to go and cherryknock the door on a sunny day when they were kids, and he had doubledared her, and she had triple-dog-dared him.

He had taken a moment too long and then stood up straight and told her he wasn't scared anyway and had hopped over the gate. He started to make his way up the garden path.

Cheryl and Emily had hid behind the hedge, holding their breath. Stu was moving really slowly, like the path was made of treacle.

"Hurry *up*!" called Emily in a sort of whisper, and Cheryl had told her to shush, and they both erupted in giggles, which they tried to stifle as Stu jumped, and turned around and pulled a face at them and waved at them to shut up.

A cold breeze had got up then, and a dark cloud that Cheryl hadn't noticed before had rolled over the sun. There was a rumble of thunder. She remembered looking up at the sky because she could have sworn that it had been a perfect summer's day, but she remembered the cloud, because it got really dark really quickly, like you wouldn't believe…

Some people said she wasn't remembering right, but she was, and she remembered what happened next, too.

She and Emily had watched Stu go up the path, like he was walking on eggs. It was all overgrown, and the path was narrow. The plants on both sides were touching him in some places.

It was the apple tree, though. There was a gnarled and twisted apple tree growing in the garden about two-thirds of the way up the path. It creaked ominously in the wind that had sprung up, and its branches waved wildly.

Cheryl had held her breath. Stu was getting closer to the door.

There was a terrible creaking.

And—it sounded mad when she thought about saying it out loud, but she knew this was what she'd seen—the tree had slowly twisted round and made a grab for Stu. And she knew this was what had happened and here was why: he yelped and shot in the air and turned around and lit up the path like it was on fire, and went over the gate in two strides and was off up Green Lane like a shot, while Cheryl and Emily went after him, and they ran to the other end of the village, up on the playing field, and they hid in one of the concrete tubes up there and didn't come out for an hour, even though it had gone back to being a perfect summer's day.

And the funny thing was, she thought, that right after Stu had gone over the gate, she could have sworn she heard someone inside the cottage *laughing*.

Anyway. Without talking about it, they all somehow decided that Stu had actually done it, had cherryknocked old Dot Trevelyan's cottage, and so they told everyone that that was what had happened: the old lady had come to the door and been mystified, while the three of them laughed behind her hedge. No one had ever believed them anyway. The place still looked like it was barely standing up from some angles, but what you could see of the garden was nice, even though it was a tangle.

That Sarah, though. She was like Dot: she would always *just show up*. That Sarah.

Sarah suddenly looked up and locked her one good eye on Cheryl's two. Cheryl started and looked away hurriedly; Paul Barlow (eighteen, but only just, and they all knew bloody well what he was selling in the car park even if he thought they didn't, but he didn't make trouble) was standing at the bar and she went over to serve him.

If Cheryl was being honest, something about Sarah gave her the creeps. And she knew she wasn't the only one. The Perkinses, and Shelley and Eddie, and the Pounds wouldn't hear a word against her, but you heard everything when you worked in the pub, and people said that it was funny, someone just showing up when you were in trouble, someone you didn't know in your home. Dot, they'd known for years, of course, but she was new, that Sarah, and she'd only lived in Crowsbrook since last October, and you didn't know, did you? There were some funny people about. And no one knew exactly what had happened to her eye either; Jake just said that she'd had a bad accident, but you could tell he didn't really know, not really, and it had happened about the same time as all that horrible business with Adam Carpenter, who had just vanished along with his girlfriend, the doctor. Home left wide open, it had been. And those three people in the cellar; made it out, they did, but only just. In the papers and everything, but no one had ever really found out who they were. Not from round here, probably. She was sure she'd read the names in the paper, but she couldn't remember.

Awful, it was. Gave her the shivers.

She served Paul Barlow his John Smith's. She wouldn't want Sarah turning up on *her* doorstep, that was for sure. Meant things were bad, usually. And you never knew what would happen.

Weird one, she was, that Sarah.

• • •

Jez was doing homework when she heard the buzzing. Her head jerked up from her books.

There was a fly in her room.

She froze. She felt sick.

She screwed up her face and grabbed the fly swatter from beside her desk. She never closed the curtains until she went to bed anymore, and this was why.

She moved slowly, noiselessly, into a standing position. The fly buzzed up against the windows, bumbling, trying to get out.

Jez didn't take her eyes off it. She moved closer, slowly. Almost imperceptibly.

The fly buzzed. Crawled. Buzzed again. Moved up the window.

SMACK!

Jez pounced. She hit it on the first go, but smashed the swatter against the window twice more, to make sure.

SMACK! SMACK!

The insides of the fly were smeared across the window. Half of its body fell onto the windowsill. Jez didn't care.

She paused, to make sure it was dead. Then, gripping the swatter grimly and moving it as little as possible, she stepped across the room to grab a tissue from the nearest box. There were several, tissues blossoming from them like helpful flowers, clean and inviting. She pulled out two, carefully wrapping one under the fly swatter. She cleaned all the parts of the fly off of the fly swatter, carefully removed the tissue from underneath its mesh paddle (she didn't want any bits of fly escaping), and wrapped the one tissue in the other. She placed both carefully on her desk, briefly, took a large, blackened jam jar from a shelf above her desk, put the tissues in it, put it down, and screwed the lid on tight. Then she went back across the room, pulled two more tissues out of the box, retrieved a bottle of Windowlene from under her bed, sprayed the squashed fly guts with cleaning fluid, and scrubbed the glass until it was spotless.

Those tissues also went in the jar, which she put on the windowsill. There was a can of lighter fluid above her desk, and she moved that to the windowsill, unscrewed the cap, and doused the tissues. It stank.

Then came the tricky part. She reached down to the floor under the window without looking and picked up a pair of sprung bottling tongs, with which she clamped the jar. She opened the window as far as it would go. The wind gusted in and spattered her with raindrops, and she flinched. *Ugh.*

She reached into the pocket of her jeans and pulled out a book of matches, and struck one, holding it with the tips of her fingers in case there was any residual lighter fluid. The wind gusted again, and the match flickered.

Nearly there.

She held the tongs as far out of the window as she could

without wobbling. The flame on the match was wavering in the cold. Hopefully it would be enough.

She dropped it into the glass jar.

WHOOMPH.

The tissues caught light. Jez crossed the fingers of the hand that wasn't holding the tongs, hoping that no one downstairs would see, hoping that Aunt Becky hadn't made an unscheduled trip upstairs for something, hoping…and watching the tissues burn. She could feel the heat from the jar. The tissues, and the remains of the fly, burned out. Some of the acrid smell drifted into Jez's bedroom. She pulled her arm inside and clapped the lid on the jar, wiped the mesh of the fly swatter with alcohol, and dumped the tissue in the bin.

She closed the window.

Can't study with flies around, she thought. She clenched her teeth, sat down heavily at her desk, and started reading again.

• • •

Sam was waiting in the rain outside Nick's House of Kebabs in Arden. He pulled his jacket closer around himself and shivered, and then pulled his phone out of his pocket and checked the time.

Seven thirty-four. Theo was late.

No, he thought. *That's stupid. Four minutes is not late.*

Maybe he wasn't coming.

He would have let you know, Sam thought to himself. *He would have.*

He would have.

Sam had known Theo for eight weeks. It felt like longer. He had been at a Christmas party with his parents, at the Keswicks' house in Crowsbrook. His family had known the Keswicks forever. His mum had worked at the library with Christine Keswick, until Christine had gotten a job managing the Waterstones in Arden, when it was still there. Christine's husband, Keith, did something with law. Sam didn't really understand what it was, only that it didn't involve wearing a wig, and it did involve going to London all the time. Mostly at the party he had smiled a lot and said all sorts of jolly things in a loud voice and ladled out copious amounts of fragrant, spicy mulled wine, hot enough to burn your hands through the glass tumbler.

The house had been full, and Sam had taken up his usual position in the corner of the busy kitchen, talking to Christine about books and helping her move things wrapped in pastry in and out of the oven. The kitchen was noisy and busy, like the whole house. The Keswicks really knew how to throw a party and their house was huge. Christine was telling him how he should read *The Goldfinch*, how some people thought it was a bit self-indulgent, but she didn't and he was nodding and looking around the room, slightly drunk (Keith was always pretty swift with the refills) and feeling okay, feeling

(*like October never happened*)

good, even, looking around and thinking how everyone was safe, and didn't know what had almost happened to Crowsbrook, to them, and how it was kind of cool that he knew everyone and—

Wait a minute, he didn't know everyone. There was a couple he didn't know by the stove, chatting and laughing with Keith and getting a refill.

"Sam?" said Christine. "You still with me?"

"What?" said Sam. "Oh. Yeah. Sure. I was just..." He looked toward the stove.

"I don't think you've met James and Siyanda," said Christine. "I'll introduce you, come on." She beckoned him over to the other side of the kitchen. "They have a son about your age. Siyanda, I want you to meet—"

And then the hottest guy Sam had ever seen walked into the room.

And it turned out that he read *Private Eye*. And was the same age as Sam. And liked bands from the nineties. Turned out they had quite a lot in common, actually. So they hung out the next day. And then the day after that. And then it was Christmas. But they caught up on Boxing Day. And on the twenty-seventh, they'd kissed for the first time, and then later on the twenty-ninth…

Anyway. Sam hadn't looked back.

He didn't really know if they were dating or hooking up or whatever, but they saw each other most days, and he hadn't seen Jez in weeks. He felt a bit guilty about that, especially after everything that had happened in October. (There was a twinge of pain in his arm; he tried to ignore it, and stretched it out and rotated his shoulder backwards a couple of times. It ached. Hopefully it was just the rain. Or his imagination.) October seemed a million years ago.

I mean, he thought, *it's not like I haven't seen her at all.* He'd run into her at school, obviously, once in a while. Although she wasn't in the Year Thirteen common room much these days. Or the cafeteria. He didn't know where she was hanging out at school, come to think of it. Right after *October* (he stretched again; it usually helped, stretching it out a couple of times)…well, he'd needed surgery for his arm; he'd broken it pretty badly…

(THAT THING broke your arm)

…and he'd needed surgery to put some pins in it, and he'd been on a lot of drugs…

(couldn't have slept without them)

…and he knew she'd been to visit, because his mum had told him, but he didn't remember. But that was only right after; they'd wanted him back at school right away, and his mum had driven him on the first day, rather than making him go on the bus, because his arm was still in a cast, and then he'd started physio right away…

(it hurt, so they gave him more painkillers)

…and he hadn't been on the bus much. And usually he'd meet Jez to do homework, but she said she had mock exams right after Christmas, so that was late November and early December, and he'd been getting better and was off the painkillers…

(when the dreams started)

…and had figured out that his mum thought that he'd been injured in a hit-and-run, and thought that the other things he'd mumbled about were the drugs talking…

(you should write a book one day, she said, *with your imagination)*

…he was starting to miss Jez and needed to talk to her or to somebody, anybody, about what had happened, but he didn't want to bother her because it had been so much worse for her, with her dad and everything…

(You could have talked to Sarah. You know where she lives. You could have talked to Sarah, and have been there for Jez.)

…and then he'd met Theo and he didn't know where the time had gone…

(and Theo wouldn't remind anyone of Gareth Lake, would he?)

He should call Jez. He should call her now. Theo was running late anyway. He pulled his phone out of his pocket. He was going to call Jez.

"Heeeeey!" He looked up and saw Theo grinning at him. He felt a jolt of excitement. "Sorry I'm late."

"No worries," said Sam, and then felt stupid. Awkward. He should text Jez. Just quickly. He could say that, right? *"I just have to text my friend."* It wouldn't be too difficult, right?

What would he say, though? It wasn't like they'd parted on bad terms, it was just…well, it'd been a while. He knew he should have texted her or something. But she hadn't texted him either. But she had exams, and he'd mostly been texting Theo…oh *shit*, Theo was going to think he was really weird. Or stupid. Or from some little town that wasn't London where people didn't know how to interact socially and…oh crap, this was getting worse by the second.

Say something. He willed himself. He opened his mouth.

"Everything all right?" said Theo, still smiling. He gestured toward the phone in Sam's hand.

Sam hesitated for a moment.

"Yeah," he said. He smiled. "Everything's fine." He put his phone back in his pocket. "Let's go."

"I've heard this is the best kebab shop in Arden," said Theo.

They went into the shop just as three women were coming out. They were older, and all three wore wide-brimmed hats and long black coats. Theo held the door for them, but they didn't say thank you. A fresh wave of icy rain whirled by after they passed, as if it had been afraid to risk falling on them. Theo rolled his eyes.

"You're welcome?" he said, as they departed.

Sam looked at his phone again. Jez hadn't texted him either.

Better do that tomorrow, he thought—again—and went to get a shawarma.

● ● ●

Sarah swayed back into her cottage from the pub at about eleven-thirty—not too late, and the shop didn't open until ten on Sundays. She grabbed at the door knob and missed.

Stupid eye. It was definitely the eye. Her depth perception had been gone for almost four months, and she was mostly used to it, but sometimes it still caught her off guard. But it was *definitely* the eye, and not the beers.

Definitely.

She tried again and caught it, and let herself in successfully.

She liked talking to the Pounds (well, listening, mostly; she still didn't really like to talk because it led to awkward questions) and had heard about their son Alan's latest misadventures with his van. He was renovating an old VW that he'd picked up for peanuts a couple of years ago; he was working on the engine and had got it going again, purred like a cat, Jake said, but he hadn't done a lot of work on the body up until now, and the rusty hulk sitting on four piles of bricks outside the garage was driving Rose mad. Sarah felt a bit bad; she knew that Alan'd probably be further along if he hadn't taken a break to fix Sarah's car, which had gotten into an accident with—well, it didn't matter, but in October it had been pretty bashed up. Looked like someone had driven it into a tree and dropped a rock on it, Alan had said. Sarah just nodded, and there had been a pause, and he had told her that it needed a new windscreen and a lot of bodywork and a respray. But he had fixed it for her, and wouldn't take a penny for it, which might have been luck or might have been Rose glaring at him from the corner of the kitchen when it came up. But then Rose said later that she hadn't minded about him working on the car and not the van and that, really, nothing would have got done on the van before Alan fixed Sarah's car because it wasn't until right after that that he'd had a run of luck with the lottery; hadn't won the jackpot or anything, but for a few weeks in a row, he'd won enough to pay his bills for a while and get the parts he needed for his van, with a bit left over. Lucky really, the way these things worked out.

Sarah sat down at the slightly battered ancient wooden table, next to a wall of bookshelves, and prepared herself for negotiating the wrought-iron spiral staircase that went up to the second floor of her tiny cottage. A spider dropped out of her hair and onto a pile of old papers in front of her. It ran over the papers and onto the back of her hand and stopped there, quivering, as if in expectation. She looked up suddenly at the sensation of movement.

"Oh," she said. "It's you."

The spider was an ordinary, large-ish house spider, but its appearance was marked by the absence of one of its rearmost legs. This didn't appear to have impeded its movement at all, but it did make it easy for Sarah to distinguish the creature from the other spiders in her house.

And there were a *lot* of other spiders in her house.

Sarah was well aware that you couldn't really tell where a spider was looking with any of its eyes (and it was even more difficult when you considered that they had eight of the things) but it seemed to her that the spider was staring at her.

"What day is it?" she said, mostly to herself.

The spider ran over her fingers and onto the pile of papers, then circled back and clambered over the monolith of her hand again. It sat there, waiting.

"Right," she said. "Feeding day, right?"

The spider ran up her arm and disappeared; at least, she couldn't feel it anymore. "Okay," she said, and got to her feet with a grunt. It was time she was in bed anyway.

She went up the wrought-iron spiral staircase in the corner of her living room, cleaned her teeth and changed into a worn-out T-shirt and pyjama bottoms, and lay down on her bed at the back of the house.

Feeding the spiders was one thing that had become easier, since she lost her eye. Funny how things worked out.

She took a deep breath and closed her eye and reached out with her

mind
body
soul

down down into the earth looking for the things beyond life the things beyond death the things that knew her loved her served her she called them: come to me come to me come and feed come and feed and I will nourish you and we will be one flesh…

come to me

come to me

come—

She called to them, and they came, rushing, over the windowsill, through the door to her bedroom, standing ajar in the darkness, between the hinges of the door, through a slender crack in the wall, up from under the bed, they flowed in their hundreds, thousands, like a silent sea teeming with life.

Spiders.

They covered her, head to toe: on her face, in her hair, over her ears, on her skin. She could feel them everywhere as they fed, could feel the energy draining out of her, could feel herself getting sleepy as the tide of spiders passed over her. She held her breath so that she didn't injure any of them by inhaling.

Feed, she thought. Feed well.

They fed well and fed long. Then, as suddenly as they'd appeared, they departed, flowing back the way they had come as easily as water. Sarah let out her breath in a rush and inhaled deeply. A final spider ran over her face, and then they were gone. She felt a little drained.

She had inherited the spiders, along with the cottage, from her great-aunt Dorothea the previous year. Her grandmother, who had raised her, had told her about such things, of spirits, helpful spirits, that were—

Well, not "passed down," exactly, she had said. *They've living things, you can't own them. You can only take care of them.* Familiars, the finders had called them, long ago. They were a big part of the family business, although her grandmother had told her they were rare these days, much like the family businesses themselves.

You feed them, she had said, *and they help you. Protect you. That sort of thing.*

They had protected Sarah the previous October, all right. When she had lost her eye. The spiders had saved her life. She had looked it up. *Scoring above the breath* they used to call it: if you drew a witch's blood above her mouth and nose—in the eye, say—and the blood fell on the ground, her familiars would hear the sound and come running. And they had. Saved her and the two kids, Jez Elliot and Sam Katz, who had been trying to help her themselves, although Sam had ended up with a broken arm for his pains. She'd seen him in the shop a few times since then; he was always polite, but not exactly friendly. She didn't mind. Kept herself to herself. It was better that way.

She was still on a mission.

She had come to Crowsbrook after her house had burned down, with everything she owned and her best friend, Eleanor, inside it. The fire had been, she had found out eventually, the result of a scheme by a London financier to mine the supernatural world for profit. Nicholas Carrington, his name was. Sarah had sworn to avenge Eleanor's death. But bloody vengeance in the twenty-first century was not as easy as it sounded, even if you had centuries' worth of your family's business resources at your disposal. And that was without the distraction of local businessmen selling their souls to Lord knows what for power and influence, like Adam Carpenter had, although he'd paid the price for it in the end. That was the first thing she'd had to deal with when she'd come to Crowsbrook, and that was how she'd ended up in the cellar of the big house on Sycamore Lane with a half-human, half-demon monster with flies living in the front of its caved-in face gouging her eye out with its claws. And breaking Sam's arm.

It was all go in Crowsbrook, she thought.

But there was something else that was bothering her, something that her great-aunt had mentioned in the letter that she had left for Sarah in the immaculately clean living room, for when Sarah had arrived at the cottage. The dark times. Dot had mentioned dark times. She'd believed that forces of evil were gathering, preparing to make another onslaught on the world that modern technology had taken from them. Sarah's grandmother had disagreed—or, at least, felt strongly that the family business should mind its own and not get involved—and the two had fought bitterly about the responsibility of the family business under the circumstances. Sarah's grandmother believed that the knowledge of the family business was its power and should be kept secret; Dorothea believed that only by trading knowledge could they even hope to breach the impending darkness. The two women never reconciled, dying apart. Dorothea had spent the years before her death travelling; she had wandered with purpose all over the world, seeking to trade knowledge for the impending fight, listening, learning, offering to share the knowledge she had, if she was asked, and writing down what she found out in hundreds of hardcover notebooks that filled the small cottage in which Sarah now lay.

And weapons. She had collected weapons. God knows how she had got them through Customs. There were three trunks of them in Sarah's spare room: charms, cantraps, spellridden items that looked perfectly normal until you picked them up and they gave off sparks. It seemed like a lot, until you considered what it was supposed to go up against.

Rising darkness aside, she needed to find out more about Nicholas Carrington. And that was proving surprisingly difficult.

She'd started off on Google, on the computers in the library in Arden, and had found out what she already knew: he was in business in London and had worked for an old company in the city that had an impeccable pedigree. He had attended an excellent and exclusive public school and had continued on to an excellent and exclusive university. And then he had joined a firm (Maunce Paxton, they were called—it wasn't exactly clear what they did), and then he had left to strike out on his own, and there the Internet trail ended. No presence on social media. No pictures. No references to his brilliant career. It was as if he had dropped off the face of the planet. The clock on the computer had clicked down to the end of her session, and she had gathered up her things and moved into the Reference section and looked up his immediate family in *Who's Who* and found that any Carringtons that were closely related to Nicholas were respectably deceased, under no unusual circumstances, for some years.

And she didn't know where to look next. She couldn't afford one of those private detective services (especially not with the cost of everything being what it was in London). The Sight wouldn't help her—it wasn't like a supernatural Yellow Pages. She was a long way from London, and she didn't know what she was looking for. And the spiders were really only helpful for gathering information in the village; they'd helped her out with the family business more than once, letting her know who was ready to come into the world and who to leave it because that was one of the things that the family business had traditionally done. But London…London might as well have been another planet. And Carrington was hidden somewhere within its swirling atmosphere, and likely knew enough dodgy Ethereal people to keep himself hidden from anyone who might have an interest in him that wasn't to his own benefit.

She hated to admit it, but she was at a dead end.

Her head was a little foggy from the beer and the feeding, and she drifted off to sleep.

. . .

Sarah dreamt.

It was foggy. She was standing on spongy ground. Leaves. Twigs. She looked down and saw they were wet. The fog was thick. She couldn't tell where she was. It looked like a wood. There were a lot of trees.

It was windy. She could see the fog moving through the trees, like clouds past the window of an airplane. She couldn't feel the wind. Couldn't hear it properly either; it was like being under water. They called them "visions" for a reason.

She looked at the fog more carefully.

Couldn't smell it either.

It wasn't fog. It was smoke. Her stomach lurched. She took a few steps forward and stumbled onto a path she knew well.

She steeled herself. She was here for a reason. She wouldn't see anything that was worse than she'd already seen. Couldn't. That couldn't happen.

She turned left and walked toward her old home.

The smoke was clearing. The fire was over. Everything was over. All that was left was the ruins. Skeletal walls. Charred beams. Rubble. Ash. Sarah stood still, behind an elderly oak.

There was nothing here. So why was she? She stared at the ruins. Her grandmother had told her that there was no such thing as coincidence. When a vision was this clear, it would be for a reason. Sarah's mind was clear now, and she watched the ruins like a hawk. Minutes passed.

Why was she here?

A figure moved among the ashes. A woman. Sarah started. How had she missed her? There was another. And another. Three women. Dressed in black. She couldn't see their faces. The first had a broad-brimmed black hat and a cane and was poking through the rubble as if she were looking for something.

Who were they? What were they looking for?

Sarah felt something tickling her foot. She looked down sharply; that shouldn't happen, not in a vision. A large adder was making its way slowly over her bare foot. She gasped.

A brick tumbled from the pile of rubble. Sarah looked up. All three women were staring right at her.

They can't see you, she told herself. *People couldn't see you, in visions.* But somehow, she knew it wasn't true this time. Whoever they were, they could see her. She was frozen to the spot. The snake slithered off.

Without warning, three large crows attacked Sarah, cawing and screaming, feet in her hair, wings beating against her face. She shouted and tried to beat them away and—

woke up with a start in her bed in her cottage at Crowsbrook. She brushed at her hair with both hands and blinked. She sat up.

What the hell?

What did any of it mean? It wasn't like she hadn't dreamt about the cottage (and the fire and the aftermath and all the rest of it) before, but this dream had felt different, and the dreams that felt different were the ones you were supposed to pay attention to. The problem was that this hadn't been different in a good way. Whoever those women were, they had seen her. And no one was supposed to be able to see a witch in a vision.

They had to be Ethereal. And then she had been attacked by crows. What did it all mean?

She went to take a drink of water from the glass by the side of her bed and breathed in sharply.

The seven-legged spider was lying dead next to it.

· · ·

Night lay on the pond. The clouds covered the moon, and the rain spattered the surface in near-complete darkness, while the wind hissed through the naked branches of the trees.

The pond had held a great evil for a long time. Old habits died hard. The thing it had possessed was gone, and it felt the lack like a phantom limb. Something in its water called out to the things that needed it. The signs in the land pointed the way. They would find it on instinct.

The shadows at the edge of the pond knew this. They could feel it: something calling, something growing.

Something coming.

The shadows cowered in the darkness and the cold.

Chapter 2

Hogarth coughed as he peeled the potatoes for lunch. He'd been coughing a lot recently; he'd had a heavy cold back in October and he hadn't been able to get rid of the cough. Disgusting, it was: felt like he was grinding up bits of his lungs most days, and the rain didn't help. Mostly he liked the rain: the school cleared out more quickly and he could start the cleaning without having to nod hello to the frazzled and distracted mums and, less frequently, dads, who would be ushering their squealing plastic-wrapped kids into cars like rain-splashed sodding spaceships with wheels. By the time he made his way home, the streets would be dark and empty. He'd read somewhere—probably in the doctor's office, in one of those crappy magazines the receptionist brought in—she didn't want them and no one else did either, the age of them— that rain was "spiritually cleansing." Load of rubbish, of course, but the rain did get rid of the kind of debris that Hogarth hated most: the kind that walked on two legs.

Not got the sense they were born with, most of them, Ma used to say.

He was a pretty good cook now. Simple stuff, though. Not as good as Ma made. He didn't go in for all that fancy stuff you saw on the telly, even if that dark-haired tart was a bit of all right. He'd taught himself right after—

Well, it was about thirty-five years now he'd been making dinner for two, as it were. Plus it seemed rude just to keep chucking raw sausages into the cupboard. Tried to learn to cook what Ma used to make, he had. He made a few mistakes to start with, but the thing in the cupboard (as he had thought of *him* back then) hadn't minded. Ate the plates a couple of times as well, so now Hogarth served his companion's meal on paper ones. It would have been expensive if he'd been paying, but he wasn't, so he didn't care.

The Bag'un was paying.

Hogarth had started thinking of the thing in his cupboard as the Bag'un about three weeks after he'd put the bag in there. It just seemed right. *Th'un that came owt' bag*, he thought. The Bag'un didn't *speak* exactly, but Hogarth could hear it, quiet and persistent, right in the middle of his skull. He didn't like company (Ma had been different; she was Ma, not company), and he didn't want company, but the Bag'un was different, too.

The Bag'un wasn't *people*. Like Ma hadn't been *people*.

Hogarth finished peeling the potatoes and put them on to boil. He had a couple of minutes before he needed to put the sausages on. Couldn't mess with sausage, beans, and mash, Ma always said, and the Bag'un seemed to like it. (The Bag'un ate pretty much everything and didn't seem to care, but Hogarth had a good feeling about sausage, beans, and mash.) He went into the hall to lay the table. He'd set up a small table and chair for himself next to the cupboard. Might as well do these things properly, even if he was the only one of the two of them that used a knife and fork.

"Hello, hello," he said out loud as he opened the cupboard.

He dropped the cutlery.

The cupboard was just a cupboard. Three shelves, some light bulbs, and the four pieces of wood that he couldn't remember why he'd kept. His stomach dropped with fear.

"No," said Hogarth. "No!"

He heard an echo in the middle of his skull, a whisper of a thought. Not the Bag'un's usual clear voice (what he thought of as the voice anyway: something between a whisper and a hiss). This was quiet as breathing. Quiet as a last echo.

…be back…

It didn't help. Hogarth stood looking at his cupboard with growing discomfort. Because this had happened once before, and when it had—

Well. Might have just been a coincidence, of course. He had told himself that a hundred times. Just a coincidence.

Thing was, when you knew someone could get that far into your head, you knew when you were lying to yourself as well. And you also knew that even when you made the effort and cooked sausage, beans, and mash, and someone told you that they liked it, and they were happy with you for making the effort, and they appreciated the care that you took of them…you knew really, you knew deep down that although everything they were telling you was true, the other true thing was that no matter how much you told yourself it was a coincidence that this had happened once before (and then the other thing, the bad thing, well, the bad *things,* had happened), you knew it wasn't really a coincidence because at the back of your mind—and this was a thing that you had never been told, not even in the way that you were usually told things, the way that made it easier to pretend that you had made it up yourself—the one thing you suspected and suspected hard was this: that sometimes they were hungry for the thing that wasn't the thing you could give them, whether that was sausage, beans, and mash or not.

Sausage, beans, and mash wasn't the only thing the Bag'un liked to eat. And it had gone out to find something else.

• • •

"You all right? You look a bit peaky." Rose inspected Sarah from over the reading glasses she'd been looking through to price tins of beans. She put down the pricing gun. "Don't tell me two whole pints knocked you flat." She frowned. "I don't want you working if you're poorly. Can't have you chundering on the supplies." The pricing gun clicked.

"Yeah, yeah," said Sarah, hurriedly. "No. I'll be fine. It's not like it's going to be busy." It wouldn't be, she knew from experience. Sunday afternoons were quiet.

"Well," said Rose, with clear reluctance, "only if you're sure. Maybe don't start the cleaning and all that for a bit; have a sit-down first." She pointed behind the counter. "Start with your break. Catch up on the paper."

"I brought something," said Sarah, lifting an old string shopping bag. There was a package in it, wrapped in brown paper.

"All right, then," said Rose. "Go and man the till and have a sit-down; I'll be out of your way in a minute." Sarah mostly worked the shop on her own on Sundays, while Jake and Rose took a well-earned break. She made her way behind the counter to the bar stool covered in torn red vinyl that stood behind it. The sponge poked out of the tear like a soft yellow hernia. She sat down and took her book out of the bag.

"Mind if I read, if it's quiet?" she called to Rose above the click of the pricing gun.

"Long as everything's clean, the customers aren't waiting, and you're not pinching the supplies, I don't care, if it's quiet," Rose hollered back. "You don't have to keep asking. Although the floor by the fridge was a bit sticky when I came down this morning. I think the bloody Amble kids spilled a can of Irn-Bru on it last night; if you could do that as soon as you've got your head together, I'd be much obliged." She looked up. "You look like you're coming down with something. I'll go and make you a cuppa." She bustled into the back.

Rose didn't have the Sight, but she was very well attuned to people she knew and liked, and she'd known Sarah for four months now, so it wasn't surprising that she could tell something was up. And Sarah knew what it was, too. The memory of the feathers against her face made her shudder.

She hadn't been physically hurt, of course—visions couldn't do that to you, she told herself. It was one of the first things her grandmother taught her; all kids knew that. However scary your dreams were, they couldn't *actually* hurt you. But then, she'd been pretty sure that people in visions couldn't *see* you either, and she'd known—somehow she'd *known*—that the three women knew she was watching them, and they were watching her right back. And she had a gut feeling that wasn't good. That was another thing her grandmother had taught her: don't ignore the feelings from your gut.

And on top of that, the last time she'd had a vision that vivid—and the *only* other time she'd had a vision that violent— was right after she'd arrived in Crowsbrook, right at the start of the business with Adam Carpenter when heavy-duty Ethereals had been on the move. *Seriously* heavy-duty Ethereals. But those Ethereals hadn't been watching her watch them.

She shivered.

Rose came back through the green and white curtain of ribbons that separated the shop from the storeroom at the back, behind which was Rose and Jake's bungalow. Rose was carrying a teapot, her hands wrapped in a tea towel to protect against the heat. "Here you go," she said. "Pot of char. Cure anything, that will."

"Lovely," said Sarah, hauling herself back to the present. "Sorry. Miles away, there." She watched Rose pour out a steaming mug of tea and hunched over it as Rose disappeared into the back rooms. She tried to take her mind off the vision of the three figures by taking out her book.

It was one of the bound collections of notes and scraps that her great-aunt Dot had left her. There were hundreds of them, a testament to her aunt's belief in the imminence of the dark times. Sarah was reading them one at a time. It was taking ages: her aunt's handwriting was tiny, and she must have been the only person left who preferred writing with actual ink to a ballpoint pen, but in a twist of apparent modernity, she had eschewed (or hadn't be able to find) blotting paper. The pages were spotty and in some places soaked into holes with the dark fluid. Most of the books that Sarah had read since she had arrived in October had dealt with the contents of Dorothea's weapons trunks, and that had been pretty interesting, although some of them needed some serious maintenance work, and Sarah had no idea how she was going to find the money for the replacement bits, let alone how she was going to find the bits themselves. How could you get cassowary feathers in Ardenshire, without attracting the attention of either the local wildlife services or H.M. Customs?

Sarah had always been more of an under-the-radar kind of person. So had her grandmother.

She sighed and cracked the spine of the book, and saw immediately that this one was different. The blotchy, drunken-spider handwriting was familiar, but this was a scrapbook, not a journal. It was full of press clippings. Annotated. She looked at the date on the first page. The clipping was from the 1970s.

BONES FOUND IN FOREST BELONG TO MISSING TEACHER, shouted the headline.

Police have confirmed that skeletal remains discovered in Thewston Woods late on Sunday night are likely the mortal remains of Miss Alice Cookson, 54, who has not been seen for almost a week. Reports that the remains are badly decayed beyond what might be expected after so short a time have yet to be confirmed by detectives, but a police spokesman assured reporters that the remains were Miss Cookson's at a press conference yesterday.

Weird. She turned the pages carefully. The old newspaper cracked; the cuttings had been stuck in with yellowing Sellotape, and some of it was coming loose. She laid the book down flat on the counter; it wasn't as if there was anyone in the shop anyway.

Murders unsolved because they should have been impossible. Mysterious beasts, barely glimpsed from car windows; animal attacks that no one could explain. Disappearances. Outbreaks of disease among livestock. All seemingly unconnected, but tracked and annotated by Dorothea. And there was one big difference, Sarah noted, between the stories regaled in these clippings and the catalogue of weapons that Dorothea had amassed as she'd travelled around the world adding to her collection.

All of the newspaper clippings were from the British Isles. She turned the pages. The Brecon Beacons. The Rhondda Valley. Dumfries. And in the towns: Leighton Buzzard. Thetford. Widnes. There were towns she'd never heard of in here. All small towns. She looked at the names of the papers: they were all local. And the dates…

The oldest one was the Cookson one from the 1970s. June 1976, it had been. After that, they averaged about one every couple of years, throughout the eighties and into the nineties and the twenty-first century.

Until 2001.

In 2001, the number of clippings went up to two or three a year.

"VAMPIRE" VIRUS DRAINS PATIENTS OF BLOOD IN WARD 4

SCHOOL CLOSED AS "MAGGOT PLAGUE" RUNS RIOT

REVELLERS' NIGHT ENDS IN "WILD DOG" TERROR TOWN MYSTIFIED BY VISITING "LIGHTS"

It was the same pattern: always small towns, always small stories, always unsolved. She turned the last page, and her mouth dropped open.

FIFTEENTH-CENTURY COTTAGE DESTROYED IN FIRE screeched the headline. ONE DEAD.

One dead indeed.

Eleanor. The person she had been closest to since her grand-mother died.

She stared at the page, at the photograph of the smoking ruins of her house, and felt sick again. She knew that her aunt had known that it had happened, of course she had. He aunt had left her a letter in the cottage; that was how she knew that Dorothea had immediately connected it to the events that she believed foreshadowed the dark times. But seeing the scene in front of her once again disturbed and unsettled her.

It also reminded her that she hadn't gotten any closer to finding Nicholas Carrington in four months.

Six months, said the voice in her head. *The cottage burned down in August.*

It had taken her a while to get the name, though, she told herself.

The clock's still ticking. You swore an oath. A blood oath.

Her grandmother hadn't taught her about the blood oath. She had learned herself.

• • •

She had been allowed to read any of the books in the cottage. Her grandmother had always made that clear. And there were plenty of books; every room was lined with them, some up to the ceiling. She hadn't sought the shelf out. She'd just noticed one day when she'd been going up the stairs (her grandmother said that she'd been shooting up like a beansprout that year, and maybe it was the first time she'd been tall enough to see it) that there was a shelf covered by a curtain way up in an alcove in the stairwell. She'd stood on her tiptoes and twitched it back; it revealed seven books she had never seen before. They were tiny, and their leather covers were dark with age; each one had a dull black ribbon around it, to hold it together.

Sarah climbed up and took one down. She laid it on the step in front of her, untied the ribbon, and opened it. The pages were loose and slipped around. She picked it up, sat down on the stairs and started to read.

Her grandmother found her seven hours later. She hadn't moved from the stair.

Sarah? said her grandmother. *What are you reading?*

Sarah looked up, slowly and wordlessly. She held up the book.

They were up there, she said simply. She pointed.

Her grandmother nodded.

Well, she said after a long time. *You know the rules. Magic is magic. Neither good nor evil. It's what you do with it that counts. But those things—she nodded her head toward the small pile of books lying next to Sarah—those things, you need to be careful of. They'll bind you in ways you don't want to be bound. And there are consequences for breaking the rules.*

Okay, said Sarah. She shrugged. There weren't many rules in the business, and they made sense to Sarah. If her grandmother said be careful, well, whatever. She'd be careful.

I mean it, said her grandmother. *You say it's all right now, but those things…those things aren't meant to be used when you're sitting on the stairs in your right mind and listening to the rain outside. Those things are for hearts that are screaming.*

Okay, said Sarah. She felt she should say something else. *I'll be careful.*

And she had been. Until the night her heart was screaming.

• • •

She pushed the memory away. There was a pocket in the back of the scrapbook, part of the cover, and there was a newspaper clipping folded up in there, too. Gingerly, she took it out, bracing herself for more photos of the burned cottage, but immediately saw she needn't have worried: the clipping was too yellowed and slippery to have come from last year. It was old. She unfolded it and studied it carefully. It was an obituary.

Mr. Obadiah Kane read the name at the top.

Mr. Obadiah Kane, head administrator at St. Joseph's Children's Home, passed away suddenly in his sleep, at the age of 52. Mr. Kane had devoted his life to the service of underprivileged children since leaving the seminary 30 years earlier, and had run the St. Joseph's Children's Home since 1977. He is described by those at St. Joseph's as "much beloved," and Sister Mary Angelica, his secretary, says that "the place will not be the same without him." Donations can be made to the St. Joseph's Children's Home Care Trust.

Then there was a phone number.

Sarah frowned. This was odd. This was just a clipping about a dead orphanage manager. She turned it over, in case the real story was on the other side, and saw part of an advert for a used-car showroom.

What the hey?

She looked at the date on the newspaper clipping. It was splotchy; had been written by hand in ink—1995.

Huh. Well, that didn't make any sense.

The bells above the shop door jingled, and Sarah slammed the scrapbook shut, pushed it under the counter, and wished Mr. York, who'd come in for his copy of the *Daily Mail,* a very good morning. Then she went to get the mop.

• • •

"MUMMY, LOOK!"

Jack was at the top of the slide. The really big slide. The slide that was so big there was a cage at the top to stop you falling off when you finished climbing up the ladder. He had been in awe of it the whole of last summer and had conquered it in December, a couple of weeks before the Christmas holidays.

"I'm looking!" called Holly, trying to sound enthusiastic (she knew the slide had been a big deal for him, but it had been six bloody weeks now and she'd watched him go down the flipping thing a lot). "Well done!"

"I haven't DONE it yet!" Jack yelled back. He sat down at the top of the slide. Holly's phone buzzed and instinctively, she looked down and pulled it out of her bag, just as Jack pushed off.

"MUMMY!"

"Well done!" called Holly again, looking up sharply.

"You MISSED it!" yelled Jack. He was frowning. Crap. Then he yawned.

"Do it again!" called Holly. "I'll watch this time." Jack ran around to the ladder, and she snuck a look at her phone.

"He's yawning a lot," said a cut-glass voice from beside her. "Still not sleeping well?"

Holly felt her stomach clench. Allegra Valentine. *Goddammit.*

Allegra settled delicately next to Holly on the bench, and Daphne Latimer and Isabella Butterworth floated down to settle beside her.

"Better," Holly lied. She'd woken up twice in the night, worried about him, and had peeked into his room. He had been lying in exactly the same position she'd left him, tense and focused, watching the cupboard like a hawk.

"Sleep is *so* important," said Allegra. "Wear them out every day and they'll be out like a light. Physical activity. Cures everything." Jocasta, Allegra's daughter, was, Holly knew, enrolled in two types of martial arts and ballet classes. She'd seen the evidence of the former on some of Jocasta's friends, among whom, fortunately, Jack was not counted.

"Looks good on the UCAS form as well," pointed out Daphne. Allegra and Isabella tittered politely.

Yes, thought Holly. *Right. Gotta be thinking about university applications, once they're in reception class.* She smiled, weakly.

"So glad to hear Jack's sleeping better, though," Allegra continued. "I mean, the assembly thing…it just makes it so much harder to for children to find their places in the social structure if they can't fit in properly." A week ago, after two weeks of disturbed sleep, Jack had fallen asleep in assembly. He was still being taunted about it. There were also disadvantages to not being counted among the friends of Jocasta Valentine.

"Yeah," said Holly. "About that. I didn't want to bring it up, but he says Jocasta's still teasing him about it." Normally, she wouldn't be this direct with Allegra, but she hadn't slept well either. "Could you have a word?"

Allegra smiled prettily. "I'm sure it's just a misunderstanding," she said, in a voice sweet as organic agave syrup. "Jocasta doesn't tease. I think you'll find Jack's a very sensitive child. Which is laudable, of course. But you need to help him become more assertive. There are classes, you know. It's never too early."

I wish I'd known, thought Holly. *I'd have taken one, and then I'd be able to tell you exactly where you and your monster spawn could get off.* "No," she said. "He was pretty assertive about telling me who'd been calling him Bye Baby Bunting every playtime for a week and egging on the other kids to do the same."

Allegra sighed. "I'm so sorry for you," she said. "But you can't take offence over every little disagreement between the children. They have to learn to express themselves and sort out their own differences. I'm sure you can have a talk with Jack about standing up for himself. But it's really not the rest of the world's job to accommodate his needs. It's such an important lesson. It'll stand him in good stead when he's older."

"Right," said Holly. "He can put it on his UCAS form." Daphne Latimer raised her eyebrows, but Allegra seemed unaffected.

"I'm so glad we had this talk," she said, beaming. "I have to take Jocasta to Wen-Do now." She got up to leave, and her courtiers rose with her.

"Bye," said Holly despondently. She checked her phone. She and Jack should be heading home for tea themselves. "Jack! Time to go!" She scanned the playground, and when she saw him, she froze.

He was crouching in front of one of the bushes in the corner of the playground, staring into the darkness underneath it with the same expression and intensity that she had seen the previous night.

"Jack!" She was by his side faster than she knew she could move. "Jack, what is it? What are you looking at?" She peered under the bush, but all she could see was darkness. "What is it? Is there someone there?"

He turned to her slowly. His eyes were wide with fear and he was trembling slightly.

"The monster," he said. His lower lip quivered. "It's started following me."

• • •

When it had happened before—when the Bag'un had gone away before—Hogarth had woken up and known that something was different. Afterward, that was. When the Bag'un had come back. Hogarth had woken up and noticed that the sheets felt different. Crisper. Newer. Like when Ma was around.

Twenty-five years ago it had been when it had all happened before, and he remembered it like yesterday.

• • •

Twenty-five years ago, the curtains that had covered his window—that still covered his window—were thick and did an excellent job of blocking out the light, but the digital clock next to his bed told him that he had slept in to mid-morning. Well, whatever. He'd been up to the Nag's Head the night before, sat in his corner, and gotten blind drunk, because the Bag'un had gone away and he was alone. Ma wouldn't have approved, but Ma was gone, too, and if Ma had been around, he wouldn't have had to go down the Pony, and he didn't have to be at work until noon anyway.

He did need to piss, though.

He braced himself and got out of bed. He was happy to find that he felt better than he had thought he would. The room didn't swim. That was good. The carpet felt soft and clean under his feet. He looked down.

He squinted at it.

He hadn't changed the carpet since Ma—well, since Ma hadn't been around. Hadn't seen the point. Couldn't get a new one the same and Ma had liked this one; it had lasted well. Been twenty years old when she—well, it must be almost forty years old now, and if he was honest, it hadn't been quite as new looking as in Ma's day, though she'd taken good care of it. At least, he'd *thought* it wasn't as new looking. Maybe it was last night's beer, but as he sat on the edge of the bed with his feet on the carpet, it seemed—well, *softer*. Less like a flour sack. He thought the colours seemed brighter as well.

Probably a hangover brewing. If it hadn't hit him yet, he was probably still drunk.

He pulled on his old dressing gown, the one Ma had made for him (couldn't buy one like that, still good it was, after he didn't know how long) and made his way to the bathroom, and then, feeling relieved, downstairs. Everything looked like it had been freshly painted. The wood on the stairs had been planed, sanded, and polished. All of the chips and scratches that came with usual wear and tear had been removed.

Looked like it had done when Ma was around.

When the Bag'un had first moved in, it hadn't been like this. There was the food, of course, and the house got warmer and less damp even though the heating bill stayed the same, but for the first years after the Bag'un had arrived, it was the way it had been since Ma—well, things wore out, and he hadn't had the heart to change them. He'd just managed as things got a bit older—it was all quality; Ma didn't hold with spending good money on rubbish. And he agreed: no sense in doing your place up like a magazine. Ma hadn't held with people who did: "showy," she called them, which was just short of being "flashy," and she wouldn't be doing with the flashy ones, not her. He had his telly and his comfy chair, and a posh ashtray where you could push a thing on top and the ash disappeared so it didn't smell or get everywhere, and that was pretty much all he needed.

But the Bag'un had filled his fridge and his cupboards. His favourite stuff. Stuff he didn't even know how to cook. Stuff he'd forgotten he liked, because he didn't know where to find it. And that was good. It was almost like—

Well, no, it wasn't, really. There was only one of Ma.

And then the Bag'un had disappeared. Seven years it had been, Seven years after he'd met Savaric at the crossroads, though he hadn't known where the time had gone. The fridge stopped filling up. Hogarth wasn't used to it. He ran out of food. He ended up buying a can of soup from the shop to heat up and have for his tea on the third day after the Bag'un had gone, but he couldn't finish it. It tasted like it was full of chemicals, and he ended up throwing it out. He went to bed hungry.

He tried not to think too much about it. This was why Ma hadn't held with people. They weren't to be trusted. Not that he'd *trusted* the Bag'un. He'd left him in his house all right, but there wasn't much worth stealing and he hadn't left the cupboard until now (as far as Hogarth knew, anyway). It wasn't like properly *trusting* people, whatever that was.

He couldn't focus, though. The Bag'un was *gone*. It wasn't in his head anymore. He was alone. The house no longer smelled of lavender. He called in sick to work. Didn't seem a lot of point. On the fifth day, well, that was when he had gone to the pub and got drunk.

But when he woke up the morning after he got drunk at the Pony, everything had changed. He looked around, and his house was—it was just *better*.

It was like when Ma had been around.

As soon as Hogarth realized, he had run to the cupboard and flung open the door. The darkness was back.

"You!" he had yelled into the void. "You! What…what? It's you!"

Yesssssssssssssss, purred the voice in his head. *Hogaaaaaaaaaaaarth*.

"What the fuck happened to my house?"

Nothing. Just the purring noise.

And then there had been the knock at the door. *What the fuck?* There was *never* a knock at the door. Nobody came to the door. Even the postman left big bits of mail on the step. Plus that was part of the rules. Nobody came inside the house but Hogarth.

"Who's that?" yelled Hogarth. "Fuck off!"

"That's not very nice," said a voice through the letterbox. Hogarth froze.

He knew that voice. Hadn't heard it for years, but he remembered it well.

"Hang on!" he shouted. He ran upstairs and pulled on his work jeans and dirty T-shirt and ran back and opened the door a crack.

He was right. It was Savaric. He stood there grinning, his teeth looking especially white. He was holding a copy of the local rag, the *Spectator.*

"All right, Mr. Merrick?" he said. "Everything to your liking?"

"The house," said Hogarth breathlessly. "The house is all fucked up."

"Fucked up?" said Savaric. He didn't seem as surprised as he sounded. "That wasn't supposed to happen. You want it back the way it was?"

"No," said Hogarth automatically. "What the fuck is going on?"

"It's complicated," said Savaric. "But you're looking after—" he yawned "—our mutual *friend,* and that comes with perks."

"Were there people," said Hogarth, "in my fucking house?"

"No," said Savaric. He sniffed. "No one goes in your house except you. And, you know. *Him.*"

"That isn't—" said Hogarth. "That's not possible. Have you seen my fucking house?"

"No," said Savaric. "But I get the general idea. Let me guess.

He went out, came back, made a few improvements. Do you like it? If you like it, where's the problem?"

"It looks like—" said Hogarth. He took a deep breath. "It looks like it *did*."

Savaric shrugged. "So trash it," he said. "It's just stuff. What do you want? New stuff?"

Hogarth stared at him, mouth open. He looked back into his house with all of its shining glass and paint and polished wood. It reminded him of when he was a kid and Ma did her big spring clean.

"Just enjoy it," said Sav. "You're going to die anyway."

"*What?*" said Hogarth.

"Figure of speech," said Savaric. "I just thought I'd check in on you because sometimes people don't react well to…" He nodded in the direction of the house's interior. "But you haven't gone mad, so that's good. Haven't got to find *him* a new house-mate. Works for me." He handed Hogarth the copy of the paper and turned to go.

Hogarth stared at him, mouth open.

"What?" he said, dumbly, and then gestured behind him. "*Why?*"

"It's complicated," said Savaric. "You help us out, he helps you out, he helps me out, and every so often, he has to go off and do his own thing so he can keep on keeping on, and all that. Everybody wins."

"How often is he going to do this?" said Hogarth. He had gotten used to the Bag'un being in his cupboard, and he didn't like surprises.

"Not that often," said Savaric. "Don't worry about it. Think of it as going for a little stroll for his health. He's just on a different timescale to the rest of us. Well, and *space* scale." He laughed, mirthlessly. "Hilarious. You helped him, didn't you? You did the—" He made a vaguely circular gesture with his hand. "The thing he asked?"

Hogarth swallowed.

"I—" he said. A growing dread was developing in the pit of his stomach. "I don't know what you're talking about."

He knew what Savaric was talking about. The toys. The thing had wanted him to buy toys, and then…well, it was sort of like a giveaway, really. It wanted him to buy the toys and leave them just inside the cupboard where he kept his mops and brooms at St. Joseph's, where he worked. On the second shelf from the bottom. At the front.

Not hidden, exactly. You could see them, if you weren't that tall. Just leave them there. That's all he'd had to do. No harm in it really. They'd been gone when he'd come back.

(along with—)

He swallowed again.

Savaric rolled his eyes. "Don't worry about it," he said. "I'll be off now, then. Have a good one." He yawned again and wandered off.

Hogarth had watched him disappear down the road and then closed the front door slowly until it clicked. Then he went to the cupboard, and opened it. The darkness was back, and he felt the Bag'un purring.

Everything was as it should be.

He had glanced briefly at the free weekly paper with its noisy headline about a kid going missing, and slung it in the bin without looking at it. Ma didn't hold with keeping up with the news. Never told you anything good, she said. He had gone back to his clean and restored armchair to spend some quality time with his telly (which no longer flickered, even though it was raining) before he was due at work.

• • •

Twenty-five years ago all that had been. He remembered it well, though. And now the Bag'un had gone wandering again.

Hooooooooooogaaaaaaaaaarth, whispered the voice in his head.

Well, this was the part he wasn't that comfortable with.

Why not? whispered the voice.

He knew what the thing wanted him to do. Somehow. He'd never been asked, never talked about it. He just sort of—knew.

He had done it before, after all. The thing with the toys.

He went into town that afternoon. Had to make a special trip, but you couldn't put these things off when they needed doing. Ma had always said that. Get it done quickly; keep out of trouble. Worked well so far. He took the bus. It ran once every four hours on a Sunday, but that was okay. He would wait.

It wasn't busy in town—not on a rainy Sunday in February. He hadn't brought an umbrella, and he stumbled off the bus and pulled his coat over his head. There was a hole in his coat and he tried hard not to hope that soon he wouldn't need to buy a new one.

He didn't have far to go. He splashed along the High Street and made a left turn when he got to Boots. He hoped the shop was still there. It had been a while since he'd visited.

He was lucky. It was. A lot of them were going out of business, what with the credit crunch and the Internet, but this one was hanging on. He stood outside in the rain for a minute or two before pressing his lips together hard and heading inside.

Felt awkward, he did. Especially in this day and age. Probably why the girl asked if she could help him as soon as he got in the door. He looked at her hard. She didn't seem suspicious.

"Um," he said. "Yeah. I need a present." He nodded for emphasis. "It's for my nephew." That was good.

"Awww!" squeaked the girl in the shop. "How old is your nephew?"

Fuck. He thought fast.

"Five," he said. Ought to do it. He caught a glimpse of himself in the glass of the counter and hoped the girl didn't question it; lots of people started over with families, though, didn't they, and it wasn't any of her business anyway. That said, he was keen not to attract attention. "What's popular at the moment? I don't have kids." He didn't like lying more than he had to. It was too much effort.

"Should be able to find you something," said the girl, beaming. "Does he like Star Mutants?"

"Oh, I think so," said Hogarth. He managed a knowing smile. "That sounds very familiar."

"Well, in that case," she said, coming out from behind the counter, "if you want to follow me, I'll show you what we've got." She led him through a brightly lit sequence of aisles until they came to a set of shelves piled high with boxes and bubble packs covered with the red and black Star Mutants logo.

"Flippin' heck," said Hogarth, involuntarily. (Ma had taught him not to swear in front of ladies, and hadn't blenched from giving him a swift clip round the ear when he'd forgotten, even when he was old enough to go to the Pony by himself.) "This is popular then?" He hadn't been making things up when he said it rang bells. He'd seen the logo on kids' lunch boxes and stickers and folders when he'd showed up early for work.

"I know, right?" said the girl. "Wish I'd had some of this stuff when I was a kid." She pushed a button on one of the packages, and the thing flashed and burped and growled.

Hogarth bought four of the action figures. Two male, two female. The show appealed to a broad audience. Clever, really.

Made his life easier.

When he got home, he left them in their bags and dropped them by the front door. He didn't want to look at them until he had to. Monday, that was—and then he wouldn't have to think about the whole business for a very long time. Maybe never again. And he would be happy and the Bag'un would be happy, and everything would be the way it had been, and he wouldn't need to think about it anymore.

Kind of the way he didn't think of the blood he'd found in the mop cupboard the day after the toys had disappeared the first time. Just a little bit, there was. On the second shelf from the bottom.

He took a deep breath. The house smelled of lavender. Ma's favourite scent.

Chapter 3

The bus rolled over the hills between Crowsbrook and Arden High, its top deck smacking thunderously into low-hanging branches. Jez had once been faintly impressed by the quality of the glass in the front windows: she'd never seen one cracked, although she'd heard some pretty resounding wallops in almost seven full years of taking the bus every morning. Now, she just stuffed in her earbuds and cranked up the volume.

It was raining again. She wanted out more than ever.

It had been bad enough back in October, before all the stuff with Adam Carpenter had happened. She had been bored back then. But now she was scared. Everything bad that was out there in the world had landed on her doorstep, and it wasn't just that the world had crystallized into a hard and uncertain place where the things that she thought could only happen to other people could suddenly, terrifyingly, happen to her and the people around her. It was that what had happened had been *isolating*. She couldn't talk to *anyone* about it. It would be pointless. No matter how well-meaning, no matter how empathetic, no one—*no one*—would believe her. She would be written off as an attention-seeking head case. She knew how people talked about teenage girls. She'd done it herself.

Rain lashed at the grimy windows of the bus and Jez managed to swig coffee out of her travel mug before the bus hit the crest of the next hill with a bump.

"Learn to drive!" yelled someone from upstairs.

The travel mug had saved her. She'd never liked coffee, but she needed it now. She was walking a tightrope where the need to study, to stay awake and to keep watch fought with a desperate exhaustion that soaked her bones. She couldn't have slept for more than twenty minutes at a time if she'd wanted to. Besides, she kept the lights on all through the night now.

She dozed in the common room, where there were people around. Sometimes in the car with her aunt Becky, if it was daylight and they were on a main road and there was a lot of traffic. Sometimes on the bus in the evenings. Before it got dark. When it got dark, the things she had seen flashed across her brain in colours saturated by exhaustion, surreal and vivid and ghastly, sharper than the drowsy world she dragged herself through while it was light.

She didn't have to be asleep to have nightmares anymore.

The bus creaked up to the stop and Jez blinked hard and pulled her stuff together. Her brain felt as though it were wrapped in a thick duvet. She tried to focus. *Double biology. Free period. Double maths. You can do this.*

She stepped carefully off the bus; she was the last one. A gust of rain splattered against the side of her face and she jerked her head away and winced.

That was when she saw them. Three of them. All women, all dressed in black. All old, but not bent. They were tall. They looked like they were looking for someone.

They didn't look like anyone's mums. Maybe crazy aunts. But this was Arden High, and if anyone had had that many weird aunts, everyone would have known about it. Bozo Ottery's cousin was a professional clown, and look what had happened to him.

They weren't doing anything. Just staring. Something didn't seem right.

Weird. Whatever, she thought. *Chance they're pedos is pretty slim.* Another gust of rain hit her in the face, and she swore and wiped her eyes. Then she realized what it was, and did a double take.

They weren't getting wet.

You can't tell from a distance.

She could, though. They had been there before Jez's bus arrived. After a couple of minutes standing in the rain, Jez's hair was starting to drip. But all three women had long, grey hair, and it looked bone dry.

Someone whacked her on the shoulder. She pressed her lips together, frowning, and turned.

"Jez!" It was Alex Appleton. "Sign my petition? We're protesting pesticides."

"Sure," said Jez, taking the pen without really listening. Alex did a double take. "Do me a favour?" Jez went on, bending her head over Alex's clipboard. "Don't look now, but do those three look funny to you?"

"What three?" said Alex.

"Over there," said Jez, trying to gesture with the pen without actually pointing. "Three old women."

"I have to say," said Alex, "I think the term *old women* is a little dismissive and condescending. We need to celebrate our seniors' breadth of experience—"

"Yeah," said Jez, cutting in. "Sorry. But over there—"

"Where?" said Alex. "I don't know if you're projecting your own subjectivity onto…well, you know what, I don't know who you'd even be projecting onto. There's no one there."

Jez looked up. The three women were looking over the school fence, peering toward the building.

"No, right there," she said, making an effort not to point. "By the big tree."

Alex laughed. "Don't know what you've got in there," she said, nodding at the travel mug, "but you might wanna cool it this early on a Monday."

Jez looked back. There was no one there. She blinked. "Whoa," she said, involuntarily.

"Maybe take a study break tonight for ten minutes?" said Alex. "Mental health is, like, *really* important."

"Right," said Jez, absently, staring at the spot where the women had been and handing the clipboard and pen back to Alex. "Yeah. Will do. Sorry about the phobia-thingy." She turned from the school gate and took a few steps toward the main road, looking left and then looking right. The women were nowhere to be seen.

"Just trying to make a better world," yelled Alex, as she disappeared through the school gates.

"Okay," Jez called back, not listening. *Fuck.* At least Alex was too woke to tell the common room that Jez Elliot had finally gone batshit crazy.

There must be an explanation. There *had* to be an explanation. People just didn't disappear. She hadn't been sleeping well. Maybe she'd hallucinated the whole thing. People who were sleep-deprived experienced visual disturbances. Maybe she'd briefly fallen asleep and dreamt it.

Yeah. Standing up. While you got hit repeatedly in the face with large drops of cold water.

Okay, well, there was nothing she could do about it now. Maybe she should phone the doctor for an appointment when she got home. Maybe she could talk to Auntie Becky about not sleeping. Auntie Becky had been living with them since her dad's accident. She was all right.

Or she could talk to Sam. But stuff was weird with Sam. He was off with other people the whole time, and they hadn't really talked, not properly, since all the stuff that had happened in October, and now it was just sort of awkward, because they hadn't talked about not talking as well as not talking about everything that had happened. Which was stupid. But that was basically what had happened. And she was reluctant to text him because she couldn't help feeling that one of the reasons that they hadn't been texting was that neither of them really wanted to acknowledge the reality of what had happened, that everything they knew existed close to the edge of a precipice, a pit of unknown depths and dimensions. It was easier to pretend that it didn't. Which sort of made it necessary to ignore the other people who could confirm that it did.

She missed Sam.

Fuck it, she thought. *I'm texting Sam.*

She pulled out her phone and a bolt of fear shot through her as she looked at the screen.

The battery was flat.

• • •

Sam's first class of the day was English, which made Monday mornings bearable. It was on the top floor of the school, which was perfect for the scenario in which he found himself right now: staring out of the window to distract himself from Saskia French's clueless witterings about Renaissance revenge tragedy. He focused on the rain, and tried to think about meeting up with Theo. The elevation of the classroom meant that he could see above the small trees that clustered around the school's gates all the way to the road, where the traffic moved in a soothing, syncopated rhythm.

He frowned. There were three women standing next to the entrance to the science labs. And they looked *wrong*. People you didn't know showed up at Arden High all the time—parents, teachers from other schools, weird inspectors with clipboards that sent the teachers into a barely concealed panic, people with tools dropping by to fix the latest thing Mickey Amble and his proto-anarchist entourage had destroyed by accident—but they all looked like they should be there. They were usually there with a teacher or a Year Twelve or Thirteen. They had to sign in and wear badges. Sam was too far away to make out for sure, but he somehow knew that these three women were not wearing badges.

"Sam?"

Shit. He'd been caught staring out the window. Mrs. Crowther didn't care too much at this stage, but it was embarrassing, especially since he liked her class.

"Sam?" said Mrs. Crowther. "Can we have you back, please?"

"Sure," said Sam. "Um." He tapped his finger on the desk a couple of times. "I'm not being weird or anything, but there's a bunch of people down there and they're not with anyone… Is that okay?" His voice trailed off. It was probably nothing.

Mrs. Crowther came over to the window.

"Where?" she said.

"Down by the science labs," said Sam. "They're wearing black."

Mrs. Crowther peered out the window.

"Huh," she said. "It doesn't look like they're there now."

Sam looked again. They had gone.

"Okay," he said. "Sorry to interrupt." A flicker of movement caught his eye on the ground. "Oh! There they are again!" And they were: they were looking through the windows of the art room.

Sam felt a chill. The art room was as far away from the science labs as you could get at Arden High without going round the back of the buildings or out onto the playing field. There was no way they should have been able to get there that quickly.

Mrs. Crowther looked.

"Nope," she said. "Still can't see them. I'll let the office know at break. If I can distract you with Elizabethan revenge tragedy…"

Sam stared into his book. A year ago, he would have assumed that he had made a mistake, because there were things that were possible and things that were not, and the line between the two was clearly drawn in his mind. But the October stuff had scared him. He had learned that more things were possible than he had thought, and that just because a thing seemed to be impossible did not mean that it was, or that it would not happen to him in particular.

He looked up at Mrs. Crowther, who was still speaking, and his eye flickered over the empty desk and chair that had, until October, been occupied by Gareth Lake. Gareth had died because of something that had not been possible. But he was still dead.

It could be a mistake, Sam tried to tell himself. *You could have made a mistake.*

He could have, it was true. It was just that it would have been far easier *before* to believe that he had made a mistake.

Saskia French was bibbling on about her theory that corruption of the aristocracy and the abuse of power were less of a concern to John Webster than the Duchess of Malfi's doomed romance. Sam tried to focus, but he couldn't even manage a cursory eye roll.

What to do? If the women had…if they were…

Ethereal. Supernatural by any other bloody name. He hated that word. If they were Ethereal, they could possibly be dangerous and would almost certainly not be playing by the rules that normal human beings did. If they were Ethereal, Sarah Trevelyan would know about them already. She had a sense for things going on in the village; she probably knew what was going on in the town as well. He had probably made a mistake. He thought about texting Jez when the class was over. Maybe she would have a different perspective. But then he remembered what Jez, ranting about Saskia French and her flaky obsessions, had told him about idiopathic stuff, where your brain would just fill in pictures and make something familiar out of random patterns, like when you could see faces in tree bark and pine planks and fake-marble bathroom tiles. She had told him about how people's memories were never as good as they thought they were, about how people had gone to jail because witnesses had sworn up and down in court with no malice that the person in the dock had attacked them, and it had turned out not to be true. Jez didn't hold psychology in high regard as far as sciences went (too many people, not enough maths), but she had less time for people assuming that they were special because they trusted their own observations. If it wasn't quantifiable, she had been fond of saying, it didn't exist.

Right about that, was she? said a small voice at the back of Sam's mind.

Fuck it, he thought. He wasn't on Sarah's payroll. He had gotten involved once before, and people had died, and he had gotten his arm broken, badly, and it had hurt like fuck. He was not signing up for that again. It was too dangerous.

Messing around with Ethereal stuff was like poking a wasps' nest with a stick. Sarah would surely know the nest was there. If it was a nest. Which he had no reason to believe that it was. He wasn't getting involved. He made an effort to focus on what Mrs. Crowther was saying, but his eyes kept returning, involuntarily, to the empty desk and chair formerly occupied by Gareth Lake.

• • •

Jack yawned. Then he started and covered his mouth. You weren't supposed to yawn with your mouth uncovered. Mrs. Seddon told them off for that. "Put your hand over your mouth," she'd say, "in case a bus comes." Everyone laughed except the person who was yawning. It had never happened to him, and he didn't want it to.

Jocasta Valentine had seen, though. *Oh, bum.*

"Does baby need a nap?" she asked, in the kind of voice she used when she was playing dolls with Celandine Latimer and Artemis Butterworth. Well, not exactly the same voice. That voice was nicer.

"No," he said, defiantly. His mouth betrayed him, though, and he felt another yawn coming. He tried to stifle it, and failed.

"Baby needs a nap!" sang Jocasta with delight. "HA, ha, HA, ha…" Celandine and Artemis joined in.

"Shut UP!" said Jack, frowning. "I'm doing SUMS."

"Baby's doing SUMS!"

"STOP it!" he said, fiercely, although he knew there was no way to stop it now. Jocasta started up a soft melody, quiet enough that Mrs. Seddon wouldn't hear.

"Bye Baby Buntiiiiing…"

The other girls joined in.

"Bye Baby Buntiiiing…"

Jack frowned and concentrated hard on Numbers. Whatever he did, they were just going to keep singing and calling him a baby. Mrs. Seddon looked over to their table.

"We don't need to sing while we're doing Numbers, Table Four."

Thank you, thought Jack, although as a non-singing member of Table Four, he felt the mild sting of the false accusation. Jocasta started up again.

"Baby's—"

Mercifully, the bell rang. Like magic, his tormentors began straightening up pencils and books while Mrs. Seddon called for them to calm down and sit quietly before they went outside. He didn't understand why she always said that. Break was for making noise anyway. Jocasta and her gang were sitting pretty, chins up and smiling, as Mrs. Seddon sent everyone out, table by table. Their table was second last, which was strange because theirs was one of the quietest, but grown-ups were strange and didn't always stick to the rules that they'd put in place. He let the girls go first, because if they got to the playground first and started playing, they might not notice him if he was the last out of the cloakroom. He walked slowly toward the classroom door, overtaken by Carlo Amble and the Noisy Boys. He just had to walk as slowly as he could but not slowly enough so people would notice. And everyone was in front of him anyway. And then, he could spend five minutes putting on his coat, and then there would only be a bit of break left. He was almost at the cloakroom. He could totally—

"Jack?" It was Mrs. Seddon. He froze. "You all right there, Jack?"

"Yeah," he said, looking at his feet. He just had to get into the playground, because it was break, and then everything would be normal.

"You sure?"

"I'm not a baby," said Jack, unhappily. He tried to stifle yet another yawn.

Mrs. Seddon looked at him hard, but she didn't seem cross. "What time did you go to bed last night, Jack?"

"Eight o'clock," said Jack, promptly.

"Eight o'clock, was it?" said Mrs. Seddon. "Your mummy's good about that, isn't she? Did you go to sleep all right?"

"I—" said Jack. He didn't know what he was supposed to say. He was supposed to say yes, but that wasn't true, and he wasn't supposed to tell lies. Lying was bad. "I couldn't go to sleep." That was true.

"Oh dear," said Mrs. Seddon. "That doesn't sound like fun. You look tired now."

"There was a monster in my cupboard," said Jack without thinking, and then he was furious with himself. He had said that he wasn't a baby, and that was the most babyish thing he could have said, and now his eyes were betraying him and welling up with tears, but he would not cry. He wouldn't. He frowned and screwed up his face as a couple of tears rolled down his cheeks. *He would not cry.*

"A monster?" said Mrs. Seddon. "Well, monsters in books are usually pretty scary." She bent down so she was kneeling at his height. "But they're just pretend, Jack. Did your mummy tell you there's no such things as monsters in real life?"

Jack couldn't speak, but he nodded. *Of course she had told him. And he knew that monsters in books were pretend. Of course he knew monsters in books and magic and superheroes and Star Mutants were pretend. Except the monster in his cupboard wasn't pretend. He hadn't seen it, but he knew. He knew. He could feel it watching him. He could smell it, from the other side of the room sometimes: a whiff of something that wasn't quite right, something that shouldn't be there. And he knew that it was watching him, and he knew that it had started to follow him. He had known it was under the bush at the playground, where it was too dark to see. And he knew that he didn't want to sleep while it was around.* His face was still bunched up with the effort not to cry.

"She's good, your mummy," said Mrs. Seddon. "You're a good boy. I bet you help her a lot, by being a good boy."

Jack nodded. "I put my things away when she says. And I have a wash when I don't want to."

"Good boy," said Mrs. Seddon. She sighed. "Do you want to go out for playtime? You're missing it."

Jack shook his head. He didn't want anyone to see he'd almost cried. His face was still wet.

"All right," said Mrs. Seddon. "Just this once, you can stay indoors. Want to help me tidy up and get ready for painting?"

Jack didn't, not really, but he knew that was the wrong answer, and he didn't want to go outside. He nodded without looking at Mrs. Seddon.

"All right, then," she said, brightly. "You can cover the tables with newspaper, and then we'll get the paint out of the art cupboard." She clapped her hands together quietly. "Let's go, kiddo."

Jack went over to the newspaper box and started unfolding newspapers to put on the table. He didn't feel better, but at least he hadn't had to go outside. He glanced at the clock. He knew that telling the time wasn't his strong point, but he did know that when the big hand reached the nine, the bell would ring again and everyone would come pouring back in, including Jocasta and Celandine and Artemis. The big hand was just past the seven now.

"I'm just going to get a cup of tea," said Mrs. Seddon. "You be all right for a couple of minutes?"

"Yes," said Jack automatically. He didn't look up from his newspapers.

"All right then," said Mrs. Seddon. "Be back in a tick." The door clicked behind her as she went out.

Jack breathed deeply. Being in a classroom on his own was nice. It was strange, seeing everything familiar without the background hum of voices and squeals and mumbling and the odd snatch of song. He spread the final sheet of newspaper over Table Four and stood back and admired his handiwork.

Nice job.

Okay, so they were going to be painting next. He knew how that worked. The paints came out of the cupboard and went in the middle of the table: one red, one yellow, one blue, one white, and one black on each table, along with a jar of water for washing your brush when you'd finished one colour and wanted to do another one. He could start putting the paints on the table. That would be helpful.

He turned around to the art cupboard and froze.

The art cupboard was a really big cupboard set into the wall of the classroom. There were shelves in it with paper in all different colours and paint and tissue paper and bits of pipe cleaner. It smelled of bits of paint that hadn't quite been washed out of the brushes properly—not exactly unpleasant. It made you think of painting. There was a big tub of felt tips as well. Enough for everyone. He liked the art cupboard.

Except he was sure that the door of the art cupboard had been closed before.

He was *sure* of it. Mrs. Seddon said it all the time after painting: "Close the door when everything's put away." He'd had to go past the cupboard to get the newspapers. He'd have noticed.

Maybe he hadn't though. Maybe he'd just been so focused on stupid Jocasta and stupid Celandine and stupid Artemis that he hadn't been paying attention. It was just a stupid door. It was the door to the art cupboard, and he liked the art cupboard.

He wished his mother was there. What would she do?

Well, she'd probably tell him there was nothing to be scared of and check in the cupboard and then show him that whatever it was in the cupboard had gone for the time being and then turn out the light and leave him alone in the dark, even though she didn't mean to.

He had to do it himself. He had to check the cupboard. He'd seen in the cupboard a hundred times. More than that. A thousand. Maybe a million. It was just paper and glue and paint and things.

He took a step toward the door and breathed in deeply. A new smell wafted toward him that wasn't the usual smell of dried paint and bottles of white glue and coloured foil. This smell was a bit like the stream where the class had gone to look at frogspawn when he was in Year One. A bit like that. It reminded him of the time his mother had taken him down to the Foxglove Pond, ages ago, when they'd first moved to Crowsbrook. It had been dark under all the trees, and the mud had been slippery. And he had seen two big shadows there, flickering between the trees like big kids who shouldn't be there. (He knew what it looked like when you shouldn't be there, because Carlo Amble was in his class.) And his mummy had asked him what he was looking at and he told her and she said that nothing was there and there was nothing to worry about. But he had seen the shadows. He had. He hadn't liked it one bit, and had eventually cried until they went back to the normal park.

He hadn't liked the Foxglove Pond at all.

He peered around the door of the cupboard. He couldn't see in it very well. It was dark.

It was *really* dark. He stretched out his hand toward the door and nudged it with his fingertip. Not quite enough to move it. He swallowed.

Then, all in one motion, he grabbed the edge of the door and pulled hard. The cupboard was completely dark inside.

When Mrs. Seddon came back, he was still screaming, although the darkness in the cupboard had vanished, and all that could be seen in the cupboard was paper and paints and bottles of glue.

• • •

Holly shifted on the slightly too-small chair.

"It sounds tough," said Mrs. Seddon. "Have you taken him to see a doctor?"

Holly could feel a sinking in the pit of her stomach. She liked Mrs. Seddon, but parent–teacher interviews always made her feel like she was being marked, and about to be told that she needed to try harder or she'd never get anywhere.

"No," she said. "I thought I'd try some other stuff first. I looked up some things on the Internet. You know. Things you can do. More exercise. Changing his room a bit. Stuff you can talk about." She looked over at where Jack was colouring, in the corner of the classroom farthest away from the art cupboard. "Phobias and stuff. But, like, age-appropriate." She sighed. "I just don't know what they'd be able to do. I don't want them giving him pills. But he can't go on like this."

"I totally understand," said Mrs. Seddon, and she sounded like she did. "But it is affecting his performance at school. I mean. You know that." She flipped through a notebook in front of her. "I'm not a medical person, obviously, and I know that it's not my business, but have you thought about trying to get him referred to a child psychiatrist?"

Holly's eyes widened. "I…" she said. "I don't know. No. I don't know."

Mrs. Seddon held up her hands. "Don't panic," she said, and smiled. "It would just be to try and figure out what's going on with Jack. What's *really* going on with him, I mean."

"Is it expensive?"

Mrs. Seddon shrugged. "You can get it on the NHS. There's a long waiting list, though. The doctor might recommend medication in the meantime. If you can pay…"

"I can't," said Holly. She slumped, inwardly. *Medication…*

Mrs. Seddon sighed. "It's up to you, of course," she said again. "But I found him staring into the cupboard and screaming. I've never heard a child scream like that, and I've dealt with compound fractures, projectile diarrhea, and a snakebite. Never. I know it's tough for you." She looked down at her hands. "Dad's not in the picture, right?"

"No," said Holly, shortly. "We don't talk. It's better like that." *He wouldn't be interested anyway*, she thought. Knew.

Mrs. Seddon nodded. "And you're doing okay? How long have you been here, now? Six months?"

"About that," said Holly. "My mum knew someone who was renting out a house and talked him into letting us have it for a bit for cheap. When she explained."

"Right," said Mrs. Seddon. "I remember." The pause was just long enough to be awkward.

"Does he—" said Holly, almost without thinking; it wasn't something she'd meant to start. "How is he—how is he with Jocasta Valentine and that lot? Here, I mean. I've noticed—at the playground and stuff." Having brought it up, she felt a sudden surge of rage. "I'm pretty sure that Jocasta Valentine and her little mates treat him like shit, excuse my language, every time they come into contact with him, and they encourage the other kids, too. I've seen it at the playground and I've stopped it where I've seen it, but he won't talk to me about it. I don't think that's the only reason he's not sleeping, but it can't help. Is there something you can do?"

Mrs. Seddon looked surprised, but she nodded. "Sure," she said. "He sits with them now, but—"

"He *sits* with them?" said Holly. She was incredulous. How had she not known this?

"I'll move him first thing tomorrow," said Mrs. Seddon, "and I'll keep an eye on him. And on her." Holly wasn't sure if she was imagining it, but it looked like Mrs. Seddon's poker face had descended.

"I spoke to Allegra," Holly continued. "But I didn't get very far."

Mrs. Seddon's face was inscrutable. "No," she said. "It can be difficult."

If Mrs. Seddon was going to be neutral, Holly decided she wasn't going to be.

"Well," she said. "It isn't difficult if you're a self-righteous organic yoga fanatic who knows better than everyone, even though you pretty much spawned the Devil… Actually—" she thought for a moment "—the kid's awful, but Allegra *lets* her be awful, which is sort of worse, I guess. But whatever. She has her 'parenting style'—" here, Holly made air quotes with her fingers "—and I have mine, which is not so much a style as sort of based on leaving the house on a regular basis after having a quick wash and making sure no one died during the night." She rubbed her head hard with her fingers. "It involves a lot less organic food is what I'm saying. But her kid is an *arsehole*, specifically to my kid, and that is *not okay*. And when I say 'not okay'—" she did the air quotes thing again "—I'm being really careful not to stand up and scream and smash things to demonstrate in a sort of hands-on kind of way just exactly how *not okay* it is. So I would appreciate it if you could do that. Keep an eye out for him. You know. While we're waiting for the—" she made the quotation marks once last time "—'*child psychologist*.'" She stood up and called to Jack. "Jack, we're going. Thanks for your time, Mrs. Seddon."

They marched out of the classroom and out of the school gates. Holly felt a shot of adrenaline as she saw Allegra, Daphne, and Isabella with Jocasta, Celandine, and Artemis outside the village hall, opposite the school. The girls were wearing white tutus and pink cardigans. Ballet class. Of course.

Holly held Jack's hand tightly and crossed the road. Jack was reticent, he was holding back a bit, she could feel it, but he was following her, albeit half a step behind. Allegra looked up.

"Holly!" she said, beaming. "How *are* you? Oh dear, Jack looks—"

Holly held up the hand that was not holding on to Jack.

"Well!" she said. "We're both well. I just wanted to tell you that if your piece-of-shit bully of a daughter *ever* upsets my son again, I will rip your perfectly Botoxed fucking face off. Enjoy ballet class."

She stalked off, Jack in tow, listening to the women gasp and the girls beginning to wail behind her. It was a stupid thing to have done and it probably wouldn't help. But it felt really, really good.

• • •

It was a stupid thing to have done.

That was Eleanor talking. *Why would you bind yourself to powerful magic like that?*

Because sometimes you needed to do the stupid thing? Sarah imagined herself saying.

For sure. But that's for stuff like tequila shots and pretty shoes that you can't walk in. This is serious.

I never bought a pair of shoes I couldn't walk in, thought Sarah. *Or run.*

She had sworn a blood oath, though. The night of the fire. The cottage had been attacked by malevolent Ethereals working for Nicholas Carrington. *Over a plant*, she reminded herself. The plant in question didn't look like much. It was a fern, and not a pretty one. But part of its magic had been the ability to bestow eternal youth. Not immortality, just eternal youth. And Carrington had seen the potential and wanted to use it to make face cream, and was prepared to kill anyone who got in his way.

Well, thought Sarah. *Not really. Mostly he was okay with people dying so he could get what he wanted and was prepared to hire beings who weren't fussy about killing to get their job done, as long as they got their payment.*

Either way, he's culpable.

The cottage she had shared with Eleanor had been part of her family's business for generations, and the family hadn't been under any illusions about how certain factions in the outside world saw them. There was an escape tunnel hidden behind one of the bookcases in Sarah's study that had been built during the times of the witchfinders. It was long, and had a low ceiling, but although it had been built for a generation of people smaller than Sarah's five foot seven, it had been built to last. It came up in the woods, about half a mile away from the cottage, and away from the village.

Sarah had made it into the tunnel. Eleanor hadn't. She'd been trapped upstairs, and Sarah hadn't been able to free her. Two of the fae—the guardians of the fern—had pulled her away and bundled her into the tunnel, and they had run. Fast. One of them had been killed by a phantom that had pursued them into the tunnel. It had taken the fern.

Sarah had been hauled screaming out of the tunnel exit by the second fae. Ansgot, their name had been. They had held her down until she stopped kicking and swearing and trying to free herself so she could go back to the cottage. Wild-eyed and covered in soot, stinking of smoke and sweat, face streaked with tears and rain, she had eventually shaken them off, growling like an animal, had pulled the knife out of her belt, and had cut her hand so that her blood dripped onto the ground.

Scoring, they called that: the shedding of a witch's blood.

When a witch was attacked and injured, scoring would call her familiars. When she shed her blood herself, scoring would call upon powers darker and earthier than the spirits who lived with her in the everyday. Lying on the ground, numb, broken, homeless, and bleeding into the dirt, she had sworn revenge against those that had wronged her. With her heart, with her blood, and with the earth.

She hadn't remembered much after that. She slept for days or not at all: dreams became like waking reality. Ansgot and another fae, Lovet, brought her food and kept her warm; they brought her things that they had found at the cottage that had not burned: some clothes, a suitcase, a few books. She did not understand how the things had survived. They should not have. She should not have either.

But she was a witch. It was easy for her to disappear.

One day, as the leaves were starting to turn, Lovet brought her a letter. It told her of her aunt's passing, and of the cottage in Ardenshire. She had somewhere to go.

She paid her debts to the fae and got on a train to Crowsbrook. And then—

You forgot the oath.

I didn't forget the oath, she thought, irritably. She would never forget that night. It was burned into her memory, flashbulb-bright.

She hadn't forgotten the oath. She just hadn't done anything about it.

How big a deal can it be? she thought. *I mean, I'll get to it eventually. It's not like I've forgotten.*

That magic will bind you, her grandmother had said, *in ways that you may not mean to be bound.*

Well, what could she do? She had looked for Carrington and hadn't found him. But he was bound to pop up somewhere, and when he did, she'd be ready.

What if he popped up tomorrow? said a voice in her mind. *Be ready then, would you?*

The voice was familiar, but not one she recognized instantly. It wasn't her grandmother or Eleanor, the dead voices that came to her most frequently. They weren't the real voices of the dead. When she spoke to them, it was mostly a conversation she imagined having with them. It was the way that she knew they were still with her, still alive. But this one was different, and it took her a moment to recognize it.

She sat up straight and her eyes widened with astonishment.

It was Nan Trevelyan. The Crowsbrook Witch. She had appeared to Sarah in a vision, when she had been kidnapped and drugged the previous October. Nan had appeared to her in a hall of mirrors that had no floor and no ceiling. A hall of illusions. Sarah had no idea why she had appeared then and had no idea why she was talking to her now.

Nan? she thought. But the voice had gone.

Nan had been right, though. If she found Carrington tomorrow, she didn't have a plan. She didn't know what to do. Revenge? What did that mean? Was she planning to kill him?

People said that all the time, didn't they? They became angry and said things like "I could murder him" or "I'm going to kill her." And then they didn't, because they had no intention of doing that.

She thought about Carrington. She didn't want him dead. She wanted him to suffer. And she could make it happen. The blood oaths hadn't been the only powerful magic in the books at the top of the stairwell, and witchcraft had never just been about helping people in and out of the world and keeping the balance between the human world and the Ethereal world. She knew how to do terrible things. And she was willing to as well.

Still not prepared, *though, are you, sweetheart?* Nan was back. *You might be able to curse up a storm, but you've never done it before, have you? Have you checked your book for what you need? Can you still bring up the rage?*

That she could do. She carried it with her every day, heavy as a rock, in her stomach, and heated with volcanic anger, fuelled by loss and grief. It was exhausting. But it burned bright. It would keep her going for a while. Give her time to work on getting her revenge.

There was no harm in a bit of a delay, after all. Was there?

She pulled out a bottle of Windowlene and a soft cloth from under the cash register and started attacking the fingerprints smeared on the counter.

Chapter 4

Father Dominic Quinn finished his last cigarette of the evening and stubbed it out very carefully. He rose to his feet, picked up the overflowing ashtray, and lumbered off toward the back door of the parochial house, to empty it.

New habit, it was. Had a bit of a close call back in October: he'd almost burned the house down, leaving a cigarette burning while he was having a nap. Best be on the safe side. He cleared his throat, opened the back door, dumped the dog-ends and ash into a metal can, coughed and spat after it. It was raining. He looked up at the sky and frowned. Rain made his knees hurt. He was eighty-four, and February was a cheerless month.

He closed the back door and locked it; his housekeeper was long gone for the night, and he would have to be up early for matins at eight. Sometimes he wondered why they didn't get someone younger to do it. Mysterious ways, indeed.

The parochial house was Victorian, and the kitchen was at the back, linked to the living room by a narrow corridor. The friar turned the light out in the kitchen and groped along the wall for the switch that would illuminate the corridor. He found it and pushed it down. The bulb flashed brightly for a second and then went out with a loud *pop*.

It made Father Dominic jump. He let out his breath in a great rush, and coughed. *Just a bloody light bulb*, he told himself. He'd ask Mrs. Flanagan to do the necessary in the morning. In her sixties, she was—not exactly a spring chicken, but she wasn't eighty-bloody-four, and he was sure she'd have less trouble with the chair and the looking up and the twisting and the getting down than he would. He could manage for the time being. He was going to bed anyway. Damned if he couldn't find his way up the stairs in the dark.

There was a little light filtering in through the leaded glass panels of the front door, from the street light outside; it cast an orange-tinged glow through the front door, bleaching the colour out of the remaining threads in the carpet. *Poverty. Chastity. Obedience.* Wouldn't do a person any good to trip up on the frayed bits, though.

The light took him to the bottom of the stairs, and he flicked the switch there. Nothing happened. He frowned. That couldn't be right. He clicked the switch up and down a few times—it was an old-fashioned one, and made a satisfying *click* when you switched it—but the house remained dark. The friar rolled his eyes. *It never rains, but it pours*, he thought. It was odd for both bulbs to burn out together, but these things happened. Mrs. Flanagan would sort it out.

He began to make his way up the stairs, his knees complaining at every step. *It's just the rain*, he told himself, and it really was; most of the time there was nothing wrong with him, nothing at all; coughed a bit from the fags, but apart from that, there was nothing wrong. Sound in body and mind. His left knee cracked loudly, and he winced. There were only thirteen steps, in the Blessed Name of Our Lady. It wasn't a bloody marathon.

He felt something brush past him.

He froze, hand on the stair rail. There was nothing in the hall. Nothing at all. There couldn't be.

He turned around sharply and looked behind him. Nothing. No one. A gust of wind splattered rain against the panes of the door. He swallowed and shook his arm out, as if to loosen a muscle.

He couldn't really have felt that, could he?

No, he decided. No, he could not. Even if you were in the business of dealing with matters unseen, matters unseen didn't usually disturb you when you were off the clock. And matters unseen were certainly not generally in the business of pushing past you on your own stairs; this was not in the gamut of things that our Blessed Lord had intended.

Father Dominic grunted and continued his way up the stairs. Unconsciously, his fingers felt for the crucifix that hung around his neck.

That was when he heard the voice.

"Faaaaaaaaaaaather…"

It was little more than a whisper, but it carried down to Father Dominic and chilled him to the bone.

"Who's there?" he cried. "Who's up there?"

"Faaaaaaaaaaaather…" the voice whispered again. It was a high voice, a child's voice, and Father Dominic realized, through his fear, that it was a frightened voice.

"My child?" he called, heart racing. "My child, where are you?"

Maybe a child had got in and had an accident, he thought. Upstairs. But his heartbeat didn't slow down. *There has to be a rational explanation*, he thought.

"Faaaaaaaaather…help meeeeee…"

His heart was pounding. There could be no child in his house; it was not possible. He may have been eighty-four, but his hearing and his mind were as sharp as they ever had been, even if his eyes and his joints were not. He had been in the sitting room all evening; anyone going past him would have had to sneak past its open door, and years of teaching Sunday school and catechism classes had honed Father Dominic's awareness of what people were up to behind him until it was effectively a sixth sense. No one had passed the door of the living room this evening.

He gripped the railing and started up the stairs.

"My child," he called again. "Are you all right? Where are you?"

"Faaaaaaather…"

The cry was more desperate now. Father Dominic's knees screamed and he hastened to the top of the stairs, coughing hard. His lungs brought up thick phlegm; he had to swallow so he would not choke. He gasped for breath and looked around him. He could see nothing.

But there was a light coming from under the door of the old linen cupboard. Mrs. Flanagan had stopped using it as a linen cupboard a decade ago, when the boiler had broken and the system had to be replaced, and people had come and…well, he wasn't sure what had happened exactly, except that eventually, they'd had hot water again, and Mrs. Flanagan had told him that if he needed a clean towel and it wasn't a Thursday, he should look in the chest in the room where he slept. He hadn't used the linen cupboard since.

He didn't remember there being a light in it either.

"Faaaaaather…"

Although Father Dominic was closer, the voice didn't seem louder. Cold dread seized his wracked body; he was still coughing, and he stared in horror at the cupboard door with the eerie light shining from beyond it. The light was pulsing.

The voice in Father Dominic's head, which he had learned to trust, through years of prayer and meditation, as the voice of his wisest self—the part of him that, sinner though he knew himself, was probably closest to his Lord—spoke to him gently through his fear: *you are a man of God. Such things will not dare harm you.*

He was not reassured. In the mortal world, there were many beings capable of doing things that they should dare not.

"Faaaaaaaather…heeeeeeeeelp…"

A child was calling for help. His fear was irrelevant. He ground his teeth together, stepped toward the cupboard door, and pulled it open, fingers still clutching his crucifix.

His face contorted into an expression of shock and horror, eyes widening as he stared. He opened his mouth to cry out, but no sound emerged.

There was a child—a boy of about eleven—sitting at the bottom of the linen cupboard, weeping; his hands covered his face. The sound seemed to be coming from a long way away.

"Father," he sobbed. *"Help me. Please…"*

The priest was frozen in terror. The boy's distress was clear, and he knew somehow that he had to help this child, and yet he found himself unable to move forward to comfort the boy.

You are a man of God, whispered the voice inside his head. *You cannot be hurt by—*

By what? Father Dominic did not know. But as he stared, two facts remained indubitable. The first was that the eerie, pulsing light was emitting from the boy himself. And the second was that, as Father Dominic stared at the distraught child lying in a heap on the cupboard floor, he could also make out the lines of the wooden boards on which he sat. The priest could see right through the child.

He steeled himself.

"Who are you?" he managed. "What do you want?"

"Father," sobbed the boy. *"It's daaaaaaaaaaaark…"*

"Who are you?" shouted Father Dominic again.

The boy looked up, and the friar felt another pulse of chills explode in his solar plexus and flash through his body. The boy's face was bloody. Half of the flesh had been torn away, revealing the blood-smeared skull beneath.

And Father Quinn recognized him.

"Father," moaned the boy again. *"Heeeeeeelp…"*

• • •

The phone rang in Sarah's cottage, just as she was getting in from work.

The phone *never* rang. She didn't even know anyone who had the number. Come to think of it, she wasn't even sure *she* knew the number. She didn't know the number by heart, anyway. It was written down somewhere. It would be on the bill.

(She got the bills sometimes and put them in a safe place. The phone company never followed up.)

She dumped her bag and took her shoes off and stared at the phone. It had come with the cottage. It was black and shiny and old-fashioned and heavy and rang with a bell. As if in response to her stare, it rang again.

Who the hell would be calling her? And at this time on a Monday evening?

That was it. It must be a wrong number. She let out a sigh. She didn't have to answer it after all.

Three minutes later, the kettle was on, and the phone was still ringing. Sarah took a deep breath and picked it up.

"Hello?" she said. "Who is this?"

"Dominic Quinn," said a voice at the other end. "Father Dominic. We met back in October."

Sarah's eyebrows flew up. She remembered the friar well; she had asked him for help, and, at first, he had been unforthcoming. But when she had lost her eye (she winced at the memory of the feel of the thick, yellow nail that had gouged it out, of the hand

and the twisted arm and the tortured body that that nail had been attached to), he had been there, waiting outside in a battered old Morris Minor to take her, half-blind and in agony, to the hospital, where they cleaned her up and gave her painkillers and a pamphlet on how her vision would readjust and offered to tell her about the glass eyes you could get on the NHS.

She preferred wearing the patch.

"Father Dominic," she said. "This is a surprise. What can I do for you?"

She bit her tongue to stop herself adding "and the Firm?" Father Dominic's employers were not known for their sympathy toward the kind of family business that Sarah's family had pursued over the centuries; indeed, several of those centuries had been stained red by the Church's lethal hostility. Sarah's family had been English, and so they avoided the worst of it, but going through her great-aunt's papers during the four months she'd been in Crowsbrook, she had found letters, very old letters, from families across the channel and in Scotland, where the fires had burned with abandon. It had not made her more sympathetic toward the Church, but she had understood, to a greater extent, Father Dominic's reluctance to help her.

"I would like," said Father Dominic, "your *advice*."

Sarah frowned. She only had a short mental list of reasons the friar might possibly call her, and "for advice" was most certainly not on it.

"Advice?" she said. "Advice on what?"

"Strange happenings," said Father Dominic. "An occurrence that is decidedly *odd*."

"Odd how?" said Sarah. "Doesn't your employer have its own protocols for dealing with *odd*?" She laid the emphasis on the last word just as the friar had.

"Indeed," said the friar, after a pause. "But under the

circumstances, I would rather not call upon the divisions that deal in those matters. The views of some of the higher-ups can be—" he cleared his throat as he searched for the right word "—inflexible."

Sarah was intrigued. "So," she said, "all right, then. What can I offer advice about?"

Again, there was a long pause. "This," said the friar, "is something of a long story. Do you have time?"

"Of course," said Sarah. There was something in the friar's voice that worried her; she felt a familiar creeping dread in her stomach, and a line from the old, famous play came to her out of nowhere: *The time is out of joint.*

The friar coughed, and Sarah heard the click of a lighter at the other end of the line. "I hope you're sitting down, then," he said. "Many years ago, I was working at a home called St. Joseph's, a bit outside of Arden; it was what, in those days, was called an orphanage. Now they call it a group home or some such, but it's really the same thing. Children with no families, or with families who can't look after them or with families who shouldn't bloody well be allowed anywhere near them, you know."

"Yes," said Sarah. She didn't want to think about where this might be going.

"It was a terrible place," said the friar. "Bloody awful. A lot of us were doing our best, but some—" he made a noise that was somewhere between a sigh and a growl "—some most decidedly were not. And so kids would run away, get in trouble with the police, bugger off to London or other cities and get into God knows what. And no one would listen. Awful." The final word fell like a steel bar.

"Is it still open?" said Sarah. She didn't really know what to say. She didn't know a lot about these kinds of places, and nothing she'd heard second-hand had been particularly good either.

"It is," said the friar. "But it has, let us say, improved greatly in the intervening years. A pile of money was thrown at it, and some people in the right places started listening, and a lot of the staff were— Well, they don't work there anymore. I'm told that it's now one of the best homes of its kind in the area."

"Are you still involved?"

"Tangentially," said the friar. "I was sick for a while; had to give up my duties. Took me a while to get back to fighting fitness, and by that time, they'd found other people to do my work and moved me to Castleton. But I still do what I can."

"Right," said Sarah, thoughtfully. She was beginning to suspect that there was more to the friar's story than he was telling. "But you're better now?"

"This was a while ago," said the friar dismissively. "I'm fine. But I suspect that there are other matters that are *not*."

Sarah waited.

"A child went missing," said the friar. "Twenty-five years ago, more or less. A boy. Eleven years old. His name was Daniel Giddens. He was last seen one Tuesday morning. It was assumed he left St. Joe's to catch the bus to Arden High. He never came back, and by several—though not necessarily reliable—accounts, he never got on the bus in the first place."

Sarah waited.

"The police were called, of course," said the friar, irritably. "But since they emphasised that children living in group homes run away all the time, and since there are no grieving parents to look in the eye, and since many children who run away from group homes also run into the police sooner or later, I personally could not help but feel that this was not, shall we say, a priority case for them." Sarah heard him take a long drag on his cigarette.

"But he was a kid," said Sarah. "He was *eleven*. What if something bad happened?"

She heard the friar exhale a cloud of smoke. "I am certain," said the friar, "that something bad *did* happen."

Sarah bit her thumbnail.

"They never found Daniel," said the friar. "I had…" He took a deep breath. "Twenty-five years ago, I had a vision of him though. Horribly mutilated and crying for help. It wasn't a dream: I was fully awake, but alone, and he appeared to me. I could not help him. I didn't know how. I prayed and I hoped and I tried to have faith. The vision only came once then. I still pray for him. Pray that he is at peace."

Sarah could hear the pain in the friar's voice.

"I had a second vision earlier tonight," the friar went on. "Daniel. As before. Mutilated and crying for help. Before, he needed my help. But—" he paused "—he had not aged in the second vision, and I do not know why I saw him. I have thought about him often since he disappeared, but since the first vision I had never seen him again until last night. If there is any way…" Sarah heard him take a deep pull on his cigarette. "If there is any way that you can find out where Daniel Giddens is, or what he wants us to do… He needs help, and we need to help him."

Sarah's heart lurched.

"What is it," she said eventually, "that you want me to advise you about?"

"Your aunt had a gift," said the friar. "An unusual one. She called it the Sight. I know that you share a lot of her talents."

Sarah did.

"You want me to help look for him," said Sarah. It was a statement, not a question. "Of course."

"Yes," said the friar. "I have grave concerns about the safety of other children. I have no basis for concluding so, but his presence felt like a warning."

Sarah had no reason to disbelieve him.

"It's not one hundred percent," she said. "Reliable, I mean. The Sight. I might be able to point you in the right direction, but that's it. You'd still have to go to the police to sort everything out."

"Right now," said the friar, "I'm not so concerned with 'sorting things out,' as you put it. I'm worried that…" He trailed off. "Let's just say I fear the worst. Likely—hopefully—it's just the paranoia of an eighty-four-year-old fool who spends a lot of time by himself. I don't know what it is that you do, but if you could do it, I'd be grateful. And a child's life might depend upon it." Again, his words fell with the weight of iron.

This was not the kind of request where anyone reasonable had a choice. And certainly, Sarah knew, not someone with the kind of abilities gained by training in a family concern such as hers.

"Okay," she said. "I'll take a look. But you know how these things work, Father. Like I said, there's no guarantees." *And rarely any easy answers*, she added silently to herself. "I'll let you know."

"Thank you," said the friar. "I appreciate it." He hung up.

Sarah stared at the phone. She would look, of course she would look, but a pervasive feeling of dread was growing stronger in her stomach. This was her village now. She had saved it once (not that many people knew) and she knew pretty much everything that was going on in it. Not everybody's business or anything like that, but it was like running her hands over an old familiar blanket: she could feel the threads and strands that held things together, could sense weaknesses that needed shoring up, knots that needed smoothing out, tangles, bumps, and anything else that wasn't going as it should. And she hadn't noticed anything. In fact, it wasn't just that. She had been keeping watch since October, looking for knots or bumps in the landscape of Crowsbrook, looking for signs that something that was not as it should be, looking for something wrong, anything—and *this wasn't there.*

The friar's in Castleton, she thought, weakly. But Castleton was a scant eight miles away, and that was close enough. She whistled slowly and got up and started preparing to look in the water.

She still had some of the water from the pond, just in case.

She took a glass bowl and a piece of black velvet that was not quite big enough to be a tablecloth out of a low cupboard in the kitchen, spread the cloth on the table, put the bowl on top along with a candle and a box of Swan matches, and then filled it with the water from a large, smudged glass jar that had been sitting on the kitchen windowsill. The water smelled slightly sulphurous. It was best to use water that hadn't come out of the tap.

Sarah held her breath while she poured it. The pond had a long history, and not all of it was good. Sarah didn't hang about by the Foxglove Pond more than she had to.

The water settled. She lit the candle, sat down at the table, took a deep breath, and began to…

connect

She stared deep into the bowl of water, into the blackness, feeling as though she were simultaneously floating and rooted firmly to her chair. She felt the earth below the old wood of the floorboards and the brick foundations of her cottage. She felt the worms, the crawling things, the moisture, the roots of plants, and she reached deep into the heart of the Earth.

Where is the boy? she asked, silently. *Where is the boy the friar saw?*

It was a tough question. The land knew nothing of names, and she didn't have anything like hair or fingernails or even a piece of clothing to connect with. She was working with nothing here. But the friar had described something bad, and the land would remember.

She needed to focus.

Where is the boy?

She reached out to the earth. In the earth, there was power.

She connected. Her mind reached out in a thousand directions. The water cleared and she *saw*.

A house. A big, crumbling house with an untidy, unfriendly garden. The water flashed.

The sun was low in the sky. Early morning.

Children. There were children. She saw them laughing together, like an old film with no sound. The house was big enough for lots of children to live in, along with the people who looked after them.

St. Joe's.

One boy. About eleven. Skinny. Getting to be in need of a haircut.

This is him. This is Daniel. She knew.

She watched him. He wasn't quite part of the laughing group. She had a sense that he wanted to be, but he was afraid to join them.

One of them noticed him standing there and yelled something. Daniel flinched. Two of the other children pointed and laughed. Daniel turned and ran off, head down, back into the house.

She was in the house now as he wound his way through the corridors and up to a dormitory room with four beds in it. There was another child in there, though, and she shouted at Daniel to fuck off and get out. Sarah's lip reading wasn't up to much, but she could figure that out.

Moving slowly now, Daniel left the room, closed the door, and slumped down against the wall to the floor. He was making a gargantuan effort not to cry.

That was when Sarah noticed the cupboard. It was opposite Daniel. She had assumed it was another room, but she realized now that all the rooms he had passed had had frosted glass panes in the doors, and this one was solid wood. It was open a crack, and there was no light coming through. She hadn't noticed that it had been open before.

Daniel looked both ways up and down the corridor. He pulled the door open and slipped into the cupboard. The door closed behind him. Sarah could have sworn she heard the click.

Time passed. It was a few seconds in Sarah's world but she knew that it was much longer for Daniel.

Then the vision smashed her through the door and showed her what no one had seen at the time. It showed her what had become of Daniel Giddens.

She cried out; the connection broke, and pain stabbed through her head. Water splashed out of the bowl, slopping over the edge of the table and onto her lap and feet. It was cold. The sulphur smell was stronger.

Sarah felt sick. She clapped her hand over her mouth and ran upstairs to her bathroom, where she dropped to her knees and vomited into the toilet bowl. She took some deep breaths. The pain in her head began to subside. She threw up again, and collapsed against the wall.

You should never break a connection that suddenly. Her grandmother. Or the part of her that knew that. But what she had seen had shocked her into movement, shocked her out of her trance.

She rested her head against the bathroom wall. The friar had been right to be worried.

The things that she had seen at the end had been unmistakable, lying partially covered in mud and water and leaves. They were bones. Long bones, with bloody chunks of meat still attached; chunks of meat that she had been able to recognize as having once been a small hand and a small foot.

Bones from which the flesh had clearly been eaten.

• • •

The shadows flickered in the dark down by the pond, between the trees. It was always dark where they were. The days and nights were the same. Nothing marked the passing of time. It could drive a living person mad.

No one was there to see them.

Sometimes the sound of sobbing drifted through the trees, but no one was there to hear it.

• • •

On Tuesday morning, Hogarth picked up the bag of Star Mutants as he went out the door and closed it quietly behind him. Going into work early. No need to make a fuss. Nevertheless, he could feel his heart beating a wee bit faster, and there was a tension in his stomach that he didn't usually feel.

Nothing to worry about, he told himself. *Just a normal day at work. Just moving some things.* It had taken him a day to work up to it, but it was just moving some things, after all. He stuffed them into his backpack anyway as he walked toward the school. *Wouldn't do to have anyone see them.* He knew that. *Just in case.*

Not that anything's going to happen.

And if it did, it wouldn't be his fault, would it? No one could prove anything. He didn't know for sure. He just did what the Bag'un asked him, and it asked nicely, and so he did it and he didn't ask any silly questions afterward either. Just did his job and looked after his friend. He wasn't doing anything wrong. Nothing he was doing was wrong. You could buy toys. No one said you couldn't buy toys. You could buy toys and give them away. That's what Christmas was, and people were okay with that.

He was pretty sure he could feel the arm of a Star Mutant digging through the fabric of his backpack into his back. He tried to ignore it. The walk to work wasn't long. Ten minutes later, he was walking through the gates of the school.

He always started work early, but he was extra early today.

He went to the broom cupboard and hung up his coat on the hook on the back of the door. He pulled on his overall and picked up the dust mop. Then he pulled the plastic bag of Star Mutants out of his backpack.

This cupboard was a good one, but it was his, and there was a limit to how much he was willing to share.

He pushed his mop down the corridor. *Star Mutants.* Hadn't had Star Mutants all those years ago. Couldn't remember what rubbish the kids had been into then.

Something else with spaceships and lasers probably. Daniel was really into—

Hogarth flinched.

All the kids were into that stuff. Then and now. All of them.

The school was silent except for the fall of his feet on the parquet and the swish of his dust mop on the floor. He looked to the left and the right as he walked through the corridors.

No one was around.

He had a cupboard in mind. It was at the end of the corridor outside the assembly hall. It was on the other side of the toilets, and then there was the end of the corridor and that was it.

He quickened his pace. When he got to the end of the corridor, he opened the cupboard, reached into the plastic bag, and pulled out a Star Mutant. He stood it on the floor. It fell over backwards. He stood it up again and propped it up with a couple more Star Mutants. He formed his purchases into a sort of pyramid so you could see what they were. It wasn't Toys "R" Us, but it'd do.

He fiddled with the door so that it was open a crack. It wasn't obvious, but you could definitely see the Star Mutants.

Especially if you were short.

He held out his hands. The door stayed still. All done. He stood up. His knees cracked. *All done.*

Now he just had to walk away and forget it. Or come back later and pick up the toys. But they'd probably be gone when he came back.

He'd cleaned the corridor last night anyway. He'd leave it for a day or so, just in case. He walked away quickly toward the assembly hall, pushing his mop, but did allow himself one quick look over his shoulder at the cracked-open door.

He couldn't see anything inside. The cupboard just looked really dark.

• • •

It started during assembly. Before assembly, they ignored him, and at first, he was grateful. He could see them whispering to each other as they lined up to go into the assembly hall, and then playing "Pass it on" while they waited for the big kids from Years 5 and 6. Jocasta whispered to Celandine on one side of her and Artemis on the other, and they excitedly passed the message on: Ernie to Amalee on the left and Anoop to Madison on the right. Round and round the message went until it got to Jacob, who was sitting next to Jack. Jack turned and leaned to listen to the message, but it never came. Jacob just sat there, frowning.

That was weird. Oh well. The message was heading the other way around the two rows of children at speed. Poppy was sitting on the other side of him, and she would tell him.

She didn't. She was sitting right next to him, and she didn't tell him.

Jack frowned. He felt like he was shrinking. He was the only one who didn't know what the message was. Why wouldn't they tell him?

The big kids from Year Five and Year Six came in noisily, and everyone stood up, so Jack stood up, too, but he wanted to run away and hide. The piano thumped out an intro, and everybody started singing. It was a song called "Give It All You've Got." Jack didn't like it much. He mouthed the words and hoped no one would notice that he wasn't singing.

They sat through a story about an elephant who eventually learned that he could do a thing none of the other animals could do, which was squirt water through his trunk and keep them all cool when it was hot, which Jack didn't really see the point of because none of them in assembly were elephants and it was raining outside anyway, but it was better than being in the classroom. Then they all got up to file out of the hall and back to the classroom.

There was a logjam at the door: one of the Amble kids in the year above Jack had fiddled with the handle and done something so it had stuck. The teachers crowded around making *tsk* noises and yelling at the kids to be quiet and calm down and shouting at Wayne Amble and asking why he would do that. The neat crocodile line devolved into a sort of mess of kids milling about. Jack craned his neck to see what was going on by the door. Suddenly, he felt a tremendous push on his back and he nearly fell over. He turned around to see who had pushed him, but there was a group of kids behind him— Jacob, and Poppy, Anoop, Talia, and Electra—and they were all looking the other way as if nothing had happened.

"Hey!" said Jack loudly. "Who did that?"

No one answered. Jacob was looking out the window. Ernie was inspecting his shoes. Anoop and Talia were talking about Star Mutants. Artemis, Celandine and Jocasta just ignored him.

"Hey!" he said again.

There was a round of cheers from the door and kids started filing out toward their classrooms again. No one spoke to Jack on the way out.

Chapter 5

By afternoon break, Jack was ready to curl up in a ball and hide under his bed.

When they'd got back to the classroom after assembly, Mrs. Seddon had moved him off Table Four and put him on Table Six with Jacob, Poppy, and Aneesha, and he was so happy he pretended he didn't see Jocasta's stupid pretend smile and little finger wave. But it didn't make things better.

No one would talk to him.

They'd started with Numbers, which was okay (not as good as Drawing or Words, but you couldn't do anything about that). The point on Jack's pencil had broken and he asked Poppy to pass him the pencil sharpener from the basket in the middle of the table. Poppy kept her head down and stared at her Numbers book. Jack figured she hadn't heard him, so he asked again, and then just stood up and got it himself, but he was starting to feel a deep feeling of dread.

At lunchtime, everyone was playing tag, and no one tagged him, even when he stood stock still right next to Poppy, who was It. As he was walking, he overheard Electra and Kyla.

"Jocasta's being horrible," said Kyla. "And it's not fair."

"If you talk to him," said Electra, "Jocasta won't invite you to her birthday party." Jocasta's birthday party was shaping up to be the social event of the year. Everyone was going to go to Jocasta's birthday party. (Jack had thought he might still be invited; people said everyone went, and that meant him, didn't it, because he was part of *everyone*.) "Besides," Electra went on. "He *smells*. He used to sit on their table and Jocasta said so. She says his mummy's so rubbish she can't buy mushrooms." She looked up and saw Jack, and turned away in disgust.

Jack felt tears stab at his eyes like needles. He ground his teeth, willing them to stay behind his eyelids. His throat hurt. *He did not smell.* He had had a wash that morning. He had had a bath the night before. How could he smell? He looked down and sniffed, just to check. He couldn't smell anything.

He didn't smell.

He didn't.

He *didn't.*

Then after lunch, he'd heard Kyla sniffing. She kept leaning over toward him and sniffing, and she wouldn't look at him.

By afternoon break, he'd had enough.

He was in the playground, in a corner, by himself. Mrs. Lycroft, who taught Year Five, was untangling Carlo Amble from three skipping ropes, a football, and something that looked like a giant lump of plasticine, and she wasn't looking.

So he ran. He ran around the side of the building where they weren't supposed to go, and he wanted to never stop running, but there was a hedge in the way and on the other side of the hedge was a road, so he couldn't. But there was a door into the building. He'd never been in that way before, but he tried the door and it wasn't locked or anything, so he went inside. It was eerily quiet. The sounds of the kids playing outside reminded him of being in the swimming pool with his head underwater. He stood stock still for a moment.

He wasn't supposed to be in there. You weren't supposed to be in the building at break unless it was pouring or you had fallen over and needed the Magic Cream on your knees or you were helping a teacher. It wasn't allowed. But he wasn't spending any more time in the playground. Not today. He wouldn't come back to school tomorrow either. Or the next day. He would go somewhere where they couldn't laugh at him or call him names or ignore him.

Except now he was indoors on his own during break. Like yesterday.

He stood in the corridor, barely able to move.

He heard footsteps and instinctively flattened himself against a wall, behind the edge of a bookcase. He heard Mrs. Seddon talking to someone. Someone who wasn't talking back. She was on her phone. Her shoes clopped off toward the staff room, and Jack breathed out.

He felt better being indoors. But break was going to end soon, and there was no way he was going back to the classroom. No way. He was going to find somewhere to hide until the end of the school day, and then he'd go away and never come back. And he would become a firefighter or an astronaut or a Star Mutant, and come back and tell Jocasta Valentine that *she* couldn't come to *his* birthday, and everyone would laugh at *her*.

He had never been in this part of the school before. The corridor had a bunch of bookshelves in it and pictures on the wall by the big kids. Jack looked at them. They were really good. They were on a big board, and Jack wandered past it looking at what the big kids had done. They'd been learning about Australia and had drawn pictures and written about them. Jack couldn't read all of the words, but he was impressed by the drawings and the handwriting.

Some of the handwriting was almost like grown-up handwriting. He wandered slowly up the corridor looking at the board. The last picture was of kangaroos jumping in front of a big red mountain with a flat top. It was really good. He liked that one.

He heard the clop of teachers' shoes again and he jumped, shot with fear. They were moving fast, and getting closer. He looked around desperately.

There was a door open a crack next to the board. A cupboard.

Clop, clop, clop.

He panicked. He hated cupboards. The thing—the monster—that had been following him watched him through the cupboards. It liked dark places.

Clop, clop, clop.

He would *NOT* go back out to the playground. He wouldn't.

Clop, clop. Clop. Pause. He could heard the teacher—Mrs. Willoughby, it was—talking to someone in another room.

She was just around the corner.

This cupboard, though…the other cupboards had been dark, really dark, and this one wasn't dark. Not quite. Not at the front. He could see something piled at the bottom. It looked like—it couldn't be, surely, but it *looked* like—something with Star Mutants on it.

He took a step closer.

It *did* have Star Mutants on it. It was a pile of Star Mutants action figures.

Whoa.

Whose were they? Were they anybody's? He didn't think so. You looked after your Star Mutants, if you had them. You didn't leave them lying around in school. Everyone knew that if someone found them, they got to keep them. Finders keepers, losers weepers.

These ones were new. They were still in the packet. Jack took another step closer. It was really dark in the cupboard, but he could see Pulsaria and Starhammer and the Red Giant.

He loved Star Mutants. He'd swapped Galacticor off of Carlo Amble, swapped two of his best Hot Wheels for keepsies. Galacticor was cool. Carlo's had broken—he was missing an arm—but that meant he fitted really well into Jack's pocket; without thinking, his hand wandered down to check. Galacticor was still there. He really, really, really wanted more Star Mutants— all of them—but Mummy had said that he would have to wait until his birthday and then if he was good, they'd see. He tried to be good. It didn't always work. There was a lot about being good that you didn't find out about until you'd got it wrong. And it was really easy to forget some of the small bits. But he was trying hard. His birthday was in August. It was ages away.

Maybe he could borrow these Star Mutants?

That would be stealing, whispered a voice somewhere in the back of his head.

He thought about it for a moment. It would be stealing if they were someone else's. But they were just *there*, in the cupboard.

The right thing to do was to go and tell a teacher that they were there, and then if nobody said that the Star Mutants belonged to them, then Jack would get them at the end of the week. But nobody would leave a pile of Star Mutants in the cupboard and then forget them.

Okay, so he couldn't take them. That would be stealing. And he couldn't tell a teacher, because then they'd know he was indoors at break time. But he could *look* at them for a bit. He could totally *look*. He took a step closer. He was crouching down by the Star Mutants now, just outside the cupboard. There wasn't any harm in just *looking*.

Mrs. Seddon was always saying that you looked with your eyes, not with your hands, but there were some things that grown-ups didn't understand. Sometimes you meant to look with your eyes, but your hands got in the way. He reached out to touch the Star Mutants, but somehow they seemed further away than they looked.

Clopclopclopclopclopclopclopclop

He darted inside the cupboard and pulled the door to, not quite closed, so he could still mostly see.

It would be fine, he thought. He would hide here until home time, play Star Mutants, and then give them back. It would be fine. He would share his toys, so whoever's they were wouldn't mind. Maybe if he shared really well, they could be friends.

He started to pull the plastic bubble off of one of the Star Mutants.

As if it had been caught by a light breeze, the door closed behind him with a click, and the cupboard became darker than he had ever imagined the inside of a cupboard could be.

He heard the shoes clop past the cupboard and out of the door that he had come in. It was fine. It would be fine. He heard the bell for the end of break, and he knew that he would not have to go back to the classroom. He breathed a sigh of relief.

Then he felt it. Cold air. On his neck.

His heart sank.

He heard a gentle hissing sound, and he knew the thing that had been in his cupboard, the thing that had followed him to school, had tricked him and now he was in its den. He was in the cupboard with the monster.

He groped for the door handle in the darkness, but it wasn't where it should have been. He screamed, but a scaly thing that was a bit like a paw but with long, rough, knobbly fingers clamped itself over his mouth. Then he felt himself being pulled backwards through the darkness.

He started to scream.

• • •

Holly was not looking forward to the school run. She was really regretting yelling at Allegra, and she knew there would be raised eyebrows and the tap-tap of perfect manicures on screens and phones that buzzed at the same time and pointed comments (nothing made to her, no, they couldn't be sure anymore how she would react, but made within her hearing to someone else, they would be, in the abstract; little comments thick with tiny thorns about Some People and how you could never be sure about Some People…)

The bell rang and the kids flooded out, brightly coloured and chattering. She watched them pour out of Jack's classroom. He was pretty good with his coat and remembering to collect his lunchbox, so he was usually about halfway between first and last out. But she couldn't see him.

Probably just helping Mrs. Seddon with something. Like yesterday. He was a good kid.

She waited for five, then ten minutes. She sighed.

"Come on, Jack," she muttered to herself as she trudged up to the door and into the school. Mrs. Seddon was in Jack's classroom putting a pile of forms into a tote bag. She smiled when she saw Holly.

"Hello again," she said. "What can I do for you?" Holly saw her eyes flick beside her, roughly to where Jack would have been.

"Um," said Holly. A horrible feeling was growing inside her. It wasn't fear exactly. It was more like a creeping realization that she was about to be frightened, more frightened than she had even been in her life, that this fear was coming, and what she was feeling now was the light breeze that heralded a tornado of destruction on a scale she couldn't even imagine. "Where's Jack?"

"He's not with you?" said Mrs. Seddon. She frowned.

"No," said Holly. *Of course he's not with me, you stupid woman.* "He didn't come out with the other kids. Was he helping you with something?" She could hear her voice becoming thin.

"Not this evening," said Mrs. Seddon. The smile had gone now and there was the faintest hint of panic in her eyes. "Were you late picking him up?"

"No," said Holly, angry as well as afraid. "No. No, I was there five minutes before the bell went. And he knows not to wander off or go with anyone if we haven't talked about it. And we have a password for if someone's picking him up and he doesn't know them or if they're picking him up in an emergency. He didn't come out of this classroom. I was watching the door."

"He must be here somewhere," said Mrs. Seddon. She pushed her chair back hard, and it scraped against the floor loudly. "Jack?"

"You don't *know*?" said Holly, aghast.

"I can't be everywhere," said Mrs. Seddon. She sounded like she was starting to panic herself. "I was in here. He was here after lunch. I didn't see him leave. Jack?" she called again. "He'll be here somewhere. Maybe he's in the loo."

They looked in the toilets. He wasn't there.

"Okay," said Mrs. Seddon. "Jack knows not to leave the school grounds. He must be around here somewhere."

Holly blinked.

"Somewhere?" she said, he voice rising. "*Somewhere?* You're supposed to be in charge! When did you last see him?"

"He was here," said Mrs. Seddon, quickly. "He was in class all day. Really he was." He voice caught a little. "He was *here*. I know this is stressful. Please don't shout at me, Mrs.—"

"It's *Ms.*!" shouted Holly. She tore off down the corridor, calling to Jack. She opened cupboards; poked under desks, looked behind bookshelves. She went down a corridor that had a big, brightly coloured display about Australia on it; he wasn't in the toilets down there, and he wasn't in the cupboard at the end. It was full of old books and dusty sugar paper.

Holly searched the school, and Mrs. Seddon told the other teachers, who helped, and then after an hour, Mrs. Willoughby, the head teacher, suggested gently that they call the police.

She put the phone down and Holly began to sob.

• • •

Two police cars zipped in quick succession past the shop. Rose opened the door and peered out.

"Oh dear," she said. "There's something you don't see in Crowsbrook every day."

Sarah looked up from the notes she was making behind the counter. "No sirens," she said. "It's probably not urgent if there's no sirens."

"Going at quite a clip, though, they are," said Rose. "Usually they're hiding behind the trees pointing hairdryers at you and telling you to slow down. Bloody hypocrites." She looked up at the sky quickly and ducked back into the shop. Ten minutes later, Mr. York came in for his *Daily Mail*.

"Thanks, Rose," he said, as she passed him the rolled up paper. "Something's up at the school s'afternoon. Crawling with policemen, it is."

"Oh dear," said Rose. "We saw them heading down that end. Really tonking, they were. Know what's going on?"

Mr. York shrugged. "Not a break-in. Everyone's been there all day. Only thing I could think of was something to do with one of the kids, but you don't like to think about that."

"Or the parents," said Rose. "But I can't think of anyone who'd cause trouble. All been in the village for years."

"Not all of them," said Mr. York. "Saw a new girl down there a couple of weeks ago. Wife says she moved in six months ago." He sniffed, put his paper on the counter, and wiped his nose with a very white handkerchief. "Not got a husband, she hasn't."

"Good on her," said Rose, pressing her lips together and lifting her chin. "Living the bloody dream." There was a glint in her eye that dared Mr. York to keep going with that line of discussion.

"Funny last name she's got, too," said Mr. York. "More consonants than bloody *Countdown*." He sniffed. "Foreigner, I reckon."

"Well, obviously," said Rose. "She only moved to Crowsbrook six months ago. Anything else, Mr. York?"

"You know what I mean," said Mr. York, darkly.

"Believe me, Mr. York," said Rose, beaming beatifically from ear to ear, "I know *exactly* what you mean." She picked up his paper. "And here's your *Daily Mail*."

Mr. York took the paper from her and lumbered off, mumbling something that may or may have involved the word *feckless*.

"Thank you!" called Rose after him, with acid sweetness. "Bloody reactionary misogynist old goat," she said to Sarah. "Good job they're all bloody perfect and nothing ever goes wrong for them. I just love that they all think it's all down to their upstanding virtue and not just sheer dumb luck." She sighed. "I bet," she said, "that they all have really boring lives. Oh well, long as they keep picking up their papers from here." The bell above the door jangled and Mrs. Bastable came in. "Hello, Jean," called Rose. "All go here today, it is."

"Not surprised," said Mrs. Bastable. "You hear about the police at the school? One of the littl'uns wandered off."

"No!" said Rose. "Terrible, that is. Did they find him? Or her," she added, as an afterthought.

"Not when I was down there," said Mrs. Bastable. "The mother's going out of her mind, of course. Sitting in an ambulance with a blanket round her when I walked past, she was. Just sitting there staring. You'd think she'd want to help to look. Single mother, she is."

"Probably the first sit-down she's had in years, then," said Rose. "Awful, though, it is. What happened? Someone take him from the school gates?"

"They don't know," said Mrs. Bastable. "He was there at lunchtime, and he was in his classroom after lunch, and after that, they're not sure. The mother said that she was there when the bell went, and it looks like she was—a whole crowd of people saw her—but they're not sure where he could have got to. They've checked the drains and the furnace and the places—well, you know, the places they tell the youngsters not to go because they're dangerous. And they didn't find him there, which is good, I suppose. But still: they can't find him, and they're wondering if someone wandered off with him."

Sarah closed her notebook and looked up.

"They were talking to Hogarth Merrick when I left," said Mrs. Bastable. "He's a funny old bird, he is."

"Who's Hogarth Merrick?" said Sarah, looking at Rose. "I don't think I've heard of him before."

"Still learning," said Rose to Mrs. Bastable, gesturing to Sarah with her head. "He's been in Crowsbrook all his life. And his family have been here forever. He'd have nothing to do with anything untoward. He'd be too scared of his mother, for a start."

Sarah frowned. She hadn't heard of Hogarth Merrick's mother either. "Do I know her?" she said. "Does she ever come in here?"

"Been dead more than thirty years," said Rose. "Thank God.

Although I wouldn't put it past her to still be keeping Hogarth on a tight leash."

Mrs. Bastable rolled her eyes. "No disrespect to the dead."

"Oh come on," said Rose. "She was a—"

"Very strong personality," Mrs. Bastable finished. "Didn't put up with nonsense, and that included nonsense from her family. If Hogarth put a foot out of line, she knew about it before he did it, and put a stop to it before he'd thought of it." She nodded, for emphasis.

"Powerful lady," said Sarah. She moved closer so she didn't miss anything. "How come her son's still scared of her?"

Rose shrugged. "Not literally," she said. "I'd hope. But she was one of those people who don't get on with other people. Kept themselves to themselves, the Merricks did. Her and the boy. I don't know what happened to Mr. Merrick. Florence Trumper said Augusta was quite the looker when she was young, and there was something that didn't work out with a man who went off to London, but I don't know if he was Mr. Merrick. I always thought he'd be dead or run off, and no one'd blame him either way, you ask me. But Hogarth's never been in trouble. He's a bit of an odd duck, but he's quiet. Worked around kids for decades and never been in trouble…"

"Doesn't mean anything, these days," said Mrs. Bastable, with a sniff. "Not getting in trouble. They're clever, they are. The ones who—you know."

"No, but he was down at whatzit's in Castleton for years. What do you call it?" Rose gestured to Mrs. Bastable. "Thingy's. The orphanage. They don't call it that anymore. The group home thing. And there *was* all that trouble, and he wasn't a part of any of it."

"St. Joseph's," said Mrs. Bastable. Sarah noticed that, somehow, she had managed to incorporate the suggestion of a sniff into the sentence, which should have been physically impossible, but didn't seem to be in Crowsbrook. "Used to be a *Catholic* place."

Ah, thought Sarah. *That would explain it.* Diversity, in Crowsbrook, meant that there was more than one family that had Methodist roots. It wasn't like the place she'd grown up in had been better, but when you spent a lot of your formative years learning that not everyone with whom you interacted shared the same assumptions that you did (in her case because they weren't necessarily from the same plane of existence), you were a lot more comfortable with the idea that people were just kind of different and it wasn't a big deal.

When you grew up in a family business, though, you were also painfully aware that not everyone thought it wasn't a big deal.

Wait a minute. St. Joseph's was the place from the clipping in the scrapbook. And it was also the home from which Daniel Giddens had disappeared all those years ago. Rose was telling Mrs. Bastable that live and let live was a fine motto to live by, and Mrs. Bastable was resisting valiantly. Sarah waited for her moment to jump in.

"Can I ask a question?" she said. "Because I was reading about St. Joseph's. In the old newspapers. At the library in Arden. Bit of local history there, am I right? St. Joseph's, I mean?" She hoped the open-ended question would work.

"Ooh," said Rose. "How long've you got?"

"Well," said Mrs. Bastable pointedly pulling her cuff over her wristwatch. "Terrible place it was. In the old days. Kids running wild, running away…all sorts. No one able to keep charge. Then the man in charge died suddenly, and it was like the people who ran it finally noticed it was there. Fixed it up, they did, and the things they found, you wouldn't believe. All sorts…you don't like to think about it. People didn't talk about it back then, not like

now, where it's everywhere, but the things that had been going on…"

"The man who died," said Sarah, frowning. "I think I read about him. Was he a priest?"

"No," said Mrs. Bastable "And they didn't think he knew what was going on, or he would have put a stop to it."

"Oh," said Sarah. "What was his name again? Wasn't there a priest there called Father Quinn?"

Mrs. Bastable frowned. "Maybe," she said, shaking her head. "I've never heard of Father Quinn, though. This was Mr. Kane. Hale and hearty he was, and not very old either. About fifty. And then suddenly he just took sick and died. They couldn't figure out why. Complete mystery it was."

"That's right!" chimed in Rose. "Gawd, this was bloody years ago. Creepy, it was. There were all sorts of rumours there might have been foul play—poison or something—but they did tests and…nothing." She shrugged. "All sorts of stories going around there were, but it didn't come to anything."

"Interesting," said Sarah. "The things you learn. So he wasn't up to anything, and he didn't know anything about what the people in the house were doing, and he died suddenly? Sounds like it would have been handy for a lot of people."

The two women shrugged. "There was nothing suspicious," said Rose. "They never found anything."

"But," said Sarah, "one of the people who worked at the place where a bunch of kids disappeared is now working at a place…where a kid has disappeared?"

"I know what you're thinking," said Rose. "But no. A lot of the kids that disappeared up and ran off. They found most of them eventually. You'd read about them in the paper when they got arrested in London. But with Hogarth it wouldn't be anything *bad*. Keeps himself to himself…"

"Wouldn't be the first time someone said that about someone up to no good," said Mrs. Bastable. "But really. Augusta Merrick's boy wouldn't dare. Come back from the bloody grave and beat him black and blue, she would. No disrespect to the dead," she added, looking over her shoulder. "Anyway, the boy'll turn up. The youngster. They always do."

"Fingers crossed," said Rose. She was all seriousness now.

"Fingers crossed," echoed Sarah. She hoped the kid would turn up. But she had a heavy feeling in the pit of her stomach. *If* a kid had gone missing…*if* there was a connection with the orphanage…then she had to consider the possibility that there was connection between the vision that Father Dominic had had and the disappearance in Crowsbrook. Which meant that she had to consider the possibility that—

She didn't want to think about it, but the gnawed bones attached to a human foot floated in front of her mind's eye.

They didn't know for sure the child was properly missing yet, though. They didn't know for sure.

She clenched her jaw. She was going to have to find out for sure. She was off work at seven. She glanced at her watch. Half an hour left.

Half an hour to come up with something.

She stared out at the rain through the glass panes in the door and blinked.

Was that—

She could have sworn she'd seen three women in black—the women from her vision—pass by the door.

Distracted, she walked toward the door and opened it.

"You all right?" called Rose, after her.

"Yeah," called Sarah. "Just…" Her voice trailed off as she looked both ways up and down the road.

There was no one there.

• • •

Hogarth was home by five-thirty o'clock, eating his pork chop by six. He'd expected to be home earlier, but the police had held him up. Just doing their jobs, of course. He'd been happy to help. Why not? He hadn't done anything wrong. Answered their questions and let him go, they had. Ma always said, don't be afraid of the police, they're there to help you.

Just don't tell them anything they couldn't work out from the other side of the front door.

They hadn't helped him. He'd helped *them*. Had a good day at work, apart from this. Got a little something on the Premium Bonds in the post this morning, ten pounds, so he'd been whistling all day; all of the teachers had known where he was because of the whistling, and he didn't have any time unaccounted for. Had his tea with the teachers at break time; ate his sarnies in the back of the kitchen with the dinner ladies at lunch. And Eamon Amble in Class 4 had been violently sick on the floor just before afternoon break; spent twenty minutes with the sawdust and shovels and hot water and bleach, he had, while Mr. Comstock sat in the corner with a green-faced Eamon and waited for his mum. Hadn't seen any of the kids out of the classroom when they shouldn't be. Of course he understood why they had to ask, officer. He read the papers. He was an older chap, living on his own, kept to himself. He understood. No, he didn't get lonely. Never got lonely. Lived in Crowsbrook all his life, he had. Knew everyone down the pub and they knew him. Liked to keep to himself mostly—

"—since your mother died?" said the officer.

Hogarth flinched at the recollection. *Coarse*, Ma would have said. You didn't talk about that sort of thing like that. *No respect for the dead.*

He smiled sadly at the officer and nodded.

But apart from that, they'd been pleasant, and asked him

to let them know if he noticed anything odd around the school buildings, and told him not to clean anything else until they'd finished, and let him go. Well, he wasn't going to argue if a policeman told him to take a couple of days off work, was he?

Very efficient, the police had been. He was impressed. Doing their job well, they were. Nice to see someone getting it right for a change, protecting the kiddies. There were a lot of weirdos about.

He finished his pork chop and went to wash up (no sense leaving it, Ma would have said, you want to live in filth?). But he couldn't help opening the hall cupboard door a crack. Just to check.

The cupboard was dark. The Bag'un was back. And Hogarth heard a noise in his head that sounded suspiciously like snoring.

• • •

As it is in the light, so it is in the dark.

There are creatures that kill to eat. There are creatures that kill for sport. There are creatures that gorge themselves on a fresh kill and who leave what remains for the scavengers. There are the creatures that eat carrion without killing at all.

And there are the creatures who kill and eat rarely, wasting nothing, protecting their meat from the scavengers in carefully crafted larders, keeping their captured flesh cool near the water until they are ready to dine, and eating slowly, a slow bite and a mouthful and a gulp at a time over the course of—

In the dark, it can be years. In the dark, they can keep their prey alive.

The thing from the cupboard was old, and it was magic, and both of these things had honed it to be an efficient and skilled predator. It grabbed its screaming, wriggling prey in its jaws using just enough pressure to hold it securely without damaging it, and set off, fast as a heartbeat through the unearthly dark in the back of the cupboard to the place where it knew it could store its food and make it last.

It wasn't far. And it was hungry. It had been decades since it had had a proper meal. *Soon*, it knew. *Soon.*

Usually the places it moved in and between were small and enclosed. It knew it was there when the space around it opened up. There was water. There were trees.

It dropped its prey on the ground. The prey was quivering and hysterical, but too confused to get up and run away.

The thing bit into the right foot, and began to munch. The prey let out a piercing scream.

The beast just wanted a small piece. Just to keep it going.

Chapter 6

By Tuesday evening, Jez had made up her mind. She had to talk to Sam about the disappearing women. In spite of all she had been through, she could not be sure that there was not a rational explanation for what had happened. She needed a second perspective. Sam might have been a bit useless with numbers, but he wasn't stupid, and he was the only person who had seen the things that she had seen, back in October.

Well. The only normal person, anyway. Sarah didn't count, and she was biased: she was used to things being invisible. Or selectively visible. Or disappearing randomly. It was what she did. Jez had seen enough evidence to convince her that all that stuff was real, but it was still profoundly unnerving to her.

She pulled out her phone and texted Sam.

You around?

The reply came right back: *Sure.*

Wanna hang out?

K.

Yours in 15.

There. Relatively painless. She threw some books in her green bag, pulled on her coat, and headed downstairs.

"Going to Sam's," she yelled into the living room.

"Okay," called back her aunt Becky. "Dinner's at eight; food is important."

"'Kay," hollered Jez. She slammed the front door behind her and headed to Sam's.

It took her fifteen minutes to get there. It used to take her ten, but she didn't cut through the graveyard after dark anymore.

• • •

Sam's mum opened the door. She made some noises about how she hadn't seen Jez in a while, and Jez mumbled something about exams and applications, and Sam's mum smiled and waved her in, and then she clambered up the stairs to Sam's room. She pushed the door open and was happy to see that it was mostly the same: it looked like someone had picked it up, shaken it, and put it back.

He had made some changes, though. The hat that had balanced for years on top of the precarious piles of papers and books on his desk had gone. The ancient beanbag was covered in some kind of soft throw blanket the colour of stone. There was a photo of him and couple of kids Jez didn't know, in a restaurant with a lot of dark wood panels and twinkling candles, pinned to the cork board. There was an electronica magazine next to his bed.

Electronica?

Oh well.

"Hey," she said. "What's up?"

"Oh," he said. "The usual. Trying to get through the days without gnawing my own leg off out of boredom. You?"

"Exams," said Jez.

"They're in May."

"They're a lot of work."

"Right."

There was a pause. Jez felt uncomfortable. Sam didn't have

music on and it was really quiet. She put down her bag, took off her coat, and sat down carefully on the throw on Sam's elderly beanbag. It rustled, ominously.

"So," she said. "Something weird happened. At school. On Monday."

"At Arden High?" said Sam, his eyes lighting up. "Surely not. Please tell me that Alex Appleton finally got it together with Lee Humbolt."

"Not *that* weird," said Jez. "Well. Sort of weirder. Different weird."

"Oh yes?" Sam was non-committal. The pause that followed swelled like a cyst.

Jez sighed and then took a deep breath in. "Okay," she said. "I'm just going to say it. I saw three women down by the bus stop at school. They were acting funny—looking over the fence and stuff, like they were looking for someone, but they didn't want to actually go in the gates. I didn't know if I should report it or anything, because weirdos and school, and Alex was there asking me to do a thing, and so I asked *her* if I should report it, and she couldn't see anyone there. And I could. And she couldn't. And when I turned back, they'd gone. Or rather—" she caught herself "—I didn't see them anymore either. And I checked the road and stuff, and they weren't walking down it in either direction or anything. On either side of the road. And you can see a long way from the bus stop. Longer than you could walk out of sight in the time—"

"Yeah," said Sam. He wasn't smiling anymore. "Gotcha."

"And," Jez went on, "I needed to talk to you about it because last time something weird happened I thought I was going mad...and...you..." She trailed off as she saw the look on his face. Sam was just looking at her, his expression flat.

"You helped me," she finished.

There was a really, really long pause.

Fuck.

He had helped her *eventually*. He had told her she was probably going mad, first, though.

"Want me to put on some tunes?" she tried.

"No," said Sam. His voice was emotionless as his expression. "No. Not right now." He pulled a packet of gum out of his pocket, broke a tab out of the blister, and started chewing in a halting, irregular rhythm.

Jez looked at the packet in his hand. "Nicotine gum?"

Sam shrugged.

"You quit smoking?" she said, astonished. She'd needled him about it since they'd become friends, shortly after he started.

"Yeah," he said. "Th— I mean. Loads of people don't now."

"Right," said Jez, shortly. "Makes sense." Sam chomped on his gum. "You were saying?" Her tone was colder than she'd intended.

Sam looked out the window. It was full dark. The rain was falling steadily, but the wind had died down. Jez could hear the water running through the gutters above.

"All I can say is what I said before," he said. "There must be an explanation. And I feel like I'm saying the thing that you would normally be saying. People don't just disappear. Weird shit doesn't just happen. Yeah, we saw some stuff in October. But we spent seventeen years before that not seeing any of that shit, and we managed just fine. Even if it existed, it didn't touch our lives. We only got involved last year because of—"

"Sarah," said Jez, quickly. "Yeah."

"Because of someone else," said Sam. "Yes." He rolled his gum around his mouth. "I wouldn't worry about it if I were you. I know it sounds horrible to say that you imagined it, so I'm not going to do that, because obviously you wouldn't make up something like that. But there's no way they could have just disappeared. There must be a rational explanation for it."

"Okay," said Jez. "But Alex couldn't see them either. And I can't think of a reason why."

"Do you need to?" Sam held up his hands. "Does it matter? Before October, you would have assumed there was a rational explanation and not given it a second thought."

"I have more data to take into account?" Jez picked absently at the side of the beanbag. "I know it's dumb. But the October stuff was *dangerous*, Sam. If it's coming back—"

"I know it was fucking dangerous," said Sam, with a note of anger in his voice. "My arm is still not the fucking same. It has pins in it. You're not supposed to get aches in your joints when it rains at seventeen, Jez. But just because a terrifying, dangerous, scary thing happened doesn't mean it's going to happen again, and doesn't mean it's going to happen to us." His voice softened. "You don't have to be paranoid forever," he said. "It's over."

"Yeah," said Jez. "I guess." She didn't feel better, but she could tell she wasn't going to get anywhere.

"It's nothing, Jez," Sam said. "Nothing happened. Everything is fine."

Jez picked at a loose thread on the throw. "You never think about it?"

"Of course," he said. "But I try not to."

"Is that why we don't hang out anymore?" Jez knew she was getting off topic, but she couldn't help it. "Because you're trying not to? Think about, I mean?"

"No," said Sam. "No," he said again. "I dunno—no. Theo—"

"Right," said Jez. "Theo, yeah." She was annoyed now. "You're not around at school either, and he's not there."

"You're always in the library."

"Not always!"

"*Yes* always. When do you eat? You don't! You don't get coffee anymore. You don't hang out in the common room!"

"We couldn't hang out in the common room together anyway!" Jez was almost shouting. Jez and Sam were in two different year groups at Arden High because Sam was three months younger, and each common room was restricted to one year group. "You don't sit near me on the bus!"

"I'm not always going right home!"

"I know! You're meeting bloody Theo *all the bloody time!*" Jez realized that she sounded like a twelve-year-old and couldn't help it.

"You're working all the time!"

"Yeah! Because I have *literally nothing else to do*! I still live in bloody Crowsbrook!"

"You mean *figuratively*, not *literally*! You *essentially* have nothing else to do! You don't *literally* have nothing else to do!"

There was silence.

"Jerk," said Jez eventually, in a small voice, not looking at him. She tried smiling, to show it was okay. After a moment or so, she steeled herself and looked up. He was doing the same.

"I'm sorry about the bus thing," said Sam. "And for the other stuff."

"It's okay," said Jez, and then realized it wasn't. "Well. It's not okay. But it's cool that you said it. I mean. We're okay. You're okay by me. Fuck."

"Oh my God," said Sam. "We have to start hanging out again; you can't even speak in full sentences anymore." Jez went to punch him on the arm, and he flinched. She stopped short.

"Okay," said Jez. "But I should tell Sarah, at least. That was the first conversation I ever had with her: if you see anything weird, tell me. I should tell her about this. I mean, even though I don't know, it might be better. She might have a better idea of whether it's a thing or not."

"Or you could leave it to her altogether," said Sam. "If it *is* her kind of thing. It does seem to be her job. She probably knows already. Why do we—why do *you* have to get involved?"

Jez shrugged. "I dunno," she said. "I feel—I dunno. *Responsible.* Somehow. After all the stuff that happened. She needed our help then, Sam. If we hadn't helped her, she would have died in that basement. And she wouldn't have been able to kill that—" she shuddered internally at the memory "—*thing.* The thing that killed Cat. And Marina. And G—"

"Yeah," said Sam, shortly. "I know. But a lot of other things wouldn't have happened as well, Jez. You're all about science. What you're saying is just speculation. We'll never know how things would have turned out if we hadn't been involved." He sighed, and pulled the packet of chewing gum out of his pocket, unwrapped another tab, and started working on it. "Maybe I'm biased, but a broken arm hurts like a *motherfucker*, Jez. You didn't get hurt, badly."

"I have nightmares," said Jez, flatly. She stared hard at the rug in front of her. She hadn't told anyone this before. "Every night. I wake up two, three times a night. Seeing stuff. Sometimes I'm in the hospital and that thing's about to come through the window. Sometimes I'm in the car. Sometimes I'm in the cellar. Over and over and over again." She rolled the thread into a ball and flicked it into the corner of the room. "And then I wake up and I'm in my bedroom. Where I saw Marina's ghost. Or corpse. Or something. And I can't move because I'm scared."

Sam looked at her, shocked. "Can't you get help?"

"My family have enough on their plate," said Jez. "Besides, what kind of help? What are they going to do? There aren't any great treatments to help you stay asleep; most stuff just helps you *fall* sleep. Plus it's not that great for you. And the alternative is going to see a therapist, and what am I going to tell them? What are they going to tell me? 'Think nice thoughts and try to avoid horror movies'? Fucking *meditate?*" She punched the beanbag in frustration, and it made a small splitting noise. "Shit. Sorry."

"Don't worry about it," said Sam. "My mum has been saying for years that she's only doing palliative repairs on it. You don't owe Sarah anything, you know."

"She saved the village, Sam. Maybe more."

Sam grunted.

"Look," he said after a moment, "I know. She did good things, and no one's ever going to say thank you, or even know. I appreciate that. But the stuff that she has to deal with is mad and dangerous, and there's nothing in place to help."

"I know," said Jez. "And I'm worried that's a reason we should be helping her."

Sam chewed fiercely for a moment and then looked up to face Jez directly.

"Yeah," he said. "It is. But how is it our job? Neither of us even has a driver's license, let alone the kind of knowledge you need to help Sarah Trevelyan. We'd be cannon fodder, Jez. The only reason we managed to get out okay last time was dumb luck. We don't know what we're doing. And it's not just about us being safe. You know that better than I do."

Jez nodded.

"I'm not saying don't talk to her," said Sam. "But it's not your job. And I'm—I dunno. I don't want to get involved."

Jez shrugged. "I'm not sure there's anything to get involved in."

"Sure," said Sam. "Fair enough. But just be careful. She's a dangerous person to know."

Jez picked at another thread on the beanbag.

"I think," she said, "that's why she doesn't have any friends."

Sam sighed. "Not our problem, he said. "Put some tunes on, will you? It's way too quiet in here."

"I hear you're into electronica now," said Jez, gesturing toward the magazine and pulling out her phone. He half-laughed.

"Theo is," he said. "I was just trying to *educate myself*, as the Interwebs say." The opening riff of "Staying Out for the Summer" leaked out of Jez's phone. "Ah!" Sam spread his fingers wide. "A classic. Take your mind off the weather. And strange women in black. And the ongoing saga of Alex Appleton and Lee Humbolt." He smiled.

Jez did, too. Then something struck her and the grin faded from her face.

"Sam," she said quietly and as evenly as she could manage. "Who said anything about women in *black*?"

Sam's face froze. The song carried on merrily, but the silence between Sam and Jez was edged with acid.

"You saw them, too," said Jez. It wasn't a question. "You saw them, *and you know what I'm talking about*. Because if you had seen them, and nothing strange had happened, you would have gone, 'oh right, those weirdos, probably from Ofsted, that or they're visiting Mr. Littlefair's music class, no worries, moving on, isn't electronica amazing?' But you pretended you hadn't seen them, *you fucker*." She stood up. "Why would you do that?" She pulled on her coat. "I said it was freaking me out. Why would you not go 'yeah, I saw that—it was weird, let's figure it out'? Why would you *lie*?"

"I didn't *lie*," said Sam, standing up. "I stand by *everything* I said. Maybe you made a mistake. Maybe I made a mistake. There's no need to assume everything's supernatural. We didn't before, and we don't have to now. Just because we know it can happen doesn't make it more likely to happen to us."

"You don't know that!" Jez was trying to keep her voice down; her throat hurt with the effort. "You don't know how this stuff works any more than I do. You can't just ignore it and hope it'll go away."

"You can't panic every time you come across something you can't immediately explain either," said Sam. "You never used to. You *always* used to look for the rational explanation, so what's changed?"

"*They were right there, Sam!*" Jez was practically hissing. "*And Alex couldn't see them! And the same thing happened to you!*"

"*I don't want to get involved, Jez!*" Sam stood up and looked hard at Jez. "Yes. I saw them. I was in English. I was staring out of the window; they looked weird. I called Mrs. Crowther over because I didn't know if they were trespassing. I *did* the responsible thing. She couldn't see them. I fudged it and said that they must have gone in one of the buildings, but I looked out of the window a moment later, and they were outside the art room windows. They shouldn't have been able to do that, but they did. I don't know what's happening, but whatever it is, I don't want to be a part of it. I don't, Jez." He pointed to the arm that had been broken. "I'm still not over the last time we were hanging out with the supernatural on a regular basis."

"You fucking lied to me!" Jez spat the words as quietly as she could manage. "I think I'm going crazy here, and instead of going, 'no, you're all right,' you're all 'yup, crazycakes; look at you, paranoid lady.' Fuck you." She marched out of Sam's room and slammed the door behind her.

"You all right, Jez?" said Sam's mum, when she reached the bottom of the stairs. "You going already?"

"Yeah," said Jez, not looking at her as she headed toward the front door. "Becky's got dinner on. And electronica sucks."

• • •

Holly sat in her living room, staring at the wall. There was a cup of herbal tea on the coffee table in front of her. It had been put on a coaster. Her heart was pounding and she was shivering. Someone had put a blanket over her.

Someone was talking. Someone was explaining a thing to her. Holly could understand that much, but it was like trying to listen to someone when you were underwater. Waterbury, that was it. Constable Waterbury. She was the community-liaison-officer person they'd left with Holly, and she was doing the old "is there anyone you can call, anyone who can come and stay with you?" routine.

Holly shook her head. There wasn't. Her mum was out of the country, her dad was dead, her brother was in Scotland and they had phoned him and he was coming, but Scotland was a long drive. And her ex-husband…well, she didn't want to call him. She'd have to at some point. Except she wouldn't, because they were going to find Jack and everything was going to be okay.

"I've got to go now," said Constable Waterbury. "But we're still working, and I'll be back tomorrow first thing to check up on you. Are you sure you'll be all right, by yourself? There isn't a neighbour or anyone?"

"I just moved here," said Holly, hoarsely. "Six months ago."

Constable Waterbury looked concerned. "Well," she said. "If you're sure. Someone probably would. If you wanted. This is a pretty tight-knit community."

Holly shook her head slowly. Constable Waterbury let herself out.

"Tight-knit" community. Tight-arsed, more like it. She had seen the looks around the school, the ones that slipped over the faces of parents and neighbours drifting out of their houses as the police cars zoomed in, lights flashing. The faces of concern and self-satis-faction: *what's going on? It must be bad. I would never let that happen to me.*

She could imagine Allegra and her cronies on the Internet right now, along with everyone else in the village.

Where were the parents?

The child obviously had no respect for his teachers and should never have been allowed to leave the classroom. Who taught him that? Education begins outside of the school!

Bleeding hearts have destroyed a generation by refusing to discipline children when needed. It's sad that this young boy had to pay the price for his mother's failure.

Parents should be held accountable. The fact that this happened in a school doesn't matter.

No doubt someone will try to sue the school. Teachers look after up to forty children in a single classroom these days, they can't be expected to be everywhere at once. Teach children discipline and they won't go wandering off in the middle of the school day. Shame on the mother.

You didn't need to read it to know it was happening. Holly pulled out her phone and then put it back in her pocket without looking at it. She took a sip of tea. It was almost cold.

She stared across the room. Wilma Bear was leaning up against a chair, sagging toward the floor, staring into the middle distance. Holly knew how she felt.

And then something in Holly's mind snapped.

Fuck this. FUCK this. Her kid was missing and she was lying on a sofa covered in a blanket like fucking Princess Snow White, like stuffed Wilma Bear, waiting for Jack to just show up again so they could live happily ever after? She sat up straight and hurled off the blanket. No. The police weren't coming back until morning, although the search was going on overnight. She'd been told to keep away, but they couldn't be everywhere, and time was being wasted. She ran around throwing things into a backpack: water, chocolate *(you shouldn't have it in the house; they think refined sugar is addictive now)*, Walter Bear. She strode toward the hall, pulled on her coat, dug out a set of wellingtons from the ottoman near the front door, dodged into the kitchen to grab a torch, and went out.

You could cover a lot of ground in a night, and she intended to.

• • •

The first thing that Sam did when Jez left was call Theo.

"Hey," said Theo. "I know you love the nineties, but phoning is going a bit far, isn't it?"

"I was just feeling the retro," said Sam. "As the kids all say. Or used to. Or something. I just had a fight with Jez."

"Jez?" said Theo. "You guys haven't spoken in months. Were you hanging out?"

"Sort of," said Sam. "I dunno. It's—ugh." He shrugged, and then remembered Theo couldn't see him. "So much drama."

"Well, what happened?" said Theo. "Was she pissed off that you're seeing someone?"

Seeing someone. It still felt a little weird, and maybe that was why the thought had not occurred to Sam. Had Theo ever said it out loud before? Sam didn't think so.

"I don't think so," he said. "She didn't mention it. We were talking about other stuff."

"What stuff?" said Theo.

Sam realized he'd talked himself into a corner. "I dunno," he said. "We were talking about some old stuff that happened ages ago, and then she decided I was lying to her and got annoyed and stormed out." He felt a twinge of disloyalty. "It's complicated."

"Why would she think you were lying to her?" said Theo. There was an uncomfortable pause. "*Did* you? Because if you did, she might have a point. Which might be less complicated."

Sam paused. "Maybe," he said. "Sort of. I told her not to worry about a thing I was worried about, and that it was no big deal. It doesn't matter what. She found out that I thought it *was* a big deal, and stormed off. I was trying to help." He took the packet of nicotine gum out of his pocket, pressed out another tab, and started to chew. "Which, needless to say, did not work."

"Sounds like she overreacted," said Theo. "Clip, clop, knock, knock. The Drama Llama comes to visit again."

"It's not like that." Sam could hear that he sounded defensive. "It'll be fine."

"Sure," said Theo, evenly. "It's not like you guys hang out much. And she's moving away in a couple of months anyway, right?"

"I guess," said Sam, but he still felt uncomfortable. He tried to change the subject. "What are you up to?"

"Not much," said Theo. "Giant pile of work. The usual. I saw those women again today, though."

"What women?" Sam had had enough of talking about groups of women appearing and disappearing for one day.

"Remember we were in the kebab shop a few nights ago, and those three women pushed past us on the way in? They look like really old Goths. Like, *really* old. I saw them again today, outside the town hall while I was getting lunch. Are they, like, a local institution or something? I asked the guy in the shop, but he didn't know what I was talking about. I guess he was making my laffa, and when he looked up, they'd gone."

Sam was silent for a moment.

"No," he said. "No idea who they are. They'd stand out a mile in Crowsbrook."

He hoped to God that they would.

• • •

Time became elastic for Holly: stretched taut and vibrating with tension. She would look at her watch and, what seemed like an hour later, she would check again and five minutes would have passed. She tramped through the fields and wood around Crowsbrook. It was slow going: she was thorough. She checked under every bush, under every hedgerow; she climbed fences, looked into ditches, poked into holes. She had never explored the country around Crowsbrook—she had been working and looking after Jack since they moved in. They went to the supermarket in Arden, and the shop, and the school, and the park, and to the pond once, and that was about it. The fields and footpaths were a mystery. More than once, she stumbled on uneven ground; hidden rabbit holes threatened to trip her. One time she stepped on what she thought was dried mud and it turned out to be the dessicated top of a cowpat. Her boot crunched through it and came up reeking. Through all of it, she kept going.

When she saw the torches of the police and the volunteers—you could tell it was the search party, they were moving in lines—she changed direction. She was ahead of them, and knew they wouldn't find anything in the ground she had already covered. On she went, until, sooner than it had any right to, the sun came up. It threw a weak and watery grey light onto the field. Holly realized that she had no idea where she was.

She turned, and saw the school in the distance. All that way, all that walking, and she still hadn't made it out of Crowsbrook. And she still hadn't found Jack.

She found her way back to the road. It was still quiet at that time, and the rain had dropped off to a light drizzle. A runner was heading toward her, lean in her brightly coloured leggings and rain jacket.

No, thought Holly. *It couldn't be.*

It was. It was Allegra. Holly looked at her watch—7:02 a.m.

How? thought Holly. *How? How? How?* She knew Allegra's

explanation already. It would start with a breezy *Oh, I just…* and end with *…it's so important to set an example, don't you think?*

Holly had never been sure for whom the example was being set.

As Allegra came closer, her eyes widened, and she slowed to a stop.

"Holly!" she said, breathlessly. "How *are* you? I am so, so sorry to hear what happened. You look *terrible*."

Holly looked down. She was splashed with mud from head to toe. She reeked of the cowshit that covered her boots. Her jacket was soaked. She ran her fingers self-consciously over her hair, and a wet leaf tumbled the ground. Allegra was clean and showered and barely breaking a sweat.

Is she wearing makeup???

Holly did not have words to describe the shame. She just nodded and mumbled agreement.

"You have to take care of yourself, you know," said Allegra. It's *so* important. Especially at a time like this. I don't know *what* I would do. You've got to keep an eye on them at *all* times, haven't you? It just goes to show. It's *so* important."

Holly just looked at her.

"I have to go," she managed.

"Oh yes," said Allegra. "Me, too. I have to get Jocasta ready for school. Oh—"

There was an awkward pause.

"You know how it is," she finished.

Holly blinked.

"I'll get going, then," said Allegra. She went to put a hand on Holly's arm. Holly flinched. "If there's *anything* I can do…"

Holly just nodded.

"…let you know," she said.

"Okay, then. See you at schoo—"Allegra began lightly and

then stopped herself. "See you soon!" She jogged off down the lane toward Sycamore Lane, where she lived.

Holly did not remember how she got home. She closed the front door and began to cry, leaning against it and sliding down it until she was a heap on the floor. She fell into a fitful, nightmarish half-doze, leaning against the front door, and only woke up when the community liaison officer rang the doorbell at eight o'clock on the dot.

Chapter 7

Savaric had a comfortable place in the trees next to the Foxglove Pond. You wouldn't notice it at a casual glance, but when Savaric was sitting there, ten feet in the air, you could see how perfectly he fit, as if the tree had been coerced into shifting its creaking form for his specific comfort. You had to look carefully, though. With his coat wrapped around him and his perfect stillness, he was somehow very easy for the eye to slide off; he could almost pass for part of the tree, if you weren't paying attention and you weren't expecting him to be there.

It was a trick that had served him well in the early days in Crowsbrook. He liked the Foxglove Pond. Always had. He spent a lot of time in the city now—had for years—and while he wouldn't have moved away for the Devil's fortune, in the old times it was nice to sit in the quiet and the dark at the familiar place and feel anticipation, the growing light, before the sun came up. It wouldn't be dramatic this morning—it was pissing with rain, for a start, and he'd seen so many sunrises now that the thrill was all but gone—but it was the principle of the thing. When he was in Crowsbrook, he paid a trip to the pond.

He'd always enjoyed its fearsome reputation. He knew what

had happened there; what had been trapped in it. But that hadn't made it evil, although that was how a lot of people in his day had seen it. It wasn't that simple. You worked these things out when you had enough time to think about them. The pond just drew things that were inclined toward darkness toward it. It called to its own.

Plus, he'd always had good luck there. He'd laughed when he'd seen the half a tree trunk there that someone had made into a seat. One of the local kids had carved into it *GL + MB 2gether 4ever*. There were always some that wandered away, to the places where no one else would go.

It had actually been a few years since he'd been in Crowsbrook, but it felt like five minutes since he'd last seen Hogarth Merrick and his little friend. *The Bag'un*, Hogarth called it. Good a name as any. Savaric didn't care: business was business and the Bag'un was one of Savaric's ongoing concerns.

He pulled an old leather flask out of the folds of his coat and took a swig.

It wasn't about money. Or power. Or fucking with people for the Devil's own bloody sake of it, which was mostly why he did things. The Bag'un was different from all of that. The Bag'un was about survival. And if there was one thing Savaric was good at, it was survival. That was another reason he was better off hanging around the pond instead of going into the village, where he knew there would be people and coppers and all of that palaver. And you'd have to be made of stone not to feel a *bit* bad. Sometimes you did when it was kids. But the Bag'un was what he was, and needed what he needed, and Savaric had spent enough time coming to terms with what he himself was and what he himself needed that he couldn't judge another creature for that. Self-acceptance was one of the hardest things you had to deal with after you'd—well, *changed*, like he had. But, as his sister had always said (and she had changed, too, of course), you had to work with what you had. The world was a hard place and always had been. His own mother had buried nine children. All except Savaric and his sister. And their mother had never forgotten a single one of them. But you had to move on. You had to survive.

He remembered his mother, thin and red-eyed and bent over the fire the morning after they buried his first brother. She had collapsed to her knees and sobbed for what seemed like a lifetime, until she saw him looking at her. Then she wiped her eyes and sniffed and got up and went to feed the pigs. She never talked about his brother again. Or any of the others.

She lit rushlights, though. Kept them on the windowsill. On the days of their births and the days of their deaths. And went to the church and said prayers for them all. The dead ones, that was.

They were still buried in Crowsbrook, in the churchyard, under generations of later bones. He couldn't go there, but he thought about them when he came down to the pond.

The pond was a good place for a good think.

He tried to mitigate the things he had to do. But at the end of the day, he was a hunter, and he was good at it. Savaric had the trick of being able to sense vulnerability, strong emotions, almost like he was hearing them. He could pick up on people who were distracted, and he had learned that, if you concentrated hard enough, you could lock on to a really strong emotion and sort of give a person a little nudge. In the head. Get them where you wanted them. So to speak. It helped that a lot of people weren't clear on the difference between what they wanted and what they needed.

The rain started to drip more heavily around him, the drops of water thudding through the twigs.

The Bag'un was just how he made his living. How he got through the world. He was effectively immortal, which really raised your living expenses over time and definitely knocked retirement on the head (though Savaric had laughed to break the drains when he'd found out what *retirement* actually was.) How many people could say they got their living through the world and harmed no one? Wouldn't exactly take long to count them, would it?

He reached down to one of the pockets of his long coat, and felt the folds. His fingers traced the outline of a small box.

Still there. He knew it would be, but he still liked to check every so often. Sort of like he did with Hogarth.

Hogarth. Bloody hell, Savaric had met some pathetic mortals in his time, but Hogarth was even mediocre at being pathetic. Oh well. He did what he was told, mostly. Actually, he did what he was told *to the letter*, which was helpful for Savaric's purpose. It was just that Savaric didn't know how he did it. He'd never met a set of rules that he didn't think would look better with some cracks in them and bent into a more interesting shape.

He took a deep breath of the damp, early morning air and exhaled a long stream of mist.

Crunch.

Savaric snapped out of his reverie sharply. Not many people came down to the Foxglove Pond. He was unlikely to be in danger—Savaric was well aware that most of the time, the most dangerous thing in his immediate vicinity was him—but he vastly preferred avoiding trouble to confronting it.

(If he wasn't causing it, obviously.)

He moved sharply, casing the pond with a predator's eye. He couldn't see anyone. He frowned.

"Below you," said a voice like a saw.

Savaric started. He wasn't used to things sneaking up on him. The sudden movement made him lose his balance and he slithered out of the tree, scraping his way down the bark to the ground.

It wasn't one person. It was three. And Savaric knew right away that they weren't people at all. Not in the human sense. His insides curdled.

They *were* more dangerous than him.

He thought quickly, stood up, and bowed. It was affected, but with this coat, he could probably pull it off. And they liked a bit of deference, this sort. When they didn't go straight to the part where they clawed out your intestines so you could see how pretty they were when the light danced on them in the daylight, that was.

"Ladies," he said. They weren't, but they looked like women at the moment. If he were polite enough, he figured, he might just get away with everything still attached to him in its current configuration.

The one on the left snorted.

"Common bloodsucker," she said, more to her companions that to him. She had a slight accent. The second shrugged, and the third sneered.

"Did you come down here to mope?" she said. *That accent again.* The other two snickered. Savaric felt his hackles rise through his fear, and hoped neither would show. He raised both hands, open.

"Business trip," he said. "Nothing that should get in your way." He hoped not, at least. Whoever was in their way was for it.

"Let us hope not," said the third. "You know this place well?"

"The pond?" said Savaric. "I used to swim in it." That hadn't been for a very long time, though. Not since before there were… well, *things* in it.

"The village, you idiot." Her voice contained a scraping of irritation. "This Crowsbrook."

"I was born here," said Savaric. "That was a while ago, though."

"You know the witch? Sarah Trevelyan?"

"Witch?" said Savaric. "I've really not kept up." Old Nan was the last witch he'd known in Crowsbrook; he and his sister had run away to the city and heard years later (heard or assumed) that she'd died after…fuck, that didn't matter. There weren't witches anymore, between the burnings and the Enlightenment. That was mostly why he was able to get on with his business and work with the Bag'un.

"We are looking for her," said the woman in the middle. She was taller than Savaric, and standing just a little closer than he felt comfortable with.

"Why?" said Savaric without thinking.

"He *is* an idiot," said the second woman. "Why do we look for anyone?"

"Broken oaths," said Savaric, automatically. He was perfectly still, ready to spring and run if any of them made a move, even though he knew that it would be hopeless. "Places where the ties that bind have been broken. Where duties have gone unperformed. Obligations not been met."

He had heard how their victims died. In torment. Slowly.

"That," said the third woman, "is why we are here."

"You can relax, bloodsucker," said the first woman. She gave a short laugh under her breath. "We are not looking for you. Today."

"Oh," said Savaric, twisting his face into a close approximation of a smile. "Oh good."

"He knows the village," said the second. "What can you tell us?"

"Nothing," said Savaric quickly. "I live in London, have done for centuries."

"Witches," said the third woman, "do not move much."

Traditionally, that was true. Wards built up on a witch's cottage over the years. Wards that were specifically designed to keep things like Savaric—like the three women—out.

Savaric sighed. "I can tell you where it was," he said. "The cottage, I mean. That's all."

"It is a start."

Savaric gave the directions. They were gone as quickly—and as silently—as they had come. He took a deep breath and let it out slowly.

Fuuuuuuuuuuck.

He wasn't sure what he'd just done, but he was pretty sure that if anyone was living where Old Nan's cottage had been, their day wasn't going to get any better.

He shook his head. It wasn't personal. It was about survival. He stared at the pond for a very, very long time without blinking.

All the witches had gone—everyone knew that. Replaced. No one needed them anymore: there was medicine and counselling and therapy and sex advice columns and meditation, and no one wanted protecting from evil spirits or runs of bad luck. If you had a run of bad luck, you were on your own.

It made his job a lot easier.

If there was a witch in Crowsbrook, though…

The herbs-and-childbirth racket wasn't the only thing they did, part of his brain reminded him.

What the witches had done in the old days—apart from the love spells and turning the milk if you pissed them off—was to keep the balance between the human and the Ethereal worlds.

He took another swig from his flask.

His concern with the Bag'un had been successful over the past few decades, costs notwithstanding. It made surviving not only easier, but decidedly more pleasant. He had lived a very long time, and a lot of it had been hard. Very hard. And if Hogarth was doing his job properly, Savaric was about to come to an arrangement with a bloke he knew in London that would set him up for—well, for a very long time. Which, when a very long time was what you had, was important. He had learned not to mind the rain and the cold: he had his coat and his good umbrella, and you could go a long way with that. But there were delights in the world that he had learned to actively enjoy. And if his arrangement worked, there would be ample opportunity. And he didn't need anyone screwing it up for him, witch or not. Because one person's nice little earner was another person's imbalance in the universe.

He put the flask away, fighting the urge to drain the bloody lot.

Right then. He took a deep breath and focused. His hunting instincts kicked into gear, and the name *Sarah Trevelyan* echoed through his head like the clang of a funeral bell. He'd sent the women to the old cottage. He should maybe head over that way himself. Keep an eye on who might be coming or going.

Obviously the women were looking for the witch, but they wouldn't need to if he found her first. If he put her out of action before they got to her. From what he'd heard about the Three, he'd be doing her a favour. And if they considered he'd done them a favour, that'd be no bad thing either.

It really depended upon who found her first.

• • •

The air shifted and crackled around the shadows.

Something had changed. Something was wrong. Someone was screaming.

And they could feel a presence that overshadowed everything with its power.

So little had happened since they had been there. So little had changed.

Together, they moved toward the sound of the screaming.

• • •

The community liaison officer had offered to make her another cup of tea. Holly wondered how satisfying it was, when you were a fully trained police officer, to be the one stuck in the houses of weepy, broken people, offering to put the kettle on for tea both of you knew they didn't want. They'd gone through the polite stuff—hello, how are you this morning, how are you holding up, did you sleep (soooo important, Holly thought, pulling a sarcastic face when the officer's back was turned)—and then she said she was going out.

"You don't have to," said Constable Waterbury. "You can—"

"Can what?" said Holly. "Stay here and look at the walls, while my son's been out there all night by himself?"

Waterbury made protesting noises, but Holly wasn't listening. She grabbed her wet coat, pulled on her wellies, and slammed the front door behind her.

More woods and fields, this time to the west side of Crowsbrook. But today was different. Yesterday, she had felt desperate. Her world had been turned upside down. She didn't know where to start, where to turn. She only knew that she had to do something.

Because how had this happened? She had tried. She had tried her best, and all she had managed was a rubbish marriage, a hasty escape, and a borrowed home in the middle of nowhere, where he couldn't even get a good night's sleep. And now she had lost him. She had tried to be a good mother and now—

Tears stabbed at the back of her eyes and pain wrenched her throat.

She'd done everything right. She'd *tried*. And she'd failed. The parts of her mind that her therapist had called "the tapes" were playing at full volume.

Oh, you did everything right? You couldn't even protect him from a six-year-old girl. You're rubbish at this. You make stupid choices, and he's the one that suffers. It wasn't enough that you failed at everything you tried; you had to bring him down with you. You can't see anything through, can you? You turned him into just another half-arsed Holly project. You might not have listened to your friends about Richard (and God knows that whole thing was another example of your stellar decision making: why not get married straight out of university to a man no one else could stand to be around for more than an hour? What were you trying to prove: that you could make him better? That you could protect him against all those people who saw and understood what he was? That you were goddamn magic?), but at least he saw you as what you are: a stupid, weak, self-pitying cunt. Ever consider that you only left because you can't handle hearing the truth?

Her face twisted into a grimace of pain, and tears ran down her cheeks. She was walking at the edge of a field, along a footpath that led to the top of a hill on the edge of the village. By the time she reached the top, she was sobbing wildly, taking great, hiccupping gulps of air.

The village and the county lay in front of her, silent and still, apart from the odd car drifting by on the main road that slithered along the far side of Crowsbrook. She couldn't see a soul. And Jack was somewhere out there.

She let out a bloodcurdling sound that was somewhere between a scream and a howl, throwing her weight against a tree trunk. It was an old oak tree and it didn't give an inch. She pounded on it with her fists, still screaming.

It was too much to bear. And yet here she was. The bark

scraped her hands and her face as she rained blows upon the solid, silent wood. The sky started to drip with rain again.

Eventually, Holly leaned her head on the trunk of the tree and placed her palms against the oak tree. Its stillness was soothing. Drops of water ran down her face.

This was where she was now. There was nothing she could do to change what had happened, any of it. And yes, she was still the same person, and the tapes still played in her head. But she could up her game.

She knew who she was. She was Jack's mother and she was going to get him back. She pushed herself away from the tree and stood upright, surveying the landscape in front of her through the steadily falling rain.

She would walk to the end of the world if that's what it took.

• • •

Jez was working in the library. She spent most of her time in the library now; it wasn't that the common room was too noisy (it wasn't, not as finals got closer), but every time she went in there, she could feel the stress vibrating in the air like a thousand over-taut cables. And it was getting worse. It didn't affect her much— she had made a point of developing immunity to all group hysterias during her time at Arden High—but she didn't want to be around it. It sapped her energy and made her less focused, and she didn't need that. So she hung out in the library, where very few people ever went, and built a protective wall out of her biology textbooks, and glared at the handful of odd eleven-year-olds who occasionally wandered away from the tiny and dog-eared Young Adult collection, and they scuttled away from her, wide-eyed, and left her alone.

She couldn't focus today, though. Her eyes were sore and

heavy and she could feel her clothes rubbing against her skin. She kept thinking about Sarah.

The last time she had pushed Sarah on something that had seemed strange, had not let it go, she had ended up getting involved in something that had upended her small world. All her assumptions about what was real and what was not—what *could* be and what could not—had been shattered. And it had been costly, too. Her dad was still in a lot of pain, still in physical therapy, still due for another couple of operations because of the car accident that had happened as a result of her involvement with Sarah. Sam's arm had been badly broken. Because Sarah had said she needed Jez's *help*.

What would happen if Sarah asked for Jez's help again?

She knew what she should do. It should be easy. Easiest decision in the world. Hanging out with Sarah had meant that people she loved had been hurt. Directly. Physically. The sensible thing to do would be to move on, and forget about everything, and do what Sam said—do what Sam was apparently *doing*—and get on with her life. She should tell herself that she didn't want anything to do with Sarah and walk away and never look back. She had seen countless didactic teen dramas, rolled her eyes through too many interminable school role plays not to know: when people were in the habit of asking you to do something risky or dangerous or that you didn't feel comfortable doing, you just said no, firmly and politely, and eventually got to work in a bank or something.

And yet.

The danger that she had faced with Sarah had been real. It couldn't have hurt people if it hadn't been. It had been real and it had been a threat, not just to Jez and her friends and her family, but to her whole community. Her friend Cat had been killed, along with her entire family, for no better reason than her father had unwittingly objected to the evil things that had invaded the village. Jez had truly hated living in Crowsbrook back then, and it wasn't much more fun now, but she had not and did not hate it enough to want to see it destroyed, to see its people living in misery, sick and unhappy and lonely and afraid.

The sensible thing would be to walk away. The *right* thing—

She didn't know what the right thing to do was. But there was a possibility, however slight, that Sarah might need help again.

It might be just a minor thing, she told herself. *It might be nothing.*

Sam could well be right, the rational part of her brain told herself. *There's a good chance that your senses fooled you. That there was something you might have missed. That they may have taken a direction you didn't know about or didn't think about. People don't just disappear.*

No, she thought. *But Sam saw them, too. And he was convinced enough that they had disappeared that he was willing to lie to me about it, just so he wouldn't have anything to do with any of that stuff again.*

She was still angry with him for that. But that aside, none of this even touched on the key thing, the thing that Jez didn't want to admit to herself, and that was that working with Sarah had been *exciting*. It had felt *real*. It had been dangerous and terrifying and it had destroyed many of her assumptions about how the world worked and what her position was in it.

But it sure as hell hadn't been *boring*.

Jez took a deep breath and sighed very slowly.

She had fallen out with Sam once before over this kind of stuff. But that had been before he knew it was real. It had been right after Gareth and Marina had been murdered by the Foxglove Pond in Crowsbrook. She had tried to take Sam's mind off it by telling him about meeting Sarah and seeing the supernatural world for the first time, and he had assumed she was making it up and had been really angry. In retrospect, she could sort of see his point, even though she hated to admit it: she had been right about all of that stuff being real and he had been wrong, after all.

They had sorted that out because she went over there with a dead fly in a jar, and it had spontaneously combusted in front of him, for no apparent reason, thus proving her right. She had basically lucked out.

She didn't know what to do this time. But a quick visit to Sarah wouldn't hurt.

Yeah, she imagined Sam saying. *You don't know that.*

• • •

Sarah couldn't concentrate. There wasn't really much that needed concentrating on at the shop, but she was restless, pacing up and down as her mind flailed about in a mire of limited information and a hundred questions.

Who were the women? Where was the kid that had disappeared? Was there any connection between his disappearance and the kid that had disappeared from St. Joseph's years before? Was there an Ethereal connection? There should be. Father Dominic's vision said there was. Her own vision said there was: even back in the eighties children didn't get abducted and eaten without there being a national outcry. And yet she had felt nothing in Crowsbrook, had noticed nothing—and this was her turf. This was *her* village. She knew everything that happened in it, Ethereal or no—

Well. *Knew* everything was a bit of a stretch. But she had a feel for it, a sense for when things were wrong. And on top of that, she had the spiders. And on top of *that*, she had the water. And only the water had spoken to her. The water from the pond.

The pond made her uneasy. She wasn't scared of it, not

exactly, but some very bad things had happened down there. Some very nasty things had come out of the pond as well. But she had survived her run-in with those, though it had cost her an eye and a lot of pain.

The lights felt too bright, and the clock was too slow. She had to leave.

Fuck it. The shop was empty, so she went into the back to find Rose.

"I need to go," she said. "I'm really sorry."

Rose frowned at her.

"Why?" she said. "You all right?"

"Not feeling good," said Sarah. "Sick. And the bus rush isn't going to help."

Rose raised her eyebrows. "Well, it's not going to help me either," she said. "But all right. Do what you've got to."

"Thanks," said Sarah distractedly. "Sorry. I won't—it's not a regular—"

"It is what it is," said Rose. "Anyway, if you're not here, I'm not paying you, so it's not just my loss." She smiled. "Hope you feel better."

"Thanks," said Sarah. She didn't feel great about lying. But she had to get out of the shop.

A few minutes later, she was winding her way through the village, past the Nag's Head, past the school, toward her cottage. The houses were further apart on this side of the village, the hedges higher and less well kept. A stray branch whipped at her face in the wind. The trees were dense enough that she was out of the worst of the wind and the rain, but water still dripped heavily on her. She shivered and pulled her coat more closely around her.

Home soon, said Eleanor's voice, in her head. Get the kettle on. Sort it out then.

She had always thought of it as Eleanor's voice. Except she

knew, of course, that it wasn't. She knew that she was just having a conversation with her memories of what Eleanor was like, which was a fancy way of saying that she was talking to herself, because Eleanor was dead.

There. She'd thought it. Eleanor was dead, and no revenge would bring her back.

It would stop Carrington, Sarah thought feebly. *He wouldn't be able to do it to anyone else.*

Yeah. But that's a different thing though, isn't it?

Sarah breathed hard and rubbed drops of water from her face.

"Hello," said a male voice behind her.

She jumped and turned around. The man was standing under an umbrella. He was wearing a flat cap and sunglasses and a long coat; the colour of the coat blended with the dark, wet trees around her. He grinned. His teeth were very white and a bit longer than usual. There seemed to be too many of them for his mouth. Also, they seemed to Sarah to be remarkably pointed.

There was no one else about in the damp gloom.

"Hello," said Sarah, frowning. She didn't recognize him. He didn't say anything else, and eventually the silence became unnerving. "Are you lost?"

"I'm looking for Sarah Trevelyan," said the man. "She lives around here."

"Why?" said Sarah. "What do you want?"

"Didn't mean to startle you," said the man. "Are you her? Sarah?"

"Yes," said Sarah, warily. "What do you want?"

"To say sorry," said the man. "It's not personal."

In one smooth move, he furled his umbrella, rolled it up neatly, and pressed a button concealed in the handle; he stabbed Sarah in the stomach with the long blade that shot out of the umbrella's tip. She gasped; he put his hand on her shoulder, pulled the blade out, wiped it with his finger and licked it, and then retracted the blade. Sarah tasted blood; she felt it spill over the corner of her mouth and run in a thin trickle over her chin. She coughed and struggled to breathe.

The man caught her as her knees buckled and pulled one of her arms around his neck. As Sarah's consciousness began to fade, she registered his strength. It was more than human.

Holding her by the waist, Savaric carried her the short distance to her cottage, opened the gate, and stowed her body underneath the hedge, in the overgrown garden.

He couldn't see the women. He would make himself scarce until they turned up.

Chapter 8

Sam wasn't on the bus after school. Jez was actually quite grateful for that. She stuck her headphones in her ears and stared out the window.

Maybe none of this happened in cities. Maybe it was just Crowsbrook. She had a conditional offer for the School of Medicine at the University of Manchester now, had received the letter at the end of January. She would be leaving Crowsbrook in eight months. Manchester was a three-hour drive away. She knew that there were all sorts of dangers in big cities (Becky had outlined them to her again and again), but she could cope with those: you could be careful and take cabs late at night and avoid the dodgy bits and mostly things would be okay, even if there *was* more crime than in Crowsbrook. Most crime in Crowsbrook was burglaries anyway, and as Sam had pointed out on numerous occasions, people tended not to burgle other people when the other people didn't have stuff that was worth nicking. Point was, there was a new and exciting world out there, and it wasn't a supernatural one.

Ethereal, whispered a voice in her mind.

Ethereal. Whatever.

The way she saw it, she had nothing to lose. She could warn Sarah, tell her exactly what she had seen, explain that there could be a rational explanation, and let Sarah figure it out. She could walk away and go home and study cell structure and let someone else sort it out.

Could she, though? Didn't she have a responsibility to see it through?

See what through? You don't know that what you saw means anything. You don't know for sure that you didn't imagine it.

Ugh, thought Jez. The bus chugged and farted its way into the centre of Crowsbrook, opposite the primary school. There were still a police car outside it, although most of the police were out and about in Crowsbrook. Jez had heard a rumour on the bus that morning that one of the little kids had disappeared. One of Mickey Amble's Agents of Chaos had been yelling about it. Jez hadn't really been listening to start with.

"Yeah," said Vicky Rice, Year Eight Bitch Queen, rolling her eyes. "People don't just *disappear*."

Jez's attention focused on the conversation with a snap.

"Disappeared right out of the fucking school," the kid said, and tossed a Tangy Tom into his mouth. "Mum came to pick him up and—" He spread his fingers like a stage magician. "Gone. Just like that. Scout's honour." He flipped the three-fingered salute.

"Yeah," said Vinay Singh. "Police came round last night in the middle of *Hollyoaks*."

"*Hollyoaks* is lame," said Vicky Rice.

"I *know*," said Vinay. "My mum was watching it. She was totally pissed at the police. Wanted to know if she'd seen any-thing. If anyone had been round."

"If anyone was a peedo."

"Fucking peedos. I told them it was you."

"Fuck off!"

"Mam said…"

Jez tuned out again. Okay, it was terrible a kid had disappeared. That never ended well, ever. But here was the thing: when Gareth and Marina had been killed, there were no police the day after. There were no door-to-door searches. There had just been a coroner's van and some tape and some vague assurances to the parents, and some rumours that the kids had committed suicide, because they were Goths, and that was the sort of thing that Crowsbrook thought that Goths did. Except that they hadn't. They'd been murdered by something ancient and malevolent and *hungry*. And it had fogged up everyone's ability to see what was going on. There had been nothing in the papers. Nothing on the telly. Marina's family had buried her in the Crowsbrook churchyard and moved away. It shouldn't have been possible, but it had happened. And it had happened because of Ethereals. She felt stupid even thinking it, but it was true: they had hidden what they had done with magic.

If there were police everywhere, it stood to reason that Ethereals were not hiding a thing they had done with magic. Not like with Gareth and Marina. It sucked hard that a kid had disappeared, but Jez had to admit that she was relieved that it was probably just some fucking psycho pervert. Other people could catch psychos. People knew that they existed. There was a horrible, awful, rational explanation for a kidnapping.

People just didn't disappear.

The bus shuddered to a halt and Jez shouldered her bag and marched off the bus into the drizzle outside. The sky was grey. She shivered.

Okay. Sarah's cottage. Darn it.

Jez hated to admit it to herself, but she was still a bit scared of Sarah's cottage. Rumours had abounded when she was a little kid that it was haunted, that monsters lived there, that Miss Trevelyan (the old Miss Trevelyan, who Jez now knew had been Sarah's great-aunt Dorothea) had been a witch. That the last one had turned out to be true had not reduced Jez's sense of unease about the cottage. Even though she had been inside it. Had drunk tea in it. Had drunk Scotch in it, actually. She wasn't sure that that had been responsible of Sarah. You were supposed to be suspicious of adults who willingly gave you alcohol.

There was no pavement in this part of the village. The road was too old and too narrow. She made her way carefully along the side of the road, peering into the thickening mist for cars.

She hadn't seen Sarah in months. Maybe this would be awkward. She hoped not. She was at the gate to the cottage garden more quickly than she'd realized. She put her hand on the gate to push it open.

Something moved in the cottage garden. Instinctively, Jez drew back behind the hedge so she couldn't be seen.

Stupid thick hedge.

Who would visit Sarah? There was Rose at the shop and all the people that she'd helped, who wouldn't hear a word said against her, but she didn't exactly have *friends*. And even the people she'd helped—well. She'd never met or heard of anyone else who had been inside that cottage other than Sam.

So who was visiting now?

She tiptoed alongside the thick hedge, bending and peering, as quietly as possible. Nothing. She understood why. Sarah had once made a throwaway remark about witches' cottages being distinct because of the high, thick hedges around them. She could hear movement on the other side.

Was it one person or more than one? She couldn't tell.

Fucking hedge.

It was no use. She couldn't see a thing. She would have to look through the gap where the gate was. She would make it look like she was just walking past to go back to the village square. She turned around and started walking at a pace she hoped looked natural. It was slower than her usual pace. She was painfully conscious that she was trying to walk more quietly.

The gate was coming up. She took a deep breath and turned her head.

Her stomach dropped. There was more than one person in the garden. There were three. And they were all dressed in black.

She stopped again and flattened herself against the hedge on the other side of the gate. Her heart was pounding. She forced herself to turn her head and look.

It was them. It was the same three women. At Sarah's cottage.

Panic shot through her. She started walking as casually as she could. When she got back to the village square, she started running and didn't stop until she reached her home, winded and wiping tears from her face that had mixed with the drizzle that was turning into rain.

$$\bullet \ \bullet \ \bullet$$

Savaric hummed as he prowled near the cottage, looking for movement.

He never really liked killing people. It was another survival thing. He did it—of course, he did. He had to. But he didn't get a kick out of it or anything. He didn't.

He didn't need a witch around either. And that one, the one resting in peace under the hedge, there was no mistaking her mind for the one that was soaked in guilt and the need for revenge and the obligation that she hadn't fulfilled. Damn near given him a headache, she had. It wasn't good to get too close to the minds of other people who were Ethereal. Witches were human, of course, but they were the closest humans to the Ethereal world, and near as damn it.

And that also meant that he didn't have to worry about anyone human finding the body. The Ethereal world took care of its own.

He heard footsteps moving in the cottage garden, the lightest of noises. They would have been undetectable to a human ear; they were unlikely to have been made by a human foot.

He opened the gate to the witch's cottage. He hoped he could catch the three before they left.

The path to the door made him faintly uncomfortable. Witches occupied a sort of middle ground, and he never trusted anyone with a foot in both camps, especially if they were charged with keeping things—*beings*—like him in line. He pulled his coat closer around him and stopped humming.

They weren't at the front of the house. Maybe they were round the back. He would have to go around the house. And they would know he was coming.

He tried to ignore the faintly sick feeling. Probably just hungry, that was all.

Sighing, he made his way around the corner of the cottage, through the sprouting herbs and early snowdrops. They were there. They looked at him, expectant and unblinking as he rounded the corner.

It would be fine. He'd done them a favour.

"Er," he said. "Found it, then? The house?"

"What do you want?" said the one in the middle.

"I found her," said Savaric, a touch eagerly. "The witch." Somehow, their stares seemed a little harder, though they didn't move.

"Well?" said the one on the left. "Where is she? She is not here?"

"No," said Savaric. "She's under the hedge."

The one on the right frowned. "The hedge? What hedge?"

"At the front," said Savaric. "Of the cottage. Over there." He nodded. "Don't worry about it. She's dead."

All three started.

"Dead?" said the one on the right.

"Saved you a job," said Savaric. "I know you're busy. You're welcome." He turned to go.

A hand heavy as a lump hammer fell on his shoulder and pulled him around. The three stood close to him, glaring.

"Dead?" said the one on the right again.

Shit. This had gone south fast.

"I was trying to help," he managed. His voice was higher than it had been for quite some centuries.

The one in the middle grabbed him by the lapels and pulled him close to her face. Savaric smelled something faintly earthy, faintly rotten.

The woman leaned in toward his face and breathed in slowly through her nose.

"You," she rasped, through gritted teeth, "are an idiot. *Bloodsucker.*"

And then Savaric was falling. Flying. He couldn't see. Everything was moving, and the wind was rushing past him. The fear shot through him like electricity. He gasped—

—and was plunged into water. The rushing of wind turned into the cold heaviness of water, its silence broken by the bubbles generated by his plunge. He opened his eyes in shock. It was dark. He didn't know which way was up.

Fuck.

They wouldn't be in here. That was a start.

Savaric didn't technically need to breathe as much as other people, but it had been a habit of his for a very long time, and not doing it was uncomfortable. He looked around him desperately. There was light above him. Not too far. He wasn't much of a swimmer, but up it was. He kicked and paddled until he broke the surface with a reflexive gasp. He shook his head, coughing, and made his way toward the shore of the—

Holy shit. He sped up, moving as quickly as he could toward the land. His feet touched the soft mud and weeds of ground and he stood out and waded out of the pond. He stood on the side of the pond coughing and shivering.

The pond. They'd thrown him in the Foxglove Pond. There were things in the Foxglove Pond that had been there since Savaric had been a boy. They had put him there to show him what they could do, if they wanted. Where they could put him. Where they could keep him.

The wind whipped through the trees. Savaric felt the cold like he hadn't felt it in years. Then he blinked.

Fuck this. Fuck ALL of this.

Savaric stopped being afraid and became very, very angry. He set off, squelching, up the hill.

He knew one person in the village with a bathroom and a clothes dryer, and he was going to pay him a visit.

There are rules, his brain reminded him.

He told his brain to fuck off, clenched his jaw, and set off for Hogarth's house.

· · ·

Hogarth was watching the telly when there was a knock at the door. He looked as his watch, then back at the telly. It was too late for the post.

He ignored it. A couple of minutes later, he heard the knock again.

Well, he wasn't supposed to let anyone in, was he? And who was going to be poldering on the door like that at this time of day? No one up to any good, that was who. He ignored it again.

The hammering on the door threatened to break it. Or at least to wake up the neighbours. Ma hadn't liked the neighbours, but she'd have been darned if she'd have given them a reason to let them get the better of her.

A voice floated up through the letterbox.

"Hogarth, you epic fucking cockwomble," it shouted. "Open this fucking door this second, or—"

Hogarth froze. He hadn't heard that voice in years.

"—and pull your fucking intestines out by the—"

Hogarth opened the door. He had been right. Savaric stood on the doorstep. He was dripping wet and covered in mud.

"All right?" he said. He stared at the dripping figure before him.

"Do I," said Savaric, his voice loaded with venom, "look all right to you?"

"You look wet," said Hogarth. Then he felt silly. Then he didn't feel silly, because the first time he'd seen Savaric, he had been completely dry in a scenario where he should really have been soaking, so the fact that he was on the doorstep dripping in the anaemic dusk just seemed like everything balancing out.

"Well done," said Savaric. His voice was soaked with sarcasm. "I don't suppose I could trouble you for a *towel*? Maybe? If it's not too much trouble?" He grinned and tilted his head from side to side. It wasn't a sincere grin and it showed a few too many teeth. He moved forward. Hogarth stayed where he was, blocking the doorway.

"Nobody," he said. "You said nobody."

This was true, and the part of Savaric's brain that often and vainly tried to tell him when things were about to go pear-shaped was trying to remind him about that as well. But he had known the Bag'un for a long time. Longer than Hogarth had. Much longer. He was wet and he was cold and he was angry, and he hadn't been this much of any of those things in several centuries, which was almost as long as he'd known the Bag'un.

He wanted a *towel*.

"Yeah, well," said Savaric. "Nobody *else*. I *told* you what the rules were. I need ten minutes and a bathroom, although I wouldn't say no to a cup of tea and a biscuit to be quite honest with you. I'm bloody cold, and I've had a hell of a day. What do you say?"

"You said nobody," said Hogarth again. "You're somebody."

"Oh, for fuck's sake," said Savaric. "Ten minutes. I will be ten minutes, and then I will be gone again. Bye bye, nice seeing you, see you in another twenty years." He peered at Hogarth's lined face. "Or not. Look, it doesn't matter. It's me. Don't let anyone else in. I can see you take this seriously. But it's *me*."

Hogarth looked at him. Ma was never one to bend a rule. But he wouldn't want to be out there, wet all day, and looking like he'd fallen in God knows what. He stepped to one side and held out his hand.

"Well," he said. "If you think it's all right."

Savaric pushed past him. "*Thank* you," he said. "Can I use your bathroom?"

"Up the stairs," said Hogarth, a little numbly. No one had been in his house except him and the Bag'un for more than three decades. It felt strange. He felt like he had no clothes on, or like someone had walked in on him in the morning when he was going for a wee.

Ma wouldn't have approved of this fella, he thought.

Savaric thundered up the stairs with his shoes on, and Hogarth heard the bathroom door slam shut. Then he heard the taps running. Then he heard the hot water heater burble into life. This was obviously going to be longer than ten minutes.

He didn't like it, having someone else in this house.

And then he heard a noise coming from the hall cupboard that sounded a lot like growling.

Apparently the Bag'un didn't like it either.

• • •

It wasn't ten minutes. Savaric was in the bathroom for at least an hour, doing God knew what. Hogarth never spent more than fifteen minutes in there at a time. There had only ever been one bathroom, and Ma banged on the door every five minutes while he was in there, to remind him. Good job he'd been to the loo before he left work.

Eventually, Savaric came out looking reasonably clean and dry. The mud was almost all gone from his coat and umbrella. Hogarth stood on the landing, looking at him awkwardly.

"D'you want a cup of tea?" he said. "Or something?"

Savaric looked at him, puzzled.

"To warm up a bit," said Hogarth. He didn't think it was odd, asking about the tea. That was what people did on the telly. "You said you wanted a cup of tea and a biscuit." He had some of the good biscuits in the cupboard.

"Oh," said Savaric. He thought about it. "All right," he said. "Milk, no sugar."

"All right," said Hogarth. He turned to go downstairs. "I'm sorry about before," he said. "It's just you said—"

"Yeah," said Savaric. "I say a lot of things. Best go back to the way things were, after I'm gone, though. Nobody else comes in the house. *Nobody.* It's really important. This doesn't change anything."

Hogarth frowned.

"If it's important," he said, "hadn't you better go, like? Less being here's probably better, if no one's allowed in."

"Nah," said Savaric again. "Damage is done. But he knows me. Got a long memory, he has. He knows me. It's fine."

I think, added the inconvenient part of his brain. *Probably.*

Hogarth gestured toward the cupboard. Savaric nodded. Hogarth pressed his lips together.

"You can't hear that?" he said, not really wanting to know the answer.

The growling wasn't as loud, but it was still there: there was no getting around it. The Bag'un wasn't happy. Hogarth felt the way he had felt the one time he was a kid and Ma had let his friend Billy stay for tea because they were having rock cakes and Hogarth knew Billy liked rock cakes because he was always pinching Hogarth's out of his lunch box and pretending he hadn't. But when Billy came for tea, Hogarth had been on edge the whole time: waiting for something bad to happen, for Billy to step out of line, for Ma to come after him with the broom or a wooden spoon or a slipper. When Billy had gone, he felt so relieved that he'd never asked anyone to come for tea again, and Ma hadn't offered. She'd never mentioned Billy again either, and Hogarth wasn't sure if that was good or bad. But right now, he was feeling very uneasy, and the feeling was getting worse. Having Savaric in his house was like having something caught under his skin that he could feel, but he couldn't get out. It was like getting dressed with the curtains open.

He'd tried that once, in the back bedroom that faced the side wall of the house next door. He'd never done it again.

"All right," he said, clearing his throat. "Tea, then."

Savaric nodded. He picked up one of Ma's ladies from a shelf in the hall and turned her over in his hands, appraising the figure.

"Haven't seen one of these in a while," he said.

Hogarth was horrified. You never touched Ma's ladies. China, they were, all wearing long, posh dresses in different colours and had their hair done up, like they were going to a party in the olden days. Ma had ordered them from the magazine that had the telly times in it. There were adverts. She would fill in the form and write off and send a postal order, and then they would send her one of the ladies in a brown cardboard box. The address had always been written by hand, and it had always been the same handwriting, Hogarth remembered. Ma would take the new lady out of the box and add her to the shelf and take a deep breath and nod briefly and then walk away. She never talked about the ladies, but sometimes Hogarth would watch her cleaning them and she seemed to be in another world.

He had touched one of the ladies once, and the clip round the ear had been swift and sharp. Then he got a beating like he'd never had before in his life.

"Can you put that back?" he managed in a voice just above a whisper. "Please?"

Savaric shrugged and put the china figure back with a *clunk*. They made their way downstairs and Hogarth put the kettle on. The growling in his head was turning into a high pitched whine of rage.

He spilled some of the water when he poured the tea. His hand was shaking.

Savaric frowned. "Something wrong?" he said. "You seem nervous."

"I can hear him," muttered Hogarth. "He doesn't sound happy."

Savaric rolled his eyes. "It's *me*," he said. "It's fine. He's whingeing a bit, that's all. Nothing's ever perfect for anyone, is it?"

Hogarth handed Savaric a cup of tea. It was in a white mug with a cat on it.

The Bag'un hurled itself through the door of the cupboard. The crash was sudden and deafening.

"Shit!" shouted Savaric.

It wasn't supposed to be out of the cupboard, out of the dark. Even in the mild light, its skin smoked as it reacted to light. It was the ugliest thing that Hogarth had ever seen. Its head and body were one misshapen lump of vaguely round flesh, split open by a jagged mouth filled with inch long, yellowing pointed teeth. Its arms were long and skinny, with outsized hands. Its one central eye was bloodshot and leaking a thick, white fluid; its skin was translucently pale and covered in coarse bristle.

It threw itself at Hogarth and Savaric; Savaric moved backwards faster than Hogarth had realized that anyone could move. Both men yelled, and Savaric dropped his mug of tea, which broke on the floor. The Bag'un tore off Hogarth's left arm just above the elbow and Hogarth screamed in shock and pain. He turned to hit the thing with his other arm, and watched it bite and swallow his wrist and forearm in two gulps.

No. Not possible.

He felt faint. Blood was flowing from the stump, a lot of blood, splashing on the floor like a thin stream of water. Hogarth swung wildly at the thing from the cupboard and connected, but when he made contact, the thing just felt like firm jelly, and his fist started to burn. The smoke alarm went off. Savaric dashed behind the creature, toward the hall, and made a grab for his muddy umbrella; in the chaos, he stumbled against the broken cupboard door, which slammed shut. The thing turned around and Hogarth slumped to the floor. Savaric, panicking, opened the door again; the darkness had gone, replaced by the empty shelves and the bits of spare wood. Savaric grabbed one of the bits of spare wood and walloped the creature as it came toward him, snarling. Hogarth winced as the Bag'un, clearly stunned, emitted a sound like a scream. Savaric bolted for the front door, hauled it open, and dashed through it. It slammed behind him, and a moment later, Hogarth heard the splintering of wood and glass breaking as the thing from the cupboard hurled itself through the door after him.

Hogarth gasped.

His house was silent.

• • •

Gone.

It wasn't after him anymore.

Gone.

He had to stop the bleeding. He grabbed a tea towel, and ripped it almost in two and started trying to wrap it around the stump of his left arm. After a couple of attempts, he got it tight, and the bleeding slowed and eventually stopped.

Breathing was an effort. But he could do it. He just needed a sit-down.

He crumpled onto the floor, trying his best not to let gravity overwhelm him. He had to stay in control.

The floor was cool and hard. He exhaled slowly. He just had to rest. Just for a minute, maybe two.

He lost track of the minutes.

Infection. That would be the next thing. He couldn't go to the hospital. They would ask. They would ask what had happened and where the other bit of his arm was, and he wouldn't be able to tell them.

He was in shock. It had attacked him. His friend had attacked him. After all this time. After thirty-five years.

It had attacked him because he broke the rules. He wouldn't have broken the rules if Savaric hadn't—

He needed to stop an infection somehow.

Bloody Savaric. It wouldn't have happened if it hadn't been for Savaric.

His arm was raw. He had to stop the infection. His mind felt hazy.

He took a deep breath, clenched his teeth and stood up. The room swam: his brain exploded in a crackle of static sparks. He stumbled against the kitchen counter, feeling for the edge with his remaining hand; he caught himself just in time.

Deep breaths. Deep breaths.

He shivered. There was a breeze coming from somewhere. He turned and took in the mess that had been made of his hallway.

The cupboard door was still open, and there was a hole in the front door. Broken glass and splinters of wood covered the carpet. The doormat was covered in spatters of rain.

The Bag'un had gone.

Fuck, thought Hogarth. *Fuck.*

Focus. The ghost of the Bag'un haunted his mind. Force of habit.

Stop the bleeding. You don't want to get infected.

He couldn't wash it, not in the state it was in. There was a different way, though. He had seen it on the telly once. He felt a little sick.

Slowly, he made his way to the back room where the washing machine was. It was where the house cleaning stuff was kept. Not that Hogarth used them much. The Bag'un took care of most of that. But there was also a high shelf above the washing machine where Hogarth kept the washing powder, and the mousetraps and the mothballs. Sitting on the end of it—unused for years—was an old electric iron.

He reached for it and swayed. He felt as though he were looking at the world from the far end of a long tunnel. He knocked a mousetrap off the shelf and it clattered down onto the washing machine. It sounded a long way off.

Would it be better to fill it with water or not? He didn't know, but he didn't think the steam would help. Best keep it dry.

Fighting to stay conscious, Hogarth plugged in the iron, turned the heat to the highest setting, and waited. As the minutes ticked by, the smell of hot dust began to permeate the small room. When it was mixed with the smell of melting plastic and a couple of sparks fizzed from the appliance's base, Hogarth didn't think it was going to get much hotter.

Right then. This was it. He grasped the handle of the iron and swore. Even the handle was hot.

Well. Best make it quick.

Hogarth's screams drifted through the hole in the front door, along with the smell of seared meat.

• • •

It was cold.

It was cold and it was damp and it was completely dark. Jack strained his eyes, but he couldn't see anything. It was that dark. Like having your eyes scrunched tight shut when the lights were off.

He didn't know where he was. He was breathing hard.

His foot *really* hurt.

The monster had gone. He had thought it was going to eat him, and he had felt it sink its teeth into his foot, through his shoe, and then he didn't remember what had happened. And then he was here. And his foot really hurt.

He reached out his hand and patted the ground next to him. He was lying on the ground. It felt like dirt. He could hear something that sounded like water, but it wasn't falling on him.

He felt like the world was spinning, like when you turned around too many times in the playground and then stopped and the world tilted one way, and then the other. He moved his hand in front of his face, but he still couldn't see it.

His foot *really* hurt. He moved his hand down to touch it, and pain shot through him as his hand registered a mess of ragged plastic, and pointed bits and wet. He pulled his hand back and whimpered.

He was frightened. He didn't know where he was or how he'd got there or how to get back. People told you not to talk to or go with strangers all the time in case they took you away, but he hadn't, he hadn't spoken to anyone. He just wanted to hide from Jocasta in the cupboard. He hadn't stolen the Star Mutants. He just wanted to look at them.

He realized with a start that one of them was still in his hand. He brought it in front of him so he could feel it with both hands. It was still fastened to the cardboard of the packaging with plastic ties, but it was Starhammer. He could tell from the mallet in his hand and the bumps on top of his head.

His face crumpled. He was hungry. He rolled onto his back and tried to sit up and managed it. He still felt dizzy. Even apart from his foot, he was bruised and sore and damp.

He drew his knees up to his chin and made himself as small as he could in the dark.

He wanted his mummy. He whimpered. Then he took a deep breath and yelled as loud as he could, with his eyes tight shut.

"*HEEEEEEEEEEEEEEEEEEEEEEEEEEEEEEEELP!*"

His voice echoed in the darkness. He tried again.

"*HEEEEEEEEEEEEEEEEEEEEEEEEEEEEEELP!*"

Nothing.

He didn't care. He was going to keep trying until he couldn't speak.

"*HEEEEEEEEEEEEEEEEEEEEEEEEEEEEEEELP!*"

Was that someone's voice? Footsteps? They echoed, too. He

frowned. You usually only got echoes indoors. And there was a breeze. You usually only got breezes outdoors. How was this place outdoors and indoors?

This was all wrong.

There was a light, too. A kind of a light. And the footsteps were getting closer. Someone was coming. No, there were more footsteps. Two people were coming.

He screwed his eyes tight shut, in case they were monsters.

And then they were there, bending over him. He could feel how close they were.

"What the heck?" said a voice. It was a male voice. A young male voice. A Big Kid.

"It's a kid," said another voice. This one was young and female. "How did a kid end up here?"

"Like we did, I suppose," said the first voice, with a note of resignation.

"No," said the female voice. "No. He's not…he looks different. Look."

It was lighter. Jack could tell, even though his eyes were shut. He put his hands in front of his face, opened his eyes enough to see, and peered through the cracks in his fingers.

They were older than him, for sure, but they were still kids. Big kids. *Teenagers.* And they were glowing with a soft, greyish light. The boy held one hand behind his back. He was holding one of the girl's hand's with the other. The girl knelt down next to Jack.

"Hey," she said, softly. "What's your name?"

"Jack," whispered Jack.

"All right, Jack," she said. "How did you get here? There's bad things here. You have to be careful."

Jack just shook his head. He looked at the girl through his fingers. She was pretty. Her clothes were black.

"What do we do?" said the boy.

The girl sighed.

"I don't know," she said. "But we can't leave him alone. He's not—" She stopped herself. "He's not like us."

"We should stay with him," said the boy. "Maybe someone will come."

"You hear that, Jack?" said the girl. "We'll stay with you until someone comes."

Jack opened his fingers a bit more. He could see the outline of trees and bushes in the dark. The girl sat down on the ground next to him.

"It doesn't matter if anyone comes," said the boy. "They can't hear us. They can barely see us. How can we help?"

"I don't know," said the girl. "We'll work something out. We have nothing else to do."

The boy snorted, but it didn't sound quite like he was laughing. The girl looked straight at Jack.

"My name's Marina," she said, and pointed to the boy. "That's Gareth."

Jack nodded. He'd seen them before.

They were the shadows.

• • •

Hogarth could barely move. He had been sitting in his laundry room at the back of the house for he didn't know how long. The laundry room was a mess. He had dripped blood all over it. There were bits of his flesh sticking to the face of the iron like chunks of scrag end stuck to the bottom of the frying pan when you were browning it. But his stump had stopped bleeding. He had grabbed a choc ice from the freezer and had eaten it to keep his strength up. Then he had thrown it up. Then he had waited and eaten another one, and that one had stayed down. And he had slept. He felt like he had slept for hours and hours.

He had been numb for the first part. One day? More days? He wasn't sure. A long time. He was surprised he wasn't dead. But he wasn't. He had just been sitting up against the washing machine, breathing carefully.

Then he got angry.

It was a slow process. He came out of being numb, and it felt like waking up slowly the morning after a heavy night at the Pink Pony. He looked around him. The room was the same, but somehow clearer, more in focus. He felt a knot in his stomach and he didn't know what it was. Then he remembered.

The Bag'un had gone. His friend. His friend had attacked him and then had left. He couldn't associate the friend in his mind with the thing in the cupboard. He had done so much for his friend over the years. Thirty-five years they'd gone through together, and then he turned out to be an ugly monster, and just up and left him, and took his arm with it. His stomach hurt.

Ma had warned him that that was what people were like.

And the Bag'un wouldn't have left either, if he hadn't broken the rules just that once. And for what? For Savaric. He'd only let him into the house because he said it would be okay, and everything else Savaric had said would be okay had turned out okay, and better than okay, really. He'd *believed* him. He'd believed Savaric when he said everything would be okay, and it hadn't been okay and now everything was bollocksed up. Because of Savaric.

You couldn't trust anyone. Ma had told him time and time again, and in the end, he hadn't listened and look where that had gotten him. He should have listened to Ma.

He'd never been in this bad shape before, and he still couldn't believe what had happened. Savaric had told him not to let anyone in, and he had done that. Then Savaric had told him it would be all right if he let one person in, and it hadn't. Why had he believed him the first time and broken the rules the second? Weakness. Weakness, that's what Ma would have said. You knew what you were supposed to do, she'd have said, and you didn't do it and now you've paid the price and you won't get your money back. Got a free lesson in life for the bargain though, so you'd better make the most of it, hadn't you? You'll know next time, that's for sure.

His stomach hurt. His throat hurt. His eyes were watery. He felt like he couldn't breathe. He banged his head on the washing machine a couple of times and that helped. He didn't want to look at his arm. He felt uncomfortably warm.

There wasn't going to be a next time.

He screwed up his face and pounded his fist into the metal of the washing machine, letting out a roar of rage as he did so. Pain exploded in his hand and he didn't care. There would not be a next time. He could fix this. He *would* fix this. He had worked hard so that none of this was disturbed and the Bag'un was happy. He had put his conscience aside so that he could live in peace and comfort. He would not have it interrupted: enough had been sacrificed. He'd lost his arm but that didn't matter: people got over that. But he wanted his friend back, and he wanted his quiet life, just the two of them, in the house that no one ever came into. It was worth a quick trip to the toy shop every once in a while.

Savaric, though. Savaric had given him all that and had taken it away, for no reason. Because he thought it would be fine. He had either worked out the risk to himself, and decided it was worth it, to get what he wanted, or he hadn't known that the risk existed, other than as a sort of abstract thing that happened to other people, but not to him, never to *him*, never to Savaric, who would always be one step ahead, except when he wasn't. Bloody Savaric. He had ruined Hogarth's life, and two of his doors, and his kitchen. And then he had run away. Ma had said, hadn't she? She'd said what people were like.

Hogarth decided two things then and there. He would get the Bag'un back somehow. He didn't know how. He would go out and look for him. He would look in all the dark places he could find until he found his old friend, and then he would do whatever it took to get his friend back.

Whatever it took.

The other thing that he decided was that he was going to hurt Savaric very, very badly.

Ma wouldn't have approved, of course. But then, Ma wasn't one for going to the toy shop either. So to speak.

He took a deep breath, pulled his feet back under him, and tried to roll forward and stand up. He wobbled a bit, but he could do it. He held on to the washing machine until he felt less dizzy. He noticed there was a dent in it, from where he had hit it with his hand. When the Bag'un came back, the dent would be fixed.

It would be fine. It really would. He could make everything better.

He picked up a cushion from the living room and lurched over to the cupboard. He opened the door and winced to see the empty shelves and the pieces of wood. It smelled faintly like rotten eggs.

Hogarth knelt down and placed the cushion on the floor. It was pretty, with a pattern of flowers on it. It had been one of Ma's favourites. He smoothed it out a few times and then carefully stood up and closed the cupboard door.

Chapter 9

There was a horrible pain just under Sarah's rib cage. It was the first thing she became aware of. She winced, crumpled her face, and then opened her eyes.

Oh.

She was lying on an old-fashioned couch—like a Victorian fainting couch, or what was it they called them? *Chaise longue.* It was covered in old, shiny leather that was dark red. Horsehair— she assumed it was horsehair—poked through a small hole in the leather.

And she was surrounded by mirrors. They were floating in the air around her, as if hung on invisible walls. The room was cylindrical and extended upward as far as she could see, mirrors floating all the way up. She knew that if she looked down, she would not be able to see the bottom either.

She had been here before. It was on the Astral Plane. Which was either a different level of existence or all in her head. Either way, if the last time was anything to go by, she was unconscious.

Also possibly dead. She couldn't rule that out. She had read everything her aunt had written and collected about the Astral Plane since October, when she had found herself there the first time. Her aunt's collection had been a bit hazy on the details.

She tried to sit up and gasped in pain. She used her hands to work herself into an upright position on the couch and looked down. Her shirt and cardigan and jeans were covered in blood. There was a large ugly wound under her rib cage. She tried not to look at it. It looked bad.

She sighed and then waited for a moment. She was still breathing. That was good. Although she had also read that after you died, sometimes the habit stayed with you.

Now what?

The only other time she had visited the Astral Plain, she had been visited by—

"Me," said a voice behind her. Sarah tried to turn and couldn't.

"Merry pickle you're in again, aren't you?" said the voice. "True witch, you." As it was speaking, the voice—it was a female voice, and sounded old—moved from behind Sarah to the side of her. She looked into the mirror at the side of her head and saw an elderly woman standing there grinning at her.

"Nan," said Sarah. The Crowsbrook Witch. One of the early ones.

"Ar," said Nan, still grinning. "Both of us already knew that. What *have* you gotten yerself into, girly?"

"I don't know," said Sarah. "Someone stabbed me. I don't know why."

"Deary me," said Nan. Sarah tried to sit up again, but couldn't manage it.

"What'd he look like?" said Nan. "This one that stabbed you."

"Funny," said Sarah. "Not from Crowsbrook. He had a long black coat and a hat." She had mostly been looking at the hat and the coat. She didn't remember much about the man's face. "Pale," she said, eventually. "Quite tall. Thin. Brown hair, kind of stringy. Strong features. I don't know what his eyes were like; he was wearing sunglasses. They covered his eyes up. Lots of teeth. Pointy ones."

"Pointy teeth's interesting," said Nan. "Fit a few people, that would."

"I was bleeding," said Sarah. "He dipped his finger in my blood and licked it."

Nan raised an eyebrow.

"Well, then," she said. "Where might you start, if you wanted to find this one?"

"Why would I want to find him?" snapped Sarah. "He stabbed me and left me under a hedge in my own garden. To die. He might have succeeded. I don't even know if I'm dead or not."

"You're still *around*," said Nan. "I'd make the most of it." She scratched her face, deep in thought. "He got *you* near the cottage. He stabbed *you*. I mean, he could have just been hunting; there are those that do that. But don't you go thinking that means he wasn't looking for you." She looked Sarah in the eye. "Who have you angered this time, girl?"

"No one," said Sarah. "I didn't do anything."

Nan snorted. "You're a witch," she said. "That's enough for some. So don't assume that everyone else needs more reason. You've stopped a bunch of the Other Ones—" Sarah heard the capital letters in Nan's voice "—from going their merry way once and from what I've heard, you put up quite the fight before. That kind of thing is going to get you noticed in certain circles. Someone could be on to you."

Sarah rolled back against the couch. Her body ached.

"Well," she said. "Looks like they won."

"The Devil's turds they have," said Nan. "You bloody get back there and do your job."

Sarah's head snapped back toward the mirror. "What am I

supposed to do?" she said hotly. "If I'm here, I'm unconscious. I might already be dead. I don't know who this man is, or why he attacked me. What am I supposed to do?"

"You want easy answers," said Nan, "you're in the wrong job. Think it through properly."

Sarah closed her eyes. Her mind felt as though it were full of fluff. She tried to think.

"He tried to kill me," she said out loud. "He tasted my blood."

"Good," said Nan.

"There are more Ethereals that feed on humans than there are human weirdos that drink blood."

"So?" said Nan.

"He's probably Ethereal," said Sarah.

"Very good," said Nan. "Anything funny happen in the village lately?"

Sarah frowned. "A kid disappeared from the village school. But the police were there. Everywhere, actually. I mean, last time, they weren't; it was different…" She trailed off.

"Carry on," said Nan, looking at her. Sarah shifted on the couch and winced with pain.

"Before that happened," she said, "the priest from last autumn told me he'd had a vision of a child. In his house."

Nan snorted. "Priests," she said. "Through the ages and across the world. More than one's had that kind of vision."

"No," said Sarah. "It wasn't like that. He's a good man. He had a vision of a child, badly injured. Like he'd been attacked by an animal." She swallowed. "Or something. And it had happened before, twenty-five years ago, when that child went missing from the orphanage where Father—where the priest worked. He asked me to look into the water to see what I could find out, and all I found was bones. It looks like the child he saw was eaten. And then came back to—" she shrugged "—ask for help? Warn him? I don't know." She closed her eyes. "And that's when the other kid went missing from the school."

Nan raised her eyebrows. "Turn-up for the books," she said. "Priest asking a witch for help. And not about the size of his todger."

Sarah ignored her. "He was worried," she said. "He asked me to use the Sight."

"A *priest*?" said Nan. "How did he know about the Sight?"

"A lot of people used to know about the Sight," said Sarah. "He knew my great-aunt. Dorothea."

Nan grunted.

Sarah felt as though gears were turning in her head, slowly and painfully. "Maybe he wanted to stop me looking for the kid," she said. "The man who stabbed me. Or thinking about what might have eaten the kid."

Nan's eyes twinkled. Sarah sensed she was on to something.

"Either he ate the kid, or he knows who did," Sarah said. "And either way, it's important that nothing changes. So he needed me permanently out of the way." She looked at Nan.

"What's that mean then?" said Nan. It didn't really sound like a question. "If he didn't eat the littl'un."

"He's protecting something," said Sarah. "He's protecting something in Crowsbrook. Something that can't leave. Something that harms humans."

"And you didn't see it before because…?"

"Maybe it wasn't doing anything before. It wasn't doing anything that I'd notice." Low-level magic was pretty common, and Sarah lived with it all the time. But she was sensitive to spikes in the way the village felt. "It was here. It was here before. It's low level, and it was part of the landscape. It just *lived* here. Oh *shit*." She thought about the police outside the school. There were enough things that ate children in the Ethereal world; folk tales were full of them, and it wouldn't matter how hard the police looked because they wouldn't be looking for *that*. "It took a child. We don't know that he's been eaten yet. If Daniel—if the first child—could appear to the friar when he was injured but not dead, then maybe…" She trailed off. "Maybe there's a chance. Some things store food."

"For some things, fear adds flavour," said Nan. "And remember, it doesn't eat live food much, so it'll likely make it last. Let's hope. What can *you* do?"

"Make a list of Ethereal things that eat children," said Sarah. "Figure out where it's likely to live and whether the child can be saved. Figure out what qualities it has and why the man with the umbrella would want to protect it. Act in accord."

"You don't know who he is yet?" said Nan. "Come on, girl. You're nearly there."

"I saw him for two minutes," said Sarah. "Then I passed out."

"No excuse," said Nan. "You saw him. I didn't, and I know who he is. There's only about seven of them."

Sarah fought the fog in her skull. Seven of them? Seven of whom? How could Nan know him?

The penny dropped. Her eyes widened.

"No!" she said. Her voice was a little hoarse. Nan shrugged.

"Makes sense, doesn't it?" she said.

"He was out in the *day*," said Sarah. She knew it sounded weak.

"Humans can fly now, I hear," said Nan. "Do it nearly every day, some of 'em. They call it *technololomancy*. Or something."

The hat. The sunglasses. The umbrella and the long coat. The clouds. Maybe it was possible. Add some sunblock, and who knew?

"Savaric Osbourne?" said Sarah. "Why?"

Nan shrugged. "No idea. Haven't spoken to him since he was knee-high to a grasshopper."

"But he's a city—" began Sarah. "He lives in the city. I heard they both did. Him and his sister."

"I told you," said Nan. "I didn't *know* him. Just a whipper-snapper, he was, in my day. There were more of them then. He's *from* Crowsbrook, you know," she added, unnecessarily.

"I didn't know. But I read about them," said Sarah. "And now—"

"At least two," said Nan. "Him and his sister. Probably a few more."

"Why would he—?"

"I don't know," said Nan. "Maybe you should ask him."

"He tried to kill me!"

"Not randomly, though," said Nan. "He had a reason. Now you've got two things to look for. Something that eats children, and someone who stabs witches."

She began to fade from the mirror.

"If," she called over her shoulder, "there's nothing else going on that turns out to be important."

She faded into the background of the mirror, and the entire room became hazy and began to spin.

• • •

The first thing Sarah was aware of was the pain. It wasn't just in her stomach. It was everywhere. She tensed and gasped. That made it worse. Her face contorted with agony.

"Relax," said a female voice. "Writhing will not help." She had a slight accent that Sarah couldn't place.

Sarah coughed. She opened her eyes. Her bedroom. She was back in her bedroom. She was in her bed, under the covers. She was alive, for now at least. Somehow, she had gotten home. Or had been taken home.

She moved her head. She could do that without too much pain. Three women were standing around her bed. The three women she had seen in her vision. Tall. Old. Dressed in black.

They didn't look happy. At all.

Sarah took an excruciating breath and tried to speak. She could only manage a whisper.

"Who—" she started, and broke into a coughing fit. She was barely able to catch her breath. "Who are you? What's happening?"

The woman nearest the head of the bed raised an eyebrow.

"Really?" she said. "You were not expecting us?"

"No," gasped Sarah. "I don't know who you are. Who are you? What are you doing in my house?"

"Saving your life," said the woman standing at the foot of her bed. "Someone stabbed you."

"Yeah," breathed Sarah. "Who was it? Did you see him?"

"Yes," said the third woman. "But it does not matter who he was."

"Important." Sarah managed the word with effort. "It's important. A child—"

"Not important," said the third woman again. Her face was deadly serious.

"A child is missing," Sarah whispered.

"Not our concern," said the first woman.

"Who *are* you?" The pain struck Sarah again and she cried out.

"Call me Meg," said the woman by the bed head. "You need to heal."

"Alice," said the woman on Sarah's left.

"Tess," said the woman at the end of the bed.

Sarah realized with a start that she was in less pain. She tried to sit up.

"No," she said. She rubbed her face with her hand; she was covered in sweat. "How did you find me? You're not from the village." *Are you Ethereal?* was the question she really wanted to ask, but she couldn't—

"Yes," said Meg. "Ethereal. Yes."

Adrenaline shot through Sarah.

You're in my head as well? she thought.

Tess smiled.

"More or less," said Alice.

"How?" Sarah knew she was shrieking, but she felt as though she was going crazy and she couldn't control her voice. "How? How is that possible? How could this happen?"

"You did it," said Meg. "You swore the oath."

Sarah felt sick with dread. The blood oath.

"You swore the oath," said "Alice, "and then did nothing."

"Disorder," said Tess. "Unacceptable."

"Disorder?" whispered Sarah. "What?"

"You swore an oath of vengeance," said Meg. "With blood. With *sacrifice*. And then did nothing."

"An affront," said Alice, "to your honour. To the sacrifice."

"To swear vengeance for a wrong," said Tess, "and not to act on the oath is to compound the original wrong."

Oh shit.

Sarah suddenly knew who they were and what they wanted. And it was bad.

"Wait," she said. "Wait. I haven't—I mean, it hasn't been—I couldn't find—it's only been—what?"

"Your sacrifice cries out to us," said Meg. "Order must be restored."

"What?" said Sarah. "I didn't—this wasn't—this—I read about the vengeance oaths. I don't—you aren't—I didn't know—"

"No," said Alice. "You are a witch. You knew the power of this magic."

"I didn't know about *you*," said Sarah.

"Humans know about us," said Meg. "Is the form confusing you?" She placed her hand over Sarah's remaining eye.

Blinding light flashed into Sarah's vision. She heard screams. The three women around her bed were transformed: she saw snakes writhing around their heads, which had changed shape and become wolf-like; they had veined, bat-like wings, and their eyes were blood red. Meg took her hand away, and the screaming ceased; the women could pass for human again.

Erinyes, thought Sarah. She was numb with fear.

Meg nodded and the corners of her mouth turned up in a predatory smile.

The Erinyes—the Furies—were old stuff. Old magic. Not quite demons, not quite goddesses, but *powerful*. They hunted down the breakers of oaths, those who neglected their duties, and destroyed them slowly and painfully. Their victims, it was said, died in torment.

"No," said Sarah. "No. This isn't—I—that man stabbed me. I was going to die."

"Yes," said Alice. "You would have died."

"You saved me," said Sarah.

"Yes," said Tess.

Sarah swallowed hard.

"Understand," said Meg, "that honour would not be served by having you die at the hands of one unrelated to your oath. You are expected to keep it."

"You saved me," said Sarah, "so you could kill me?"

"You broke your oath," said Meg. "You dishonoured your own sacrifice. You compounded the wrong you swore to avenge."

"I've been busy," said Sarah. She immediately felt that she'd never said anything so stupid.

"You are healing fast," said Tess. Sarah hadn't noticed before, but she was. The pain was still strong, but not unbearable. She didn't feel as though she was going to die anymore, which was unfortunate, because she was pretty sure she actually was.

"No," said Sarah. "Wait. I can explain."

"Why would you try?" said Meg. "Have we said anything that was wrong? No. Do you know what we are discussing? Yes."

Sarah thought fast.

"I need time," she said. "To prevent another wrong. Another disorder. Your job is to maintain balance and make sure obligations are kept. Mine is to maintain the balance between the human and the Ethereal world. A child has been taken by the Ethereal world. The balance is imperilled. I need to sort this out."

The three women looked at her.

"It's an obligation," said Sarah. "A duty." She watched the women's faces. They didn't move.

"Your heart," said Meg eventually, "is speaking its truth. Whether this is true or not is irrelevant. This is an obligation you take seriously."

"I do," said Sarah, earnestly. "I do. It's my job."

"You take your job more seriously than your obligations to those closest to you," said Alice. It was almost a question.

"No," said Sarah, defensively. How could she explain to the Erinyes when she had trouble explaining it to herself? "It's different. Difficult. The circumstances—"

"We are aware of the circumstances," said Tess. The women looked at each other in one fluid motion and nodded.

"You can fulfil your obligation," said Meg. "You have three days. Order must be restored."

"Three days?" said Sarah. "But I don't even know—"

"It is an age," said Alice. "We will see you then."

And they were gone. The room was silent.

Three days. Holy shit.

You could get a lot done in three days. If you knew what you were doing and had a clear plan. And hadn't just been stabbed in the stomach by a—

Savaric Osbourne. Swindler. Chancer. Monster. Blood-drinker. Amoral trickster. Suspicious of everyone. Friends with no one. And afraid of nothing, they said, except his own sister.

And he was on her turf. Somewhere. And he didn't want her around.

It was going to be a rough three days. She didn't want to think about what was going to happen at the end of it.

• • •

Holly's feet hurt. At least one blister had burst and her shoe was rubbing her raw heel with every step she took. The muscles in the arches of her feet and in her calves were also complaining. She'd been on her feet almost non-stop for more than three days, with brief breaks to go home, change her mud-spattered clothes, make food she could barely eat, and try and manage a couple of hours of fitful sleep before the stress shook her awake again and she hauled herself out of bed, heavy-eyed and stumbling, to keep looking for her son. It was as if there was a bright light, bright as a floodlight, at the back of her mind, always present, always there to remind her, waking her up when she shifted uncomfortably or the house creaked.

"Every parent's nightmare." That was what they said, wasn't it? It was funny how, when it happened, sleep came in minutes, not hours, and dreaming was impossible. It was almost as if your brain could only deal with one nightmare at a time and didn't want to risk doubling up. So you nodded off, like you were back in a boring class in high school, jerking awake as soon as you realized you were asleep, hoping that you hadn't been caught, that no one had *seen*.

The big thing, though: everyone had seen *that*. Everyone knew. She'd avoided the school at turning-out time (what was the point?), but she knew what it would be like: no one meeting her eye, the dads absorbed on their phones, the mums positioning themselves so they couldn't quite see her, the occasional *shush* when one of the children asked a question a bit too loudly. And she knew why, because it killed her to admit it, but she had to: she'd have done the same if this had happened to someone else.

She would have. And she knew why as well. The realization had been as sharp as the pain where the skin had split and burst on her foot. She would have done it for protection. Not against bad luck, or the evil eye, or the fear that what had happened was contagious, but because having a kid was *terrifying* and the world was mad and getting madder, and you had to keep your kid safe in it, and *it kept bloody changing*, changing faster than you could keep up. So you tried to make it seem like everything was okay—pretend away the spaghetti-covered T-shirts and mouldy swimming kits and unbrushed teeth—because if you were perfect, that was a sign that you were doing everything right, and if it wasn't okay, if anything was wrong with your kid, if your kid wouldn't sit still, or couldn't get the hang of reading, or farted during storytime, then it was on you. You'd got the formula wrong and fucked it up. And not only had you probably ruined your kid's life and future, you'd brought the possibility of failure into a place where that was the worst thing in the world. Because the possibility of failure meant that your kid was unsafe.

So if you failed and they cut you out, they couldn't possibly fail, could they?

Holly laughed wryly and mirthlessly to herself. You could hope.

She had thought that there wasn't anything in the world worse than losing your kid. But she had been wrong. She had lost her kid and survived.

The worst thing in the world was not knowing if *he* had or not.

A second blister burst in her shoe. Her sock began to feel like sandpaper against it. She kept on walking.

Chapter 10

Jez peered through the gap in the hedge and into the overgrown cottage garden. This time, there was no sign of the women. She fumbled with the latch on the gate and marched up the garden path, not looking left or right. There was nowhere to hide anyway. She raised her fist to knock on the front door and hesitated.

Was Sam right? Was she ripping off a scab that would be best left alone? She thought of the flying monstrosity that had attacked her in the autumn and shuddered, blinking and rubbing her eyes as the memory swam before her: the thick wings, the rough, bristled carapace, the deadly proboscis. But the women had been here. Sarah knew about them. And Jez had to make sure everything was okay.

Plus, Sam had lied to her, so fuck him.

She knocked on the door. After a moment, Sarah answered.

Jez opened her mouth to say hello, but before she could manage it, her face twisted into an expression of horror. Sarah's clothes were covered in blood.

"What…" she managed in a croak.

Sarah looked down. "Inside," she said, gesturing with her head. "Better make it quick." She stood aside as Jez bundled herself through the door, and then closed it and fastened it with the multiple locks that festooned its back.

"What," said Jez, doing her best to shout in a whisper, "the living *fuck* happened to you?"

Sarah looked down at her stained and torn clothes.

"Oh," she said flatly. "The usual."

Jez threw up her hands in frustration. "The usual," she said. "Right. Of course. Was it the three women? Did they have anything to do with it?"

Sarah frowned. "How did you know about the three women?"

"I saw them," said Jez. "They were here. They're Ethereal, right? Not everyone can see them? I saw them. Alex Appleton couldn't."

"No," said Sarah. "It wasn't them. But yeah. They're Ethereal."

"Are they good?" said Jez. "Are they bad? Are they dangerous? What do they want?"

Sarah lowered herself into an armchair. "Jez," she said. "I've got quite a lot on my plate at the moment."

"What's going on?" said Jez. "Is it dangerous? Is the village in danger again?" Sarah looked different from when she'd last seen her. That had been back in December: in the hope she could get some sleep, Jez had dropped by to see how she was getting on and had stayed just long enough to ascertain nothing bad was happening. Two months ago. Not long, but Sarah looked somehow older. And very tired.

"What happened to you?" asked Jez.

"I got stabbed," said Sarah. "But I'm okay now."

"Stabbed?" said Jez in horror. "Who gets stabbed in Crowsbrook? What's happening?"

"A couple of things," said Sarah. Her tone was bleak. "A man I don't know stabbed me. Right near here. And dumped me under the hedge in the garden."

Jez frowned.

"But he wasn't…" she started. "He was a human, right? Just because you didn't know him doesn't mean he wasn't from the village. Or that he wasn't human."

"He tasted my blood," said Sarah. "I think he was Ethereal. And I think I know who he is."

Jez felt sick.

"Who is he, then?" she managed. She wasn't sure if she wanted to hear the answer.

"A two hundred percent chancer," said Sarah. "His name's Savaric. He's a vampire."

Jez sighed and made an effort not to roll her eyes. "Of course he is. How do you know it's him if you don't know him?"

"Like I said," said Sarah, "I don't. But…" She shrugged and then winced. "It's complicated. There's a lot happening."

"I'm okay with complicated," said Jez. "I can do complicated. And I still live here, and I'm not okay with people getting stabbed near where I live. What's the lot of things that are happening? Is it like with the flies?"

Sarah shifted in her chair. She was never comfortable talking about her business. But she had talked to Jez before, and while the kid could be annoying, she had helped with the business in October. Had saved her, actually, Jez and her mate Sam had. Sarah had to assume at this point that Jez could keep a secret.

Plus it would be helpful to talk this through while she was conscious with someone who wasn't in her head and who didn't disappear at random.

"Okay," she said. "So. The friar rang me."

"The friar?" said Jez. "Father Dominic? How's he doing?"

Sarah shrugged. "No one's stabbed *him*."

"Well," said Jez," that's good. What did he want?"

"Help," said Sarah. Jez looked up sharply and frowned. "I

know," she went on. "I was surprised as well. But he'd had a vision. And he said my aunt had helped him in the past."

"A vision," said Jez. She was skeptical.

"He said he'd had a vision of a child that had been hurt," said Sarah. "Like a ghost. It appeared in his house. It was a boy who had disappeared years ago, from a group home where the friar used to work. He was never found, but the friar had the same vision back then: the boy injured and calling for help. He was worried that something bad was going to happen. And he wondered if there was anything I could do to find out what happened to Daniel." The rain splattered heavily against the windows, and she shivered, although it was warm in the cottage. "That's the boy who disappeared," she said. "Daniel. I looked in the water and I saw bones. Bones that looked like whatever's left over after something with really big teeth has finished eating."

"And there haven't been large predators like that around here for about a thousand years," said Jez. "That anyone knows about, anyway."

"Exactly," said Sarah. "Sort of. Think of the number of folk tales that feature things that eat children. That's basically what we're left with."

"And then another kid did disappear," said Jez. "Jack Czajkowski."

Sarah nodded. "And I got stabbed on the way home from work."

"Right," said Jez. "By the—ugh." This time, she couldn't stop herself rolling her eyes. "By the *vampire*." She snorted. "What's he got to do with anything?"

"This is where it gets complicated," said Sarah. "There's only a limited number of things that eat children that could exist in Crowsbrook." She pushed a spiral-bound notebook across the table to Jez. There was a scrawled list on the top sheet with every item except one crossed out. "I'm ninety percent sure this is it."

Jez read the word that wasn't crossed out. "Poggelin? What's a poggelin?"

Sarah held up one finger and pushed another book across the table. The book was old, but unlike a lot of Sarah's books, which were the collected notes of various members of her family and had been passed down through the centuries, this one was typeset. Jez flipped a couple of pages: it seemed to be some sort of encyclopedia of monsters. She frowned and flipped back to the open page:

The poggelin ys a most uggly creature, lyke a fowle kynd of toad, and the size of a Ram, she read. *He lyveth in dark closets and chests, for all are as one to hym, fiend of hell that he ys, and hys greatest joy ys to watch mankind thrugh the cracks when they are open which sustaineth him. He hath but one enormous eye, and that yn the centre of hys head, and in hys head there resideth a Stone of great beauty. Any man who hath the stone possesseth a great gyft, for he can see what the creature can see when he looketh into it, and he can watch hys fellow men as the Poggelin watcheth, but without hys Stone, the poggelin needeth mankind wondrous sorely. If he is deprived of hys stone, he becometh tame in some degree and he will lyve in one place only and wyll befriend one person who dwelleth in that place, and he wyll destroy all others who enter into yt. But thys be not the worst of him, for the poggelin hath a desperate need to feed, and he wyll use hys fowle magic to get it, and wyll snatch children to feed his vile hunger...*

Jez looked up.

"What in the shit does that mean?" she said. "All are as one to him and he has a stone in his head?"

"They live in the dark," said Sarah. "In cupboards and

drawers and wardrobes, all that kind of thing. But they're intradimensional."

Jez looked at her, one eyebrow raised. She knew better than to tell Sarah that that was impossible or couldn't exist, and yet once again, what the witch was saying made no sense.

Other dimensions, though…well. The maths suggested there might be something to that. And the maths didn't lie.

"Intradimensional," said Jez. "Go on."

"They exist in the spaces between our world and…" Sarah trailed off. "Other ones. I don't know what other ones. The net result from everything else I've read about them—" she gestured to three teetering piles of books on the table "—is that they can move between cupboards without having to deal with the inconvenient space in between. If they're in one cupboard, they can potentially be in all of them."

"Oh for—" Jez stopped herself. "That's not p—" She stopped at the plosive, paused, and let the breath out slowly. "How?"

"Don't know," said Sarah. "And right now, it's not the point. It eats kids. It comes with a stone in its head—" she held up her hand as she saw Jez shaking her head and taking a deep breath "—and if you get the stone out of its head, you can see what it sees. And it watches people from their cupboards."

Jez frowned. "They watch?" she said. "So, like, every time you leave the wardrobe door open…"

"There's probably something watching you," said Sarah. "Two somethings, if the poggelin's missing its stone."

Jez shuddered. She could deal with tech tracking you; she understood that, and she knew how to turn it off. This was something else.

"So the bloke who stabbed you," she said. "He's just a dodgy vampire who likes to watch people?"

"I don't think so," said Sarah. "If he is who I think he is, he'll have a much bigger plan for the stone." She spread out her fingers. "You can watch *anyone*. Now ask me how a known con artist could make the most of that in the twenty-first century. And why he would want to prevent someone whose job is to stop shit like that—that would be me by the way—from finding out."

Jez raised her eyebrows. "Makes sense," she said. "If he has the stone, he's making... I dunno, if not money off it, then *something* off it; he wants you to be stopped. And he wants his pog-thing to keep feeding so it can keep making him whatever it's making for him." She rubbed her forehead. "And it took Jack." A thought occurred to her. "So," she said. "Jack's dead, then?"

Sarah ran her hands through her hair. "I can't say for sure."

"So he might still be alive?"

"Maybe," said Sarah. She gestured to the books again. "No one describes how it feeds. But it doesn't feed often. It might store its food. Things that don't eat often sometimes do. And Daniel— the kid from the friar's vision—was probably alive when the friar saw him the first time. Ghosts tend to be anchored to one place."

Jez ignored the last part. "We have to find him," she said. She jumped to her feet. "We have to find him and kill the pogge- whatsit." She looked at Sarah. "Come on. We have to at least try."

Sarah looked down. "Yes," she said. "That's just one of the things that's happening though." She plucked at her bloodstained shirt. "Vampire's aren't idiots," she went on. "And he's been killing people for a long time." She looked up, directly at Jez. "I should be dead," she said. "But I'm not. Because of those women you saw."

"The women in black?" said Jez. "The ones that were here?"

Sarah nodded.

"I saw them at school," said Jez. "Like I said. Not everyone can see them. Alex Appleton couldn't." A thought struck her.

"She's pretty good at not seeing people, though. She's been not seeing Lee Humbolt for about four years."

"Oh right," said Sarah. "They saved me from the stabbing. Not Alex and Lee. The women. They're revenge deities."

"Revenge?" said Jez. "Wait. Does this have anything to do with—"

"I swore a blood oath," said Sarah. "Apparently they come with deadlines. I've got three days to find Nicholas Carrington and wreak bloody vengeance. After that, it's painful slaughter by chthonic goddess."

"Shit," said Jez. "They were looking for *you*."

"They found me," said Sarah.

"Shit," said Jez again. "But you—you have a plan, right? You don't just swear vengeance without, like, figuring out what vengeance is going to look like, right? You knew what you were going to do, right?"

"Not," said Sarah, "really. No."

"What?" said Jez again. This made no sense.

"I was angry," said Sarah. "I was gutted. I was homeless. I wasn't thinking straight. I wanted someone to pay. I wanted *him* to pay. I wanted him to suffer like I was suffering. Everything was gone, Jez. *Everything*. You don't—you're not—it's hard to—"

"Gotcha," said Jez. She didn't think she actually did, but she sort of understood what Sarah was trying to say. You didn't think straight when you were upset, and the witch had been through a lot. "But—I dunno—when you got here, you seemed—I dunno, I don't want to be rude, but you seemed—" She swallowed hard. "Okay? Ish?"

"I had to be," said Sarah. "The Carpenter stuff. I had to have my shit together. I'd been living under a tree for two months."

"But—" said Jez. She made a mental note to come back to the tree thing later. "Three days? Where is he?"

"No idea," said Sarah.

"Do you have a plan?"

"Nope."

"So," said Jez, slowly, "you can save yourself or save Jack."

"Not really," said Sarah. "I can attempt to save myself or attempt to save Jack. No guarantees either way."

Jez's brain whizzed wildly as she tried to compute all the variables. When she looked up again, Sarah was looking straight at her.

"How are you?" she asked.

The question caught Jez off guard, in the middle of her calculations. She took a deep breath. "Fine," she said. "Fine. I guess."

If Sam had been there—and if he had known—he would have pointed out that yeah, she was fine, apart from the obsessive need to destroy every winged insect she spotted in the house, the nightly terrors that had her waking repeatedly in a sweat, and the fact that her dad was still barely able to walk after the car accident that had nearly killed him in October. But Sam wasn't there, he was with Theo, and he didn't know, and Jez didn't say anything.

"Sure?" said Sarah. Jez shrugged.

"How've you been?" Jez asked the witch. "Apart from—" She waved her hand across the table. "This."

"Not bad," said Sarah. "Not bumping into things as much, for sure. Adjusting to life without depth perception. Reading. The books in the house. You know. Getting stabbed."

Jez nodded distractedly. Sarah was the only thing protecting the village from malicious Ethereals. If anything happened to her, the village would be vulnerable. But if she tried to take her revenge upon Nicholas Carrington—even if she were successful—Jack was screwed. Jez read the news, and she knew that the chances of finding a missing child unharmed dropped off a cliff after the first forty-eight hours. And it had already been more.

She took a deep breath.

"Maybe I can help?" she said. "With your stuff? What do you think?"

"I think," said Sarah, "that I don't want to scare anyone."

Jez stopped and looked at Sarah with a flash of anger. "I'm not anyone," she said. "Don't patronize me. I saw what kind of things can happen. If there's something dangerous going on, I want to know. I want to *help*."

"Thanks," said Sarah. "I appreciate it." It didn't sound comforting when she was covered in blood. "Don't you have exams coming up?" she said. "And your dad's still on the mend, right?"

"Yeah," said Jez. "But this is real. And it's dangerous. The village is dangerous. You can't write a good exam if you're dead."

"Dreams aren't real," said Sarah, looking at Jez carefully. "But they can really fuck up your exams as well, if you're dead *tired*."

Jez looked at the ground. She had tried so hard to hide it. She told herself that she would not cry, and ground her teeth together.

There was a long pause.

"Every night," she said, eventually. "It's every night. I just don't want it to happen again. To anyone. To me."

Sarah nodded. The kid had been through a lot.

"I don't want to put you at risk," she said. "But I could use someone to help me think this through."

"Yeah," said Jez, nodding quickly. "I can do that. You need someone who knows the village, right? To help with that." She gestured toward the book on the table. "The bag-thing. You have to start somewhere." She picked up the notebook and pen that Sarah had used to make the list of monsters. "I can totally do this." She doodled on the pad for a moment, then gestured toward the piles of books. "How accurate is this book? Like, it's not just stories, right?"

Sarah made the fifty-fifty gesture with her hand. "We have to assume," she said. "It's the most I have."

"Really?" said Jez. "No one—" she gestured toward the books "—no one else ever met one?"

"Can't say that for sure," said Sarah. "All we can assume is that no one ever met one and lived."

Jez looked at her.

"What?" said Sarah. "Scientific observation. I thought you'd appreciate it."

There was a heavy pause. Jez snorted with something that may have been humour.

"Anyway," she said. She tapped the open book in front of her. "According to this, it's living in one place. With one other person. Who lives alone?"

She frowned and looked up at Sarah.

"Nope," said Sarah. "Let's assume that if there was a magical, one-eyed toad the size of a sheep and with a hole in its head living in my cupboards and eating children, I'd have noticed."

"Right," said Jez. "Yeah. Of course. Who else lives on their own in the village?"

She started thinking hard. Florence Soames and Mary Vine both lived alone, but they met at each other's houses every day for a cup of tea, so that couldn't be it, because the book said that no one else could go in the house if the monster was living in it. Miss Forge held the coffee mornings for the church at her house, so that wasn't it, and anyway, Jez couldn't imagine an Ethereal entity getting by her stroppy fox terrier unnoticed. Mr. Badgerley had lived alone for some years after his wife had died, but then he had died, too, so he wasn't likely to be looking after a poggelin in secret. She ran through the streets of Crowsbrook in her mind, looking at each house and listing its residents. Park Road. Crows Hill. Green Lane. She doodled a little and tapped on the notepad with her pen; a couple of times, she started to write a name, and then crossed it out.

Sycamore Lane. School Road.

Holy shit.

She wrote a name down on the pad.

"Hogarth Merrick," she said out loud. "He's weird enough." She tapped the pad a few times with her pen. "He lived with his mother for years. She was *completely mad*. Never used to talk to anyone, or even make eye contact. Just used to rush past you, looking at the floor. The old people say there was a story there: she used to be normal when she was young, and then she met this bloke from the city, and *then*—" Jez raised one finger and lowered her voice "—she *went away for a year* and came back with Hogarth and tried to start a rumour that she'd got married and he was in the army and all that; Florence Trumper says they all knew it was a heap of crap, which is my word and not hers, and everyone was laughing at her because she'd been all high and mighty before with her fancy man from the city and all that, and then she stopped talking to everyone. Except Hogarth. Probably. And then she died—this was, like, years ago, before I was born, but seriously, buy Florence Trumper three sherries in the pub one night: you'll get all the details—and he just stayed and lived in the same house happily ever after, getting drunk at the pub four nights a week and never talking to anyone. There's a long-standing rumour that he's a pedo, but there haven't been any complaints, and there aren't any stories. Like, usually if someone's dodgy and everyone knows about it, but nobody does anything and it's just a thing everyone knows, there are usually *stories* at least. People say that stuff probably because he's a bit odd and works at the school. He works at the school! There's that connection as well. Might be worth a shot, right?"

"Sure," said Sarah. She sounded tired. "Yeah." Something

caught in her memory like a thorn. "He was working somewhere else where a kid went missing. Rose was talking about it, but she didn't think he was involved." She frowned. "If it's living with him, what would we do? What would I do?" Her brain felt as though it was wrapped in cotton wool.

"I dunno," said Jez. "You could knock on his door or something. Try and get invited in. If he asked you in for a cuppa, at least you'd know it wasn't him and the thing wasn't there. I could do it, if you want. Except you can do that thing, can't you, where you can do magic that makes you look like someone else. Maybe that's better. Oh!" She remembered. "You can go in places with your mind as well, right? Go in and have a look round, really quickly, without actually going in. You could—" She threw up her hands. "I dunno," she said. "Yeah, if you try something, you might die. But you might die in three days anyway. Also, you're going to die *eventually* anyway. So what the hell?" She got up, went to the kitchen, grabbed two mugs from the draining board, came back into the living room, bent down to a small cupboard she knew from before, opened it up and took out a bottle of Scotch. She poured two slugs sloppily into the mugs and pushed one toward Sarah.

"I'm pulling my A-levels out of my arse on no sleep," she said. "You have to *try*."

Sarah sat up slowly. She leaned forward and put her hands around the mug and sipped from it intently. Jez picked up her mug, sniffed at it, and left it. It had been more of a gesture. She picked up the pen again, turned to a new page in the notebook and drew a line down the middle of the page. She wrote "Poggelin" at the top of one column and "Stabby bloke" underneath it, and then "Bloody revenge" at the top of the other column and "Women in black" under that.

"The other thing we could try to do," she said," is to find

Savaric." Her face crumpled into puzzlement. "What kind of a name is *Savaric*, anyway?"

"An old one," said Sarah. "He's been around for a really long time. That's why he's sort of famous."

"Okay, well," said Jez. "He knows where the poggelin is. He knows how everything works. He can tell us more about whether the kid is alive. He might have the stone, which might help us find the kid. You can tell him to get lost and leave Crowsbrook alone. There's loads of reasons to find him. And, and, and—" she leaned forward for emphasis "—he's not likely to think we're going to be looking for him, because he doesn't know who I am and he thinks you're dead, so there's that. Have you got any food?" She got up to go to the kitchen.

"Maybe," said Sarah. "You could probably make toast. So we have two ways to try and find the poggelin and therefore find out what's happened to Jack."

Jez disappeared into the kitchen. "Also," she yelled from the kitchen, "we need to find out how to kill a poggelin." Sarah heard clattering and a loud clank of plates that made her wince. "To stop this happening to other kids." She reappeared in the doorway. "Somehow."

"There's probably something in the trunks," said Sarah, mentally running through a vague inventory of the cobweb-draped storage room above their heads. "Between that and the books, we could probably figure something out." Jez's energy was making her feel slightly better about the poggelin situation. There was no indication that poggelins were immortal, even if Ethereal beings tended to live a lot longer than human ones, and a lot of things that weren't immortal would die if you stuck big enough pointy things in them in the right places.

"The first thing is to find out where the kid is," said Jez, coming back into the living room with a pile of toast covered in purple jam. "Like, right away. If he's alive. And if he's still alive, we have to get him back." She thought for a moment. "How does that intradimensional thing work? Can he exist in between the dimensions?"

"I don't know," said Sarah. "It's not like Dot left a schematic. But if all the spaces are as one, he probably doesn't have to. It's just a question of navigation. What a world." She sighed. "A creature that shouldn't exist. That we know nothing about. That might actually be able to give some insight into layers of our world that we know nothing about. Except it eats children, and would destroy the balance between the human and the Ethereal realm of existence, so we have to kill it." She shook her head. "Okay. So that's a vague plan for the Crowsbrook problem."

"What about the bloody vengeance plan?" said Jez. Sarah fell silent.

"I have to find Carrington," she said eventually. "And then I have to get to Carrington. But I don't know what to do when I get there."

"What were you planning to do?" said Jez. "Kill him?"

"I guess," said Sarah. "Yes. I was. But he's just a person. It won't solve everything."

Jez looked at her stonily.

"He's *evil*," Jez said. "He basically killed your friend because he wanted to make a lot of money selling face cream. He sold out Adam Carpenter—who was supposed to be *his* friend—and we don't even know what he got out of it, but people *died* in Crowsbrook because he set up Adam. The Greenwoods: an entire family. Gareth and Marina. Pauline Spinner; she used to clean Adam's house and then quietly disappeared, and no one seems to be able to remember her except me. And possibly Sam. Adam's girlfriend, Julia Fletcher; she was a *doctor*. She *helped* people. Adam died. And yeah, I know you could argue that he was greedy and stupid and an arsehole, but he didn't know what he was getting into, and I bet Carrington did, and he pulled Adam into this stuff anyway. And for what? That's not okay. It's not just about you. He treats people like they're nothing. You need to stop him."

"I'm only supposed to protect Crowsbrook," said Sarah. "I mean, technically. My job."

"Yeah," said Jez. "And how many family businesses were there when they wrote that job description? Because I bet there are a lot less now. You *know* about this. You can't just leave it up to someone else to solve it. There isn't anyone else. And he doesn't follow the rules."

"Ever killed anyone?" said Sarah, suddenly and sharply. "Because I haven't— I mean, I've never killed a human. And I'm not exactly looking forward to it. And it's not exactly following *the rules*, whatever that means."

"You have to find him first," said Jez. "Focus on that."

"Big spells can take seven days," said Sarah, almost to herself. "What am I going to do, bash him on the head?"

"Use your imagination," said Jez, tapping maniacally at her phone. "I've come up with some really creative things I wish would happen to Saskia French on a Friday afternoon in history, and that was only a single period lesson. I can still remember most of them, and I haven't taken history in two years. Eleanor was your best friend. You didn't ever think of *anything*?"

"It's not the thinking," said Sarah. "It's the doing."

"Use magic," said Jez, still bashing her phone screen. "Problem solved."

"I can't," said Sarah. "There are repercussions for doing that."

"Yeah," said Jez. "You just told me. Are these repercussions worse than the ones where you get tortured and then killed? And if they're the same, do they at least kick the painfully slaughtered bit down the road so that you have a time to work out if the painfully slaughtered bit can be avoided? How," she went on, smacking her forehead and throwing down her phone, "is this Carrington bloke so invisible? It's like he doesn't exist in the twenty-first century. Can't you find him with magic?"

Sarah shrugged. "I can try."

Jez whirled on her. "You never *tried*? Oh my God. I'm going to slaughter you painfully myself."

"You don't know what it was like," said Sarah. "My life. Before I came here."

"You said you were living under a tree," said Jez. She was tapping rapidly at her phone again. "That's all."

"I wasn't exaggerating," said Sarah. "I lived with the fae. I don't know where we were. In woods. No one ever came by. No mortals, I mean. They brought me food and water and a blanket, and I didn't move for weeks. I had some burns, and they treated those, too. One day I was able to sit up, and eventually I went back to where my house was. And that's where I found the letter telling me about Dorothea."

Jez put her phone down slowly.

"No one came looking for you?" she said.

"No," said Sarah. Jez's phone buzzed. She ignored it.

"*No one?*"

"No," said Sarah with some irritation. "It's the job. You don't make a lot of friends because firstly you're strange and secondly you can't talk about what you do."

"But you had Eleanor."

"Yes," said Sarah. She winced. "And then I didn't." She frowned hard, and with a great effort stood up. "I need to make you some tea for the dreams. I can do that. And it won't take long."

"I'm in then?" said Jez. "I can help with this?"

"Don't wreck—"

"My exams," said Jez. "I'm not *going* to. I've worked too hard. Besides," she went on, "I'm pretty sure I'm up to the second term of the first year of medicine now anyway. Just in case it came up."

"You read ahead?"

"I told you," said Jez. "There's nothing to do in Crowsbrook. Might as well make sure you can get out." She stood up. "You make the tea. I'll start trying to figure out how to kill a poggelin, and then we can work out how find Carrington together."

She stomped over to the bookshelf and started pulling down books.

• • •

Jack felt better now the big kids were here. It was still scary, but not as much. His foot still hurt. And the monster hadn't come back, which was good.

Marina sat on the ground next to him. Gareth was still standing up and walking about, like Mr. Beecham did when he was doing assembly.

"Where are we?" asked Jack. "Are we in Crowsbrook?"

"Yes," said Marina. "Do you know where the pond is?" She pointed, and part of the darkness glittered in her light. "That's the pond over there. Be careful; you have to stay away from the edge. There are bad things in it."

"I know," said Jack. He didn't know how he knew, but he knew. "Is it night? I was at school."

Marina looked sad. "It's always dark here," she said. "I don't know if it's day or night. It's just dark. All the time."

They had no idea how much time had passed since—since that day in October, when she'd taken Gareth down to the place where she would sit and think and write in her journal, sharing the pond's wild beauty and sinister atmosphere. She had been drawn to its isolation and the faint sense of danger that she had ignored, down there, alone, because really: how dangerous could a pond in a country village be, once you knew not to swim in the weeds, or walk on the fragile film of ice that covered it in the winter? So she had taken Gareth down there, and they had both died.

Gareth wasn't one to hold a grudge. He had told her again and again that she couldn't have known. And she knew it was true. But she still felt the pain of something that was not quite guilt, something that said that if she had listened to her gut and not her heart, then maybe one of them at least would have survived.

Jack was talking again and she brought herself back to the present.

"How did you get here?" he was saying. "Are you a ghost?" She frowned, and saw him looking intensely at the light.

"Something bad happened," said Marina. She didn't want to frighten him more than he was already. "I don't know. We're probably ghosts. I think."

"Am I a ghost?"

"I don't think so," said Marina. "You look different. You're not glowing." *And you're bleeding*, she thought, but didn't say it out loud. Half of Jack's foot appeared to be missing: it ended in a stump of tattered flesh and shards of bone. She didn't know how he was so calm. Maybe he couldn't feel it. Maybe he hadn't noticed.

Maybe it was just this awful place.

"What was the last thing you remember," she said. "Before you ended up here?"

"I was in a cupboard," said Jack. "I hid from Jocasta Valentine in a cupboard and something grabbed me. It was a monster. There were Star Mutants." He waved Starhammer to make his point.

Gareth nodded. He looked like he was thinking.

"He's not supposed to be here," he said. Jack felt worried. He didn't want to be in trouble.

"It was an accident," he said. "I came here by accident."

"No, hon," said Marina. "It's all right. We just don't know—well. Mostly, people like you don't come here. They can't. And we don't know how to get you back to your—back home, I mean."

"His mum's going to be going barmy," said Gareth. "My mum—"

"Try not to think about that," said Marina. Her voice wobbled a bit. "It won't help right now." She turned to Jack again. "Do you remember anything else? Anything at all?"

Jack shook his head. He'd had his eyes shut. All he remembered were noises.

"If we can't get out," said Gareth, "how did he get in?"

"I don't know," said Marina. "I don't know."

She looked at Jack.

"We can stay with you, though," she said. "We've been here for a while. We'll stay with you. We can do that."

Gareth snorted.

"It's not like we have a choice," he said.

• • •

After twenty minutes of clattering in the kitchen, Sarah handed Jez a jar wrapped in a tea towel. Its heat radiated into her hands.

"Thanks," said Jez. She looked at the jar. "That's a couple of nights sorted. I thought you said magic took time?"

"It does," said Sarah. "This is just complicated tea-making. And you don't drink it all at once. You put a couple of drops in a glass of milk or hot chocolate or whatever before bedtime. Last you a few months, this lot will. You don't have to keep it in the fridge, but you should probably keep it in the dark, if you can. Under your bed or something." She stepped back into the kitchen, and Jez heard the clink and rustle of herbs being put back in jars.

She jumped as a rustle and a louder *clank* came from behind her, and spun round to see the letterbox in the front door wedged open with a copy of the *Arden Spectator*. A draft began to blow through the gap. Jez got up, pulled the paper out of the letterbox, went back to her seat and sat down heavily. Two spiders scuttled over the arm of the chair and disappeared across the floor and behind a curtain. Jez's eyebrows shot up as she remembered the spiders, and she leaped to her feet and checked for more before sitting again, more gingerly. "Sorry, guys," she muttered.

She unfolded the paper.

LOCAL BOY MISSING yelled the headline. She went cold.

Of course. Of course it would be in the papers. That would make perfect sense. It was the kind of thing that made the national papers, let alone the local papers. Why would it not?

Because—she knew, she didn't have to remind herself—*this is Crowsbrook*. And things that happened in Crowsbrook didn't always make it into the outside world. Because people didn't notice them, or believe them. Or even remember them, after the fact.

She turned back to the paper. Maybe there would be something here that could help. Anything.

The village of Crowsbrook is reeling after five-year-old Jack Czajkowski disappeared from Crowsbrook Primary School on Tuesday. The boy was last seen by his teacher, Sheila Seddon, at afternoon break. Mrs. Seddon assumed that Jack had returned after the afternoon break, but when his mother, Holly Czajkowski, arrived to collect him at the end of the day, he could not be found.

Blah, blah, every parent's nightmare, blah, blah… Nobody had seen any strangers. Nobody had seen Jack come back in from break. She threw the paper down on the table in frustration and sighed, staring at the photo of the familiar school surrounded by serious-faced police officers.

She frowned and looked closer at the photo. One of the Amble kids mugged back at her, having successfully photo-bombed Midge Appleton's shot of the police outside the school. She snorted.

Then she started.

The Amble kids!

She stuck her head into the kitchen.

"I just thought of something," she said from the doorway. "It's probably stupid, but if anyone saw anything that day, or knows anything about what happened, it'll be the Amble kids. They've got eyes bloody everywhere. I don't know how they do it, but they do. Plus there was a rumour on the bus that Jack Czajkowski used to play with Carlo Amble sometimes. Mickey Amble goes on the bus. He's a bit of a terrorist, but he might be able to answer a serious question if he's not in front of his mates." *And if I can get him to stay in one place for five minutes*, she thought. "D'you want me to see if I can have a word?"

"It's worth a shot," said Sarah. She thought for a moment. "If you could see if—I dunno. If you could borrow anything of Jack's, that'd be helpful, too. Then we could do the water thing again. I could, anyway." She looked directly at Jez. "Thanks."

"It's not much," said Jez. "I'm just talking to a twelve-year-old."

Sarah looked amused for the first time.

"You're talking to Mickey Amble," she said. "I'd offer you a protection charm, but I don't think it'd do any good."

Chapter 11

Maggie Amble opened the door when Jez knocked. Maggie was the Amble matriarch. Sometimes when Jez had been racked with insomnia, awake at 4:48 a.m., and at her wits' end at the prospect of another half-wakeful day, she thought of Maggie.

In Crowsbrook, Maggie was held to be a saint made of nails.

"He's not in," she said, when Jez asked for Mickey. "He's probably up in Ghost Town. Tell him he'll be back for his tea at six or else."

Ghost Town was a Crowsbrook legend. It was in the woods, on the edge of the village: the remains of the buildings that had accompanied a tiny airstrip that had been used during the Second World War. The huts had fallen into disrepair, and the woods had claimed them. But so had the Amble kids. Ghost Town was Mickey Amble's kingdom. Jez thanked Maggie, and set off for the woods.

The sky was darkening with heavy clouds when she arrived at the edge of the woodland. It smelled of wet earth and rot; the branches of the trees were February-bare and bony. It was quieter here; the underbrush and the trunks of the trees muffled everything, but she could hear the calls of crows in the treetops and the sound seemed to echo. She headed off the road and down the footpath that led into the woods, slowing her pace, peering between bushes, looking for the secret signs that all the Crowsbrook kids knew showed the way to Ghost Town.

Turn right at the broken fencepost. Follow the path that isn't really a path until you get to the tree that was struck by lightning. If you get to the rocks, you've gone too far.

She couldn't see anyone.

No one at all.

She turned right and snaked slowly down the path that wasn't really a path. It was just a sort of clearing worn by generations of feet. It was narrow and covered in slugs.

She took a risk. "Amble?" she called.

An empty pop can came flying out of the gloom and whizzed past her ear, flicking remnants of Coke on her face. She winced and wiped it off.

"Amble!" she snapped. "Was that you?"

She heard a newly deepened chortling from within the trees. Then, nothing. She picked her way forward through the shrubs and the silence.

"I want to talk to Amble," she said, more loudly. "It's important. Serious."

"Seeeeeeeeerious?" hissed a voice from behind the lightning tree, and the snickering began all over again.

Jez looked at the sky for a moment and ran her hands through her hair. She turned at the lightning tree and saw a dilapidated hut with broken windows, covered in weeds. There was a tattered tarp patching part of the roof. There were no lights on inside.

It had gotten darker outside, too.

"Amble!" she shouted. "Where are you? I need to talk to you."

The door of the hut opened with a bang, apparently of its

own volition. Jez carefully stepped inside, looking above and around her for booby traps.

It was dark in the hut and it took a moment for her eyes to adjust to the light. A short, skinny boy sat on a large and ancient swivel armchair in front of her, framed by two tattered flags, one on each side of him, and two lieutenants, who stared at her coldly.

Mickey Amble.

"What do you want?" he said. "The fuck are you doing up here?" It wasn't a hostile question, more one of genuine puzzlement.

"The missing kid," said Jez. "Jack Czajkowski. Your brother used to play with him, right?"

"Carlo," said Mickey Amble. "Yeah. Shit." He took a final swig from a can of Fanta, crushed it expertly, and tossed it out of the broken window, where the clattering sound it made suggested strongly that it had not been the first can disposed of in such a manner. "Some pedo or something, right?"

"Nobody knows," said Jez. "You know Jack?"

Mickey looked at her as if she'd asked him to give her a lift to the chip shop. "He's fucking five or something. No. Fuck."

"You know his mum?"

"I've seen her around. She's hot." The lieutenants laughed, affecting a deliberately low register.

"Who does know them?"

"Who cares?" said one of the lieutenants. Mickey Amble elbowed him sharply in the ribs, and he yelped and shut up. Jez looked at Mickey Amble and raised one eyebrow.

Mickey sighed. "Fuck. Look, I don't know her. I heard my mum talking about her. The mum. Her name's Holly. She hasn't been in the village long. She got a divorce and moved to Crowsbrook. Went to the church in Castleton for a few weeks but stopped. Mum went over to her house once to see if she was all right. She wouldn't open the door." He looked at the ceiling, trying to remember.

"Anything else?"

"She's fucking crazy. Hasn't been home since her kid—she's just been wandering around Crowsbrook like a mentalist poking hedges with a stick. Came up here a couple of days ago. Wayne Badgerley yelled at her, but it was like she couldn't hear him."

Jez flinched at Wayne Badgerley's name. She'd met his great-grandfather once.

"Like he was fucking *invisible*. Sprayed her with almost a full bottle of Tizer in the end, and she didn't even turn around." Mickey Amble frowned. "You know," he said, affecting an overly elegant accent, "it seemed *quite rude*."

"Yeah?" said Jez. "Where does she live?"

"Two doors down from us."

"Two doors down?" said Jez. "*Two doors down* and this is all you've got? She ignored you so you sprayed her with pop?"

"You'd have to have seen her," said Mickey. He stuck his arms out in front of him like Frankenstein's monster and crossed his eyes. "Totally out of it. Like a fucking zombie or some shit. One that can poke bushes with a stick, obviously. Accidentally walloped Bill with it. Show her your leg, Bill."

Bill pulled up the leg of his trousers to reveal a revolting purple bruise.

Jez looked at the bruise. "What kind of stick?"

"A fucking big one," said Bill, with feeling. "Part of a fucking tree or something. I dunno. A big fucking lumpy stick." He covered up the bruise. "Fucking mental case."

"Jack's just a fucking kid," said Mickey. "Some old bat's probably taken him in and fed him and hasn't seen the news for a week. He'll show up."

"Thanks," said Jez. She wished she had Mickey Amble's faith. "Let's hope. Jack used to play with Carlo, right?"

Mickey nodded. "Yeah. So what?"

"Carlo borrow any of his stuff?"

Mickey narrowed his eyes. "You think Carlo fucking thieved his stuff?"

"No," said Jez, quickly. "I just wanted to—if Carlo's got something that's Jack's, can I borrow it?"

"Why?"

"Long story," said Jez. Mickey shrugged. Jez suddenly realized that Mickey understood the value of not being asked for an explanation better than she did.

"You would," he said, "have to have words with my younger brother on that. Don't get your hopes up, though. Sense of possession like a steel trap, that boy's got." The lieutenants nodded slowly in agreement.

"He here?" said Jez.

Mickey gestured with his head. "In the back."

Jez made a move toward the tarp-covered door that separated Mickey's reception hall from the rest of the shack. The lieutenants moved in front of her.

"You," said Mickey, "do not have backroom privileges. Bill, go and get Carlo." Bill disappeared behind the tarp. There was a loud angry scream, and the sound of Bill swearing, and a moment later, Bill reappeared with a seething Carlo under his arm. Mickey nodded to Bill, who put Carlo down, and Mickey beckoned the disgruntled Carlo over to him.

"Carlo," said Mickey. "You remember Jack?"

"Yes," said Carlo. "He swapped my Star Mutant. Galacticor."

"Did he give you anything?"

"Two Hot Wheels," said Carlo proudly. "Keepsies."

"So he's got Galacticor, then," said Jez. "Does he like Star

Mutants?" She wasn't sure how this line of questioning was going to help, but she wanted to avoid any further accusations about what she might or might not be alleging about the property rights that attached to a swap.

Carlo nodded. "Lots. Galacticor fits in your pocket as well. Because of his arm."

Jez frowned. "What about his arm?"

"It came off," said Carlo. "But he's still all right. You could probably *mend* it."

"Oh." Jez drew it out into a syllable of fascination and wonder. "So he fits in your pocket. Did he fit in Jack's pocket?"

"'S'what I *said*," said Carlo. "He fits in your pocket. Because he's only got one arm. He fits in Jack's pocket. He's there *all the time*."

"Does Jack keep him in his pocket?" Jez was thinking rapidly. *If Carlo still has the missing bit…*

"Yeeees." Now it was Carlo's turn to draw out a syllable. "Wanna see my Hot Wheels?"

"No, you're all right," said Jez. She decided to take the long shot. "But that arm that fell off. You still got it?" Maybe there would be a connection between the two pieces of the toy. Bits of quantum theory fluttered vaguely through her mind.

"Can you mend it?" said Carlo. "I thought I lost it. When I swapped Galaticor. Then I found it, after."

"Maybe," said Jez, quickly. "Can I borrow—"

"She really needs it," said Mickey to Carlo. "Lendsies."

Carlo frowned.

"Please?" said Jez.

Carlo contemplated her for a moment. "All right," he said, and wandered off behind the tarp. A moment later he was back, brandishing a small piece of plastic.

"You have to look after it," he said, as he handed her the tiny limb. "Because maybe someone can mend Galacticor."

"I will," said Jez. "Can I give it to Jack, if I see him?"

Carlo thought for a moment. "Okay," he conceded. "But he's got to put it back on Galacticor." He trundled off into the back room.

"That was easier than I thought it'd be," said Jez.

"He's a good kid," said Mickey, shortly. "Anything else?"

"That's it," said Jez. "Oh. Your mum says your tea's at six or else."

Mickey nodded slowly and reverently. "All right, then," he said. He waved his hand regally. "Off you pop."

Jez exited the shack with grace, and then started a steady jog back to the village, with the arm of Galacticor safely in her pocket.

• • •

Hogarth was lying in bed. It had taken him a full hour to move from the laundry room at the back of the house through the hall and up the stairs to his bedroom, but he had done it, for all the times the world had tilted on its side and threatened to drown him in a wave of static. He had done it.

He was fully clothed and had piled up pillows and blankets around him to try to keep out a cold that had wrapped itself around his bones like a layer of cold clingfilm under his flesh. He was lying on his right side and the ragged stump of his left arm stuck out from under the blankets; he couldn't bear to have anything touch it. The flesh at the end was red: seared and tattered. He shivered. His mind raced. He tried to grasp the thoughts as they slid past, and it was like trying to hold running water.

The thing. The thing that had come from the cupboard. It couldn't have been there. He thought he'd seen—

Things like that didn't exist.

"Don't be daft," said someone that sounded like Ma. He gasped and looked up sharply. There was no one in the room.

"Those things are just stories." There it was again.

He thought he saw his breath, he felt so cold.

Round it had been, like the toads he used to squash on his way home from school (all of them had done it, it wasn't just him). Round with—

"You're lying to me," said Ma again, more loudly. He jumped and sniffed. He could smell her talcum powder, the lavender kind.

What the—

No, no, he had seen it, he had. The thing. The thing that couldn't be his friend, because his friend was nice, and the thing in the cupboard wasn't nice; it had hurt him and—

"I know what people are like," said Ma. "I just didn't think that *you* would be like *them*."

But he hadn't been a person. He had been magic and he had lived in the cupboard and—

"I trusted you," said Ma. "You and your fancy promises. And what did I get? A load of old rubbish."

"No," croaked Hogarth, out loud. "No. It wasn't. It *wasn't*."

It hadn't been. It *couldn't* have been. He had shared everything with his friend. He had shared *food*. The hours since that—that *thing* had roared out of the cupboard had been—

He didn't have the words. He moaned into his pillow. Because it had been good and now there was just him and only him and the agony of his arm and only him and that was all and it might go on for ever and ever and ever and there was no one else.

He wanted to scream. He clenched his eyes tight shut.

The things he had done—

The things he had done because—for—

People said that, didn't they, they said they'd do anything, but he really *had* and it was fine, it wasn't like anyone was ever going to find out, but he had, he had done it, he had put the toys there, done it twice because—

the Bag'un

—had asked him to and it had made for a happy home, and he hadn't done anything really bad, not really, it wasn't like he'd hurt those kids, because he hadn't—

He *hadn't*, it wasn't him. It was—

It didn't matter. He had done it because he'd been asked and that was something, wasn't it?

"I'd have done anything for you," said Ma. He opened his eyes. She was standing next to his bed looking down at him.

No. Looking *through* him.

He gaped at her.

"Well," said Ma. "Look what you've done now." She gestured downward, but below the waist, she was swathed in mist.

Like he didn't know what he'd done.

"What did you expect was going to happen?"

Hogarth mumbled something about not knowing.

"You're a bigger bloody fool than I took you for, then," said Ma. "Of course you didn't." She sighed. "You disgust me."

Hogarth moaned again from under the covers, a single word.

"Help?" said Ma. "God helps those that help themselves. And even then you've got to catch Him on a good day. Get up, you lazy bugger. You want things to get better? Get up and make them better."

He didn't know how he could. Ma turned away. She was fading. He didn't know how that was possible.

"Cursed, I've been," said Ma, almost to herself. "Cursed with you, I was."

She was right. He'd only ever disappointed her.

And that was it, wasn't it? It was so easy to put things in a cupboard when someone asked you. Couldn't get that wrong, could you?

"Get up, you lazy bastard." His mother's voice echoed in his ears, though he could no longer see her.

She was right, of course. She was always right.

Shaking, Hogarth took a deep breath and held it as he pushed back the blankets and swung his feet around to the floor. With a colossal effort, he sat up. The blood rushed to his head and the room swam. But he was going to do it. He was. He had to.

He was going to find the Bag'un.

He closed his eyes and listened hard. In the distance, he thought he could hear something growling.

• • •

"So what's up here then?"

Sam shrugged and made a face as he and Theo made their way up the winding path to the top of the hill behind the village hall. "Nothing. This is Crowsbrook."

"It's very *quaint*." Theo put a heavy emphasis on quaint, and Sam knew he was trying to be nice.

"Yeah," said Sam. "If you drive through it fast enough."

Theo was from London. He had told Sam stories about London that made Sam feel like a thirteen-year-old being included in an adult conversation for the first time. It was wild. It was sexy. It was exciting.

You're supposed to go to Manchester with Jez, a voice at the back of his mind reminded him.

Yeah, he thought. But how serious were we about all that stuff?

You created the Catalogue. Remember the Catalogue? The List of Reasons Not to Give Up and Die?

He remembered it. It seemed kind of stupid now, like just another game played by much younger kids. It had been fun at the time. But Jez was going in September, and he would be stuck in Crowsbrook for another year, and she would have her own stuff going on in Manchester. It wasn't like it was the actual nineties, after all. They both had phones. They would stay in touch. They would *totally* stay in touch. Wherever he was. Wherever she was. It would be fine. Why was he even thinking about this? He was with Theo.

"You've gone quiet," said Theo.

"Quiet as a Crowsbrook Saturday night," said Sam, making a sweeping gesture with his hand. A drop of rain fell on it and he looked at the sky. "Crap."

"Nobody about, then?" said Theo with a cheeky glint in his eye. He slipped his arms around Sam and kissed him.

Sam broke away and looked over his shoulder.

"Relax," said Theo. Sam thought he heard a touch of disappointment in his voice. "There's no one for miles."

"Mr. and Mrs. Bastable live over the crest and to the right," said Sam, automatically. "They walk their dog up here. And the bloody Amble kids are everywhere." The rain started falling steadily.

Theo looked up at the sky. "Not now they aren't," he said. "You worry too much. And you have to leave this place. It's not doing you any good."

You don't know the half of it, thought Sam. He put his arms around Theo, and in a minute they were kissing again, and nothing else mattered.

Theo stepped back and stumbled. They broke apart, slightly breathless.

"Whoa," said Sam, reaching out to Theo who caught his

arm and regained his balance. "Whoa." His phone buzzed in his pocket, and he pulled it out and looked at it.

The phone was powering down. Out of battery. He tried to ignore the lurch in his stomach.

He turned back to Theo and smiled. "Where were we?"

Theo said nothing. He was staring across the field. Sam felt his hand shake slightly. "They the dog walkers?"

Sam looked across the field to where Theo was pointing, and terror shot through him. It was the women in black.

He snapped out of his fugue.

"Look at your phone," he whispered to Theo. "Check your phone?"

Theo frowned. "What?"

"Check your phone," said Sam. "Please don't ask. Just look at it."

Theo raised his eyebrows and shrugged. He pulled his phone out of his pocket.

"Battery's flat," he said. He grinned. "Oh well."

"Fuck!" Sam was looking between Theo and the women. The women were gaining on them. "We have to go! Now! Run!"

"What the fuck? It's just people." Theo waved. "Hello!"

"I said, shut *up*!" Sam grabbed Theo by the shoulders. "We have to get out of here!"

"You say hello to everyone here," said Theo, looking hurt. "I was just—"

The women turned slowly and focused on the two of them.

"Oh *shit*," said Sam. *"Run!"*

He grabbed Theo's arm and set off. They stumbled across the field, through the thick weeds and wet grass.

"What the fuck is going on?" panted Theo. "Who are those people? Do you know them?"

Sam was out of breath as well. "It'll be fine," he said. "Don't ask. It'll be fine. We'll go back to yours and—"

"My place is outside the village on the other side," said Theo. "It would make more sense to go to yours, except that *literally nothing is making sense right now.* What the fuck are you doing? We need to—"

He was cut off. The women were upon them.

Except they weren't women anymore. Sam had a vague impression of the ancient human faces they had been using, but what he could actually see in front of him looked more like snarling dogs with bloodshot eyes and shaggy hair. They had tattered, veined wings, like the wings of bats, which were criss-crossed with scars. They smelled like leaf mulch and rotting meat, and they were right up in his face, one after the other, sniffing him, growling, moving round him, moving *through* him, it seemed. One pushed a snout into his face, and he saw with horror that what he had assumed was matted hair was thousands of tiny, slender snakes, attached to the head by their tails, but moving independently—and angrily. Their hissing mingled with the growls from the dogs' throats. Sam glanced at Theo: he was frozen in terror. One of the dog-headed beings brought out a studded metal flail from folds of skin that were almost like robes. It was an ugly weapon: the tails on it looked as though they were covered in broken glass and razor blades. Sam could see a dried brown piece of what looked like thin leather still attached to it. He didn't want to know what it actually was.

We haven't done anything. The thought came into his mind from nowhere. *We're innocents.*

The creatures seemed to pause. Sam took a deep breath.

"We haven't done anything," he said out loud. "You have to believe us. We haven't done anything."

The creatures growled low, and moved back. Sam couldn't believe it.

Was that all they had wanted?

Then, they darted forward suddenly, and they were in his head. He knew they were in his head, sifting through his thoughts and memories, stirring up his mind like someone turning a compost pile with a pitchfork. He screamed, and somewhere, seemingly in the distance, he could hear Theo screaming, too. Then his mind settled, and he blinked, and they were out of his head and he looked around and the creatures were gone. The only sound was the rain falling on the grass.

Theo was the first to speak.

"What," he said, "the *fuck* is going on?"

Sam could barely breathe. It was happening again. Everything was happening again. He crouched on the ground and put his head down. He felt Theo's arm around him.

"It's okay," said Theo. "It's okay. We're okay. They're gone."

"I know." It was barely a whisper.

"This—I—I don't know what we just—it's—"

"Crowsbrook." Sam was still hyperventilating. "It's Crowsbrook."

"Crowsbrook? What do you mean 'It's Crowsbrook'?"

"It's—" Sam's world began to swim back into focus. He no longer felt as though he was under water. He noticed the water on the grass in front of him, and the raindrops falling on the back of his neck. His breathing slowed to normal.

He could do this. He lifted his head and looked at Theo.

"Crowsbrook is—" he began. "I don't know where to start. Weird stuff happens here. And not many people notice. Somehow, it's really good at hiding the—" he gestured, searching for the words, and gave up "—the fucking *monsters*. The weirdness. Two kids from Arden were murdered down by one of the local ponds last autumn."

Theo raised his eyebrows.

"Right?" said Sam. "From Arden High. They were killed in the village. And this is the first you're hearing of it, right?"

"Yeah," said Theo. He was staring at Sam, and Sam couldn't tell whether he was intrigued or horrified or thought Sam was mad, or all three, or just two.

"Yeah," he went on. "In any normal place, it would be the first thing you heard. It would be a fucking urban *legend* by now. But this is Crowsbrook. Ask anybody what Ethel Spinner said to Mary Vine at the harvest barn dance in 1964 that means that you can't put a Spinner and a Vine at the same table at the Scouts' Annual Fundraising Dinner and Dance today, and everyone'll give you a word-for-word. Ask about the two kids murdered down by the pond four months ago, and they'll look at you like they're trying to remember something from before their first birthday, and eventually go 'yeah… I think I heard something about that.' It *hides* things, Theo. It hides the things that it doesn't want anybody to see. But they're there. And they kill people."

Theo was silent for a moment.

"We need to get help," he said eventually. "We need to get help."

Sam nodded and set off. Theo stood up and started after him.

"Where are we going?" he said. "You look like you know where you're going. Is there, like, a Committee of Dealing with Weird Shit or something? Like, people who know about this?"

"Nope." Sam kept walking.

"Well, where are we going?" Theo caught Sam's arm and stopped him. "You need to talk to me. This is some heavy-duty bullshit. There are monsters. What the fuck happens next?"

Sam suddenly felt very tired. He looked Theo right in the eyes.

"The only logical thing," he said, "under the circumstances."

He took a deep breath. He knew how the next part would sound, and he didn't care anymore. He just didn't want to die, and he didn't want Theo to die either.

"We go to see the village witch."

Chapter 12

Jez hammered on the door of the cottage, breathing heavily. She had the plastic arm of the action figure. She knew that Jack's mum was going a bit crazy. It was going to be fine. They had three days, and the Internet, and she had never missed a deadline in her life. She could figure out something to tell Becky and her dad if she had to go away for twenty-four hours to find Carrington. It would be fine. She put her hand in her bag and tapped a finger on the miniature oversized plastic bicep.

Sarah opened the door with her eyebrows raised and gestured her in without a word.

"I found him," said Jez. "Mickey. And Carlo was there too." She pulled the toy arm out of her bag. "He gave me this. It's Jack's. Well, it came off a toy that Carlo gave to Jack. He said Jack keeps the rest of it in his pocket. I think. But either way, Jack really likes Star Mutants. Will that help?" She turned into the living room. "I—"

Her voice died away. Sam and another bloke about the same age were sitting there already. Jez knew—she didn't know how, except that it made sense—that this was Theo.

Sam and Theo were holding mugs of tea. The silence in the living room was excruciating.

This, Sarah reminded herself, was one reason why she didn't seek out other people.

"What are you doing here?" said Jez to Sam.

"Jez," said Sam. "This is Theo." Theo stood up and held out a hand. Jez gave him a cursory attempt at a smile into which she put no effort. She stuck her hand with the action figure in it toward Sarah.

"Here you go," she said. "For the water." She turned back to Sam. "What are you doing here?"

Sam sighed. "We saw them," he said. "The women. Up on the hill. They're—"

"Oh," said Jez. "Oh. Oh, did something weird happen? Something a bit spooky? Maybe, like, scary? Oh gosh, who could have predicted that?"

"What?" said Theo. "What is *your*—"

Jez rolled her eyes. "I told him to be careful. He didn't believe—"

"You didn't tell me to be caref—"

"You lied to me! You specifically said—"

"Yeah, because this shit is—"

"Dangerous," said Sarah, quietly. Sam and Jez were instantly quiet. "It's dangerous. We all know that."

Jez stood in silence, staring into the middle distance, lips pressed together.

"So now what?" said Sam. "Who were those women?"

"They weren't looking for you," said Sarah. "Don't worry."

"I wouldn't want to be the person they *were* looking for," said Theo quickly. Jez's head snapped up and she opened her mouth to speak, but thought better of it and closed it again.

"You saw them," said Sam to Jez. "And now you're here. What's going on?"

Jez shrugged. It was Sarah's turn to roll her eye.

"Same old, same old," she said. "Don't worry about them. Unless you've done something really bad."

"What were they?" Theo was insistent.

"Furies," said Sarah. "Dark goddesses. Old ones. Really old. They deal with…" Her voice trailed off. "Problems. Disorder. They deal with disorder. Ever read the *Oresteia*?"

Theo nodded.

"Well," said Sarah. "Them. Murder members of your own family? They'll have you for sure. But they were also a sort of catch-all bogeyman you could threaten your kids with. Talk back to your teacher? Furies'll get you. Town council not listening to you? Furies'll have 'em. Serve your guests third-rate wine and olives? Watch your back. You failed in your *duty*. And they don't like that. They're attracted to *guilt*."

"Jesus," said Theo.

"Don't worry," said Sarah. "I think they've mellowed quite a lot. They only go after the big stuff now."

"Still," said Theo. "It's a bit of a problem if you're going to get a cosmic monster-bollocking for things you didn't even know were things."

There was a pause.

"I like you," said Sarah. "You can stay." She rubbed her temple. "If you want. We've got a bit of a situation here, though. And you can't talk about any of this."

"I worked that out," said Theo. "No evidence: can't prove anything. I start talking to anyone who isn't Sam…or you—" he gestured around the room "—and everyone's going to think I'm barmy."

"You catch on quick," said Sarah. "I'm trying to find a thing that might have eaten one of the kids from the village. You didn't happen to see anything else up there, did you?"

"No," said Sam. "Just the—things. What kind of monster eats children?"

"I thought all of them," said Theo. "I mean, when I thought they didn't exist." He picked aimlessly at a loose thread in the cover of the chair.

"It's teamed up with a human," said Jez. "We think."

"We don't have to worry about that," said Sam. "Humans aren't the problem here."

"Adam Carpenter was a human," shot back Jez. "At one point."

"Who's Adam Carpenter?" said Theo.

The silence became awkward.

"A dead man," said Sarah, eventually, looking at the floor. "He made some bad decisions and ended up dead. Tangling with monsters can do that for you; once you let them know it's okay to act through you…" She looked back up at Theo. "This is dangerous. You need to be absolutely clear about that. You can leave now, if you want," she went on, lifting her head and looking up at Theo. "You can leave and never worry about this stuff again. You don't have to get involved."

"That's not true though, is it?" Sam's voice was filled with barely suppressed anger. "I tried, and the monsters keep coming back. Jez told me about the women days ago, and I told her I didn't want to get involved. People die," he said, turning to Theo. "She's not kidding. People died. A fucking horrible goat-man thing stomped on my arm and broke it. Her dad was almost killed when a flying demon monster thing attacked his car," he went on, pointing to Jez. "And there's a reason Sarah only has one eye. No offence." He gestured to Sarah. "She's not joking. This stuff is *fucking dangerous*. She says you can walk away, but I tried and you can't. It's like once you know, the village has got into your head and it won't let you…"

He stopped speaking and shook his head. Theo put his arm around him.

"We don't have to," he said. "We've told Sarah. She says we can go…"

Sam looked up, sharply.

"You don't get it," he said. "I'm sorry, but you don't. Last year, we went on a *website*. Me and Jez. We were there for a minute or two at most. And these things knew and came after us. I would be looking at newspapers in the shop, and they'd fiddle with the text of a newspaper that was *already printed* to send me messages. Once they know you exist, they won't leave you alone."

"He knows that," said Jez. Everyone turned to look at her.

"What?" said Sam. He looked from Jez to Theo.

"He already knows that," said Jez. "Actually," she said to Theo, "you might not. But you sort of do."

"What are you talking about?" said Theo.

"You saw them, right?" said Jez. "You saw the women. Not everyone can, but you did. Like, most people would have been up on the hill watching Sam freak out and they would have thought he was mental or something, but you could see them."

Oh my God, thought Sam. *She's right.*

"I told you," said Jez, looking at Sam. "I saw them by the school gates, but Alex couldn't. You saw them from the classroom window, but Mrs. Crowther couldn't. You can see them, though," she said to Theo. "So some part of Crowsbrook's got to you already. Or something."

"I just moved here," said Theo. "In December."

Jez shrugged. "Anything weird happen to you since you've been here?"

"Only this," said Theo. He looked worried. "I think. What do I do? What do *we* do?"

There was a heavy pause.

"What we can?" said Jez. "That's what we did last time. I mean, we don't really know what we're doing or anything, but it helped that there were more of us. I know you have that thing about no one else knowing," she said to Sarah, "but he already sort of knows, even though he doesn't, because, you know, of what I just said. Can you drive?" she asked Theo.

"Yeah," said Theo. "I don't have a car though."

"'S okay," said Jez. "It just might help, is all." She pushed her hair out of her face. "The women aren't our problem. We have to sort that out soon, but not now. Right now, there's a kid missing and we're trying to find him. We think he's been snatched by a monster. The Ethereal kind. So Thing One is that we have to find him."

"Do we know he's still alive?" said Theo.

"We're hoping so," said Jez. "They don't eat often. Every twenty-five years or so." She looked at Sarah and then back at Theo. "The last time we think this happened and a kid got eaten was a couple of decades ago, and Sarah thinks he was partly eaten alive, which is gross. But it's more fixable than a kid being dead. Plus," she took a deep breath. "A lot of things that don't eat often store their food. Easiest way to keep food fresh over a couple of decades would be to keep it alive for as long as possible."

Sam looked across the room at Sarah. "You're very quiet," he said.

"She's not feeling well," said Jez, quickly.

"They were looking for me," said Sarah, quietly. "The women. I made a mistake."

"Jesus Christ," said Sam. "What did you—"

"It's the blood, death and revenge thing," said Jez. "*Focus*, Sam. Please? Missing kid."

"Well, it's a bit difficult to focus when you—"

"Okay," said Theo. "Okay. Calm down. He said you're a—"

He paused for a moment, working up to the word. "Witch. Can you find the kid with—er—magic?"

Jez smacked her hand against her forehead.

"Seriously?" she said. "You think I wander around collecting bits of Star Mutants as a hobby? That's what that's *for!*" She pointed to the disembodied plastic arm in Sarah's hand.

Theo looked at the arm and then back to Jez.

"Sorry," he said. "I'm having trouble seeing the connection."

"It's sort of like a séance," said Sarah. "You ask the thing to find its owner, and it sort of connects and sends out a signal, like a—I dunno, like a radio beacon? I don't know how it works. I just know how to do it. Mostly we used to use it the other way around. For finding lost things." There was an awkward pause. "I mean, technically, I've never done it this way round before. But, I mean, it should work. In theory."

"That's not how radio works," said Jez. "Just so we're clear." She pointed at the toy arm. "I got this off Carlo Amble. Who gave the rest of it to Jack."

Sam raised his eyebrows. "You got something off an Amble kid? You know everything you own is Mickey's now, right?"

"Who are the Amble kids?" Theo frowned.

"The Amble kids have a bit of a reputation for holding property in common," said Sam. "They'll share everything they own, but if what's theirs is yours, it sort of works both ways."

"Mickey said it was okay," said Jez. "And we had no other op—"

"Mickey Amble?" said Sam. "Seriously? Agent of Chaos Mickey Amble? Sorry, *head* Agent of Chaos Mickey Amble? The potential for this to go horribly wrong and backfire is—"

"Less shitty than a possibly dead kid?" said Jez. "Mickey Amble's is strictly a pranking operation."

"It's different for you," said Sam, stonily. "I prefer being off his radar."

The room fell silent.

"So," said Theo eventually. "What's—what's the deal with the women and the big mistake? If you don't mind me asking. Like, we're all—this is—this is a bit mad, innit? D'you mind me asking?" He half-laughed, embarrassed. "I just don't know what's happening. Or what you'd have to do. To piss them off that much, I mean. I just don't want to do it, you know?" He laughed awkwardly. "Sorry. That was awkward. Whatever you did. I'm sure you're—"

"Someone killed my best friend," said Sarah. "I swore a heavy-duty oath of revenge. Blood and sacrifice. Then I didn't do anything about it, and—" She held up her hands. "Some people didn't like that."

"People say they're going to kill people all the time," said Theo. "But that's just words. Isn't it?" He looked at Sam. Sam's face had frozen.

"These women," he said, slowly. "They're not…they couldn't be."

"They might be," said Sarah, looking him in the eye. "They're the Erinyes."

Sam started shaking his head.

"No," he said. "No, this is insane. They're *gods*. You can't take on gods. You can't."

"No," said Sarah. "You just have to do what you can. I'm not an oracle," she went on, seeing Sam's expression. "I'm not a mage. I'm a witch. My job is to help keep the balance between the mortal world and the Ethereal worlds, and help the people in the village with the borders between the mortal and immortal worlds. Births. Deaths. Finding lost things. I don't know every-thing. The really powerful stuff, the kind that sees you ruling lands and counselling kings? My grandmother just said it wasn't worth messing with. And I've got to be honest with you: I think she was right."

"But you could fix so much!" said Sam. "Injustice and stuff. You can do that kind of magic! You already did!"

"Yeah," said Sarah. "And look where it got me." She stood up. "I don't know what to tell you."

"How are you feeling?" said Theo. "Sorry, I know we've only just met, but it sounds like you have a really difficult job. Are you all right?"

Sarah swallowed the rest of her drink. "I have to be," she said. "I don't have a lot of time to sort things out." She plonked the plastic black and green arm on the table. "Anyone want to see what Galacticor's arm can do?"

Theo shrugged. "This is mad," he said again. "This is like little girls at a sleepover."

"You don't have to stay," said Sarah. "But this isn't a spectator sport. It's make-your-mind-up time. Stay or go: pick one."

Theo didn't move. He shrugged.

"Okay," said Sarah. She pointed at Sam. "There's a black tablecloth in that drawer," she said, pointing. "Clear off the table and cover it. Dump the stuff wherever; floor is fine. Just don't lose my place in any of the books." Sam got up, and Sarah went into the kitchen; after a minute or two, came back with a metal bowl of water inside a larger glass bowl. She placed it on the now-clothed table and gestured. "Pull up a chair," she said. "All of you. I'm going to need all the help I can get with this."

Jez, Sam, and Theo gathered around the table and sat down.

"It's like a séance," said Sarah. "Except we're trying to make a very specific connection. Between Jack and the—" She nodded toward the plastic arm. "Whatever that is. Can someone put it in the water, please?"

Jez picked it up and dropped it in the metal bowl. It made a *plop* sound, and then bobbed to the top and floated. "Is that all right?" she said. It looked ridiculous.

"Yup," said Sarah. "Should be fine." She shifted in her chair and then held up her hands. "We have to hold hands," she said. "It's tradition."

"What does it do?" said Jez. Sarah looked at her.

"It's tradition," she said again. "It's supposed to strengthen the connection."

"I thought the connection was between the thing in the bowl and Jack?"

"That's a different connection," said Sarah. "This isn't an exact science."

"It's not a science," muttered Jez, frowning.

Sarah breathed deeply, but remained patient. "The theory I'm working with," she said, "which is unproven but is based on centuries of esoteric knowledge developed by practitioners in secret—"

"It's never a good idea if you can't see the methodology."

"No," said Sarah. "I see your point. But this is the world that I live in, and this is my job. And I don't have any other ideas."

"Yeah, but—" There was a thud from under the table. *"Ow!"*

"I think what Sarah is trying to say," said Sam, "is that since we have limited time, let's maybe get on with whatever it is we're doing." Jez glared at him from across the table. "Hold hands, you say?" He held up his own, and Theo and Jez clutched them on either side.

"This is the hard part," said Sarah. "You have to focus on connecting the plastic thing in the bowl to Jack. It might help if you—" she pointed at Sarah "—and yes, I know you're going to have to suspend some serious disbelief for this, but it might help if you think of it as *asking* it where Jack is. It won't give you an answer," she said quickly, as she saw Jez open her mouth, "but it'll sort of theoretically strengthen the connection between them. We won't be able to get an answer, but we should be able to hear what's going on between Jack and—" She gestured. "This thing."

"Galacticor," said Jez. "He's a Star Mutant."

"I didn't know you were a fan," said Sam, raising an eyebrow.

"I got a tutorial off Carlo Amble. It was short though. Not sure I could pass a test."

"Yeah," said Sarah, "it's not good for the focusing bit either. Come on. Close your eyes. Breathe. Try to focus."

Jez tried. Part of her brain was telling her the whole thing was stupid. That it wouldn't work. That they were only wasting time. That Mickey Amble was right, and Jack had probably just wandered off and been picked up by one of the nice old ladies in the village who didn't get out much and—

Kept him overnight? Didn't tell anyone, with the police swarming over Crowsbrook like warrior ants?

FOCUS. This is pretty much a last resort.

She tried to ask the bit of plastic where Jack was.

Hi, Galacticor. Arm of Galacticor. You remember Jack, right? He sometimes plays with you. She felt stupid.

You have to TRY.

Okay, she thought, *have to try harder than that.*

We need to find Jack, she thought. *Help us find Jack.* Okay, maybe that was it. Just keep repeating it over and over and over again. *We need to find Jack. Help us find Jack.*

The water bubbled once, as though something had farted in it. Theo jumped.

"Whoa," he said. "What the—"

"Focus," said Sarah, quietly. "We need to find Jack."

We need to find Jack. We need to find Jack. The thought hammered in Jez's mind.

From the bowl around the water came a faint sound.

"What's that?" said Theo. Sarah hushed him sharply.

"Focus," she said. "It's working."

We need to find Jack. We need to find Jack.

A cry came out of the bowl. A child's cry. Sam drew in his breath sharply.

"What the hell?" said Theo.

"It's working," said Sarah again. "Focus. Listen."

The cry came again, a slow wail.

Mummy. I want my mummy.

"Where are you?" whispered Sarah.

Help. I want my mummy.

Jez felt chills run through her. They had found him. They had found someone, anyway. Someone in distress. It had worked.

"Tell me where you are."

It's dark, whimpered the voice. It's dark and wet…

"Where?" said Sarah. "What can you see?"

The voice just sobbed.

Trees. Bushes.

Sarah frowned. "What else?"

Shadows. Shadows like big kids…

The voice was louder and clearer, and Jez jumped.

I can hear you. I want my mummy…

The voice collapsed into sobs again.

"Oh shit," muttered Sarah. "Okay," she said to the voice. "Trees and water. Can you see anything else?"

Big kids.

"What? What do they look like?"

Big kids. Dressed in black.

"Women? Are they ladies? How many are there?"

No. Two. A boy and a girl. They're called Marina and—

Jez opened her eyes a crack and snuck a look at Sam. His eyes were wide open, and his face looked horrified.

"Okay," said Sarah. "We're coming to find you. We're coming. Hold on." She muttered something that sounded like it was in another language, and let go of Theo and Jez's hands. She reached behind her and snapped on the light. "Okay," she said. "You can stop focusing now."

Jez blinked. "What," she said, "the hell? How? What? How could you just leave him there?"

"Because we know where he is now," said Sarah. "We know where he is and we have to get there before anyone else does."

"What?" said Jez. "What?"

"The connection," said Sarah. "If this was science, I would describe it as sort of like an open frequency. A party line, if you like. It's not a private connection, and it basically sends out a sort of meta-signal that says 'hey, every Ethereal in the neighbourhood, something's happening.' They won't know what, unless they listen in, but…" She shrugged. "But we should get moving just in case."

"Right," said Jez. "No. We've done this before. I'm not going without—" She made a stabbing motion. "Pointy things. Weapons."

"*Weapons?*" said Theo. "In *Crowsbrook*? What in the name of guns and gangs—"

"Not *weapons* weapons," said Sam. "We don't have them." He made a vague gesture in the direction of the room upstairs. "Jez means—Sarah has a collection of magic stuff."

Theo nodded slowly.

"This," he said, "is completely mental."

Jez looked at him, hard.

"Yeah," she said. "You said. What's your deal? What's his deal, Sam?"

"I don't know what you mean," said Theo. He looked puzzled.

"Last year," said Jez, "I found out all this stuff was real and it *blew my mind*. I sat in that chair there and fucking *bawled*, and that is not something that I do on a regular basis, here or anywhere else. I told Sam it was real, and first he thought I was attention-seeking and delusional, and then he thought I was mental. But *you*—" she held up a hand "—you, you've just met a bunch of revenge goddesses, and you're just *sitting* there going 'ooh, mad.' Plus, we don't even know why you were able to *see* the stupid goddesses. Not everyone can. We all can, though. Why can you?"

"I don't know," said Theo. "What's your problem, anyway? You're sitting over there glaring at me, glaring at Sam… I'm trying to be nice while it turns out this whole village is bonkers and you're just sitting there going 'bitch stole my best friend—'"

"Oh, for God's s—"

"What? Like that's not true?" Theo gestured to Sam. "He talks about you, you know. Manchester, the bands…and you've totally ignored him for months."

"I did not! *He* ignored *me*!"

"Whatever. You're just having a go because it's not just the two of you anymore. Where are you going?" Theo turned to Sarah, who had got up and was leaving the room.

"Getting weapons," she said. "This is so not any of my business, I can't even start. I'll be back in a mo. With *popcorn*," she said with sudden emphasis. "And if you're not done when I get back, I'm going by myself. That didn't go that well, last time," she said, turning to Theo. "Just so you know." She went upstairs and they heard the click of the door opening and closing.

"Where are we going?" said Theo. "Does everyone know something I don't?"

Jez snorted. "Maybe *Sam* can explain it to you," she said, bitterly. "Except he's a bit upset right now. Wanna know why?"

"Jez, stop being an arse," said Sam. He looked shaken. "Do you *really* want to go back there?"

"No," said Jez. "But we have to. The kid's down there. *Jack's* down there." She shook her head. "Not going is not an option."

"Things," said Sam. "There are going to be things down there."

"Are you worried about 'things'?" said Jez. "Or are you worried about the—" she made air quotes "—'big kids' in black?"

"Fuck *off*, Jez! I don't get how this is all so simple for you! People got hurt! People died!"

"More people would have died if we hadn't stopped it!"

"It was an accident that we did that! We were *lucky!*"

"Luck is *bullshit!*" spat back Jez. "This isn't about *luck*. This is about doing what's right."

"Oh right!" Sam was on his feet now. "Why are you so fucking concerned with saving people when you don't even get that it's human to be afraid? To not to want to do the thing that has to be done, because what you might lose is huge? Have you not almost lost enough? They came after your goddamn family and now you're just like, oh well, as long as I'm doing what I think is right, it doesn't matter who gets hurt because *I'm doing the right thing.* Everyone you want to save is *human*, Jez. You need to start figuring out what that means."

He shook his head and stopped speaking. After a moment, he sat down.

"I just want to stop more people dying," said Jez, quietly. "There isn't a lot we can do about a lot of things, Sam. But this is a thing we can do something about."

"Yeah," said Sam. He sounded choked up. "If *we* don't die. How are you not scared?"

"I am scared," said Jez. She shrugged. "I'm trying not to think about it."

Sarah came back downstairs with a sheet-wrapped bundle of stuff. She plonked it down on the table and it rattled.

"Here you go," she said, unwrapping the sheet. "Pick your— well, not poison. Pointy thing?"

They crowded round the table for a better look. The bow and arrow was there again. So was the bamboo stick with the point and the feathers. Jez picked it up and looked at it.

"Where did this come from?" she said.

"Kettering," said Sarah. "It was made by a Victorian magus who wanted to make it look like what he thought a weapon from somewhere in Africa would look like, so he could scare people in Northamptonshire. Needless to say, he didn't do a lot of research. It's pretty powerful, though." She picked it up and gave it a shake.

"What's it do?" said Sam.

"Stabs people," said Sarah. "But there's a needle in the point that's attached to a vial down *here*—" she indicated with her finger "—that you can fill with your Ethereal poison of choice."

"Not magic, then," said Theo.

"It sort of is," said Sarah. She looked at Jez. "You'll appreciate this. It's supposed to be sixty-seven percent more accurate than a regular pointy thing. If you throw it."

"It's still better if you're a good thrower," said Jez. "That the same?" She pointed to the bow and the quiver of arrows.

"Basically," said Sarah. "Different poisons, but you don't know what you're going to meet down there. There's this." She held up a dagger with a dull grey-blue blade. "Blue slate. If it doesn't kill an Ethereal, it'll at least slow it down a lot."

"What's this?" Theo gestured toward something that looked like a rock on a chain.

"It's exactly what it looks like," said Sarah. "Until you pick it up."

Theo picked it up.

"Holy shit," he said. He passed it to Sam, who looked puzzled and then nodded, and who then passed it to Jez.

The rock was huge. But it was light. It was about the size of a human head, but it weighed just enough so you could swing it on the chain and aim it. Jez almost smiled.

"But it does the damage it looks like it could do, right?" said Jez.

Sarah nodded. "Yup."

"I notice," said Sam, "that none of these are really defensive weapons?" There was a definite question in his voice.

"We don't want to defend ourselves," said Sarah. "We want to go down there, get the kid, and come back out. Jez and I went down there last year with *no* weapons," she said. "And we're still here to tell the tale."

Yeah, thought Jez. *Just.* She thought of the ancient-looking insect-human hybrid that they had fought the previous year and shuddered.

"I still don't understand," said Theo. "Where are we going?"

Sarah looked at the weapons. Sam looked at the floor. Jez looked out the window.

"The Pond," they said, in unison. "The Foxglove Pond."

• • •

Holly was limping now. Constable Waterbury had finally got the message and buggered off, probably because Holly was barely home. Waterbury couldn't keep her there. This was the most important thing she'd ever done. And besides, she had to know.

The feeling gnawed at her insides. The not knowing. The suspecting. Her mind tried repeatedly to game out an impossible situation, and again and again came up blank: *you need more information.* And this was the only way that she had any hope of getting it. Of finding out how this ended.

She needed to know how it ended.

She remembered the first time she'd seen videotapes, back in the eighties. It was one of her earliest memories. Her dad used to make her laugh, winding the tapes back so they could watch the snooker balls come out of the pockets on the table, and skiers skiing up the mountains, and cars going backwards and then running it forward so people in the Old Vic in *EastEnders* were arguing silently at five times the speed of life, and her mum had yelled at her dad to stop *EastEnders*, even though she couldn't hear what was going on, because she didn't want to know what happened before she watched it.

But that was what Holly wanted now. To fast-forward to the end. To know, whatever happened, what it would feel like. Because when you were in it, when something life-shattering happened right in front of you, you had no choice but to deal with it. You could faint, you could scream, you could cry, but you didn't have to live with the heavy grind of uncertainty. You *knew*.

She decided to cut through the churchyard. She frowned. It was unlikely Jack was there (he'd be as likely to be there as any-where, though, wouldn't he?), but she suddenly realized that she hadn't checked it before.

She had only been there once. *Through* there, really, on the narrow, stony path that led to a gap in the laurels on the far side of the church, away from the village centre. She'd been raised Catholic, and the nearest Catholic church was in Castleton. She went there once when she'd first moved to Crowsbrook looking for—well. She didn't know what for. She'd stopped going when she was in secondary school, and at first her mum had been angry and tried to make her, and eventually they reached an uneasy truce where Holly would not go because she was pretending to do homework, and her mum pretended to believe her. In Castleton, she had sat through a Mass that brought her comfort in its familiarity, like an old song from childhood, but little else. She had felt the gulf between what was expected of her and what she actually was too acutely, and had slipped away, holding Jack's hand, as soon as it ended, looking at the floor and pretending not to see the kind smiles and table groaning under cups of tea, coffee, and orange squash.

She had never been back. She couldn't face it. Sometimes, when she thought about it, she didn't even remember why she'd been.

It was coming to her now, though. As she made her way past the ancient stone walls, through the crooked headstones sinking into the soft earth, the wind dropped. The village was still and silent. She looked up at the tower, built like a fortress, with crenellations outlined against the sky. She had read somewhere that it was over eight hundred years old. Eight hundred years. For eight centuries, the people of Crowsbrook had gathered in that place to celebrate. To give thanks. To confess. To meet. To ask for help.

Her feet were burning with pain, and she was cold. She was wet. She realized that she had gone to the church because she didn't know what to do and she felt she had nowhere else to go.

Maybe that was the trick, she thought. It didn't matter if anyone was listening. Or it did, but either way, there was nothing you could do about it. Maybe the trick was to give up trying. To admit that you couldn't do it. To be honest with yourself: to stop trying to drive a car that had no petrol in the tank and was emitting smoke and had at least one flat tire. To stop and ask for help.

Part of her had known this at the tree (*poor old tree*, she thought, *taking a beating for no good reason*). Part of her had known then that she wasn't up to the task. What she was up to was persisting. But she couldn't get it done alone.

You never knew. There might be someone listening.

She closed her eyes.

Help, she thought.

"You'll have to speak up, lass," said a voice nearby.

Holly's eyes snapped open. An elderly man was standing in front of her dressed in a raincoat, a striped pullover, and corduroy trousers. There was a tweed cap on his head and he supported himself with a walking stick. The strangest thing about him, Holly thought, was that he was pale enough to be oddly colourless. Maybe it was the early evening light. He gestured toward his ear.

"Bit deaf," he said.

Holly opened her mouth and then shut it again.

"I—" she said, eventually. "I didn't say anything. Sorry."

"Ah," said the old man, "I thought you wanted help."

Holly's eyes widened.

"I—" she started. "Who—"

"Badgerley," said the old man. "Edgar Badgerley. I look after the churchyard."

"Oh," said Holly, staring. There was something odd about him, but she couldn't quite put her finger on it. "Nice to meet you."

"You want help," said the old man, "you have to ask. And then listen." He shuffled off around the side of the church. Holly stared after him.

"What?" she said out loud. "What? Wait!" she yelled and set off after him at a run. "Wait!"

She rounded the corner of the church.

He wasn't there.

But that wasn't possible. He wasn't moving fast at all and she had been running. She pounded round the next corner of the church.

There was no one there.

Frantically, Holly ran around the church one way and then the other. The old man was nowhere to be found.

"What the fuck!" shouted Holly, not caring all of a sudden that she was cursing in a churchyard. "What the fuck! What is *wrong* with this place?"

"Nothing," said the old man's voice from just around the corner. "I look after the place, in a manner of speaking, and I should know. On that note, please try to avoid verbiage in the churchyard, madam."

Holly went to move. The old man tutted and she stopped in her tracks.

"I told you," he said. "All you have to do is ask."

Holly pelted round the corner and froze.

There was no one there.

It wasn't possible. She burst into tears. She had thought, over the past few days, that she had cried as much as a person could cry. Turned out she was wrong about that as well.

She leaned against the wall of the church and slid down it to the ground.

"Help," she whispered through her sobs. "Help."

The wind picked up again and she shivered. It made a soft sound as it passed through the stones of the belfry above, whispering like a voice on the wind.

Mummy?

It was followed by a sob. Holly felt it like a knife in her chest.

She swung around, straining to hear. Had she misheard? Had she imagined it? She couldn't have. Her heart was pounding.

"Jack," she screamed, as loud as she could. "I can hear you! I'm coming, Jack! Where are you?"

She barely managed to catch the words.

Trees…and water.

And shadows.

She heard him again, unmistakable this time. It was a whimper, but it was enough. She leaped to her feet. She knew where she had to go.

Chapter 13

Allegra Valentine hunted through her ice-white, glass-fronted kitchen cabinet and tutted to herself. No raisins. She wasn't really a huge fan—they were terribly wrinkly, after all, and really quite high in sugar—but Elida Allbright-Nye, her favourite food blogger, was adamant that they added fibre and what she called a "comma of sweetness" to her signature jicama-and-celeriac-root Saturday night supper: just enough to pause briefly and enjoy, but not enough to bring the fine-tuning of one's physiology to a crashing halt. Allegra was about to curse the lack of raisins, then took a deep breath in readiness for calling upon her inner goddess to centre herself, then noticed a small handprint at thigh-height on her stainless-steel fridge.

"Goddammit, Jocasta, you little shit," she muttered to herself.

Inner goddess, inner goddess. It was fine. Everything was fine. It really was fine! You could probably get raisins at the little shop, if it was still open. She never went to the little shop; she found it faintly grubby and the stock had been there for too long, but this was an emergency. And she'd be supporting a local business, albeit one that was overpriced and rather dusty.

Elida was all about supporting local businesses, especially

if they were on Vanuatu, or produced silk-infused face wipes or water bottles with cleansing crystal elements or handcrafted vegan tampons. This was why Elida was Allegra's favourite. She was just so *down to earth*.

They said Gwyneth was a big fan as well.

Okay, then. The little shop.

Jocasta was in the playroom, and Oliver was watching the football highlights in the living room. She told him where she was going and reminded him to check on Jocasta in seven minutes (Allegra did want her to cultivate her independence, but at the same time, safety was important, so she did like to check in with her every ten minutes or so; she had an alarm on her phone to remind her), then she put on her shoes, and left the house.

It was deathly quiet in the village. All you could hear was the wind in the trees and the rain. She shivered as she squelched along. It had always looked so pretty in the photographs, the country-side. She just wished someone had told her about the mud. Not that there was anything wrong with mud; as a spa treatment, you couldn't beat it for exfoliation and external hydration, but there was a difference between artisanal mud and the cheap kind that ruined your Valentinos.

Her foot splashed into a deep puddle and she rolled her eyes.

In the twilight, she saw a figure approaching her and her heart sank. That was the other thing they didn't tell you about. You were always having to *talk* to people you didn't know. *Hello. Nice day. Lovely weather.* As if you didn't have things to *do.* She never knew one small village could have so many old people in it. And a lot of them were poorer than she'd expected as well. She'd never say anything, of course, but *really*, some of them, the way they went about—

The figure moved closer. A man. She recognized him and her heart sank further. It was the odd-job man from the school. One of the local characters. Bit of an alky, she'd heard. Well, Daphne Latimer swore he was always at the Nag's Head, although how Daphne would know was beyond Allegra; she couldn't imagine little Daphne slumming it at the pub. Although they couldn't help it, could they, the alkies? Empathy was *so* important. Still she didn't want to—

He was moving a bit oddly, wasn't he? She hoped he hadn't had a stroke or anything; all she wanted was a bag of raisins, not another evening of sirens and panic. She took a sharp breath. She would do what she had to, of course. A vision floated before her of herself, receiving accolades and commendations in the village for helping a poor old man who had had a stroke; she began to compose a few lines of her speech, but her phone buzzed in her pocket, reminding her to check on Jocasta, and she pulled it out and stared at the screen. She glanced up; he was still coming in her direction. She could always pretend to be texting so she didn't have to—

Her foot made a misstep on the uneven road and she looked up sharply. Her stomach turned to ice.

The man was only a few yards away. His skin was virtually grey and his mouth was hanging open. His clothes were covered in blood and his left sleeve—

Oh shit—

His left sleeve was hanging empty by his side. She could see the outline of the stump inside it as he moved. She knew—it was the blood, the blood all over his clothes—that the loss was recent.

Raw.

She could barely breathe. She stopped moving. Her phone fell from her hand and into the puddle with a dull splash.

The man turned toward her slowly, like someone moving in a nightmare. He looked right through her.

"Evening," he croaked.

He shuffled on past. She could smell the metallic tang of the blood mixed with the smell of unwashed clothes and alcohol.

Allegra Valentine fainted. Her body landed with a thick splash in the non-artisanal mud.

• • •

Once, when Hogarth was small, he had been unable to sleep for a whole night. He had tried to get up and play with his toys—around a quarter past three it must have been because he remembered hearing the big clock in the hall go—but he hadn't been quiet enough, and Ma had got up in her curlers and given him a hiding and told him to go back to bed. But he still couldn't sleep, and he had lain there, wide awake and trying to count sheep until his alarm clock had gone off and he'd had to get up to go to school. He had tried to tell Ma, but she wasn't having any of it, and he had gone off to school with his head feeling like it was stuffed full of cotton-wool and the world looking—wrong. He couldn't say how. It was too bright. Or too colourful. Or just a little bit off, like it wasn't really real. He hadn't been able to put his finger on it. But now, the world looked wrong in the same way. And he was moving through it as if it wasn't real.

The lady had fallen over, but she would probably be okay. He knew her type and they always were. The important thing was to find his friend.

He had been able to hear the noise when he had been in his house; he'd had a sense of where it was coming from. But the further he got from his house, the less he could hear. All he had was the stomach-churning sense of loss and the whistling of the wind.

But it was okay. He would find his friend. He would. He was going to find his friend now, he was.

When you lived with someone for a long time, you knew

what they would do when things were bad. When Ma was upset, she would lock herself in her room, and he could hear her sobbing to herself for hours at a time, and then it would go quiet, and much later, sometimes even the next day, she would come out with her face set and her hair curled and her eyes full of stone, and she would never say a word about it. But he had learned. He could sense, every once in a while, that the clouds were gathering and she was about to head for her room. It was true it was usually preceded by him getting a hiding, but that wasn't the thing that gave it away. There was something in the air. You just knew, after a while.

And he had lived with his friend for a long time, too. Not that this had happened before, of course not, but it was like with Ma: you got a sense of what someone was like, even the parts they didn't readily show you. Especially when they got inside your mind like his friend had done.

It would be all right. He would find his friend again, and he would make the cupboard nice again, and everything would be like it was before. And he would promise that no one would ever come inside the house again. He had made a mistake, but he would make it right. That was the important thing. He needed to make it right. He would say sorry. He would mean it, too. And he would get him all the—

He would get his friend whatever he needed to be happy. He had made his friend unhappy and that was bad. But he could make it right. He could.

His brain floated on a soft cushion of endorphins. His arm still hurt—if he thought about it, he could still feel the part that was missing—but it was almost as if it was a long way away, something that was happening to someone else.

He still couldn't reconcile what he'd seen come out of the cupboard with his friend. The destruction, the violence—no, that wasn't like him at all. But it was fine. It really was. It didn't matter, because it was just a one-off anyway. It wouldn't happen again. Savaric was gone, and he wouldn't come back, not if he knew what was good for him, and he had been right and Savaric had been wrong, and he wouldn't let anyone in his house ever again, not if he got his friend back. He was probably misremembering the thing that had come out of the cupboard. Trick of the light. The shock of it. There would be a good reason. Maybe he had made a mistake. That wasn't the friend that lived in his head and soothed him and looked after him.

Why are you going where you're going?

That was the voice in his head that he tried to ignore. That he mostly did ignore. Didn't have anything sensible to say. Why shouldn't he go and look for his friend?

Because you know where he's gone. But you don't know why. But you know you wouldn't go down there otherwise.

It would probably be fine. He hadn't been there since he was little. It was probably different now.

Didn't like it much then, did you?

Ma had taken him down to the pond to feed the ducks, except there weren't any ducks, only crows. There was a flock of them down on the ground and he had run over to look at them and they had all flown away and he had found out what they were all doing there: there was a dead hare lying on the ground with its insides on the outside and they'd all been picking at it. He screamed, and one of the crows had cawed at him from a nearby branch, raw meat stuck to its beak.

Ma had told him not to be so mardy and had marched him home with his arm in an iron grip.

"I try and do nice things for you," she'd said, "and all I get is grief."

He had tried. But there were no ducks.

Maybe there were ducks now. There could be. It had been years.

The ducks weren't important, though. He was going to the pond to find his friend.

• • •

"Is this the quickest way to the pond?" Sarah didn't think it was, but she was still relatively new to the village and she couldn't swear to all its secret shortcuts.

"No," said Jez, striding ahead. "It's not, but I want to go past Hogarth Merrick's house just in ca—holy *shit*," she concluded, stopping in her tracks and staring straight ahead.

"Where's…" Sarah's voice trailed off as she followed Jez's gaze. "Oh."

They took in the smashed door, with the planks still dangling in the breeze and the door creaking on its hinges in the wind.

"Okay," said Jez. "Okay. It doesn't mean—"

"How big would you say that hole was?" said Sarah. "About the size of a large sheep? You were the one who wanted to go past Mr. Merrick's in the first place."

"You can't assume—"

"Nope," said Sarah. "But we can get a move on. Look at it this way: it doesn't prove anything. But it doesn't disprove our theory either."

"I don't like this," muttered Sam. "I don't like this at all." They had wrapped the spear in a pillowcase to avoid funny looks, but Sam was gripping it, ready to spring without unwrapping it.

Theo took a few steps toward the door. Sam grabbed his arm.

"What are you doing?" he demanded.

"It's raining," said Theo. "If there was someone home, and they could do anything about it, the door would be closed. We should make sure no one's hurt."

"What about the kid?" said Jez.

"It'll only take a moment," said Theo. "Seriously. You coming?"

"No," said Sam. He looked hurt and then sighed. "But I can keep an eye on things out here. I'll yell if anyone from the Neighbourhood Watch shows up." Theo opened his mouth to say something, but Sam shook his head, and he closed it again. Sam nodded his head toward the open door. "Go on," he said. "We haven't got a lot of spare time."

"Thanks, Sam," said Sarah. She stepped inside the house, with Jez and Theo close behind.

The first thing that hit them was the smell: like the windows hadn't been opened for decades, while the rest of the house grew a film of mould and dust and sweat. Jez coughed and covered her mouth and nose with her sleeve while they looked around in horror. The place was falling apart. A thick layer of dust lay over everything, and the carpet was threadbare. There was a horribly familiar, coppery note in the thick air.

"Brace yourselves," said Sarah. They turned into the kitchen.

"Holy *shit*," said Theo.

Gouts of dark red blood were splattered over the kitchen walls and worktops and over the floor. A trail of blood led out of the kitchen and toward the back of the house.

"This is mad," said Theo. "What kind of place *is* this?"

Jez ignored him.

"We have to follow that, right?" she said, flatly, gesturing toward the ground. "Just to check."

Sarah nodded. Jez shrugged. They headed toward the laundry room, with Theo following. The smell was growing worse.

Sarah opened the door, and shuddered when she saw the scene in front of her. Jez cried out. The blood. The iron, with bits of human meat still sticking to it.

"Holy shit," said Theo again. "What the hell happened here?"

"Home cauterization," said Jez, staring at the iron.

Sarah looked faintly sick.

"Would that even work?" said Theo. His face was contorted with horror.

Jez swallowed.

"Probably not," she said. "I mean, he gets points for thinking. But there's no way an electric iron would get hot enough to do it properly. The metal has to be, like, glowing; I don't know what temperature it has to be because they don't really do it anymore; it's really something you would only do if you were out of other options, because it doesn't—it's a bit of a gamble, right, because you're basically, you can make stuff worse *really* easily if the metal's not hot enough, which it wouldn't have been and…*fuck*, that's horrible." She looked at the floor and back to the iron. "Okay, he's not here. Let's go."

They made their way back out to the front door, past the foot of the stairs.

"What about upstairs?" said Theo. "What if he died in bed?"

"Then there's nothing we can do to help him," said Sarah. "We can come back for dead people when we're sure everyone who's alive is okay."

Theo hesitated. He glanced up the stairs. Sarah shrugged.

"If it'll make you feel better," she said. She swung herself around the newel post at the bottom of the stairs and started up them, with Jez and Theo in hot pursuit.

"The blood doesn't go up the stairs," she yelled over her shoulder. "So there's probably no one…" She got to the top of the stairs and paused. "Bathroom," she said, pointing to the open door. "Bedrooms." The other two doors were closed.

"Closed doors," said Theo. "Great."

"Stick together," said Sarah. "It'll be safer."

Theo gestured across the tiny landing. "How far apart can we get?"

"Seriously, mate," said Jez. "If the village witch tells you to do something because it'll be safer than not doing it, you probably want to listen. Even if you're not in Crowsbrook." She turned to Sarah. "Bathroom?"

They crammed into the tiny room. It smelled of damp and the ceiling was covered in mould. There was a pile of damp towels on the bathmat.

"Jesus," said Theo. "How do you let your pad end up like this?"

Sarah was staring into the bath.

"What does Hogarth Merrick look like, Jez?" she said. "How long's his hair?"

Jez frowned. "I dunno. Not long. Short. He's a bit thin on top, I think. I haven't seen him in a while."

Sarah pulled a long strand of hair from the bath.

"One of two things," she said. "Either something happened that has nothing to do with any of this, and we're currently covering a crime scene in our DNA or—" she held up the hair to the light "—someone with long hair came into this house and the poggelin didn't react well to it." She looked at Jez and Theo. "Maybe I'm biased. But my money's on the latter."

She moved over to the mirror, holding the long hair between her thumb and finger, and staring at the image. Jez watched her, realization growing.

"No," she said. "Seriously?" She moved closer to Sarah and both of them peered into the mirror. It reflected the two of them, and the delicate pincer of Sarah's fingertips holding nothing at all.

"No," said Jez again, with wonder. "This is *physics*." She pressed her face closer to the mirror. Sarah moved her hand forward. There was nothing there. Jez turned her face, and the long black strand hung limply from Sarah's hand.

"He was here, wasn't he?" said Jez. "Savaric?"

"Who?" said Theo. "Also, what the hell is a poggelin? It sounds like a retro toy."

"It's a—" Sarah started.

"Monster," said Jez. "Different kind from earlier. Also, Savaric Osbourne's a vampire. Welcome to Crowsbrook. Bedrooms?" She stomped out.

"Is she always like this?" said Theo to Sarah.

Sarah shrugged. "No," she said. "And yes." They followed Jez out of the bathroom and across the tiny landing where she was waiting outside one of the closed doors.

She's learned, thought Sarah. Jez made eye contact with her, and she nodded. Jez opened the door.

The curtains in the bedroom were open, but Sarah thought it probably wouldn't have made a lot of difference if they hadn't been. They hung in rags from a rusted rail. The bedsheets were in holes.

"What the hell is this?" said Jez, picking up a tattered, holed garment from the floor. "Dressing gown?" She held it at arm's length and grimaced.

"Everything is so fucked up," said Theo. "How do you live somewhere this small and not have people notice that all your stuff is falling apart?"

"People see what they want to see," said Sarah. "Magic makes it easier for them to do that. If there was a monster living in your home, wouldn't you do your best not to see it? And to make sure that no one else saw it either? *Especially* in a place the size of Crowsbrook?"

Jez and Theo were silent.

"Well," said Jez after a while. "No one's hurt in here. One more room to go."

They crossed the landing and Sarah turned the handle on the

third bedroom door. She felt it grind and pushed the door with her hand. It didn't move.

"What?" said Jez. "Is it locked?"

"I don't think so." Sarah frowned. She pushed harder. The door didn't budge.

Jez's stomach sank.

"This isn't good, is it?" she said.

"I don't know," said Sarah. "I really don't."

Jez pulled her phone out of her pocket and tapped the screen. It lit up. She still had a fifty percent charge.

"Whatever's going on here," she said, "it's probably not a monster. So there's that."

"You have an app for that?" said Theo. "What kind of village is this?"

"They drain the batteries," said Sarah. "Anything Ethereal drains the batteries. It's probably a thing you should know if you live here and want to stay living here."

"And anything Ethereal is magic?" said Theo. "Right?"

"Magical," said Sarah, putting her shoulder to the door. "Or monstrous." She gave it a shove. "I think it shifted a bit."

"One more good one," said Theo, and put his hand on the door. They pushed together and the door burst open with a grunt. A thick cloud of dust billowed from the floor and moved upward. Jez coughed.

"No one's run the Hoover round here in a while," said Sarah. She pushed the door open further.

The three of them looked in on a woman's bedroom. The curtains were closed. There was a single bed, perfectly made in the centre. There was a shiny pink bedspread on it. It was old-fashioned and had been mended in a couple of places, and it was covered in a thick layer of dust. There was a dressing table made of dark wood pushed up against the wall; it had a big mirror and a little stool pushed underneath it. There was a powder jar on it made of blue glass, and four perfume bottles, and a tarnished silver lipstick case, and one crumpled tissue.

"Whoa," said Theo, stepping in and looking around. "Everything's not…fucked up."

Jez looked for the light switch and flipped it. A soft golden light filled the room, filtered through a heavy glass shade.

"Whoa," said Theo again.

Everything was covered in dust. Years of dust. Jez crossed to the dressing table and picked up the lipstick case. It left a stencil of its form in the dust. She blew the dust off the case and put it back, fitting it carefully into the space it had come from. The drifting dust irritated her nose and eyes. She winced and sneezed.

"What the…" said Sarah.

"It's got to be his mum's room," said Jez. She opened one of the drawers in the dressing table. It was full of carefully folded pairs of tights. She closed it and opened another. Piles of underwear. "Oh," she said, and quickly closed it. She opened another. "This stuff hasn't been touched for decades. Ah!" She shouted as a spider ran across her hand and made her jump. "Jeez," she said to Sarah. "You can't keep them under control?" The spider ran across the top of the dressing table and stopped next to an envelope. It was covered in dust, like everything else, and had yellowed with age. Someone had ripped it, and its contents, into two pieces.

"What?" said Theo.

"It's like he just closed the door and that was it," said Jez, still opening and closing drawers.

"Technically," said Theo, "everyone's okay and we're now breaking and entering. Why are you talking about spiders?"

"Door was open," said Jez, not looking at him. "We wanted to check everything was all right." She opened a jewellery box. Green stones glittered in the yellow light.

"And now you're going through the jewellery?" said Theo. "Twenty minutes ago you were all, 'Holy shit, kid in danger, come on Sam, get your shit together, let's go rescue kids,' and now you're going through a dead woman's stuff for reasons unknown while Sam freezes his arse off in the rain outside. Why—"

Sarah tuned them out and watched the spider. It zigzagged across the dressing table and stopped at the letter.

Sarah picked up the pieces of the letter, turned them over, and felt a jolt in her stomach. The envelope was addressed to Augusta Merrick, but the handwriting was a familiar, tiny, spider-like scrawl.

Dot didn't write to people unless it was important, and both she and Augusta were dead. Sarah slipped the two halves of the note out of the neat slit in the top of the bisected envelope and read the letter through quickly. Her eyebrows shot up.

"Okay," she said, putting the pieces of the letter back in the torn envelope and the bits back in the rectangle they had left in the dust. "Put everything back the best you can and let's go."

"What's with the—"

"Explain later," said Sarah, as Jez put the box back in the drawer and closed it with a thud. "Now help me get this door shut."

They nearly managed it, but it wouldn't close all the way. Jez was pulling at the door handle when there was a shout from downstairs.

"Oi," yelled Sam up the stairs. "You might want to get down here."

Jez shot down the stairs, with Sarah and Theo in hot pursuit.

"Are there people?" said Jez, bounding out of the broken door and a few metres down the road and back, just in case. "Is anyone coming?"

"No," said Sam. "But this woman just freaking *ran* past here heading along the main road to the pond, and I'm pretty sure she's not getting ready for the parkrun. It was like something was on fire." He looked at Sarah and pointed across the field. "Shortcut to the pond is that way. Long way is that way." He swung around and pointed along the road. "That's the way she went."

Sarah looked at them.

"Okay," she said, and pointed to the field. "Apparently the shortcut's that way."

Chapter 14

Jez didn't want to go down to the pond.

It had been four months but she remembered it like it was yesterday: the anticipation of going down to the place where two people from her school had been murdered, her heart thumping and her chest tightening with anticipation of what she would see. Blood mixed with the mud and the water? Rags of flesh caught on the thick branches by the water's edge? It had seemed unlikely. They didn't—the authorities, whoever was in charge of that sort of thing—didn't usually leave that sort of stuff lying around after all. But that had been the most unnerving thing: when they arrived at the top of the footpath that wound its way down the steep slope to the dark water at the bottom of the hill, there had been a bit of police tape, and that had been all… no officers, no investigation, nothing that suggested anyone human cared at all. And they had made their way slowly down the slippery, muddy footpath virtually in silence, and they had got to the bottom and Jez had asked Sarah something, just a normal question, she didn't even remember what it was now, and Sarah had shut her up sharply, staring across the pond like a mentalist. Jez had followed her gaze, had looked where she had pointed and—

Christ. It had been horrible. It was one of the things that tore through her mind while she was asleep. And it had hurt her father badly, to make a point.

But was that even the worst of it? It had been trapped in the pond for hundreds of years. Jez didn't know much about monsters or magic or any of the other things that shouldn't exist and somehow did anyway. But she knew chemistry, and she knew physics, and she knew that there wasn't much that could be submerged in water for centuries and not lose at least a few molecules, contaminating the purity of the fluid around it.

It wasn't a comforting thought.

• • •

Sam didn't want to go down to the pond.

Granted, he hadn't been there when Jez had first gone down there with Sarah, and seen…well, he hadn't been able to believe her for the longest time because it just sounded mad.

And then he'd found out it wasn't mad.

He'd seen things that weren't possible. A demon had flown out of the woods he'd driven through a thousand times and more and attacked the car they were travelling in, and he'd seen it turn to dust once Sarah had killed it.

He had gone up there one time a couple of months after, with Theo, looking for some privacy. He hadn't said what had happened there—he wasn't stupid, he knew how it would sound— but there was nothing growing there. Even in the winter, with the leaves rotting brown on the ground and the frost hanging heavy on the spider webs, you could see where the thing had died, if you knew how it had fallen and remembered the shape of its leathery wings.

Jez drove him nuts. And she was right, of course she was: you had to stand up to things that weren't right. It was just that when you grew up in Crowsbrook, you sort of grew up with an understanding that even if you felt like you might be prepared to die for a cause, you probably wouldn't be called upon to actually do it.

It was different for Sarah. She'd grown up knowing about this stuff.

And it was different for him than it was for Jez. Her family had been attacked, as a warning. He had been hurt himself. His arm still wasn't right. He could use it again, but it still hurt. There were other things that could happen to you, apart from being killed. You could lose people. People that you had thought it would be impossible to lose because it would hurt too much. More than any human—maybe more than any Ethereal—could handle.

And Sarah knew that as well as either of them.

• • •

Theo didn't want to go down to the pond.

He couldn't put his finger on why. Of course, he saw the way that Sam tensed up when the pond was mentioned, and the way that Jez tried to bullshit her way through her obvious fear, and that Sarah (the village witch? Jesus Christ, where had he moved to?)—Sarah, the only adult—took all of this stuff seriously.

And looked unnerved.

But there was something beyond that. Something he couldn't put his finger on. It was—okay, it felt mental to even think it, but it felt like something he couldn't see was pressing on his stomach to try to stop him moving forward.

He was feeling a bit sick to be honest. Because it was like a weird and stupid role-playing game, except he'd seen those things up on the field, and Sam had said that things like that were a thing in the village, and now it didn't feel like his parents had moved to the middle of nowhere anymore. It felt like his parents had moved into the middle of a war zone, and they hadn't even noticed.

He remembered when he was small and had been scared of the monsters in his cupboard, and his mum had told him not to be silly. And his gran had looked at him, when he nearly fell asleep over his tea of bread and cheese and lettuce and beetroot (she called it a "help yourself" tea, because everything was in little dishes on her table, and that was just what you did). She looked at him and she saw how he wasn't sleeping, and she phoned her friend Mrs. Thomas, and Mrs. Thomas had come over and looked at him, without smiling, and had poked around in his cupboard while his mum was out, and had burned some things that smelled funny, and had exchanged some meaningful glances with his gran, and after that, he'd been able to sleep better, because the monsters had gone, after that.

And he hadn't thought about that for years, because it was daft, wasn't it: believing in monsters in your cupboard when you were a kid. You knew it was made up, even if you didn't understand it. Because it had to be. Because that was the only bit of your life that was like that. Because everyone went out of their way to tell you that things like that weren't real, even when you read about them in books or saw them on the telly or in games. You knew it wasn't real. It couldn't be real.

But he'd seen the way his gran looked, and he knew when she was joking and when she wasn't. And when he'd said there was a monster in his cupboard, her face said that she knew that it was real.

Her expression had been a lot like Sarah's.

• • •

Sarah didn't want to go down to the pond.

There was a knot in her stomach that had nothing to do

with getting stabbed. The pond was a place where there was heavy-duty magic, and its magic was…well, it was like watching an animal that was nervous, getting ready to defend itself. When you saw a dog prowling with its hackles up and its teeth bared, you didn't go and scratch its head and give it a treat.

She knew it would be bad. It had been bad before. You did what you had to do. She just didn't want the kids to get hurt. The stuff from the trunks would protect them a bit, but any fight was unpredictable.

Why are they here, then? Why did you let them come?

That was the thing, though. She hadn't "let" them come. They'd come anyway. And Sam didn't even want to, but somehow Jez had talked him into it. Peer pressure was a bugger.

It was like before. They had known they could walk away, but they hadn't done it. She knew she probably shouldn't feel grateful, but she did.

One monster. Four humans. What could possibly go wrong?

Everything. The answer was *everything*, and then some. Because the point was not the monster. The monster was the thing that was in the way of getting to the kid. And the kid was the point. If the kid was still alive.

Intradimensional monsters were tricky. They could use space in ways that humans couldn't; their laws of physics were different. Jack was down by the pond: he'd told them so himself. That wasn't the problem.

The problem was that he might not be in the same reality as they were.

She felt for the handle of the slate dagger under her coat, drew it, and gripped it, low and ready to cut. Slate could do a lot of damage to things in the magical world. She just wasn't sure if one of those things was the fabric of reality itself.

• • •

Jack didn't want to be at the pond even though Marina and Gareth were nice. Marina sang him a song about Halloween and said it was her favourite time of year and asked what his favourite time of year was. That was easy. Christmas. He liked the lights and the smells and the tree and Father Christmas coming down the chimney. He wasn't sure how it all worked but he wasn't complaining. Halloween was okay, but sometimes the shops were a bit scary.

"Can we go?" he said. "We can go to my house." Sometimes in stories it was scary when ghosts were in your house, but he knew Gareth and Marina now, and they wouldn't run around with sheets on, going "Wooooooo!" or anything. And he was pretty sure that he could find his way back to his house from the pond. He'd only been down to the pond once before, but he remembered where you turned off the road and went down the footpath, and he'd been past that bit hundreds of times. Maybe thousands. And he knew how to get from there to his house.

He hadn't tried standing up yet. Marina had put a scarf over his foot and he couldn't see what it looked like. But if he couldn't walk on it, then someone could carry him.

"I can show you where I live," he said. His mummy could make everybody tea.

Gareth looked at him sadly. He looked up and across the dark pond and up the hill, where the trees stood out against the black sky.

"We'd love to," he said. "That sounds really nice. But we can't go too far away from the pond. It won't let us."

It wasn't enough that there was no day and no night. There was nowhere to go and nothing to do: they didn't need to eat; they didn't need to sleep. All they had was time.

Gareth worked on poems in his head; they kept him sane.

Marina sang songs that she used to like, working her way through one album at a time, trying to remember the arrangements even as the memories faded.

The boredom was excruciating.

Jack frowned. "Why? Is there a fence?"

"We don't know," said Gareth. He looked at Marina. "If we knew that—"

Jack's face began to crumple and his heart sank. "I want my mummy," he said. His voice wobbled.

"I know, I know," said Marina. "I—"

They heard a low growl rumble through the stillness, not close, but moving toward them. Marina and Gareth snapped their heads up to look in the direction it came from.

"Shit," whispered Gareth. He looked around rapidly. "We have to hide him. We have to."

"What's happening?" whimpered Jack.

"It'll be all right," said Marina, though she didn't sound sure. "It'll be all right. But we need to find you a hiding place, and you need to stay still and quiet."

The sound rumbled again. This time it was definitely closer.

"It's that thing," said Gareth. "Whatever it was that took him in the first place. It's coming back."

• • •

If it was going to be anywhere, Savaric knew, it would be down by the pond.

He had hightailed it out of bloody Hogarth's house as soon as the thing had smashed its way out of the bloody cupboard under the stairs; he'd seen what had happened to Hogarth and he wasn't up for spending his next three years regrowing a limb. Too much energy; too much explaining.

And besides, it would be *embarrassing*.

It was bad enough that he was having to do a fast rethink on his upcoming arrangement with the bloke in the city. He'd been doing small jobs since he'd found the Bag'un (what a stupid bloody name, couldn't fathom why it was stuck in his head). He couldn't lose this opportunity.

It was the Devil's own luck this village was so quiet. He'd made a beeline for the pond and shot up a tree (the claws came in handy sometimes) and pulled his coat around him until he was well hidden and sat completely still so he could *think*.

And wait. If there was anywhere it would go, it would be down here. And he wasn't going to bloody miss it. There was a bag in his pocket with that thing's name on it. And he had his umbrella. And his cosh, hidden in his cuff. The bloody thing was practically bulletproof, unless you knew its weak spots. And he did, since he'd pretty much created them.

It wasn't really so much spots as a spot.

Bloody hell. He hated not being able to use a mobile phone. He was used to it, but it pissed him off, seeing them everywhere and not being able to use one. Right now, he had a meeting in the city in twelve hours and he had no way of letting his contact know that he might be running late. It would have been fine when the world moved slower; he had nothing but time, after all. But now…now things were different.

It wasn't two separate worlds anymore. And his world was having to speed up. And if he didn't adapt, he'd be left behind.

He felt in his pocket. The stone was still there. He had checked it, to see if he could figure out what was going on, but it was dark.

The thing didn't have a friend, and it didn't have a stone. It was going to go where the nearest concentration of magical energy was. And that was the pond.

How did he know? That was what he had done, hadn't he? There were things you learned, over the years.

He crouched in the crook of the tree and looked down at the pond. There was nothing. Just dark water and mud and dead-looking trees. He was lucky there weren't any leaves. The branches by themselves were thick enough.

He sat there and waited. It would come there eventually.

He hoped that it would be sooner rather than later.

• • •

Holly's feet thudded against the ground as she ran toward the pond. She didn't even feel them anymore.

She didn't know what had happened at the church. It didn't matter. She didn't give a shit. She had been told to go down to the pond. Jack was by the pond. He had been without her for so long, on his own, out in the world. Outside? Had he been outside all this time? She couldn't think of him outside for all this time, cold and alone, and with no snacks and no Walter Bear and vulnerable and…she couldn't think of it. She couldn't. She just had to find him and take him home.

She could feel Walter Bear's bulk in her backpack as she ran along the roads toward the break in the woods that marked the footpath down to the pond. Her lungs burned.

There it was. There was the gap. She glanced across the road without stopping; it didn't matter, she couldn't hear anything coming, it was fine. In an instant, she was across the road and slipping and sliding down the path toward the pond.

It was starting to get dark. She lost her footing, slipped, twisted her ankle, and went down on one knee in the mud on the hill. *Ouch.*

"Jack!" she shouted. "Jack, I'm coming!"

Was that a response? She listened hard.

"Jack!" she shouted again.
There was something. She scrambled down the hill.
It didn't sound like Jack.
But it sounded like *voices*.

Chapter 15

In the darkness, the ugly growling sound grew closer. Marina drew Jack to her.

"It's okay," she said. "It's okay." She wasn't sure it would be. She was dead already, but Jack wasn't. At least, she didn't think he was. He felt alive. She couldn't explain it, except that he felt different than Gareth. Gareth was all spirit. Jack was more solid; more vital. Her head snapped up and she looked around.

Something glinted above her. She looked up, sharply. Glowing in the air, almost as if picked out by a black light, was the shape of a dagger.

"Look!" She stood up. The dagger was at waist height.

"What the hell?" muttered Gareth. "What is it?"

"I don't know," said Marina. "A knife? It looks sharp. Maybe we can do something with it, if it's real. As, like, a weapon. Or something. I don't know." The growling sound came again. "Grab it!"

Gareth reached for the handle of the knife. The strange light around it grew brighter for a moment. He moved his hand toward it tentatively. The finger on his right hand that was only bone tapped against it with a *clack*. His fingers closed around it, lightly at first and then more firmly.

He pulled.

• • •

Sarah felt the knife jerk. She tugged at it; it felt like someone was holding it. She moved carefully, until she was holding it in front of her. It still felt like someone was holding it. Tentatively, she let it go.

The knife stayed where it was, stuck in the air.

Huh.

She gave it an experimental twist. There was a sound like the rending of thick canvas, and a black mark appeared above the blade. She frowned, bent down, and peered closer.

An eye peered back at her. She stepped back and swore, almost letting go of the knife. It sank a little deeper into the whole.

Her grandmother had taught her always to introduce herself. It took your mind off your mortality, albeit briefly.

"Hi," she said, clearly. "I'm Sarah Trevelyan. Witch. You?"

The eye blinked.

"You can hear me?" he said. Definitely a *he*. The eye vanished for a moment. "There's someone there," Sarah heard him say. "They can hear. I can talk to them."

"Hello?" said Sarah. "Hi. Bit of a rush here. Looking for a small child and possibly a monster."

"You can hear me!" The voice sounded delighted. "This is amazing! Are you alive? Are you in the real world?"

"One of them," said Sarah, cautiously. "Yes. Alive. Land of the living."

"We died," said the voice. "Here. We died at the pond."

Sarah's eyes grew wide. She rummaged through her brain. The kids. The kids from the pond. It had to be. Ghost stories were as old as time: when you died violently and unfairly, there was something in the place where you died that kept you there unless someone managed to make things right. When you died violently and unfairly because of magic…

Well, you had to hope that it happened somewhere nice.

"Gareth?" The name rose to the surface of her mind.

"Yes!" The voice was excited now. "Did you say you were a witch? Can you get us out of here?"

"Maybe," said Sarah. "Don't know. Maybe in a bit. Looking for a kid at the moment; bit of a long story. There's a chance the kid may be where you are. Have you seen him?"

"Yeah," said the voice. It was serious, with the lightest touch of disappointment. "He's here. We think he's alive. He's not like us. How do we get him to you?" The eye turned away again. "We think there's something bad coming."

Sarah pursed her lips and whistled. Her grandmother had also taught her about the power of educated guesses and calculated risks.

Then there were the guesses in the dark and the risks that you had to take without knowing what would happen.

"Pull down," she said. "Pull down hard. We have to cut—"

She stopped herself. Cutting reality would be bad.

"Just keep hold of the knife," she said, "and pull down. Hard."

She gripped the hilt of the dagger hard.

"Three," she said. "Two. One."

She pulled down hard and felt an equal force on the other side of the blade. There was a tearing sound, and then a rushing wind through the gap as she crouched.

Light poured into Gareth and Marina's space as if a curtain had been pulled apart. The trees in silhouette vanished, and were replaced by light; Marina blinked and narrowed her eyes. She saw that the trees were real on the other side.

Sarah's mouth was open as she pushed the soft edge of the

tear to one side, and peered through the dimensions. She saw two pale teenagers and a five-year-old in the darkness.

"Push him through!" she shouted. "Get him over here!"

Gareth let go of the knife, gobsmacked. Sarah tried to move it and couldn't.

"Help me!" she yelled. "We have to do this together!"

The roaring came again; it was almost on top of them. Gareth glanced over his shoulder. A single eye glittered and blinked in the light. He turned around, and they pulled the knife to the ground.

Everything that happened, happened fast.

"NOW!" shouted Sarah. Gareth grabbed her wrist and they pulled the knife downward; Gareth's fingers became mist in the light. He pulled his arm quickly back into the darkness. The poggelin roared with rage. Marina pushed Jack through the widening gap. He was filthy. Theo darted forward and snatched him up as the poggelin paused between dimensions.

It blinked and squinted, grunting with surprise and discomfort, turning away from the sudden brightness.

• • •

Jez felt a jolt of fear. This was what they were up against—

—this time.

She gripped the bamboo spear with both hands and pointed it in the direction of the monster, feeling the adrenaline course through her. Sure, it was bigger than a fly. But the stick was bigger than a fly swatter, and a lot pointier. And you could do a lot of damage with pointy things.

She looked at the monster. It blinked again, its snakelike pupil contracting fast. It turned its head slowly, still blinking.

Jack.

Jez realized it was looking for Jack. She made the beginnings of a sideways dart, to hide the boy, or to move him or to tell him to run, and slammed on the brakes as soon as she realized that moving in his direction would only draw attention to him. She froze, mind racing, spear braced.

Everything paused for a fraction of a second. It felt like a lifetime.

• • •

Sam stared open mouthed into the tear in the world. It was as if the scene around him—the pond, the trees, the grey sky—had all been a colour photograph, printed on canvas and stretched across a frame that covered something unbelievably dark. And now the knife had slashed through the screen—a piece of it was flapping in the winds that seemed to rush through from the other side—and he could see a dark and eerily lit version of the scene around him through the tear, as if it was only the light leaking through the rift from Sam's world that illuminated the world on the other side.

He could hear voices from the other side.

He blinked, his mind struggling with half-remembered ideas that Jez had told him about from books she had read about theoretical physics and dimensions and string theory, and peered into the rift. There were faces on the other side. Faces that were strangely familiar. Jez had never said anything about faces.

Oh no.

The realization felt like a punch in the gut and he flinched. His mouth fell open and his breathing became shallow as he recognized the pale faces of Gareth Lake and Marina Butterworth. He cried out involuntarily.

• • •

Jez's gaze snapped over to Sam and then to where he was looking. She gasped.

Gareth and Marina. The dead Goth kids. She hadn't been friends with either of them, really, and she'd stayed away from the people who joined their suddenly expanding group of post-life friends, but it had been unnerving and sickening to have something so violent, so final, happen so close to where she ate and slept and studied and hung out with Sam...

Oh no. Sam...

She glanced over at Sam. He was staring, horrified, into the gap, his face a rictus of disbelief and terror. Sam had been in love with Gareth and had taken his death badly. Very badly. And this...to see him again when he had started to recover...

Shit.

Jez glanced around frantically for Theo. He was standing beside a large oak tree, holding Jack in one arm with the rock raised in his other hand, eyes wide. She dashed over and shook him by the shoulder.

"Get Sam," she said urgently. "Get him away from..." She gestured toward the tear. "That thing, whatever it is. Get him away from it."

"What is it?" said Theo. "Is it dangerous?"

"Don't know," said Jez, quickly. "Probably. It is for Sam, though."

"Why?"

"It's complicated," said Jez. "Just grab him and take him further away from it than he is now. Not too far away from Sarah. I can explain later. It has to be you."

Theo just stared at her. Jez gave him a push. "Now! Go! He'll listen to you! Go!"

• • •

Sam was still staring into the hole. Adrenaline was coursing through him. He hadn't believed it when he first saw it—and he'd seen a lot of things he hadn't wanted to believe since Sarah first came to the village—but this one had kicked the air out of him.

Gareth Lake. Seeing him felt like the moment the track dropped away beneath a rollercoaster you were on by accident.

He felt sick.

There was an arm around his shoulder.

"Come on," said Theo. "Come with me." He motioned with his head. "Come on. We can go—"

"No," croaked Sam in a barely audible voice. "I should—" He pointed toward the tear.

There was a sound from across the pond; the sound of someone crashing through the bushes.

• • •

"Jack!" screamed Holly from the other side of the pond as she began to run toward the group.

Instinctively, Sarah, Jez, Sam, and Theo turned toward Holly. Jack started to scream for his mum.

• • •

This was it, Savaric knew. This was his moment. The Bag'un was disoriented; well, he could understand that. It had just crossed the boundaries of a dimension; it was blinking, stupidly sniffing for its prey. Savaric ended up with a headache if he spent too much time near the boundaries of a dimension. He'd put up with that and a lot more tonight, though, if he could get the thing back.

He dropped out of the tree behind the poggelin and dove onto it, trying to grab it in a wrestling hold. He had the bag with him, but the damn thing was strong, and it was big: like a long-lived plant that had just spent twenty years in a perfect greenhouse. Savaric was stronger than any strong human, but he knew he was in for a fight: the creature beneath him thrashed and growled, growing used to the light. He was sure he could have it, though: he moved the bag to cover its eye and—

"YOU!" roared Hogarth, crashing through the trees, one arm and one stump reaching madly forward. He launched himself toward Savaric and caught him in a broadside; Savaric lost his grip on the poggelin, and fell under Hogarth's momentum. Hogarth punched him hard in the face and Savaric saw stars.

He was *annoyed* now.

"Hogarth, you pointless twatbadger!" he yelled, rolling over and clouting Hogarth on the side of his head before he could have another go. "Get the goddam—" He looked around frantically, scrabbling to get purchase in the mud.

Shit. The thing was fast. It was too far away for him to grab again, and it was wary of him now.

It wouldn't like being around all these people either.

The monster lurched forward toward Jack, single-minded and bristling, teeth bared. Jez lunged forward with the spear, but Holly snatched it away from her and stood between the monster and Jack, snarling. Jez stumbled back, mouth agape.

• • •

"Come on then!" Holly yelled. "Come on, you fucker!"

It glared at her, eyes full of hate, and she didn't care. This was it: this was the moment that you assumed would never come. The moment where you forgot everything except for your kid and how you would do anything to protect him.

It opened its mouth just as she lunged forward and upward: the spear sunk into the roof of its mouth and snapped. Holly whipped the splintered shaft back as the sharp teeth closed around the top of her leg. She stabbed wildly at the creature's single eye: viscous fluid spurted from puncture wounds in its surface. The teeth clamped down, and she felt something warm and sticky soaking her clothes. The pond and the trees suddenly felt very far away.

The most important thing now was to finish this.

She wrenched the stick out of the creature's eye socket and started flailing wildly at its head, stabbing at the bristled skin. The stick barely left dints; the splinters at the end began to deaden and blunt. Holly felt the thing let go of her leg and heard a snuffling sound; she realized, with a flash of horror, that it was sniffing—that it was still looking for Jack.

In the moment of realization, she noticed the hole in its head. She was starting to feel dizzy. She raised the splintered stick.

• • •

"Shit!"

It seemed unreal to Hogarth. The boy, the man with the bag that he'd met at the crossroads all those years ago, his friend from the cupboard out here in the open and so angry. The rage was all around Hogarth and making him afraid. His friend had never been this angry before. The tension in his stomach was ferocious. He had to make it better. Savaric wasn't helping. His head throbbed from where Savaric had hit him. He saw Savaric trying to get up again and grabbed at him; his phantom hand went through Savaric's leg and his remaining one wasn't strong enough to gain purchase. Savaric kicked Hogarth's hand away without looking. Hogarth grasped at his clothing, trying desperately to stop him.

He remembered when Ma had been angry. She'd never been angry like this. But it never went well when you tried to interrupt someone who was angry.

• • •

Savaric threw Hogarth to the ground and rushed toward Holly. It was injured, badly injured, and its eye was one of the two things that made it valuable, but he could probably save it. There was no way…she couldn't know…he just had to hope that she wouldn't notice…

• • •

The poggelin snarled, turning toward the sound of Hogarth and Savaric's battle. Holly gathered the last of her strength and drove the sharp splintered end of the stick into the hole in the poggelin's head. It screamed. She felt the stick meet something hard and pushed. The poggelin thrashed beneath her, snapping frantically. Hands grabbed at her, trying to pull her off, but she huddled over the top of the creature's head and held on, kicking at the man behind her, forcing him to step away. She clenched her teeth and leaned on the end of the stick with all her weight. There was a dull cracking sound, and the stick sank deep into the monster's head with a squelch. Holly fell against its cold, rough skin, and the monster collapsed on the ground.

• • •

Hogarth roared. He knew that his friend was dying. He could see the thing in front of him—the thing that had taken his arm, collapsed on the ground before him, a stake in its brain, twitching as the sparks of life went out—but it wasn't just that. The voice, the connection that had sustained him for so long, had fallen silent.

There was no sound at the pond.

He was alone. He hadn't been alone since Ma died, except for those few days before he met Savaric. He moaned and heard the sound as if it came from another place.

He still couldn't believe that his friend looked the way that he did; the shock of finding out what it looked like was still fresh. But he had spoken to it. Had shared food with it. Had shared his life with it. He whimpered and knelt down in the mud next to the body and rested his forehead against it.

Ma hadn't held with crying. He tried to think of something else as a couple of drops ran down his face and splashed into the February mud. He could hear voices nearby, but it was if they came from another world.

• • •

"That's not good, right?" shouted Jez to Sarah.

Sarah was focussed on healing the rift, willing it to close and seal. It was new magic. She had never done it before, but she wasn't sure that anyone else had, either.

"It should close, soon," shouted Sarah over the noise rushing through the gap.

"Wait!" called Marina, through the gap. "What about us? We can't leave! Why can't we leave the pond? We just want to—we could go anywhere! Literally anywhere—hills and forests and castles and cities and deserts and mountains! We could walk all over the world! Why can't we go somewhere else?"

"I don't know!" The gap was closing now. "I can't do anything right now!"

"Who are you?" gasped Gareth. "Please help us! We can't leave! You don't know what it's like!"

The last rag of reality whipped in the breeze coming through the gap, closed over it, and sealed it with a quiet whipping sound. There was a silence and a stillness that lasted an age.

It was broken by Theo.

"What," he said, "the fuck?"

The world snapped back to normal speed. Jez looked around and saw the woman lying on the ground, pale and lifeless.

Shit. She know the symptoms. This wasn't even medicine. This was basic first aid. Grey skin, shallow breathing…even without the blood soaking into the undergrowth, she could tell Holly was in hypovolemic shock due to exsanguination, or in basic English, bleeding out. She scrambled across the woodland floor and in an instant, she was looking at…*yeesh*. Jez wasn't squeamish, but the wounds in Holly's upper thigh were deep and ragged.

When the thing had bitten her, it must have hit an artery.

"Fuck," said Jez out loud. *Bedside manner.* This was basic stuff. First aid. "Can you hear me?" She shook Holly's shoulder. "Hello? It's all right." She wasn't sure at all that it was. "It's all right. I know first aid." She looked again at the wounds. They were wet, but they were barely bleeding. *Shit.* This was bad.

"It's all right," she said again, firmly. She pressed her hands across the holes in the flesh. She couldn't tell if the flesh was cooling under Holly's running tights, or whether her own shaking hands were just cold in the February air. "It's going to be all right. It's all right."

Her words hung in the air.

• • •

It was, Holly knew. It was going to be all right. She had done it. She had passed the test. She—

She was a *good mother*.

It was all right.

She could rest now.

Chapter 16

Silence fell on the pond like heavy velvet.

It was broken by Savaric swearing under his breath. He kicked the corpse of the poggelin. It squelched. Then he smacked Hogarth in the head. Hogarth sobbed. The poggelin didn't move. Savaric spun on his heel and turned to Sarah.

"You're remarkably resilient," he said, his voice edged with bitterness.

Sarah shrugged. She was still breathing heavily from the effort of closing the gap, and she felt tired. "You're on my patch."

"Easily fixed," said Savaric, pressing his lips together and thrusting his hands in his pockets. He turned to go.

Jez blocked his path.

"No," she said. "No, you don't. You can't just dump a child-eating monster here for a few decades and then wander off."

Savaric looked at her, witheringly, and then looked back at Sarah.

"As I said," he said, "I'll be off now."

"No," said Jez. "Tell me who you were working for."

"I wasn't working *for* anyone," said Savaric. "Not my style. And none of your business."

"Was it Asilida?" said Jez, breathlessly. She didn't want to ask, but she had to know. "Was it?"

Savaric frowned.

"What do *you* know about Asilida?" he said. "And no. I wouldn't work for them for a thousand years' board. Bunch of suits." He snorted. "Or one suit in a bunch of…anyway. Bye."

Jez dodged in front of him again.

"Then what did you want?" she said, her anger rising. "People are dead. Why did you come here? What did you want?"

Savaric turned to Sarah. "Who is this?" he said. "Your work-experience girl?"

A cry from Theo interrupted them. He stifled it immediately, but they turned to look. The women in black were standing by the pond.

"Shit," muttered Savaric. He turned to Jez. "Thanks a bunch."

"I didn't call them," said Jez. "I don't even—"

"No," said Savaric. "But I could have been long gone by now."

The women made their way over to Sarah.

"You are still here," said Alice. "Why are you still here?"

"This is my *patch*," said Sarah. Her voice was steady. She had nothing to lose. "This thing—" she gestured toward the dead monster "—was eating kids on my patch." She looked at the three women in turn. "I told you. I had to find the child first. And I found the child. It was an imbalance. We keep to ourselves. You keep to yours. I keep the balance."

Meg frowned and prodded the rapidly decaying corpse with her toe. "How did it come here?"

"Him," said Jez quickly, pointing to Savaric. Savaric rolled his eyes. All three of the women in black looked at him.

"Why?" said Tess.

Savaric sighed.

"It's how I make a living," he said. "I used it to…gain information, let's say. It's a steady business."

"Who do you get 'information' for?" demanded Jez, making air quotes with her fingers. "Is that it? Do you get information for Asilida?"

"Who is this?" asked Savaric, looking about him.

"I live here!" shouted Jez. "And I want it not to be messed up by monsters!"

"The balance is important," said Tess. "The monsters have their own places. Even the monsters of the home and hearth." She walked over to the dead poggelin and pushed the still-keening Hogarth away with her foot. She bent over to inspect it.

"The stone," she said. "We have heard of this. And you have the—" She gestured with her hand toward the corpse. "You have the device that lets you see what it sees from the dark? And you have the stone?"

"Yes," said Savaric quickly. His previous experience and his fear told him not to prevaricate. "It's worthless now."

"Do you know Nicholas Carrington?" blurted Jez. Sarah looked at her sharply. Savaric's head snapped round.

"What?" he said. "How do you know—"

"How do you know him?" said Jez. "Where can we find him?"

"Why do you want—" began Savaric. Tess spoke again, cutting him off.

"This is good work," she said, looking at the dead poggelin and then at Sarah. "Order has been restored."

"Thanks," said Sarah. "I think."

"Your broken oath stands as an injustice in the cosmos," said Alice. "You must set it right. You have three days."

"Two days," said Sarah, without thinking. "I had to—" She gestured around her.

"Three days," said Meg. "We will see you in three days."

And they were gone.

"Look at you," said Savaric to Sarah. "Ten out of ten and a gold star for negotiating with the immovable object. Objects. Plural."

"You know Carrington," said Jez, jabbing at his chest with a finger. "We need to know where we can find him. You have to tell us."

"No, I don't," said Savaric. "I really don't. And I'm going now."

"Is he in London?" said Jez. "You're from London, right? Is he there?"

"What is *wrong* with her?" said Savaric to Sarah.

"It's easier if you tell her," said Sarah. "Or rather, it will be."

"What?" said Savaric. Then he felt the point of a sharp object in the upper left quadrant of his back.

"The thing about pushing a stake through someone," said Theo, as if to himself, "is that it's pretty effective. Whether they're a vampire or not."

Savaric began to laugh.

"Oh, you people," he said, chuckling. "You think you've got a handle on everything, and you haven't even scratched the surface. You study your little old books, and you witter away about good and evil, but you don't think about the other great unholy two-some that keeps your world going and mine. Survival and preda-tion." He turned to Sarah. "You 'keep the balance.'" He made the same air quotes that Jez had made earlier, with a grimace. "The 'balance' is based on the assumption that we stay in our world, you stay in yours, and that's what's best for everyone. But our world is hard, and yours is easier. For us." He leaned closer to her. "And if you're the only one left, it's remarkably undefended."

"That a threat?" said Sarah, looking him dead in the eye.

"It's a *fact*," said Savaric. "I don't give a shit either way; it's not going to make a difference to me." He jerked his head toward the dead poggelin. "Especially not now. But if I were in charge of keeping the balance, I might want to look beyond my *patch*. Because the things that that lot—" he gestured to Jez, Sam, Theo, and Hogarth "—the things that that lot think are long gone are getting ready to come back. They think we're a joke, you know. You can see it every October. Plastic teeth and cardboard hats and ghoulies and ghosties and long-legged beasties with friendly, friendly smiles. And they forget that they put the lanterns out and spat on the ground and knocked on wood to keep us away. Because we're *dangerous*."

"Sounds like you've picked your side," said Sarah.

Savaric shook his head. "It's a default, not a side. You can't change what you are. I'm telling you as a professional courtesy. Like I said, it doesn't make a difference to me. I've lasted this long. I'm probably going to last a lot longer." He looked at the ground and then back up. "I'm from here. I knew Nan."

Sarah's eyebrows shot up.

"What?" she said. "So you're saying you owe me? You tried to kill me. You did kill me."

"Nothing personal," said Savaric. There was a sardonic twinkle in his eye for a moment, and then it vanished. "What's your connection with Carrington?"

"What's yours?"

"Business arrangement," said Savaric. "Prospective one. Tanked now. You?"

Sarah looked steadily at him.

"There's no way you don't know," she said. "Where is he?"

"Don't know," said Savaric. "As I said, they don't let the likes of me near the likes of him. He's in London, but that doesn't help you much."

"You stabbed me," said Sarah. "You owe me."

"I really don't."

"You really do."

Savaric pursed his lips and let out a long, quiet whistle. Then he produced a small notepad and pencil from the folds of his coat, scribbled down a number, tore out the page, handed the page to Sarah, and made the notebook and pencil disappear back into his coat.

"Here," he said. "Call her. She'll know something. Only don't tell her—"

Sarah looked down at the piece of paper in her hand and then back at Savaric.

"This is a mobile number," she said. "How does she—"

"I don't know, all right?" said Savaric. "Just don't tell her you saw me. But she'll know something. She always does."

Sarah shrugged. "Okay," she said. "I'll give her a call. But don't think I can't find you again if you're trying to put one over on me."

"I've got nothing to lose," said Savaric. "It doesn't make a difference to me who's in charge. But the fire wasn't right. There. I said it." He looked up at the sky. "I'm going now," he said, turning round and facing Theo. "Don't try anything." He took the stick from Theo's hand, snapped it in two and dropped it. Then—and afterward, no one could remember quite how, except he was fast (faster than any of them had thought anyone who looked like Savaric could be)—he was gone.

Theo looked around him, as if for the first time. He saw Holly lying still on the blood-drenched ground.

"We should call an ambulance," he said. "Or do artificial respiration."

"It's too late," said Jez. "Also, your phone's dead." Theo pulled it out of his pocket and checked it; she was right. "We can call from Sarah's place; say there was an animal attack or something. Jack's going to need an ambulance as well."

"What do we do with that, though?" said Theo, pointing to the poggelin's corpse, on which Hogarth was still resting his head. "What do we do with him?"

"It'll be fine," said Jez. "I don't know how, but it'll be fine. This place covers things up really well." Her eyes were welling up. She stared at the ground, willing the tears to go away and not daring to look at Sam. Her eyes darted toward the poggelin, and she saw that already, where it lay on the ground, its flesh was beginning to turn into dust.

"Come on," said Sarah to Jez. "Someone needs to phone an ambulance. And we should get Jack away from this place."

"You can't leave them," said Sam, suddenly. "They're stuck here. You can't leave them!" His voice was rising. The wind picked up. "It's cold! It's wet! They've been down here for months and they *can't leave*!" He was shouting now. "You can't be the one who looks after everything and then leave them here. They can't leave!"

Jez felt her insides sinking. This was worse than she had expected.

"Sam—" began Theo.

"What, she gets to just walk away from the pond and the—" he gestured around "—everything that she caused since she came here, and they have to stay here?" Sam's eyes were wild. "This place is evil, Jez. They need to be able to leave!"

"I will," said Sarah, as calmly as she could. "I didn't know they were here. I will try to help them. But I have to—"

Sam snorted. "Oh right, here come the excuses. 'I can't. It's not the right time. You have to wait. Be patient.' This is affecting real people! Right now!"

"They're already dead, Sam," said Sarah, quietly. "I will help them if I can. But they're not in our world anymore, and I don't know—"

"This is your job! It's your job to know!"

"Sam! You're not helping!" Jez turned to him frowning. "You're being an arse! She can't help anyone if she's dead. Let her sort out the three-day thing and then—"

"Oh, great. And if she dies doing that, they'll be here forever!"

The pause hit like a cricket bat.

"I'm going to call an ambulance," said Sarah, after a while. "I'm going to take Jack with me and make sure he's okay. Then I'm going to make some phone calls and go to London."

She looked at Sam.

"See you when I get back," she said. She took Jack's hand, murmured something to him that they couldn't hear and lifted him up and carried him away from the pond.

• • •

Theo caught up with Sarah and Jack a few minutes later.

"D'you know London well?" he said.

"Never been," said Sarah. "You?"

"I'm from there," said Theo. "I mean, I could…if it helps, I could come with you. Help you get around and stuff. If you want."

Sarah shrugged. "It'll be dangerous."

"This was dangerous."

"This is very dangerous," said Sarah. "You seem clever. You saw what happened here today. Someone died." She looked at him. "Someone almost always dies."

"That man said that it was only you," said Theo. "Keeping the balance. You need help?"

"Yes," said Sarah. Her voice was small. "But I don't want to put anyone in danger. Jez doesn't care: she's full of fire and righteousness." She gave a short laugh. "You ever wonder why they send teenagers to war, spend some time watching her. Sam, though…" She looked directly at Theo. "Sam's scared right now, and he's completely justified. He's right to be scared and he's right to want out. If you go all in…" Her voice trailed off.

"If we don't do anything," said Theo, "what happens? Like, I know there's your stuff, but the things that bloke was talking about…that Savaric…talking about the balance being upset, and their world coming into ours…that's heavy stuff."

Sarah sighed. "Yeah," she said. "My great-aunt saw it coming. They're here. I mean, it's happening already. She cut out the newspaper articles…every time something odd happened, all over the country. She got good at looking for it as well; Jez wasn't kidding when she said that the other world was good at covering itself up." They had reached Sarah's cottage, and she unlatched the gate and they went up the path together. "They never went away. And you have to remember: they're not all evil. There are a lot of—" she swallowed "—Ethereal beings who don't do or wish any harm to humans. Most people, whatever world they're in, want the same things: they just want to get on with their lives with a minimum of suffering and maybe do their best to try and make things a little better." She unlocked the cottage door and it swung open with a creak. "But some of them don't." She nodded toward an armchair, and Theo put Jack down in it and closed the door behind him.

"Crap," he said. "That's frightening."

"Yup." Sarah moved toward the phone. "Going to throw some things in a bag. Then I'm going."

"I know you," came a voice from the chair.

Sarah and Theo froze.

"You're from the train." Jack's voice was thin and tired. "You're a witch."

Sarah looked at him, and a vague memory flickered through her brain.

"Best keep that a secret," she said eventually, and picked up the phone to call the ambulance.

• • •

The ambulance and the police had come. There were blankets and stretchers and tape and big Alsatian dogs and a nice constable called Lizzie Waterbury who seemed quite upset herself when she found out about Holly.

Sam wasn't talking. Hogarth was in shock. Jez said that she and Sam and Sarah had come down there and found the three others, and it looked like an animal attack. It sort of did, and no one asked questions, and neither Jez nor Sam was surprised. They wrapped Hogarth in blankets and took him away, and then they covered up Holly's face and put her on a stretcher and took her away, but with no sirens blaring.

Then it was quiet at the pond again.

Sam hadn't said a word. Eventually, Jez broke the silence.

"It's not her fault," she said. "It would have been the same if she hadn't come. It would have been worse."

"We don't know that," said Sam. "You're always saying we shouldn't speculate on what *would have* happened if we don't have the data to make a proper prediction."

"I know," said Jez. "But we do. All of the stuff that happened in October would have happened anyway, except it would still be going on. She just stopped it. Same happened here."

"She didn't do anything though," said Sam. "She just cut

the—she just let the monster through. The woman who died actually killed it."

"She couldn't have done that if it hadn't been in this world though," said Jez. "You can't keep blaming her for things being fucked. The only difference is that we know about them, because we know her. And we can either help her or—"

"This isn't politics, Jez," said Sam. "It's not a case of someone yelling at us if they don't agree. This is life-or-death stuff. I have a right to be afraid."

He looked at her.

"We're going to London with her," he said. "I know it. You know it. Probably Theo's coming with us. I'm not going to blame him if he doesn't, but he probably will. It's going to be dangerous, and it's not our town. We know what it's like here. There, we don't. Theo has a better idea, but there's no way anyone can know a city that size the way that we know Crowsbrook. But we're going to go, and we're going to help her, and if she doesn't manage to do what she has to do, we'll be there when…" He held up his hands. "We're going to go. But I don't want to. I don't want to go, and I don't want to die. But I'm going to go anyway. But I have a right to be scared."

He stood up and looked around at the trees and the pond.

"I don't know if you can hear me," he said, loudly. "I hope you can. We're going now, but we're going to come back. And when we come back, we're going to try and help."

He swallowed.

"I miss you," he said. "Every day. I miss you a lot."

He turned to Jez.

"You're coming, right?" he said.

"In a mo," said Jez.

The poggelin was turning to dust, dust that glittered briefly in the light. Jez frowned as a familiar shape caught her eye. She picked up a stick from the ground and started working in the undergrowth, in the weeds and the leaves and the mud, where the remains of the poggelin lay. In a minute or two, she had uncovered the unmistakable form: the side of a human skull. A small skull. A child's skull.

She let out a long breath.

It had to be Daniel Giddens.

• • •

They said his mummy wouldn't be coming back. Jack had cried for a very long time. He wasn't sure that he really believed it.

He lay in a bed at the hospital while they tried to work out what to do with him. His uncle was visiting from Scotland. He didn't care. His foot still hurt. They'd had to chop off his foot, but it hurt like it was still there. He didn't know how it still hurt, if it wasn't there. Everything was fuzzy. He didn't want to go back to school. He imagined what Jocasta would say about him only having one foot. One of the nurses had said that he would have to learn how to balance again, but that would happen later: right now, he wanted to go home. He had Walter Bear (who was still drying out) and Galacticor (one of the policemen had put him back together, and he was pretty much as good as new) and Starhammer, who was probably his now, as long as he didn't have to take him to school to see if he was someone else's.

Everything was fuzzy. He slept, and then he was awake, and then he was asleep again. He wanted a glass of water. He pushed the button and he asked the nurse and she brought him a glass of water and left it on the bedside table when he'd had a drink.

But he was thirsty. Ten minutes later, when she'd gone, he rolled over in bed and pulled himself up to have another drink. He reached for the glass and just for a moment—he didn't know why—he looked down at the nightstand.

There was a cupboard in the bottom of the nightstand. It was open a crack. And Jack could tell there was something looking at him.

The glass fell out of his hands and smashed on the floor, and Jack began to scream.

• • •

Theo went out to meet up with Jez and Sam and Sarah phoned the friar. It rang for a long time before he picked it up.

"Hello?" he said. "Parochial house. Father Dominic Quinn."

"Father," said Sarah. "It's done. The thing that got Daniel Giddens. It's dead. It attacked another child and took him. But the child's alive."

She heard the click of the priest's lighter, and the inhalation of smoke.

"Well done," he said. "I thank you. God bless you. You do good work. Like your aunt."

"Thanks, Father." She didn't know what else to say. "I have to go to London," she managed eventually. "For work." She took a deep breath. "I might not come back."

"I hope you do," said the friar seriously. "We need you up here."

"You know what my job's like," she said. "I'll do my best."

"I'll do what I can for you," said the friar. "Look after yourself. I'll talk to you when you get back."

"If," said Sarah. "Probably better to think of it as *if*."

There was a pause.

"That bad," said the friar, heavily. He sighed. "I'm sorry to hear that. May all that is good go with you."

"Thank you," said Sarah.

She didn't put the phone down. There was a question that still nagged at her.

"Father," she said, eventually. "What happened at St. Joe's?"

"Terrible things," said Father Quinn brusquely. "Things that you can't forget once you've heard them."

"I know," said Sarah, trying not to imagine. "But the man in charge. Obadiah Kane. What happened to him? He died suddenly, didn't he?"

"He did," said the friar. Sarah waited for him to go on. He didn't.

"I found a newspaper clipping," said Sarah. "In my aunt's scrapbooks. About when he died." She tapped her finger on the receiver; she'd come this far, so she might as well ask the question. "Why would she have kept that?"

Sarah heard the friar inhale deeply on his cigarette.

"I told him," he said. "He knew. But he didn't do anything. I don't know why. Brushed me off. Said the kids were lying. You could see the bruises. You'd have had to be mad not to know, and evil not to do anything. I said I would go to the police, but he told me they wouldn't believe me either, and I knew he was right. I couldn't believe what I was hearing. That anyone could—that anyone—I drove. I borrowed one of the cars and I drove. I had to get away for a few hours. I ended up in Crowsbrook. There was the legend, you know, that Crowsbrook had the pond with the Devil trapped in it, and I wanted to go there. Because I wanted to tell the Devil exactly what I thought of him."

He puffed on his cigarette. Sarah waited.

"I sat by the pond for a long time," he said. "I didn't know where to start. And then someone came. A woman."

Sarah felt chills.

"I looked upset," said the friar. "I must have. I was. She asked what was wrong and I told her. She didn't say anything, but she nodded and said she would look into it. I laughed. She shrugged, and pulled a jam jar out of her bag and filled it with water. I assumed she was mad."

He let out a final exhale. Sarah heard the soft crunch of the cigarette being stubbed out on a pile of ashes in the ashtray.

"Kane died three days later," said the friar. "The police were there immediately, and people from the government. Things started getting better. Even for the time, they could see things were wrong. The change was phenomenal. The kids got help. You know that these things, they never go away, and I do not mean to minimize what happened by saying that they began to heal. By seeing the people responsible punished."

"Kane wasn't punished," said Sarah. "He was dead."

"Funny you should say that," said the friar. "A week after he died, I got a telephone call. From the woman by the pond. Your great-aunt, of course. She asked me how things were."

Sarah was perfectly still.

"I said they were better," continued the friar. "I said that without thinking, and then I started mumbling something about respect for the dead. She said something about how occasionally the dead were best forgotten sooner rather than later, that I shouldn't argue with her on that one. She said goodbye, and then I realized that I didn't know her name and I hadn't given her mine. So I told her, and she did the same. I asked why she had phoned, and she said that it was her job to make things all right. *Then* she hung up. It was many years later that she told me what she had done. Many years and many cups of tea."

"It was her?" said Sarah.

The friar coughed. "She looked in the water," he said. "She saw what I said was true. She did—what I could not have done. And things got better. She never celebrated what she did."

Sarah couldn't speak.

"God bless," said the friar. "And thank you for following up on Daniel."

He hung up.

Sarah wiped her eyes and put down the phone. There was a knock at the door. Theo, Sam, and Jez. Of course it was. She opened it, and she was right.

"All right?" she said. "What do you two want?"

"A lift," said Sam. "Theo says London's fun."

"Haven't you got school?"

"Technically," said Jez.

"No," said Sarah. "There's no way that telling your parents that you're at each other's houses is going to work for three whole days while you bugger off to London."

"Not without help," said Jez, holding out her hands. "Please?"

"You're asking me to do magic," said Sarah. "You."

"So we can help *you*," said Jez. "Totally makes sense. Even if magic doesn't."

Sarah's mind raced through the possible solutions. On the one hand, magic took energy. On the other, having Sam, Jez, and Theo with her would help. Then again, she didn't want to put the kids in danger. That said, if they could keep her alive, she'd still be around to protect them and the patch.

It was a heavy conundrum. But a quick, hard glamour…so that no one would notice they were gone…

It only had to last three days.

"Okay," she said at last. "Give me twenty minutes. And I have to make one more phone call once we're on the road."

Epilogue

They had to take the rest of his arm as well. They said he could get a fake one, in time, and he could get physio on the NHS and a bunch of other palaver, but he didn't care. He just wanted to go home.

Then they took him home after a few days, someone from the council did, when he said he lived by himself and there wasn't anyone to pick him up. And then they saw his house looking like it had been done over, and they said animals must have got in there as well because there was blood in the kitchen, must have been a fox with a bird or something, but they didn't spend too much time thinking about it because the state of the place…well. It was a mess and no mistake. Even he could see that. And he couldn't quite remember it being in that state before, he couldn't have let it get that bad, the carpet threadbare and falling apart, and the door coming off its hinges, and the curtains all tattered and faded. They said they'd have to send someone round from a different department in the council to sort it out, and he was about to say that they couldn't because no one could go in the house except him, and then he remembered it didn't matter anymore.

They said he should sleep in the one good room. They

cleaned it up specially. Ma's room. He didn't want to, but they had him on all kinds of pills, and they made him sleepy and he didn't want to fight, so he went into Ma's room to have a lie down. He didn't remember leaving the door open either. That wasn't something that he'd have done, surely? The door to Ma's room was never open. But there were lots of things he didn't remember doing. Maybe kids had been in while the door was broken. You couldn't trust people, you couldn't.

He was nervous as he felt for the light switch, and then felt better as the warm golden light flooded the room and he smelled the perfume and the soap mixed with lipstick and dust. That was what he remembered all right.

Then he saw the letter on the dressing table, in two pieces. He frowned, slowly. He knew Ma always ripped letters into two pieces before she threw them away. But she threw them away. She didn't keep them. This one was still in the envelope, and the envelope was in two pieces.

It was Ma's letter. But here it was, on the dressing table.

Ma had always said his curiosity would be the death of him. He'd mostly squelched that. You didn't need to know everything, did you?

He wasn't really sure how he got over to the dressing table and the letter. The stupid pills, probably. They were making him feel dizzy—or something was—so he sat down at Ma's dressing table. It was nice. He could see why she liked it.

The pieces of the letter still fit together. It was old. It was dated the year before he was born, six months to the day, in fact, and it was from someone called Dorothea. The envelope didn't have an address or a stamp, just Ma's name. It couldn't have come through the post. The handwriting was small and difficult to get the drift of. It was like a spider had spent too much time at the Pink Pony.

He squinted in the yellow light.

Dear Augusta. All right, now. That was Ma's name. That was easy enough to read. That was what the *a*'s and the *t*'s and the *s*'s looked like. And the *e*'s. He was getting the hang of it.

> *I hope that you do not mind me writing to you, but I feel that I need to warn you that the young man with whom you are stepping out is Not as he Seems. I have had cause to know him—and his family—for a long time, and I hope that you will believe me when I say that he is Not to Be Trusted. Young Savaric has always been Wild, and I do not see this abating, though he has been known to me for longer than I might care to mention. I might advise you to extricate yourself from his company and should you need help with your current—*

There was a large ink blot here. Hogarth struggled to make out the letters. *Pre. Di. Ca—*

Ma never asked for help, though. Proud to get by on her own she was.

Funny: he remembered old Dorothea. They always said she was a witch, but she would help people if they needed. The young girls especially.

Flipping heck. Those pills were making him sleepy.

He lay down, in his clothes, and turned out the light.

• • •

Down by the pond, the shadows wept.

They didn't know how long they had been crying. Of course they didn't. There was no light to mark the passage of time.

• • •

Lil huddled down into the faux-fur collar of her coat, took a deep breath and opened the door of the taxi. The rain spattered onto the pavement and she pulled a face. Oh well. She'd be at the club soon. She didn't care. The rain didn't bother her.

Plus she knew a shortcut.

She reached the lights and, instead of turning down the main road, headed down a dingy side street. She knew the area like the back of her hand.

Her high heels glittered in the street light and made a satis-fying *clop* as she walked. They were among her favourites. It was going to be a good one tonight. She liked a night out. Liked a bit of a knees-up. Always had.

She cut sharply to the left and ducked into an alley between two buildings. A bunch of restaurants kept their bins back there, and if she was having an early night, sometimes she'd see the kitchen staff putting out the rubbish after the restaurants were closed, and a few rough sleepers hanging around in the shadows, watching to see if they were getting rid of anything good.

Clop, clop, clop. A rat scuttled across the alley in front of her.

She hit the end of the alley and turned into another street, closer to the main road. Not far now.

That was when she heard it. A low sound. No, wait. A *lowing* sound. Like a cow.

Followed by giggles. Masculine ones, yes, but still. *Giggles.*

Lil raised one perfectly plucked eyebrow and kept walking.

The sound came again. Louder. Shorter. Interrupted by giggling.

Lil was pretty sure she heard the words "…fucking *whale*…"

Clop.

She stopped. Her back was to the three men. There were three distinct voices at any rate.

(Three sets of footsteps she could pick out without thinking…)

Lil ran the tip of her tongue around the edges of her top teeth.

"Oi, darlin'!" shouted one of them. "Wanna pie an' a pint? Or ten?"

"She's already had 'em all!" hollered another.

More giggles. Drunk.

Lil didn't care. She wasn't in the mood.

She hadn't been in the mood for quite a few centuries.

She was in their faces before they realized it. She could smell the beer on their breath.

"Pie and a pint?" she said, smiling dangerously. "Well, I'd love to."

"We can see that," said one of them, still smirking. The other two, who still weren't quite sure how Lil had caught up with them so quickly, looked at her, baffled.

"How—" said one, "did you—" He stank of beer. Lil wrinkled her nose. It wasn't even good beer.

"Well," said Lil. "I may be a lady of size—" she gestured to her figure (she was wearing a sparkling silver club dress, another of her favourites) "—but that doesn't mean I can't *move*. When I want to." She was eyeing them from head to toe, still smiling. Hat and his friend Football-Shirt were starting to look a bit uncomfortable. Pie-and-a-Pint was still grinning.

"Pie and a pint," he said again. "Fat cow."

Lil was unperturbed.

"Like I said," she said, "I'd love to. One problem though…"

With fingernails like talons, she tore out his throat. Blood jetted from his severed carotid artery. He clutched at his neck as he fell on his knees and then slumped to the ground.

"I don't eat junk food," said Lil, stepping over the pooling blood toward Hat and Football shirt. Hat made a run for it, but Lil was too fast. She grabbed him from behind, stuck a claw in his belly and ripped upward. His intestines tumbled out onto the pavement with a splat, and Hat fell after them.

Arsenal was running. Lil caught up with him and wrapped one arm around him, lifting him off the ground.

"Life lesson," she said. "And pay attention because it won't last long, and I guarantee—" she smiled sweetly "—it'll stay with you for the rest of your mortal days."

Arsenal was breathing hard. His eyes were wide.

"Help!" he shouted, wriggling, trying to free himself from Lil's embrace. "Somebody help! Police!"

Lil placed a finger on his lips.

"*Shh*," she said. "Now listen carefully."

With the hand that wasn't wrapped around his waist, she dug a nail slowly into the soft skin of his neck. The blood welled up and began to drip steadily. It grew to a trickle. With an expert shake, Lil twitched her coat sleeve out of the way. The blood began to splatter on the ground as she drew her nail slowly across his throat.

"Don't," said Lil, "shout crap at women you don't know on the street. Because some of them might kill you dead. Oh," she added a moment later. "Too late."

She dropped his corpse and it fell on the ground with a heavy thud. Lil stepped delicately around the widening mixture of rain and blood.

She liked London.

Clop, clop, clop. She pulled out her phone and dialled a number.

"Yeah," she said, after a couple of rings. "Clean up in Aisle Three, darlin'. Archibald Road. No," she said, after a pause. "Full of booze, they were. I'd've bloody come home singing, and I've only just gone out. Chuck 'em in the river." She hung up and started walking again.

Her phone rang. She frowned. She pulled it out and looked at it. Unknown number.

Whatever. She answered it.

"Yeah?" There was a pause. "Maybe. Who wants to know?"

Lil frowned, and then broke into a delighted smile.

"Sarah Trevelyan," she said. "Well. You're the talk of the town, round here…"

TO BE CONTINUED...

Acknowledgements

I'd like to thank the following people for invaluable feedback and support while I was writing and producing this book: April Bially, Ian Calverley, Shannon Corregan, Tobin Elliott, Pat Flewwelling, Christine Gilbert, Paul Kendal, and Avivah Wargon.

Special thanks to Heather Martin, the copy editor, Nelson Gonzalez, the compositor, and Avivah Wargon, the proofreader, for their amazing work. The action figure of Galacticor on the cover was sculpted by Colin Betts, and photographed by Janet Weldon Murray; thanks also to Stuart Murray for additional photography. The cover design was created by Carmen Leah at Pink Kloud. Huge thanks to all.

And thanks to you, reader, for getting this far…

About the Author

Claire Horsnell grew up in a small English village and maintains that it would have been a lot more interesting with witches and monsters in it. She now lives in Toronto.